The Great Martian War

Counterattack!

By Scott Washburn

ZMOK
BOOKS

The Great Martian War - Counterattack
By Scott Washburn
Cover by Ben Mirabelli
Zmok Books an imprint of
Winged Hussar Publishing, LLC, 1525 Hulse Road, Unit 1, Point Pleasant, NJ 08742

This edition published in 2017
Copyright ©Winged Hussar Publishing, LLC and Scott Washburn

ISBN 978-1-945430-11-4
Library of Congress No. 2017958000
Bibliographical references and index
1.Science Fiction 2. Alternate History 3. Alien Invasion

For more information on Winged Hussar Publishing, LLC, visit us at:
https://www.WingedHussarPublishing.com
Twitter: WingHusPubLLC
Facebook: Winged Hussar Publishing LLC

Produced with miniature mart at:
quietmartianfront.com

The Great Martian War
Counterattack!

By Scott Washburn

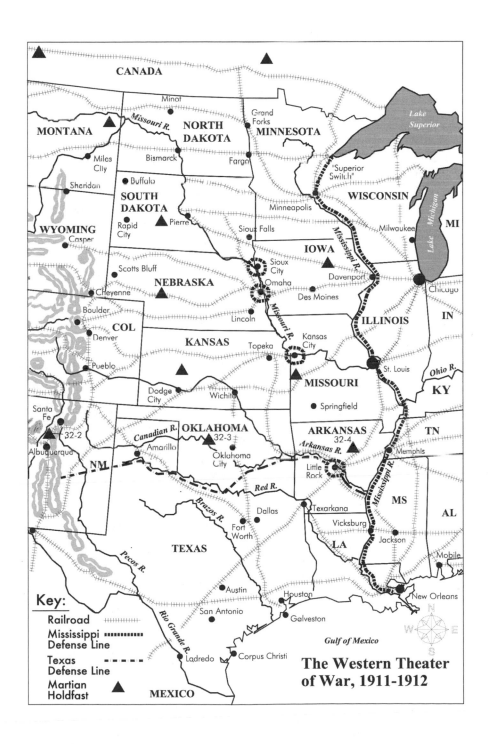

The Western Theater
of War, 1911-1912

Key:
Railroad
Mississippi Defense Line
Texas Defense Line
Martian Holdfast

Prologue

Cycle 597, 844.7, South of Holdfast 32-4

"Subgroup 2-3, destroy that weapon emplacement to your left. We will be enfiladed by it if it is not neutralized."

The subgroup leader acknowledged the command and Qetjnegartis looked on in satisfaction as the three war machines of the unit concentrated the fire from their heat rays to obliterate the prey-creature heavy projectile thrower. The clan was launching an attack to destroy a fortified prey-creature city which had resisted several lesser attacks in the past. Nearly all of the vast, flat plains between the mountains to the west and the large river to the east had fallen to the Race during the great offensive a half-cycle ago. But several cities, located on rivers, and thus not dependent on the enemy's usual - and vulnerable - transport system, had held out and fortified themselves. Qetjnegartis' clan, busy constructing new holdfasts and increasing their numbers, had not had the means to reduce these irritants until now.

At the end of the long advance, Qetjnegartis had questioned the decision to suspend offensive operations and consolidate, but it had to admit that the vastly increased strength of the clan was a comfort. They now had three fortified holdfasts, with a fourth nearly completed, and over two hundred members. In less than two-tenths of a cycle that number would swell to over three hundred as a new generation of buds matured. Qetjnegartis briefly regarded the pulsating sack on its side where its own bud was growing.

What a difference from those perilous days, a cycle ago, when the Bajantus Clan had been reduced to just eight individuals, clinging to a half-ruined holdfast! Extinction had been a real possibility, but the prey-creatures who inhabited this world had not taken advantage of the clan's weakness and the danger had passed.

Qetjnegartis hoped that the Race, here on the target world, had not made that same mistake.

While it was true that the clan and the Race were stronger, the evidence indicated that the prey-creatures had grown stronger, too. Warriors in huge numbers were massing on the far bank of the great river. Unlike the earlier armies, these new forces seemed well supplied with the heavy projectile throwers and the armored gun-vehicles which had proved alarmingly effective against the Race's fighting machines. In addition, they were building strong defensive works incorporating a cast stone material which was very resistant to heat rays.

Fortunately, the place they were attacking now had few of them. Most of the defenses were simply heaped piles of dirt and loose stones. Even though this bolstered the prey-creatures' defenses significantly, it was not as effective as the stone.

"The enemy fire has been nearly suppressed, Commander," reported Fadjnadtur, the second-in-command. "Shall we advance?"

Qetjnegartis evaluated the information coming to it over the tactical network. Brief but repeated thrusts against the city's defenses appeared to have destroyed most of the heavy weapons on this side of the perimeter. Projectiles were still falling periodically from more distant weapons, but not in great numbers. Had the enemy been weakened enough to permit a final assault? It had no wish to risk heavy casualties here. Every member of the Race was expendable, of course, but only if the objective was worth the cost. The clan had grown strong, but not so strong that it could throw away lives frivolously. This prey-creature enclave was an annoyance, but nothing more.

Still, the information indicated that an assault might succeed without unacceptable loss. Experience had shown that once the fighting machines closed with the enemy, the prey-creatures often lost cohesion and would flee. Although not always; Qetjnegartis' thoughts went back to a savage fight in a mountain pass where the prey had fought to the last and inflicted terrible casualties - nearly slaying Qetjnegartis in the process.

"Commander?" prompted Fadjnadtur. "A decision is required."

Qetjnegartis was annoyed. Fadjnadtur had arrived with the second wave of transports and was a close bud-mate to Valprandar, who had taken over from Qetjnegartis and been in command until it was slain at the end of the great offensive. It was clear that Fadjnadtur was not pleased that Qetjnegartis was back in charge again and had shown this sort of disrespect on several occasions.

"And a decision you shall have *subcommander*. All groups, concentrate for an attack on area twelve."

With the great increase in the strength of the clan, its fighting forces had been organized along traditional lines. Three fighting machines constituted a *subgroup* commanded by one of the three; three subgroups made up a *group* with a separate commander in its own machine, and three groups, a total of thirty machines, plus a machine for the commander, made a *battlegroup*. Qetjnegartis had a full battlegroup with it today and now all its machines - plus the command machines of itself and Fadjnadtur - were concentrating against a single portion of the prey-creature's defenses.

This tactic had been used with great success before. The majority of the prey-creatures' forces - the foot-warriors, the heavy projectile throwers, and the armored gun-vehicles - could not match the speed and agility of the Race's fighting machines. Therefore, the Race would begin an attack spread out along the prey's lines, probing and doing what damage they could without risking heavy losses. Then, once the enemy had been weakened and the location of its major weapons mapped, the attack force would concentrate against a single spot and break through before the prey could react. Qetjnegartis hoped to do the same thing now.

The machines swept in from right and left into a tight grouping and then advanced at full speed. The ground they passed over was mostly flat, featureless, and easily traversable. Fortunately, there had been no inclement weather for several days and the soil was firm. After a period of the heavy precipitation—so common on this wet, wet world - the soil could become a soft and sticky mass which would slow or even immobilize a fighting machine. There were no such troubles today and they quickly closed on the enemy defenses.

The fire from the prey-creatures intensified as they drew near, but it was not severe. The larger weapons on the line had been destroyed by the earlier forays and the long range fire couldn't adjust for their rapid movements quickly enough to be effective. There were several groupings of larger projectile throwers in trenches close behind the main line and Qetjnegartis ordered these to be blanketed with the toxic eradicator dust. They ceased firing almost immediately. The remaining fire was mostly from the smaller, portable weapons carried by the foot-warriors, although there were still some of the slightly heavier, rapid fire weapons. Those could be dangerous and heat rays stabbed out to silence them as the range decreased.

As they neared the line of trenches, the fire had almost ceased. The enemy works were blackened and burned by the extreme temperatures the heat rays produced. Clouds of smoke wafted skyward from fires which burned in many places. Beyond the trenches lay fields strewn with wreckage, and beyond those were the structures of the city itself. Many of the closer ones were ablaze. Not a living foe could be seen...

Suddenly, one of the lead fighting machines lurched forward and came to a halt in a strange bent-over position. Had it been hit? Perhaps a limb damaged? Qetjnegartis had seen no explosion from a projectile thrower. Another machine moved to assist and then it too stumbled and nearly fell. It staggered backward and then stood upright again.

"Report! What is happening?" demanded Qetjnegartis.

"There are pits in the ground, commander. Hidden pits. If we step upon them, the limbs of our machines will crash through for half their length. Jandrangnar's machine is stuck, and mine nearly became so."

The entire advance had stopped and enemy projectiles from distant throwers were starting to find their range. "Spray the ground with your heat rays! Uncover these traps! The attack must resume at once. Madgprindle, assist Jandrangnar."

Immediately heat rays blasted the ground in front of them. Qetjnegartis had no idea if this would reveal any of the pits, but there was no other option. The advance resumed and only one other machine encountered a pit before they were across the line of trenches. There, they paused to regroup.

The enemy fire was almost entirely stopped now, except for a few projectiles still falling around Jandrangnar's machine. And there were no prey-creatures to be seen anywhere. This was unexpected. During one of the great battles of the past offensive, the clan had smashed through the enemy lines and were immediately confronted with masses of fleeing prey and a few disorganized counterattacks by reserves rushed to the scene. But here there was... nothing.

"Group 1, turn east. Group 2, turn west, Fadjnadtur accompany them. Follow the line of entrenchment. Destroy all you encounter. I will take Group 3 into the city." The battlegroup split into three segments as directed and went in search of the enemy. They surely had not destroyed all of them.

The city to Qetjnegartis' front had been badly damaged by earlier attacks and the structures closest to the defense lines had been reduced to piles of blackened rubble. The smaller structures used by the prey were often constructed of flammable materials and would be completely consumed by the heat rays in this oxygen-rich environment, leaving little behind. But the larger structures were made of sturdier materials and their destruction produced large mounds of debris— treacherous footing for the fighting machines. That was the case here and few easy paths forward could be found.

Despite this, the leading machines of the group advanced, firing into structures which had not yet caught fire. Occasionally there would be returning fire from prey inside the structures, but their weapons did no damage. Qetjnegartis followed along behind the rest. The lack of significant resistance was... unsettling.

"Fadjnadtur, report your situation."

"We are proceeding as you ordered, Commander," came the immediate reply. "The trenches are mostly unoccupied. Very little resistance. We seem to have broken them."

"Do you see any of the prey fleeing?"

"Only a few. The rest must have fled already." Qetjnegartis checked with the commander of Group 1 and it reported the same thing. Had the prey-creatures truly all fled?

Its attention was brought back to the situation at hand when a building collapsed right across the path the group was taking. Flames from it leapt skyward and it was apparent the path would be blocked for some time. Qetjnegartis hesitated for an instant and then commanded, "Split up. Subgroup 3-1, go right, the rest of us will go left. We will reassemble on the other side of this." Three of the machines turned and went down the passage as directed. The others turned left.

The structures were taller here, higher than the fighting machines, and closely spaced. They could only proceed single file and they were closed in on either side like they were in a mountain pass.

"Commander!" a sudden communication came from Fadjnadtur.

"What is it?"

"We are being attacked! Prey-creatures are emerging from underground chambers! Hidden heavy projectile throwers are firing at us! They are behind us, too! We are being attacked from all sides!" A moment later the commander of Group 1 reported the same thing.

"Can you defeat these attacks?" asked Qetjnegartis.

"Unknown," replied Fadjnadtur. "More of the enemy are arriving and we are taking damage."

This had all the marks of an ambush. The prey-creatures had feigned weakness to draw them in! As if in confirmation, an explosion billowed up nearby, shaking Qetjnegartis inside its machine. "Commander! We are under attack!" exclaimed the leader of Group 3.

Prey-creatures were appearing from the buildings and out of the rubble. Some were firing weapons, others were throwing explosive bombs. Several of the rapid-fire weapons began firing from the upper floors of the structures and more bombs were thrown down from the rooftops. One bounced off the cockpit of Qetjnegartis' machine and exploded an instant later, slamming the machine sideways. Smoke engulfed it, blocking vision.

A flood of information came over the tactical net, too much for even Qetjnegartis to process immediately. Subgroup 3-1, which it had sent off alone, was under heavy attack both by the foot-warriors and by armored gun-vehicles, which had appeared from between the buildings. Group 1 had encountered more of the pit traps and had been attacked while they were trying to extricate themselves. Fadjnadtur and Group 2 were in a crossfire of heavy weapons which had been concealed in the rubble. All were taking damage and the actual strength of the enemy was still unknown. The situation was degenerating at an alarming rate and even Fadjnadtur's plaintive, *Commander, what should we do?* was no consolation.

"All groups withdraw," it commanded. "Fall back to our starting positions. Leave no one behind!" A chorus of acknowledgments came in reply.

Qetjnegartis turned its machine back the way it had come, spraying the tops of the buildings around it randomly with its heat ray. It paused to allow one of the others to lead the way and then followed. The structures on both sides were burning, but enemy fire came from them, too—the creatures were risking immolation to carry out their attacks. It ordered its subordinates to increase their speed.

Suddenly, the machine in front of it, piloted by Sladgenupral, went tumbling forward, to crash in a heap on the ground. Its legs were tangled in a heavy cable and thrashed futilely, unable to get free. Qetjnegartis was quite certain that no cable had blocked the passage when they came the other way. Instantly, swarms of the prey-creatures erupted from the buildings and, seemingly, from the ground itself to attack the downed machine.

Qetjnegartis knew that these enemies would be carrying their explosive bombs and try to place them on the vulnerable parts of Sladgenupral's machine. It activated its heat ray on the low-power, wide-angle mode and swept it across the prey-creatures and the crippled fighting machine. At this reduced power, it would not harm Sladgenupral, but it would still be lethal to the enemy. Score of the miserable animals were slain in moments, but not before some had achieved their purpose. Five or six explosions hammered at the machine, sending bits of it hurtling skyward and filling the space between the buildings with smoke and dust.

It continued to sweep the heat ray into the smoke and was soon joined by a subordinate who came up beside it. The smoke dissipated and they could see that the fighting machine was badly damaged. Telemetry indicated that Sladgenupral was alive, but injured. Qetjnegartis moved forward to extract it, while its subordinate deployed a carrying pod. Some fire was still rattling off the skin of its machine, but the main enemy attack had been destroyed. Qetjnegartis reached the wreck and used its manipulators to pry open the hatch.

"Commander! Beware!"

Almost simultaneous with the warning came a heavy blow to its machine. An enemy vehicle had emerged from gaps between the buildings and opened fire. Another trap! Qetjnegartis brought up its heat ray, reset it to maximum power, and then fired at the vehicle. Another impact, even more powerful than the first, struck and sent Qetjnegartis staggering back. To its dismay, daylight was seeping in through a hole in the cockpit! It twisted the machine sideways to turn the vulnerable spot away from the enemy and continued to fire the heat ray. The enemy vehicle exploded and the immediate threat was eliminated. But how many more were still waiting?

"Commander, are you all right?"

"Yes, but this machine is damaged. Quickly, recover Sladge-nupral, and let us leave this place."

This was done and the group managed to break clear of the structures and into the open. The other two groups were gathering along the enemy trench line to provide covering fire. Qetjnegartis noted that three of their machines were missing. The battlegroup reassembled and quickly fell back until they were out of range of the enemy weapons. There they halted to evaluate the situation.

One of them dead, three injured, four machines destroyed, and half the rest damaged; and the enemy city still there. Not a good result at all. Qetjnegartis was not pleased.

This is intolerable.

* * * * *

June, 1911, Fort Myer, District of Columbia

Brevet Colonel Andrew Comstock sat down at the breakfast table and picked up the morning edition of the *Washington Post*. The headline story celebrated the recent victory at Little Rock. Andrew already knew the full details from his military briefings and chuckled in amusement at the paper's fanciful descriptions of the 'gallant defense'. Well, it had been pretty gallant, and he had to hand it to the troops who had succeeded in beating off the Martian attack. Andrew had seen for himself the consequences of an unsuccessful defense and he could imagine the chaos inside Little Rock once the enemy had pierced the defensive lines. That the men had not panicked, but instead had stuck to their posts and then struck back, spoke well of them—very well indeed. Most of the garrison was made up of the 77th Division which had survived the long retreat from Santa Fe last year. Veterans for sure! Andrew had shared part of that journey with them.

His wife, Victoria, swept into the room with little Arthur on her hip and a cup of coffee in her other hand, which she gracefully slid onto the table next to him. "Good morning, dear," she said, smiling. "Breakfast will be ready in a little bit."

"Thanks."

She disappeared for a moment and then came back and sat down at the table with her own cup. Arthur tried to grab it away from her when she took a sip, but she fended him off successfully. "What will you be doing today, dear?"

"Oh, the same as always," he replied absently, still paging through the paper. "Reading reports. Writing replies. That sort of thing."

"Will you be taking any of those inspection trips again soon?"

"I'll be going to Aberdeen, Philadelphia, and then up to Long Island in a couple of weeks, why?"

"I was... I was hoping we could look for a house soon." Andrew put down the paper and looked at his wife. She was smiling faintly as she bounced the baby gently in her arms.

He glanced around at their comfortable surroundings. Since their marriage, a little less than two years ago, they had lived with Victoria's parents in their cozy home at Fort Myer, just across the Potomac from Washington. His father-in-law, Brevet Brigadier General Hawthorne, was also his boss at the Ordnance Department. They got along well and the house, which was government property, was more than big enough for all of them - and a couple of servants, too. He was perfectly happy staying here.

But Victoria had been hinting at getting their own place for a while now. Her mother was a delightful lady, but Andrew had noticed a growing tension between her and her daughter. Victoria clearly wanted to be the mistress of her own home...

"You're getting the salary of a full colonel now, dear," she said. "We should be able to afford it."

"My permanent rank is only major. If the war should end, I'll go back to that quicker than..."

"And how likely is that?"

"It'll end eventually..." he said lamely.

"Not any time soon," she countered. "I've heard you and Dad say so a dozen times when you thought I couldn't hear."

There was no answer to that, but fortunately, the maid chose that moment to come in with their breakfast, so he didn't have to. He busied himself with his food, but he could sense his wife's gaze on him. Yes, the war was not going to end any time soon. The Martians had landed in 1908 and things were still going their way. They had occupied nearly all of the Great Plains from Canada down to Texas and from the Rockies to the Mississippi. Except for the path through Texas, the country was cut in two.

Andrew had been an eyewitness to much of it. He'd been with the army when it first encountered the Martians in strength. He'd been through defeats and victories, he'd sat in on conferences with the President and high-ranking generals, and he'd conferred with brilliant scientists and engineers trying to devise better weapons to fight the merciless foe. And at age twenty-five he was a bird-colonel drawing the amazing amount of $333.33 a month, plus allowances. Even his permanent rank of major paid $250.00. Yes, they probably could afford a home of their own, even with the money he sent to his widowed mother.

"There are no empty residences left here at the fort," he said, not quite ready to give in. "And have you seen the prices in the city? Every decent place has been snapped up by generals, congressmen, diplomats, or lobbyists." It was true: the wartime expansion of the military and the government had swelled the city's population to the bursting point. There was a serious housing shortage.

They are building a lot of nice new houses in Alexandria," said Victoria, teasing the baby with a piece of bacon. "Electric lights, indoor plumbing..."

"How would I get to work from way out there?"

"We could buy an automobile."

"If we could find one! All the auto manufacturers are building vehicles for the army these days, you know."

"Well then we might still find a place closer by. With all the comings and goings, surely some houses become vacant. We can at least try. Please, dear?"

He realized this was one battle he couldn't win. "Of course, love. Perhaps this Saturday."

"Thank you, Andrew! Oh, it will be lovely!"

"Uh, huh," Andrew went back to his paper. He snorted when he saw the article on page four mentioning that the Panama Canal was scheduled to open in a few weeks. In normal times that would have been the headline story on the front page.

But these weren't normal times.

* * * * *

July, 1911, Panama City, Panama

Lieutenant Commander Drew Harding sprawled on his bunk aboard the battleship *USS Minnesota* and tried to ignore the heat. It wasn't possible, of course; it was well into the rainy season now and even when it wasn't raining, it was terribly humid. The steady breezes off the Pacific would bring some relief, but little of that could find its way into the steel bowels of the large warship. Harding was wearing nothing but his underwear, but he was still dripping with sweat. He was tempted to go up on deck to get some of that breeze, but that would mean putting on his uniform. He gave up on that idea and closed his eyes. His next watch wasn't for a few hours and perhaps he could sleep for a while.

He was just dozing off when the door to his quarters banged open, bringing him awake again. It was his roommate, Hank Coleman. "Wake up, sleepy head!" cried the man with appalling cheerfulness.

"Why?" growled Harding.

"Mail boat! You've got a letter!"

That brought him more fully awake. Mail delivery to Panama was pretty regular, but he didn't usually get anything. His mother wasn't much of a writer, his father was too busy, and his girlfriend had broken things off when he'd opted for sea duty. He rolled over and put out his hand. "Gimme."

"Looks important!" continued Coleman. "From Washington! Maybe it's your promotion to admiral!" Even more interested, he sat up and looked at the letter. It was from Washington, but then he recognized the handwriting.

"Nope, it's from a friend of mine in the Army Ordnance Department, Andy Comstock."

"What're you doing hanging around with the army?" asked Coleman.

"Oh, we used to meet a lot when I was on Admiral Twining's staff on the Ordnance Bureau. There were all these meetings to discuss new weapons and such. I was just an ensign then and he was a second lieutenant and all we did was fetch coffee for the brass and clean up afterward. Well, it wasn't all drudgery, they'd have these really fine dinners after the meetings at the officers' club, and we got to tag along. Twinning didn't skimp on the liquor and we'd get pretty potted by the end of 'em. Comstock was a good guy and we've stayed in touch." He tore open the envelope.

"And now you're the gunnery officer on a battleship," said Coleman. "Bet he's jealous."

"Ha! Don't bet on that. He's a full bird-colonel now!"

"Really? I know they're promoting everyone right and left these days, but a colonel? Wait, you mean he's *that* Comstock? The one who did all that stuff out west when the war started?"

"None other."

"And you're friends with him? Wow, how about an autograph? Can I touch you?" Coleman leaned over and poked him in the shoulder.

"Beat it, you goof!"

Coleman smirked and strolled off, banging the door shut behind him. Harding snorted. Hank was okay, but he could be a jerk at times. He pulled Andy's letter out of the envelope and unfolded it. It was dated almost two weeks earlier, but that was about normal for mail delivery. It started off in the usual fashion: *how are you? I'm fine, etc. etc.* Then there were several paragraphs describing Andrew's infant son. Drew had little interest in children and the man he remembered hadn't either, so the proud gushing was both boring and a little surprising. He'd noticed the same phenomenon with his older brother and a cousin. *The little imps do something to our brains...* He resolved to continue avoiding them.

The next page was more interesting. Andrew's description of a recent joint meeting between the army and the navy ordnance staffs, like the ones Drew had just mentioned to Coleman, had him laughing with a few sarcastic comments about people they both knew. But then he wrote: *The big topic for the meeting was that the stand-in for the land ironclads has started testing. I'll be going up to Philadelphia to see it in a few weeks.* Ah, Drew had been wondering how those projects were going. Both the army and the navy were developing enormous war machines, commonly called 'land ironclads'. They were going to be like warships on caterpillar tracks. But constructing and perfecting machines of that size was proving very difficult and they were still a long way from being ready. So a smaller and simpler version was being built as a substitute. He was pleased that they were into the testing phase already.

But enough about me, continued Andy, *what have you been doing? Enjoying your exotic location? Entertaining the lovely señoritas? And what about the canal? They say it's about to open, have you been through it yet?*

As a matter of fact, Drew *had* been through the canal, just the previous week. The *Minnesota* and a dozen other ships had been among the first to make the passage. It had been as impressive as all get-out. The enormous concrete locks had lifted the ships up to the level of Lake Gatun and then back down to the Pacific on the other side of the isthmus. It had seemed almost miraculous; the *Minnesota*, all sixteen thousand *tons* of her, raised eighty-five feet simply by opening some valves to let water into the locks, and then set back down again, gently as a feather, by letting the water out of the other set of locks. The cruise along the lake, artificially created by a dam, had been impressive, too, especially the enormous excavation at the Culebra Cut, which sliced right through the Continental Divide.

It had been a little scary, too. The Cut was still very unstable and there had been swarms of workers still moving earth there as they cruised past. Drew had seen stones and even large boulders tumble down the slopes into the water. A few small rocks had actually bounced off the ship. It wasn't safe, but the rush to get the canal open had over-ridden safety concerns. The Martians were starting to move south from Mexico and until the army could get its forts built, the navy was the canal's primary defense. They needed to get more ships on the Pacific side and the long haul around Cape Horn was very difficult these days with most of the old coaling stations in Martian hands - er, tentacles.

But now there was a strong fleet on both sides. Drew was glad to be with the Pacific Fleet. It was a bit cooler on this side and Panama City was far more pleasant than the city of Colon on the Atlantic side. Not all that pleasant, though, and the *señoritas*, Andy mentioned had been noticeably absent.

The fact of the matter was that Panama had been turned into an enormous refugee camp and construction zone. Huge numbers of refugees, hundreds of thousands of them, had fled to Panama from both north and south to escape the Martians. Most had been put to work building the canal and their added labor had gotten it open far ahead of schedule. Many of the rest - mostly women and children - were growing the food needed to feed all the workers and themselves. Vast cities of tents and shacks had been erected to house them, although many simply slept in the streets of Colon and Panama City. More people were coming in all the time and the refugees now far outnumbered the native Panamanians. The locals didn't like that at all and they had turned sullen toward all foreigners, including the *Norteamericanos* Fortunately, the army had plenty of troops here to keep order. Few people - even the Panamanians - even bothered to pretend that the United States wasn't running the place now.

But everyone was wondering if they had enough troops to defend the canal in the event of a serious attack. The construction crews which had built the canal were now working full steam on building concrete fortifications, but they weren't even close to being finished. It was probably going to be up to the navy for the near future. Drew was hoping to get a crack at the beasties at some point.

Andy finished up his letter with the expected best wishes, but there was a postscript after his signature: *I've been meaning to ask you and I finally remembered to put it in this letter. Do you have any relatives out west? I met a girl on my first trip out there named Rebecca Harding. Same last name as yours. Her family was killed in the first Martian attack. She had an aunt in Santa Fe, but God knows what's happened to her. I was just wondering if maybe you are related.*

Drew's eyebrows went up. He had a passel of grandparents, aunts, uncles, and cousins, but as far as he knew, they all lived in the Albany region, where he had grown up. Still, if anyone knew, it would be his grandmother. He hadn't written to her in ages. He checked the time and saw he still had a while until he had to get ready for duty. He rolled out of his bunk and sat down at the tiny desk the cabin boasted and pulled out a sheet of paper.

* * * * *

August, 1911, Memphis, Tennessee

Captain Frank Dolfen took a tight hold on the reins of his horse as one of the roaring airplanes flew overhead a little too close for comfort - for both man and beast. "Damn it!" he muttered as his horse shied.

"By Jove!" cried the rider next to him. "Those blighters should be more careful!"

Dolfen regained control of his mount and glanced at the man. He was British, which could be instantly discerned from his accent, and almost as instantly from his uniform. This was nearly the same shade of khaki as the one Dolfen wore, but it was cut differently and had a number of small bits of decoration you would never find on an American uniform. And there was his hat; he wore a distinctly British, off-white pith helmet with a gleaming brass regimental badge on the front. The man's name was George Tom Molesworth Bridges, but as he was quick to inform everyone, he went by the name of 'Tom'. He held a brevet rank of major.

"Yeah, they should," agreed Dolfen. "But you know fliers."

'Not really, old man. Are they all like that?"

"Pretty much, from what I've seen. All as crazy as jack rabbits. 'Careful' doesn't seem to be in their vocabulary."

"And you say we'll be working with them?"

"That's the plan. Don't know if it will really work. Come on, the headquarters tent is over there." He turned his horse toward a large tent on the edge of the field the fliers had turned into an aerodrome a half-dozen miles north of the city of Memphis. As they got closer, they saw a large sign erected in front of the tent proclaiming it to be the headquarters of the 9th Air Group. It had an insignia with a red '9' and a yellow lightning bolt going through the hole in the 9. There were a number of men in the area of the tent along with a couple of women in dresses and a scattering of children, too. With the huge refugee camps in the area, the military posts were a magnet for people looking for work or extra food. It was like that back at Dolfen's own camp, too.

They dismounted, and Major Bridges bent to give one of the kids a coin to hold both of their horses. "Whew!" he said straightening up and pulling out a handkerchief. "Hot as India! Is it like this all the time?" He mopped sweat off his face.

"For another coupla months. Summers are hell, but the rest of the time it's not bad." Dolfen led the way into the command tent, past a sentry who came to attention for Dolfen, but looked in puzzlement for Bridge's rank. Technically, as a major, the Britisher rated a present arms, but the sentry obviously didn't know what he was. Until a few hours ago, Dolfen hadn't either.

Things were bustling inside the tent. Orderlies were moving to and fro with papers in their hands, clerks were hammering away on typewriters, and there were several people talking on field telephones. Electric lights hung from the canvas roof. Dolfen identified himself to a harried lieutenant who led them to, and then without ceremony, abandoned them with the group's commanding officer. This was a lieutenant colonel named Selfridge. His first name was also 'Tom' and Dolfen had briefly met him in the first days of the war. He was a good looking fellow, and like most of the officers these days, very young in Dolfen's eyes. The skin on the left side of his face had a smooth and shiny look to it - compliments of a Martian heat ray. Selfridge held the dubious distinction of being the first American pilot to be shot down by the Martians.

Selfridge popped to his feet when he saw them and greeted Dolfen enthusiastically. "Hello, Captain! Good to see you again! Come up a bit in the world since our last meeting, eh?"

"We both have, sir," replied Dolfen. Selfridge had been a captain and Dolfen just a sergeant when they'd met during a desperate retreat to get away from pursuing Martians. "This is Major Bridges, compliments of the 4th Queen's Own Hussars."

"Ah! Our British liaison!" exclaimed Selfridge. "I'd heard rumors we'd be getting one, but I wasn't sure I should believe it. Glad to meet you, Major!" He extended his hand and Bridges took it without hesitation. Dolfen had heard tales that Englishmen didn't like to shake hands, but he'd noticed no such reluctance with Bridges.

"A pleasure to meet, you, Colonel," replied the major. "Of course I'm technically a liaison to Captain Dolfen, here, but I'm sure we'll all be working together."

"That is the point, isn't it? To coordinate our ground and aerial forces?"

"Yes, sir," said Dolfen. "And my commander wants to send out my squadron the day after tomorrow. Are your fliers going to be ready to support us?"

"Yes indeed! My boys are champing at the bit to get out there!" replied Selfridge enthusiastically. "We've been restricted to training flights on the east side of the river and I can tell you that we're getting tired of that! But come on, let me show you around!" He grabbed his cap and led the way out of the tent back into the bright sunshine.

"I have four squadrons in the group," said Selfridge, waving his hand to take in the whole operation. "With four flights of four aircraft in each squadron, that makes for sixty-four altogether. Of course that's on paper. There are always aircraft out of service for maintenance or repairs due to accidents—always having accidents. On any given day we can usually put fifty in the air."

"Now that I take a closer look at these machines," said Bridges, "they seem more familiar. I do believe we have something rather like them."

Selfridge laughed. "I'm not surprised, Major! This is a British design we are building under license. They're Burgess-Dunne D.8s, to be exact. A nice aircraft! Faster and a lot more stable than the old Wright Flyers I cut my teeth on. Very easy to fly. We've modified them to make two-seaters out of them. We have a gunner in the front with his machine gun and the pilot sits behind him. It can carry a hundred-pound bomb, too."

Dolfen studied one of the aircraft sitting close by. It was the same horribly flimsy-looking wood, canvas, and wire contraption like others he'd seen, but the crewmen, instead of being completely in the open, sat inside an enclosed area, like some oversized bathtub or canoe. The motor and propeller was at the rear, right behind the pilot's seat. But the biggest change from the other models was the fact that the wings were angled back on each side of the center. So instead of just being long rectangles, the wings were shaped like an arrow, or a military rank chevron. It made them look like they were moving fast even when sitting on the ground.

"How far can they fly, Colonel? How long can they stay in the air?"

"With extra fuel instead of a bomb, they can go about three hundred miles and stay in the air almost five hours."

Dolfen frowned. "So assuming you want to get back, you can't go more than a hundred and fifty miles from here? That's going to limit how deeply we can penetrate into enemy territory, sir."

"True, although we do have a forward airfield on the other side of the river, so staging from there would give us a few more miles. But, Captain, me and my staff had an idea the other day that I want to run by you."

"Sir?"

"Well, as I understand it, your squadron isn't just horse cavalry anymore, is it?"

"No, sir. We have one troop on horses, one on motorcycles, and a troop of ten armored cars. We'll also have a battery of field guns towed by motor trucks attached to us most of the time."

"Good! So that means you'll also have some supply trucks along? To carry ammunition and food, and gasoline for those motorcycles?"

"A few..." admitted Dolfen, not much liking where this seemed to be going. Cavalry was supposed to be light and mobile. If you started loading it down with a big supply train...

"Well, we were thinking that if we sent along a few trucks carrying gasoline and maybe a few spare parts and a mechanic or two, we could set up temporary airstrips wherever there is a flat field to land on..."

"Plenty of them over there, sir. Flat as a griddle cake all the way to the Rockies."

"Exactly!" said Selfridge, smiling. "That way we could follow along with you out to the maximum range of our planes. You could set up a strip and we could land and refuel."

"I guess that could work, sir. As long as the trucks don't break down. Nothing but dirt roads out that way and not very good ones."

"Communications will be a critical factor, Colonel," said Bridges. "How will we coordinate our movements?"

"A good point, Major. But thanks to you British, that should not be a big problem."

"I don't follow you, sir."

"Those wonderful radio transmitters you've supplied us with, Major."

"Oh, those things. Can't say I know much about them, Colonel."

"They're marvelous! They have a range of hundreds of miles, batteries which last almost forever, and they don't weigh ten pounds. We've got one for each flight leader and more back here at headquarters. You have some with your squadron, too, don't you, Captain?"

"A few, yes, sir. We're still learning how to use them properly. I've only got a few men who can send and understand the Morse."

"True, they're just spark-gap transmitters, but with practice we should be able to tell you what we can see and you should be able to call us when you need help. And that's what this first mission is going to be, isn't it? Just practice?"

"More than that, sir," said Dolfen. "We'll be out there in territory where there are Martians. My orders are that if we find the enemy and have a reasonable chance of beating them, we are to attack."

"Well that sounds like fun, Captain! My boys are itching to take a crack at the bastards."

"Pardon me for asking, Colonel," said Bridges. "But do you really think these machines can survive to get close enough to hurt a Martian tripod? I've seen them in action and they're not easy to destroy."

"I guess we'll find out," replied Selfridge. Some of the joviality left his face and he nodded. "A lot of us are going to get killed, I'm sure. But if we can take some of them with us, it will be worthwhile, right, Captain?"

"Yes, sir. And I'm thinking that if we can coordinate what we do, my troopers attacking at the same time as your fliers, we might give them so much to worry about that they can't stop us."

"Yes. That was exactly my thought, too. I was there at the Battle of Prewitt, just like you, remember. The enemy tripods are nasty customers, but they can only fire at one thing at a time. If they are engaged with your cavalry and armored cars and field guns and then my boys come flying in, well, we could overwhelm them."

"Sounds good... in theory, Colonel," said Bridges.

"Well, that's what we are here for, isn't it? To put the theory into practice? Let's go back to my office and we'll take a look at the maps and plan out our operation."

* * * * *

August, 1911, Memphis, Tennessee

"All right, let's try it again. Slowly let out your breath and then squeeze the trigger." Rebecca Harding stepped back and watched Abigail LaPlace struggling with her rifle. The weapon, a Springfield 1903, was really too large and heavy for the girl, but when Becca had been put in charge of the marksmanship instructions, she'd insisted that they use the standard army rifles. Abigail shifted the sling on her arm and took aim. Becca gritted her teeth at the way the rifle's muzzle was drifting around. It settled down to near-immobility and Becca's hopes rose, but then the girl's whole body seemed to twitch and the gun went off with a bang. Becca didn't need to use her field glasses to check the target to know it had been a clean miss, but she said: "Better. Keep at it." Actually it *had* been better, at least the girl had kept her eyes open this time.

Abigail, and all the other women around her, were part of a 'militia' organization which styled itself the 'Memphis Women's Volunteer Sharpshooters'. While they were from Memphis, and they were women, and they were surely volunteers, they had a long way to go, in Rebecca's opinion, to earn the 'sharpshooter' part of their title. Their unofficial nickname was the 'Memphis Belles' and that seemed a far more accurate description to Becca. Theoretically, there were over a hundred members of the company, most from the finest families of Memphis, but it was rare for more than thirty of them to show up at a meeting at the same time. There were about that many here today.

She walked down the firing line to where the next shooter, a much older woman, was methodically working the action of her rifle. Loading and firing with confidence, a considerable pile of empty brass was accumulating around her feet. "You're doing well, Mrs. Halberstam."

"Please, Becca, you can call me Sarah," said the woman, opening the bolt and lowering the rifle so the butt was on the ground. "And thank you."

"You've obviously done a lot of shooting, ma'am."

"Some. Bird hunting, mostly. Never with one of these, though," she said, waving a hand at the Springfield. "It's got quite a kick."

"Yes, but we need some real power to hurt the Martians."

Halberstam smiled skeptically. "Not going to hurt one of those tripod machines, even with one of these from what I've heard."

"No, probably not," admitted Rebecca. "So what're you doin' here?"

"What are you?"

She shrugged. "Felt like I needed to be doin' *something*!"

"You're a nurse aren't you? That's surely doing something."

"I guess, so. But after two years of it, it doesn't seem... enough."

The older woman nodded. "You want to hit back at 'em. Hurt them yourself."

"Yeah."

"Killing one wasn't enough?"

Rebecca winced. She wished she'd never shown anyone the newspaper clipping she'd gotten from a local paper which recounted her exploits back in the first days of the war when she'd killed the pilot of a wrecked Martian tripod. But without that she'd never have been let into the group. It was for the upper crust and Becca was literally from the wrong side of the tracks these days. But the newspaper had done the trick and the group's leader, a formidable woman named Theodora Oswald, had been overjoyed to welcome Becca into the organization. She was the uppermost of the upper crust in Memphis, it seemed, and clearly her family had a lot of money. They owned a huge estate outside of town and it was now the headquarters for the sharpshooters. There was a shooting range and a drill field set up and plenty of colored servants to provide drinks when necessary. And she - or perhaps her husband—clearly had political pull, too. The fact that a hundred Springfields and fifty thousand rounds of ammunition had magically appeared at her mansion proved that.

"One was just a start," said Becca eventually. "We need to kill 'em all."

"Yes, it surely seems that way. Well, back to work." Halberstam raised the rifle and slid a cartridge into the breech. The Springfields had a five round magazine, but for safety reasons, Rebecca insisted that they load and fire individual rounds.

She continued her inspection of the shooters. Some, like Halberstam, weren't bad, and some, like Abigail, were probably hopeless, and most - as she'd feared when she first heard about this group - thought it was some sort of social club rather than a military organization! They clearly took far more interest in their sporty uniforms than they did in drill or marksmanship. The uniforms were ridiculous: buckskin jackets with a dangling fringe on the bottom and down each arm, billowy pantaloons tucked into calf-high boots, and a jaunty hat with a feather. Becca refused to wear it and stuck to her nurse's uniform.

She reached the end of the firing line and looked over to the 'parade ground' where Sam Jones was teaching the other half of today's group the rudiments of the manual of arms and the basic marching steps. Or trying to, anyway. His charges showed all the discipline of a flock of chickens. Sam was an enigma to her. When she'd first seen him, he was a bearded, raging scarecrow, rescued from the Martian fortress near Gallup, New Mexico. He'd been a part of General Sumner's army and was captured when it was destroyed in the first battle with the invaders. Rescued, he'd refused to go back with the army—or give his right name—and had attached himself to Rebecca's hospital unit. He was nervous like a skittish horse. But he had volunteered to help her out here and his knowledge of the drill showed that he'd probably been with an infantry unit. He would disappear for days at a time, but so far had always come back.

She turned to go back down the line, when Mrs. Oswald appeared with several servants bearing pitchers of lemonade. She declared the day's efforts at an end and called all the ladies together for refreshments. Becca shook her head; they hadn't been at this for more than an hour. Of course, it was very hot. The women and girls clustered around... chattering about nothing in particular as far as Becca could tell. They seemed like nice people, but few of them appeared to have a clue of what the war was really like or about.

Oswald made some sort of speech and blathered on for quite some time before Becca could make her escape. She promised to come again next week. She rode her horse, Ninny, back toward Memphis, Sam walking beside her. "So how'd they do today?" she asked. "You able to teach 'em anything?"

"Not really. Like tryin' to herd cats. Pointless."

"So why you bothering?"

"Same reason as you: beats sitting around doin' nothing during our off-hours. Gets me out of camp. And some of 'em are kind of cute."

Becca chuckled. "Can't say I noticed. But yeah, it probably is pointless. In a fight, none of them will be worth spit."

Their way took them along the river where thousands of men were at work constructing fortifications. The Mississippi Line, as it was being called, had been little more than the river itself when Becca and the battered remains of the army's II Corps - plus a huge number of refugees - had straggled across the bridge into Memphis fifteen months earlier. They'd marched all the way from Santa Fe, each day fearing that the Martians would appear to finish them off. But they'd made it across the river - barely - and the Martians had pretty much left them alone ever since.

No one could explain why the enemy had gone dormant for so long, but no one was really complaining. The respite had given them a chance to build some real defenses along the river. They'd started with the cities and towns; places like New Orleans, Baton Rouge, Natchez, Vicksburg, and Memphis. Then on up the river to Cairo, St. Louis, Davenport, and Minneapolis. Each place had been turned into a fortress bristling with cannons. At first these had just been in earthworks, but now those were being replaced with massive concrete walls high enough that a Martian machine couldn't get across. More and bigger guns were being mounted, too. And now they were extending the concrete walls, creeping along the river, north and south from each fortress. Given time, they could link them all together in a - hopefully - unbreakable barrier.

"Those monsters are gonna have a heck of a time getting across here!" said Becca, pointing at the works.

"The river is over a thousand miles long, Becca," replied Sam. "It'll take years to make it all look like this."

"Maybe so, but there's a lot of swampland along it too. And they've got gunboats patrolling. We can hurt 'em anywhere they try."

"I hope so."

But Becca wasn't all that interested in the *defenses*. Just holding them back wasn't good enough. They needed to be driven out! Driven back! Wiped out! No one seemed to be saying much about that.

"Someday," she muttered to herself. "Someday we'll kill them all."

* * * * *

August, 1911, Rock Creek Park, Maryland

"Come on, Leonard! This is bully, isn't it?"

Lieutenant General Leonard Wood, Chief of Staff of the United States Army, watched the President of the United States disappear around a bend in the trail ahead of him and spurred his horse to catch up. He glanced behind and saw that the President's military aide, Major Archie Butt, and the squad of escorting cavalry had fallen far behind.

Wood had spent a large chunk of his youth riding in far more rugged locations than Rock Creek Park, so galloping at full speed down the easy paths here didn't bother him. The object of his pursuit, Theodore Roosevelt, was an equally experienced horseman and was probably in no danger, but the thought of some freak accident befalling the President sent a chill down his spine in spite of the summer heat.

He sighed in relief when he caught sight of Roosevelt again and saw that he had reined in his horse and was halted next to the creek, in a little glen. Wood slowed as he came up beside him. "You shouldn't ride off alone like that, Theodore," said Wood, knowing his scolding was pointless.

"Oh, I know, Leonard," laughed Roosevelt. "The woods are just crawling with Martian assassins!" He waved his hands at the luxuriant greenery. Shafts of sunshine penetrated the canopy overhead, producing shifting patterns of light and shadow. It was a beautiful spot.

"There aren't any Martians around here," admitted Wood, "but there could be assassins of the two-legged variety."

"Oh, tosh! Who would want to kill me?"

Wood didn't answer, but the tiny twitch in the President's eye told him that he knew that there were lunatics around who did wish him harm. Prior to the Martian landings, Roosevelt had been one of the most popular Presidents in American history. In the immediate aftermath of the invasion the people had rallied around him and his popularity rose to new heights. But that was nearly three years ago, and the war was going on and on. There had been terrible defeats and damn few victories. Millions of Americans had been driven from their homes and even those who had not been directly affected were being asked to make more and more sacrifices. Yes, there were people angry enough, or crazy enough, to do the unthinkable. After all, Roosevelt had first become President because of an unthinkable act—in a time of peace and prosperity.

Major Butt and the escort finally caught up and formed a perimeter around Wood and Roosevelt. The President dismounted and gave the reins of his horse to one of the troopers. He stretched and strolled toward the creek. Wood groaned silently. *He's not going to...? Yes, he is. Damn it.*

"Come, Leonard, it's so blasted hot, let's take a dip."

There was no escaping it, so Wood swung off his horse and followed. Roosevelt was stripping off his clothes and dropping them on the bank of the creek. *Well, at least it's not November!*

Roosevelt's excursions to Rock Creek were famous - or infamous in some circles. In the early years of his presidency he would lead parties of senators, congressmen, ambassadors, and just about anyone who wanted to talk to him out here and then, in all weather, strip buck naked to wade or swim in the creek and climb the cliffs on the opposite bank. People wanting to gain his ear - and his respect - had little choice but to follow suit. Wood had managed to avoid most of those trips, but he did remember one frigid March day where there was ice floating in the creek...

He peeled off his sweat-soaked uniform and followed his leader into the water. He had to admit that it did feel good on a day like this. Major Butt was standing on the bank looking very uncomfortable. The man watched Roosevelt, looked back at the smirking cavalrymen, and then shrugged and started unbuttoning his coat.

"Oh, this is splendid!" said the President, submerging himself up to his chin. "It's been too long since I've done this!"

"We've all been a trifle busy," said Wood. "I'll be up until midnight catching up from this little jaunt."

"Don't try to make me feel guilty, Leonard! It won't work!"

"Oh, I *know* it won't. Never has."

Roosevelt laughed and rolled over on his back in the water. "But you know, the idea of Martian assassins sets me to thinking."

"Oh?"

"Well, sometimes I wonder just how much they know about us. Do they have any notion about how our governments work? Who our leaders are? If they ever had the opportunity to assassinate me—or the Kaiser, or the Tsar—would they even go to the effort?"

"Well, they surely must know that we are organized in some fashion. We have cities and armies and navies. Things like that don't just happen spontaneously. And they must have some sort of government of their own."

"True, true, but they might think themselves so superior that they don't even consider how we do things. I mean do we worry about who is the leader of a herd of cattle or a flock of chickens? To us they are just a resource to be exploited."

"Hmm..." grunted Wood, not much liking the comparison.

"And their complete refusal to try and communicate indicates the Martians feel the same way toward us."

Wood had to admit that it certainly could be true. There had been some attempts to communicate with the invaders. All had failed—often with fatal consequences to those making the attempt. Parties advancing under flags of truce had been reduced to ash. There was a report out of Russia of a group of Orthodox Bishops, marching forward with icons held high, being vaporized. More cautious attempts, using blinking lights from a distance or the new radio signals, had been ignored. It was plain that the enemy had not come to talk.

"So, it will be a war of extermination."

"From our point of view it will have to be," said Roosevelt. "There's no choice. But from their point of view..." he shrugged. "If they do just think of us as cattle..."

Both men fell silent. There was no longer any doubt that the Martians did feed upon humans—and other large warm-blooded animals. But whether that was just an expediency forced upon the Martians during the initial phase of their invasion or a long range policy was unknown. Although reports from scouting missions into Martian held territory in Asia and Africa told of huge pens holding human captives, far more than would be needed for immediate food supplies. It was an unsettling thing to think about.

Major Butt joined them in the water. "You do have a reception tonight, Mr. President," he said diffidently.

"Yes, yes, I know. We'll be back to the White House in plenty of time, Major."

"Well, at least the Canal is open," said Wood, trying to bring up something good.

Yes!" replied Roosevelt, brightening. "Wish I could have been there. Just so blasted much work here, I can't get away." His expression quickly darkened again. "And not just running the war; the politics have become downright suffocating!"

Wood nodded. Yes, the massive wave of patriotic fervor in the first year or so, when Roosevelt could get anything he wanted out of Congress, Wall Street, or the people had long since disappeared. When it came to wars, Americans were notoriously impatient. They didn't balk at making sacrifices or risking death on the battlefield, but they wanted to *get on with it*! Get it done with so they could go back to their regular lives. They wanted 'splendid little wars', like the ones with Spain or Mexico. When they got a long, bloody one, like the Civil War - or this one - they tended to get angry and lose confidence in their leaders.

As they were now. Millions of people had been forced to flee the states and territories in the heartland. Except for a few fortified outposts in places like Little Rock, Kansas City, Omaha, and Sioux City, which could be supplied by river, the Great Plains had been overrun. The farms which had produced such bounty were abandoned and food prices were soaring. Mines and factories were working around the clock, so everyone had a job and wages were also on the rise, but everything cost more and wartime necessity had seen many of the worker safety and child labor laws, championed by Roosevelt in his early years, suspended. Conditions in some places were very bad. More and more women and children were being pulled into the workplace as the men were sent to the army. The factory owners were making fortunes, but the new taxes needed to pay for the war were mostly falling on the middle class. The fabric of American society was being strained as never before.

The American people had the grit to take all of that, of course, but only if they could see that their efforts were paying off. At the moment, the payoff was hard to see. Discontent was rising and the congressmen and senators were listening to their constituents. Committees had been formed to look into how the war was being handled - Wood himself was spending an inordinate amount of time on Capitol Hill answering congressmen's questions these days. Everyone had ideas on how it could be done better. Roosevelt was not getting his way nearly as often as he wanted and it only looked to get worse.

And next year was an election year.

1912 could see the most important presidential election since 1864. Maybe the most important ever. Roosevelt's third term in 1908 was unprecedented. A fourth term in 1912 might prove unacceptable. The opposition was already on the move.

"Did you see that letter of Miles' in the *Post* yesterday?" asked Roosevelt suddenly - as if he was reading Wood's mind.

"Yes. Yes, I did," replied Wood. General Nelson Miles had been a hero in the Civil War and more recently had been the Commanding General of the U.S. Army. Roosevelt had forced him to retire in 1903 so that the post of Commanding General could be abolished to make way for the current system with the Chief of Staff in charge. Miles had never forgiven Roosevelt and had tried to win the Democratic nomination for President in 1904. He'd lost that fight, but now he was back and with much wider backing. He'd written a letter that was savagely critical of Roosevelt - and Wood - and the way the war was being run. It was being reprinted in papers all over the country.

"His hat is in the ring for sure now," said Roosevelt sullenly. "You'd think he'd be too old for this sort of thing. He's what? Seventy-two?"

"Seventy-one, I think," said Wood. "Still hale, though. Remember when he rode ninety miles in one day just before you retired him to prove he was up to the task?"

"Yes, the show off. But he'll be the Democrats' choice for certain. I mean who else do they have? Bryan's been a pacifist his whole career and Wilson doesn't have any military credentials at all. They need a fighter."

"Well, he's certainly that."

We've got a fighter - what we need is a victory!

"By George! Look at that!"

Wood spun around, but saw nothing. Butt was looking for assassins and reaching for the pistol on his hip - only to realize it was on the pile of clothes on the bank.

"What?"

"I think I saw a cave swallow! They're rare in these parts. I think it landed somewhere on the cliffside. They sometimes make nests in crevasses."

Wood relaxed. Roosevelt and his damn birds! He was a noted expert on them and had written several books.

"Let's take a look, shall we?" The President paddled toward the far shore.

Wood sighed and followed.

A victory, we need a victory - and soon.

Chapter One

Cycle 597, 844.8, Holdfast 32-2

Qetjnegartis found Ixmaderna where it had expected: in its laboratory. While Ixmaderna never balked at any task assigned to it, construction, combat, or production, it had always been clear to Qetjnegartis that its greatest interest was scientific in nature. Now that they had the time to build a proper holdfast, with a well-equipped laboratory, and that every clan member was not so urgently needed for other tasks, Ixmaderna had the freedom to indulge its interests.

"Greetings, Commander," it said when it caught sight of Qetjnegartis. "It is a pleasure to see you again."

"As it is you." Ixmaderna was unfailingly courteous and Qetjnegartis often found itself mimicking the behavior. "I have just arrived back from Holdfast 32-4. Is all well, here?"

"Yes, it is. Resource gathering is going as planned, and production is at nearly full capacity. There have been no attacks on this holdfast and our scouts report no significant prey-creature military forces within three hundred *telequel*." It paused for a moment and then continued. "I have heard the news of the attack you led against the prey-creature city, Commander. An unfortunate setback, but hardly critical."

"No," said Qetjnegartis, "But it is still irritating. Attacking the enemy in one of their cities which they have had the time to fortify is much more difficult than in the open field. I am concerned because our observations indicate that the cities are far more numerous - and far larger - the further east we advance. We are going to need new techniques to overcome this problem."

"New techniques and new equipment, Commander," said Ixmaderna. "We are not the first clan to encounter these difficulties. Others have reported the same thing, and the engineers on the Homeworld have been working to develop machines which may help us overcome them."

"Indeed? Have they come up with anything?"

"We just received a transmission today. It contained the construction template for an interesting device. Here, let me show it to you." Ixmaderna moved to a large display screen and activated it. The image which appeared was very similar to a machine commonly used in mining, but with some significant modification. Qetjnegartis immediately noted the scale and realized the size of the device.

"It is not piloted?"

"No, it is far too small for that. It would have to be controlled remotely. There are also instructions for adding the necessary devices to our fighting machines - or the holdfast controls - to do that."

Qetjnegartis considered this. "It will take training to employ these properly, but I can see how they could have been used to good effect in the recent battle. And being unpiloted, they would be completely expendable. We will need such devices in future operations. Very well, you have my authorization to begin construction. I will take thought on when and how to deploy them."

"Very good, Commander," said Ixmaderna, clearly pleased. "It shall be as you command."

"Are there any other things you wish to discuss?"

"Actually, yes, if you have the time, Commander."

"I do. Proceed."

"I have been studying the intelligent prey-creatures," said Ixmaderna.

"I thought you were focusing your studies on the non-intelligent creatures of this world?"

"So I was. But the life on this world is all of identical construction and there is little of significant interest at a strictly biological level - except for the dangerous pathogens, of course, but other groups, more capable than I, are pursuing those lines of research."

"You insult yourself, Ixmaderna, You are as talented a scientist as anyone I have met," said Qetjnegartis.

"You are kind, Commander. But in any case, I turned over the routine cataloging of the non-intelligent life to an assistant, and I began to explore ways of controlling the larger non-intelligent creatures which I thought might be of use as food-animals. I hypothesized that if we could develop ways of easily controlling these animals, we could dispense with any need for the intelligent prey-creatures in that role. We could exterminate them completely and rely solely on the non-intelligent beasts."

"An interesting idea," said Qetjnegartis. "Using the intelligent ones as a food source has always posed problems. If we simply confine them, as we did at first, then the challenge becomes one of feeding them until we require them. Unconfined, they are dangerous and will try to flee. Can what you suggest be done?"

"At first I was optimistic, Commander. We have observed the prey-creatures controlling large numbers of them seemingly with ease. My attempts have been far less successful. The non-intelligent creatures are panicked by the sight, sound, and smell of us and our machines. Some grow so terrified they injure or even kill themselves in their desperation to escape. Even ones born in captivity have proven uncontrollable. Perhaps with time that will change. But I have had some new thoughts and that brings us back to my study of the intelligent prey-creatures."

"Indeed?"

"Yes, I began studying their young ones and what I've found is truly remarkable."

"How so?"

"The prey-creatures reproduce sexually, as all the lower creatures do, of course. The embryos develop inside the female and are then expelled when sufficiently matured to survive."

"That is not remarkable, Ixmaderna, most lower creatures do the same."

"True, Commander, but what is remarkable is the length of time it takes these young creatures to fully mature. From my observations, it takes approximately fourteen of the local cycles for them to reach sufficient maturity to reproduce, and then another four to reach their adult size."

"Really?" asked Qetjnegartis in surprise. That was an extraordinarily long period compared to life on the Homeworld. "But how can you be sure of that? We have only been on this world for two cycles—four of the local cycles."

"That is true. I have not been able to observe any single creature grow from birth to maturity. But by dividing the creatures into groups, sorted by their size and weight and behavior, and then seeing how they develop over several of the local cycles, I have been able to extrapolate the total amount of time it would take one to go from the least developed group to the most developed. I may be in some small degree of error, but I am confident my observations are still valid."

"Why such a long time? Are all the creatures on this world like that?"

"That is the other odd thing. No, they are not. The non-intelligent creatures develop much faster. They are born with a basic set of abilities and just a few of the local cycles bring them to adulthood. But Commander, the thing of greatest import is the fact that the newly born intelligent prey-creatures appear to be completely ignorant of... well, everything."

"What do you mean?"

"Exactly what I said, Commander. As far as I can determine, the newborns have only their autonomic functions. They cannot move, feed themselves, or even communicate with their parent, except in the most rudimentary fashion. They are utterly helpless and would not survive without help. Everything must be learned as they mature."

Qetjnegartis was very surprised. When the Race reproduced, it did so by budding off a new being. It would grow in a sac on the side of the parent's body and when it had matured sufficiently, it would detach. Shortly before detaching, the parent would transfer a great deal of basic information to the bud. From the moment it detached, it was capable of routine functions. While its intellect and advanced skills would develop later, as it experienced new things, it was a useful member of the Race immediately. But if these prey-creatures were a hindrance rather than a help for such a long period... "How could such a species even survive, let along become the dominant one on this world?"

"It does seem unlikely, doesn't it?" replied Ixmaderna. "I can only speculate that any potential competitors were even more primitive."

"Extraordinary. If this is true, our conquest of this world seems assured. But how does this relate to your earlier statement about controlling the non-intelligent creatures?"

"I am only speculating at this point, Commander, but it occurs to me that if the infant prey-creatures are truly such a blank, then perhaps they could be trained—by us."

"Trained? To do what?"

"Well, anything, I suppose," replied Ixmaderna. "My initial thought was to use them to control the non-intelligent animals. Perhaps we could keep small numbers of trained prey-creatures to control large numbers of the non-intelligent animals. There might be other useful tasks they could be set to do, as well."

It took a few moments for the full implication of this to be processed by Qetjnegartis. "Could they be trained to fight other prey-creatures?"

"I... don't know, Commander. There may be some instinct against fighting their own kind, some sort of automatic loyalty..."

"The level of armaments the first expedition encountered would argue against that," said Qetjnegartis. "They reported warriors with weapons and powerful fighting machines on the oceans. Clearly they must wage war on each other."

"True," conceded Ixmaderna. "It might be possible. Of course, considering the very slow level of development, it will be three or four cycles—six or eight of the local cycles—before we would know if we've been successful."

"I understand. But this is significant enough that I believe it should be pursued."

"That is excellent... Of course to do this properly, I will need expanded facilities, a good supply of captured prey-creatures, perhaps an assistant or two..."

"I will order it done."

"My thanks, Commander."

"This has the potential of repaying the clan many-fold. No thanks are needed. But Ixmaderna... There is another matter I wished to discuss with you today."

"Yes, Commander? What matter is that?"

"You touched upon the subject, just now: instinctive loyalty."

"I see," said Ixmaderna, waving its tendrils in sudden under-standing. "You are concerned about the buds."

"You have noticed this yourself?" Qetjnegartis was surprised.

"Yes. The buds created here do not have the automatic submission to the seniors who have arrived later. It is an interesting development."

Interesting! Ixmaderna's habit of understatement could be called 'interesting', but this was far too dangerous for that! The entire social structure of the Race was based upon the absolute submission of younger members to the older members within their clan. A member would submit to the will of its progenitor, or its progenitor's progenitor, or their bud-mates, up the line of ancestry for as far as it existed. But while the buds created on this world would submit to those who were here when they came into existence, they had no such submission to those still on the Homeworld or those who arrived from there after they were budded.

"I find it a very *alarming* development, Ixmaderna," said Qetjnegartis. "Since you have observed it, do you have any explanation for it?"

"Only an untested theory, Commander."

"Share it with me."

"If you insist. I'm reluctant to take a stance on something like this with no data to..."

"Share it with me."

"Very well. There are several theories that attempt to explain the known phenomena of our automatic dominance and submission. The most widely accepted—and the one I subscribe to - is that there is a mental link that exists between every member of the Race."

"I'm aware of that theory," said Qetjnegartis.

"Yes, it is theorized to be similar to the mental melding we can achieve when we grasp tendrils, but that it exists without physical contact and at a very weak - and hence subconscious - level. When a bud achieves consciousness, this subconscious link imprints the new being's place in the hierarchical structure of the Race. It instantly knows - and accepts - the dominance of all those there before it, and likewise its dominance of all who come after it. The problem in proving this is that no trace of this link has ever been detected even though reason dictates that it must exist within the electromagnet spectrum."

"Perhaps." Qetjnegartis had heard some lesser-accepted theories that postulated some entirely unknown method of transmission.

"If we accept that the link is electromagnet in nature," continued Ixmaderna, "then it must obey the inverse-square law. The strength of the link will weaken over distance. My theory is that the link is already very weak. It is strong enough to function within the relative small space of a single world, but too weak to function across interplanetary distances."

"Ah, I see," said Qetjnegartis. "To the buds created here, the others on the Homeworld would be too far away to detect and thus would not be included in their imprinted hierarchy."

"That is my theory, yes. Sadly there is no way to test it."

"Perhaps not, but it explains what we are observing." Qetjnegartis paused. "I need to consider the possible consequences of this. There could be some serious issues. Very serious issues."

"As you say, Commander."

"Ixmaderna, it would be best if we do not mention this to anyone else."

"I will obey Commander. But surely the other clans are noticing this, too."

"Perhaps so. But if anyone is going to raise an alarm, it will not be the Bajantus Clan.

* * * * *

August, 1911, Shoreham, Long Island, NY

Colonel Andrew Comstock breathed in the warm air and reflected that this was actually a rather nice place when it wasn't covered in snow. The other times he'd been here it had been in late fall or the dead of winter. He didn't need his greatcoat today! It would have been uncomfortably warm, in fact, if not for the breeze off Long Island Sound.

He was here to see the latest invention developed by the brilliant but erratic mind of Nikola Tesla. He'd met the man on a number of occasions and learned that the only thing you could predict about him was that he'd be unpredictable. Andrew glanced at the huge Wardenclyffe Tower, a metal monstrosity almost two hundred feet high, and was surprised to see that not only was it not, apparently, going to be in use today, but it looked as though some of it had been dismantled. When he'd gotten the message from Tesla that he wanted to demonstrate a new 'electric gun', he'd assumed it would be some improvement on the earlier adaptations he'd made to the tower. It appeared he'd been wrong.

He spotted Tesla in a nearby field, standing next to a strange device and surrounded by a group of men, some of whom he realized were newspapermen. "Blast him!" he snapped.

"Sir?"

He looked to the man accompanying him and raised an eyebrow. Lieutenant Jeremiah Hornbaker was his new aide and Andrew wasn't quite used to having him around. He'd been making inspection tours like this since before the war and almost always alone. But he was a colonel now and rated an aide. He'd actually rated one since he made major, but never got around to requesting one. Hornbaker was lanky, eager, and incredibly young - much like he'd been not so many years ago.

"Tesla!" he said jerking his head toward the tall, impeccably dressed figure. "He doesn't have the slightest regard for procedures or security. He probably invited those reporters before he bothered to inform the Ordnance Department he'd be making this test today!"

"I see, sir. But it seems as though he's built something, there."

Indeed it did, and unlike the Wardenclyffe Tower, this actually looked like some sort of weapon. There was a boxy structure about the size and shape of an automobile with all manner of pipes and tubes and wires spilling out of it. Above that, however was a long tapering cylinder, like a cannon barrel, mounted on a rotating mount. Cables came from the box and disappeared into the cylinder. There were thick rings of a white ceramic material at intervals along the length of the cylinder until at the end they stopped with a white ball where the muzzle should have been.

"Ah, Major Comstock!" cried Tesla when he caught sight of him.

"It's colonel..."

"So good of you to come! Gentlemen, this is Major Comstock from the Ordnance Department! He and I have worked together for years producing weapons for the war against the Martians!" He grabbed him by the arm and displayed him to the group like some prize show animal. Andrew refrained from mentioning that so far, Tesla's work had yet to produce a single working weapon for the war effort.

Well, that wasn't entirely true. Tesla had managed to get a half-dozen captured Martian heat rays operational. They weren't terribly practical weapons, requiring enormous power generating plants to make them work. Five of them had been incorporated in the defenses of St. Louis, it being seen as the critical lynch-pin in the Mississippi Line.

"Mr. Tesla," said Andrew, "what have you built here?"

"Ah! Yes, right to the point! Good!" He turned and waved his hands at the contraption. "As I was explaining to these gentlemen, using knowledge gleaned from captured Martian machines, I have created the first electric cannon!" Andrew glanced back at the Wardenclyffe Tower and Tesla instantly noticed. "Yes! You were here for my first experiments, but I assure you that my new device is as far advanced beyond that as a machine gun is from a bow and arrow!

"Some of the problems with my first device - as you so ably pointed out, Major - was the short range, the difficulty in aiming, and the large power generators needed to operate it."

"And you have solved these problems, sir? I can't help but notice the cables leading back to your generator building," said Andrew, pointing to several cables as thick as a man's arm running to the large brick building at the base of the Wardenclyffe Tower.

"Ah! Yes, the device needs to be charged up by a significant source, but once charged, it is independent and can fire several times without recharging. You see, I have made use of that remarkable Martian wire which has no electrical resistance. Amazing!"

"Where did you get the wire?" asked Andrew sharply. The stuff was being strictly rationed, since the only source of it was from damaged Martian machines which had been captured. And even though each machine could yield thousands of miles of it, it was proving so useful for the new British-designed radio units and the experimental coil guns, it could only be acquired with Ordnance Department approval; and Andrew was damn sure none had been authorized for Tesla!

"Oh, I have my sources," replied Tesla with a smirk. "And I only needed a few hundred miles for this. But as I was saying, using the wire as a storage battery I have been able to accumulate an electrical charge of an unprecedented intensity. It can then be projected through this large tube, where I have additional coils of the wire. From there, the electric charge will leap to the target." Tesla pointed to an object in an adjoining field. It had to have been at least five hundred yards away.

"It can fire that far?" asked Andrew, surprised. The earlier demonstrations with the tower had only had a range of about fifty yards.

"Indeed yes! With future improvements I believe it can fire even farther. But here! Let me demonstrate! I charged the coils earlier today, so it is ready to fire!"

Andrew instinctively stepped back. The bloody thing was already charged? He'd seen what happened when one of the Martian storage batteries failed first hand and he had no wish to be close to some homemade copy of Tesla's! "Come on," he growled to Hornbaker, "let's move over there." He led the way to where a low stone wall provided a bit of shelter. Quite a few of the newspapermen followed him.

"Whenever you're ready, sir!" he shouted back at Tesla. The man waved and started fiddling with his device.

One of the newspapermen came up beside Andrew. "So, Colonel," he said, "you've been working with the doctor for a long time?"

"I wouldn't actually say *working* with him. I keep up to date with his activities - most of them anyway—and come to confer with him and observe demonstrations like this when events warrant."

"Is he as brilliant as they say?"

Andrew shrugged. "His mind works on a level I can scarcely conceive of, sir. If that's brilliant, then I'd have to call him brilliant."

"Some say he's a charlatan. Spending huge sums of government money and producing nothing."

Andrew wasn't touching that one! All he needed was to be quoted in the paper saying something bad about Tesla. "I guess we'll find out in a few minutes, won't we?"

Tesla waved again and shouted something Andrew couldn't quite make out. His hearing wasn't as good as it used to be. Getting caught on the edge of the blast of an exploding tripod last year hadn't helped. But he assumed Tesla was ready and that something would soon happen.

It did. A loud hum filled the air that got higher and higher in pitch until it faded from his ability to hear. Hornbaker groaned and muttered *ow*! Several of the other watchers were wiggling fingers in their ears. A moment later a blue glow appeared around the tube of the machine. It was the same color as a Martian tripod getting ready to explode and Andrew tensed to duck behind the wall...

Then sparks and crackling arcs of electricity were crawling up and down the tube, and an instant later a blindingly bright bolt of what could only be called lightning leapt away from the end of the tube and in an instant struck the distant target. The bolt persisted, connecting tube and target for a few heartbeats and writhing like a snake. There was a blast of flame from the target and then the bolt was jumping around the target, striking the ground in a dozen spots, almost too quickly to see. An enormous crack, like a thunderbolt, shook the air and then the light was gone. The *boom* rolled away across the landscape and out onto the Sound.

"God in Heaven," whispered the newspaperman. Except he wasn't whispering, he was shouting. Everyone's ears were stunned.

"I don't think anyone will be calling him a charlatan after this," Andrew shouted back.

The crowd pulled itself together and went back toward the cannon where Tesla was fairly dancing in delight. "Did you see? Did you see it?"

"Saw and heard! That was amazing, sir!" And it had been, it really had. The captured heat ray which Tesla had demonstrated had been impressive, but that was something which already existed. Tesla had only figured out how to make it work. But this! This was something totally new. "But what did it do to the target?"

"Let's go see!" Without further ado, Tesla skipped toward the target, leaving nearly everyone behind with his long, quick strides. Andrew hurried to catch up. He was sweating by the time they crossed the field. But the target was...

"Is that part of a Martian machine?"

"Of course! I had to make sure my cannon could actually damage one!"

"Where did you get it?" Andrew was sure Tesla hadn't been authorized this either.

"A friend supplied it. But look! Look what I did!"

The target had once been the curving rear plate of a tripod's head. Now it was a cracked and smoldering wreck. Black streaks marred the gleaming metal and there were holes in several spots. Thousands of the tiny hexagonal metal flakes that made up Martian armor were scattered all over. The thing had been propped up with several steel angles, but these were damaged, too, and the whole thing was leaning over drunkenly to one side. There were scorched patches on the ground all around, too. In a few spots the grass was still burning.

"Well? Well? What do you think?" demanded Tesla.

Andrew walked around, looking at the remains and directed Hornbaker to take some photographs with his Brownie camera. "You certainly did significant damage to it, sir." He put his hand through one of the holes, careful not to touch the edges - the thing was clearly still hot. "It would normally take a large caliber shell to do this sort of damage." It was impressive, but considering the size of the apparatus and the facilities needed to charge the thing, he was wondering if it was any improvement over conventional artillery. Then something else caught his eye. Just to the rear of the armor there was a... puddle of metal. Something had melted and then solidified again. It wasn't part of the armor; it had a golden color. "What's that, sir?"

"Ah! You have sharp eyes, Major!" said Tesla coming over next to him. "This is how I overcame the targeting problem!"

"And how did you do that?"

"The first few times I fired the cannon the electric charge would - as you'd naturally expect - simply jumped to the nearest object which would ground it out. The challenge was to get it to jump to where *I* wanted it to go."

"I can see that, sir." He remembered an early trial of the tower-device and how the bolt hit several unintended objects.

"Well, the breakthrough was when I discovered that the power, once stored in the Martian wire, took on a distinct and very unique frequency. You are familiar with electrical frequency, are you not?"

"In a general sort of way..."

"Good! Well, the frequency of the Martian current is quite unique. And I discovered that by attuning my projector properly, I could make the electrical bolt jump to a target that resonated at that frequency in preference of any other target! Brilliant, is it not!"

Andrew opened his mouth to agree and then stopped and looked at the puddle again. "So that's the Martian wire?" he said aghast. "Destroyed?"

"Only about a mile of it," said Tesla waving his hand as if it were nothing. The stuff was worth ten times its weight in gold right now! And melting would leave it useless. "I needed to make targets, you understand."

"Targets?" said Andrew weakly. "H-how many?"

"Oh, a dozen or so. I had to refine the technique, you understand. I really could use some more of it, now. Can you take care of that, Major?"

Andrew opened his mouth - he wasn't sure what was about to come out - but unexpectedly Lieutenant Hornbaker stepped in. "Excuse me, sir, but how did you prevent the bolt from jumping to the storage battery in your cannon? Seems like that would be the closest target."

Tesla spun around and stared at Hornbaker as if he'd never seen him before. "Who are you?"

"This is Lieutenant Hornbaker. He works for me," said Andrew.

"Ah, I see. Well, that is an *excellent* question, young man! And it took all of my inventiveness to find the answer!" He launched into a lengthy explanation of which Andrew could follow very little. The gist of it seemed to be that somehow Tesla had managed to alter the frequency of the current in his storage battery so that it would not attract the bolt.

"Doctor, so you are saying that your cannon will unerringly send its bolt to find a Martian power unit that's within range?" asked Andrew. "It will never miss its target?"

"That has been the result so far," confirmed Tesla. "At least within the effective range. If the range is too long, misses have occurred. But I should add that I believe the range will be determined by the *amount* of power stored in the target. The amount I could put in my little target batteries," he waved his hand at the puddle, "is tiny compared with what a Martian tripod must have. The effective range against one of them might be many times what it is here!"

Andrew took a deep breath and looked from the target to the cannon and then back to the target. Now *this* was something! A weapon which could wreck a tripod and *never* miss? The problems with the size of the device and the need for generators to charge it up seemed far less serious now!

"Mr. Tesla, I... well, first, sir, let me shake your hand!" He stuck his hand out, remembering too late that Tesla abhorred shaking hands. But to his surprise, the man took it and shook weakly. He quickly let go. "Congratulations, sir! This is an amazing achievement! Truly amazing! My superiors will be extremely interested in this. Can you provide drawings? Specifications? We will want to build a lot of these devices."

"My assistants are working on them now, Major," said Tesla beaming in delight. "Of course we will need a great deal of the Martian wire to build many of these."

"I'm sure we will get it." *Somehow...*

The reporters crowded in now and bombarded Tesla, and himself, with questions. Tesla was more than willing to talk about his genius, but Andrew had to temper his responses to avoid making any sort of statement he'd come to regret later. Eventually he broke free, and he and Hornbaker headed back to the train station.

"That was really something, sir," said the lieutenant.

"Yes, it was. And I still can barely believe it."

"Sir?"

"Oh, I've been coming to see Tesla for years and he's... well, as I'm sure you noticed, he's a bit of a blowhard. He promises the sun, moon, and stars, but up until now hasn't delivered much of anything. So for him to now come up with this. And he wasn't even *supposed* to be working on this, mind you. It's a surprise. A real surprise."

"But a pleasant one, surely."

"Yes indeed. I just hope I can get General Crozier to believe it. And use it."

"Will that be difficult, sir? I thought the general was open to new ideas."

"Oh he is. But I know he's skeptical of Tesla. He'll be cautious about committing a lot of resources."

"Maybe we should get him up here to see this."

"We might have to."

They reached the train station and Andrew found a telegram waiting for him. He read it and frowned. "Trouble, sir?" asked Hornbaker.

"It's from the Baldwin people. They'd like to put off the demonstration until tomorrow. Problems with their device apparently. I suppose we can just layover in Philadelphia..."

"Or we could go right on down to Aberdeen and see what Goddard has to show us, sir," suggested Hornbaker. "Then back up to Philadelphia the next day."

"Yes, yes, we could do that. Goddard is ready to go now from what his last message said. Good idea, Jerry. Check the train schedule while I send a wire to Goddard to get ready for this afternoon."

"Yes, sir."

The arrangements were made and soon the two of them were on a train heading south. Andrew immediately slumped down in his seat and pulled his cap over his eyes to try and catch some sleep. Hornbaker had his face pressed to the window of the car, taking in the sights. The young man was from some backwoods place in Kentucky or Tennessee and was still amazed by how built-up the east was. Andrew had seen those sights enough times not to need to do so again - although they did seem to change a bit each time he came through here.

America's mobilization to meet the demands of the war was changing the landscape and changing the society as well. New factories and smelters were springing up everywhere. Thousands of chimneys belched smoke into the skies and heaps of slag grew into small mountains. Winter time snows stayed white only a few hours before soot turned the drifts black. Vast marshaling yards were filled with tanks and guns waiting to be shipped to the front. Training camps turned out new soldiers, a hundred thousand each month. Women and children were working in those new factories so the men could go fight. Everyone was involved - everyone. Andrew's own wife was growing vegetables in a garden which took up nearly the entire back yard of her parent's house at Fort Myer and organizing the wives of other officers to do the same. With the loss of the Great Plains, there was a growing food shortage. It was finally sinking in that this was a war for survival. He dozed off thinking about the house and the garden.

Late afternoon saw them at the Aberdeen Proving Grounds in Maryland, north of Baltimore. The army had a large base there to test new weapons. Andrew had been here frequently over the last few years. In fact he'd been here just a month ago watching a field test on a new device which was hoped could help blast a way through the walls the Martians threw up around their fortresses. It had looked promising, although with the current state of the war, they were unlikely to need the thing for a while.

The weapon being tested today was one the army had great hopes for. The war against the Martians was unlike any ever fought by men. The enemy employed large, heavily armored war machines which were virtually invulnerable to the rifles and machine guns used by ordinary infantry. On rare occasions a damaged tripod might be taken down by some lucky fusillade of bullets, but that was exceptional. To make up for this, the infantry had been supplied with small bombs. These could wreck a tripod—indeed, Andrew and a small group of men had done exactly that a few years before—but it was difficult and incredibly dangerous. Not every infantryman had the nerve to make such an attack. And despite the tremendous output of America's factories, not every soldier could be supplied with a tank or an artillery piece. Somehow the masses of infantry which made up any army had to be made effective again.

What was needed was a weapon powerful enough to damage a tripod from a distance, and yet small and light enough that infantry soldiers could carry them into battle. A little less than two years ago, a young engineer named Robert Goddard had accosted Andrew on the streets of Boston and insisted he had just the weapon for the job. Andrew had been skeptical at first since the army was being flooded with 'great ideas' for winning the war—most totally impractical. But Goddard had been accompanied by Charles Munroe, an explosives expert who Andrew already knew of from his work in the navy's torpedo factory in Connecticut. The two of them together had proposed a shaped-charge explosive device delivered by a small rocket. Developing it had not been as simple or easy as Goddard had promised—but then few things were—but at last it looked as though the problems had been solved. Or Andrew surely hoped so.

Aberdeen was on a stretch of ground hugging Chesapeake Bay. It was mostly low, flat, and in places, swampy. Scraggly clumps of trees grew here and there and swarms of mosquitoes everywhere. The weather was clouding over, but the wind had died and Andrew found himself sweating under his wool uniform. A motor staff car met them at the railroad station and carried them along dirt roads deep into the base. From time to time loud booms shook the air as artillery and explosives were tested. The car passed a few firing ranges where artillery of many types and sizes were being fired. They finally arrived at a secluded field where a small group of people were waiting for them. He spotted Goddard right away. The man, though little older than Andrew, was almost completely bald and never seemed to wear a hat.

Goddard trotted over to greet them, smiling broadly. "Welcome, Colonel! Glad to see you. As soon as I got your wire I had things set up here. Glad you could come today, it's supposed to rain tomorrow."

"Your weapon isn't affected by the rain is it?" asked Andrew.

"No, no! We've made it quite waterproof. We were told right from the start that whatever we came up with would have to be able to stand up to field conditions. I was just thinking that the demonstration would be a lot more pleasant if we weren't standing in the rain."

"Yes, I see. So, what do you have for us?"

"I *hope* I have the final prototype for the Anti-Tripod Rocket Launcher. We've been testing it almost non-stop for the last week. Over two hundred rounds fired with no serious mishaps."

"That implies some not-so-serious mishaps, Dr. Goddard," observed Andrew.

"Well, yes, there have been a few misfires and a few duds, but that's to be expected. There have been no injuries and no unintended damage. And the performance has been excellent. Here, let me show you." He led the way to where several tables had been set up. On one was sitting the launcher. This was little more than a piece of hollow tubing about three inches in diameter and about four and a half feet long. It had a crude aiming site, a curved wooden piece that would allow the operator to rest the tube on his shoulder, a pistol grip near the middle and another near the front, and a small box that was only a few inches square near the rear. The other table held a dozen of the rockets themselves. These were a little less than two feet long with a bulbous nose, a thin central section, and four guiding fins at the rear.

"Looks like a stovepipe," said Hornbaker.

Goddard chuckled. "Yes, that's what the men are already calling it. I imagine that will prove a lot more popular than the ATRL." He picked up the tube and handed it to Andrew. "About thirteen pounds, only a little more than a standard rifle, so the men should have no problem carrying them. The production model will have rings to attach a carrying sling. The rockets are a little over three pounds each, but a bit awkward for carrying. I've sent the specification to the Quartermaster Department, as you instructed. They are going to develop a carrying rig which will hold eight rockets and which can be worn like a back pack. I'm thinking that the weapon can be used by a two-man team. The rocketeer would operate the weapon and the other man could carry the rockets and act as the loader."

"The exact method of deployment is still being worked out," said Andrew. "Ideally there would be one of these for each squad, but it will be quite a while before they are available in sufficient numbers for that. For now, we'll try to get a few to each company. But show me how this works." He handed the tube back to Goddard and then nodded to Hornbaker, who got out his camera.

"It's very simple to operate, Colonel; come with me," said Goddard. He started walking out into the field, one of his assistants following with a rocket. Andrew and Hornbaker trailed along. When they were about a hundred yards from the tables, Goddard stopped and swapped the tube for the rocket. "The launcher is just a hollow tube to guide the rocket in the first moments of flight until its moving fast enough for the fins to provide stability. The loader inserts the rocket halfway into the rear of the tube." The assistant put the tube onto his shoulder and Goddard slid the rocket in. "This is the only tricky part. First, you pull out this pin, which arms the warhead. Then you tug loose this wire and wrap it around this little coil attached to the tube." He did so and slid the rocket the rest of the way in. A small click of metal indicated that it was somehow secured in place and wouldn't fall out if the tube was tilted. "Okay, it's ready to fire. If you'd move over here next to me—there's quite a back blast and you can't be right behind it when it fires." All three of them moved about a dozen yards to the side of the firer. "Whenever you are ready, George."

The man nodded and directed the tube toward a distant target about two hundred yards away. There was a moment as he adjusted his aim and then there was a loud roar and a blast of smoke from the rear of the tube. The rocket flew out the front and in a surprisingly short time crossed the distance to the target and exploded. The explosion wasn't particularly loud or impressive, to Andrew's disappointment. Goddard waved to the men around the table and one of them trotted forward with another rocket.

"The propellant in the rocket is very stable under normal conditions and has to be set off by an igniter," explained Goddard as he loaded again. "The ignition is electrical. We have a standard National Carbon zinc-carbon Leclanché dry cell in this box attached to the tube. It is good for a few dozen firings. I'm thinking that we could have a new battery included with each carton of rockets." He looked right at Andrew and pointed at the arming pin on the rocket. "However, once this pin is removed, the rocket is dangerous to handle. The firing pin is in the rear and the sudden deceleration of hitting the target will drive it into the explosive. Even simply dropping it could cause it to detonate. So the pin should only be removed just prior to firing."

Andrew frowned. "We'll need to hammer that into the men using it. Hornbaker, here, will be putting together the operating manual for this and he'll need your notes and any other useful advice you can give."

"My pleasure, Colonel." He finished loading and George sent another rocket against the target. "Would you care to give it a try, Colonel?"

Andrew blinked in surprise. "Uh, sure, why not?" Another rocket was brought forward and Andrew put the launcher up on his shoulder the way he had seen the assistant do it. Goddard loaded and patted him on the shoulder.

"You're ready, Colonel. Flip up the cover over the trigger and press it when you want to fire. Give us a moment to move aside."

Andrew shifted the tube so that his eye was close to the rear sight, which was nothing more than a metal tab sticking out with a small hole in it. He lined it up with another metal bar attached to the front of the tube. He could see several marking spaced vertically on it. "How is the sight calibrated?" he called.

"Oh, sorry!" replied Goddard. "The top mark is for one hundred yards, the second for two hundred, and the last for three hundred."

"Ah, I see. Okay, here goes." The range to the target looked about two hundred yards to him, so he lined up the second mark on the target. He flipped up the little cover over the firing button and gingerly pressed the button underneath it. There was an instant's delay when he heard a tiny crackling sound, then a loud whoosh, and he was engulfed in smoke. He heard the bang as the rocket detonated, but he couldn't see a thing until the smoke dispersed. The others walked over to him, Goddard grinning. "Did I hit it?"

"A little over, sir," said Hornbaker. "Close though."

"It does take a little practice, Colonel," said Goddard. "Of course a real tripod would be a much bigger target than what we have here."

"There's no recoil at all," observed Andrew.

"Of course not," said Goddard. "That's the nature of a rocket launcher."

"But what can it do to the target? Can it blast through the Martian armor? That's' the whole point after all."

Goddard's smile faded. "Let's take a look at the target, shall we? It's a piece of a Martian machine we were given for testing."

They walked down range to the target, which Andrew saw was the curving piece of the cockpit of a Martian tripod about six feet in height and width - not unlike the target Tesla was using that morning. It was rather badly battered with cracks and holes and divots taken out of the surface. But the holes and most of the divots had red paint dabbed on them. "We only had the one target," explained Goddard. "So after each series of tests we paint the hits so we don't confuse new hits with old. Here these are the new hits we made just now."

Andrew looked close and saw the newest divots in the armor. And that's all they were, divots. "We didn't penetrate."

"No, Colonel," said Goddard. "But this sample is from the most heavily armored part of a tripod. The drawings you've provided show that other areas are not so well protected."

"We need a weapon which can kill these things, Doctor!"

"Sir, I must remind you that even regular artillery usually requires multiple hits to destroy an enemy machine," said Goddard stiffly. "The rocket launcher has a similar destructive potential as a four-inch gun. To make it powerful enough to punch through the armor with a single shot would require a weapon far too large and heavy to be employed by ordinary infantry - although I would like to pursue the development of such a weapon. We were directed to create a weapon which infantry can use and this is it."

"Well, yes," said Andrew damping down his disappointment. "It's certainly safer than the bombs we've equipped the poor sods with, and far better than nothing. Sorry, Doctor, I suppose I let my hopes get away from me. But you say that this is ready to go into production?"

"Yes, Colonel. There are several facilities which are only waiting your approval to begin work."

"Very good. I'll talk to General Crozier and we should have that approval in a few days."

"Excellent!" said Goddard, recapturing his good humor. "I'll be involved for a few months getting the factories up to speed. After that, I'd like your permission to pursue a few new ideas I have concerning larger rockets and possible multiple launchers for a barrage system. Charles Munroe is already working on a larger shaped-charge warhead and..."

I'll pass that along, Doctor, but for right now, please concentrate your efforts on production of your stovepipes. We need to get these into the hands of our troops as quickly as we can. The Martians may be quiet for the moment, but that won't last!"

Chapter Two

September, 1911, east of Augusta, Arkansas

"Where the hell are they?" growled Captain Frank Dolfen. "It's been three hours since we called for them!"

"Yes, and I don't know how much longer we can hang about here before those blighters notice us," said Major Bridges. The two officers were lying on their bellies on a small rise in the ground that passed for a hill on the flat eastern edges of the Ozark Plateau. They were seventy miles west of Memphis and about an equal distance northeast of Little Rock, staring at a new Martian fortress. Like the one Dolfen had spent weeks looking at near Gallup, New Mexico two years earlier, it was a ring of raised earth and stone about forty feet high and three miles in diameter. At the moment, there were two Martian tripods not a mile off, apparently on patrol. Clouds of dust in the distance hinted at others. Dolfen, Bridges, and a pair of troopers had snuck to this position during the night.

They were waiting for a group of Air Corps bombers to come and attack. Not Colonel Selfridge's planes, but a different group with much larger machines. They had attacked the place several times before, but reconnaissance from the air hadn't been able to determine what sort of damage was being done. So the request had gone out for some reconnaissance from the ground and Dolfen's squadron had been the lucky ones to get the job.

But the bombers were late.

"They better show up soon," said Dolfen. "Take a look at those clouds off to the west. A storm's coming for sure. A few hours off yet, but they sure won't want to be flying once it gets here!"

"Might be useful for us, though, old boy. Give us a spot of cover to make our withdrawal."

"True. I don't relish the idea of staying here until dark." He looked north. They had put the horses in one of the small gullies that crisscrossed the area, but once they mounted up they would be visible for miles.

They waited another half hour as it got hotter and hotter; it might be September, but summer wasn't over yet. "Maybe I should try the radio again."

"I'd advise against it. We found out in Afghanistan that those beggars can track our signals if we broadcast too much. Might lead them right to us."

Dolfen frowned, but the Englishman was probably right. Despite his foppish manner, Bridges did seem to know what he was doing. An experienced cavalryman and a good rider who had fought Martians himself, defending Britain's colony in India. They settled down to wait some more, but only a little while later Dolfen heard a faint buzzing. He rolled over on his back and swept the eastern sky with his field glasses. "I think I hear something."

"Yes, I do, too. Can you see them?"

"No, I... wait. There they are!" He pointed to a swarm of dark specks.

"I don't see... oh, yes, now I do. How many do you think?"

"Looks like about thirty to me..."

"They certainly are high up, aren't they? Can barely see them."

"They have to stay high to avoid the heat rays. The bastards can torch a plane two miles up, so they stay a bit higher than that."

"Can they even see the target from that high?"

"I sure hope so! Don't want them hitting us by mistake. But the walls of the fortress must look like a giant bull's-eye from above. They'd have to be blind not to see it."

The specks slowly crept across the sky. As they got closer, Dolfen could make them out clearly. They were twin-engine planes built by the Glenn Martin Company—or so Colonel Selfridge had told him; Dolfen had little interest in the nuts and bolts of aviation. Even so, he was impressed by the size of the bombers. He remembered the tiny and flimsy craft that were the best available just a few short years ago. *We're learning. We're learning fast. But will it be fast enough?*

"I looks like the Martians have seen them, too," said Bridges.

Dolfen redirected his attention from the planes to the enemy. The tripods, which had been striding back and forth, for all the world like human soldiers on sentry, had stopped. He half-expected them to lean backward to look up like a human, but they did not. They were faced in the direction of the oncoming planes, however, and they had raised their heat rays.

"Sure hope those blokes have their altitude right," said Bridges.

"Amen to that."

The planes were nearly overhead now and Dolfen flinched when the buzz-saw shriek of the heat rays pierced the air. On a bright day like this, the rays were hard to see, but they were clearly directed skyward. He looked up at the planes again and focused his glasses. The formation flew onward in a stately fashion, and to his relief, none of them burst into flames. Looking closer, he thought he saw small objects falling from them. "I think they just dropped their bombs!"

He tried to follow them down but lost sight of them. He lowered the glasses and looked out toward the enemy fortress. The seconds ticked by, and after a dozen or so, he thought he heard a whistling sound. A half-dozen more and suddenly geysers of smoke erupted from the walls. A heartbeat later, the deep rumble of the explosions made the ground tremble. More geysers and more booms but then it was over. The echoes died away and the smoke and dust from the bombs merged into a single huge cloud which slowly rose and drifted east. Dolfen eagerly brought the glasses to his eyes and scanned the fortress for damage.

"Anything?" asked Bridges.

"Not... not much, damn it. Maybe a couple of their ray towers wrecked, and a few craters in the wall. Nothing burning, it doesn't seem." He cursed again. "I suppose I shouldn't expect much. General Funston bombarded the Gallup fort for *months* without doing any serious damage. The reports we got from inside said that pretty much everything was deep underground. The only way to root 'em out is to go in there and do it ourselves."

"Pity," said Bridges. "Still, it can't hurt to let the bastards know we can hit them even at this distance."

"Yeah, I suppose. Seems like a lot of effort for little harm, though." He looked back up at the bombers and watched them turn east and disappear. Looking west, he saw the storm was still building and definitely closer. Another hour or so and they'd have a real gully-washer from the look of it. "I think we'll have all the cover we need to get out of here pretty soon." He told the two troopers to make sure the horses were ready.

He studied the fortress through glasses a while longer, making notes on a pad of paper. He was just putting away the glasses and his notes when there was a sudden commotion from the gully where the horses were being kept. Loud whinnying, followed by human cursing, and then to his dismay one of the horses bolted out of the gully into the open, dragging one of the troopers who clutched its reins.

He sprinted toward it, but Bridges got there faster and managed to halt the beast. Dolfen was there a moment later and between the three men they got the horse under control. "What the hell happened?!" demanded Dolfen.

"A goddamn jackrabbit, sir!" said the exasperated trooper. "I flushed it out of a bush by accident and this fool horse thought the thing was gonna eat him, I guess!"

"Oh, for God's sake! The damn thing ignores bombs and heat rays, but it's spooked by a rabbit?"

"Bloody hell," said Bridges. "The cad has gone and given us away, Captain. Look."

Dolfen spun around, and to his horror the two tripods he'd seen earlier were now heading their way! "Shit! Mount up! Ride!"

All four men jumped into their saddles and spurred their mounts into motion, leaving a fair amount of their gear lying on the ground. There wasn't a second to spare and they all knew it. Even the horses seemed to sense the danger, and being rested, they tore across the prairie as fast as they could.

Dolfen looked back and cursed. The Martians were far closer than he'd like, very nearly in heat ray range already. He probably had as much experience being chased by Martians as any man alive and he didn't like what he saw. A galloping horse could outdistance a tripod pretty easily, especially on flat ground like this, but a horse would get tired and the enemy machines never did. Worse, the two on their tails looked to be scouts. For the first few years of the war, the Martians had only had one type of fighting machine. They were powerful, tough to destroy, and while faster than a man on foot, significantly slower than a horse. But in the last year or two, they'd started to see other types. One was a bit smaller, less heavily armed and armored, but significantly faster. The army had designated the first types as 'attack tripods', and the smaller ones 'scout tripods'. Scouts still couldn't keep up with a galloping horse, but they didn't lose as much ground as an attack tripod, and when the horse had to slow down...

Bridges clearly saw it too. "Going to be a damn near thing to get back to your squadron before they catch us up, old man," he shouted. There hadn't been any covered spots close to the enemy fortress big enough to conceal the whole squadron so he'd left them about ten miles away and gone forward in the night with just Bridges and the other two. "Could you use the wireless to call them to us?"

"It takes five minutes to set up!" he shouted back. "Those bastards would have us before we could get the message off! Turn to the west!" he yelled to all of them. "Head for the storm!"

They veered to the left toward a wall of black clouds that was growing and building at an amazing pace. He could see flashes of lightning and gray sheets of rain connecting the clouds with the ground. It was a real squall line, and if they could get in there, they had a good chance of giving the Martians the slip.

A strong gust of wind suddenly hit them in the face and Dolfen's hat was torn away. Dust clouds were kicked up and stung his eyes. A few large drops of rain started hitting them, driven by the wind hard enough to sting. Glancing back, he could see that the Martians were coming on. If they could stay ahead of them for a few more minutes...

He heard the heat rays fire, but they were faint, barely to be heard above the wind. A sudden warmth on his back made him wince, but it wasn't bad, just like standing in front of a fire. They were still out of range. But the horses didn't like it and they put out a burst of speed. A moment later the heat cut off.

The rain was heavier now and the wind even stronger; bits of debris went flying past. They galloped across an abandoned wheat field and jumped the remains of a wire fence, the wreck of a farmhouse still stood in the distance.

"I say! What the devil is that?!" cried Bridges suddenly. Instinctively, Dolfen looked back at the Martians, but they were just as they'd been. What was the Englishman talking about?

"Over there!" The man pointed. Dolfen stared ahead and swallowed down sudden fear. Barely visible through the rain was a rotating column of dust and debris. It was dark, although slightly lighter than the clouds behind it, bits of stuff drifted around it and a roar like a freight train was growing.

"A twister!" cried one of the troopers.

"A what?" shouted Bridges.

"A tornado! A cyclone!" yelled Dolfen. It was almost directly in their path and seemed to be moving toward them and to the right, as though it would pass to the north of them. It was still a ways off, but it was moving fast. He stared at it a moment longer and then made his decision.

"Follow me! Head north!" He turned his horse to the right.

"But sir!" screamed one of the troopers. "It's headed that way, too! We should go south!"

"Better that than the Martians! Now come on!" he spurred his horse, although it hardly needed more encouragement to run. The tornado was now off to his left, but the distance was closing with terrifying swiftness. Would they be able to get past it? If he'd guessed wrong, it would herd them right back into the Martians' heat rays - if it didn't kill them outright.

Closer and closer the thing came. It was enormous, easily half a mile wide, maybe more. He had caught sight of a few small ones during his time in the army, but always from a safe distance. This close, the power of the thing was unbelievable. He shifted his course more to the east, trying to get around it.

The wall of darkness filled half the world now, blotting out everything to his left. Larger objects were hurtling past, but the wind was now coming from behind them, pushing them onward. Bridges came abreast of him, hat gone and mouth wide. He was shouting something, but the roar was all-encompassing; nothing else could be heard.

And then the noise and the blackness was more to the rear of them, the sky ahead was brighter. Had they made it past? He twisted around in his saddle and yes, the tornado was crossing behind them! Exhilaration filled him. They could swing west again and find cover before the Martians could...

The Martians!

He suddenly caught sight of one of the machines. The damn thing was standing right in the tornado's path! Didn't the fools know what it was - or what it could do? Apparently not, because the tripod was standing its ground and as he watched, it fired its heat ray right into the oncoming funnel-cloud.

The ray had no effect whatsoever. It did ignite some of the debris the tornado was carrying and for a moment streaks of red fire wrapped around the funnel. But then the edge reached the machine and it was lifted bodily into the air! Dolfen watched in wonder - and jubilation - as the enemy was carried up and up until it disappeared in the cloud. He continued to stare, hoping to see the tornado spit the bastard back out again and watch it smashed to bits on the ground, but there was nothing. Clearly it had killed the invader somewhere Dolfen couldn't see. Of the other tripod there was no sign; destroyed, too, or retreated, he didn't know.

"By Jove! That was really quite something, wasn't it?" said Bridges coming up beside him again, a lunatic grin on his face.

"Sure was! But come on, let's find some cover just in case the other one is still there after it passes!"

* * * * *

Cycle 597, 844.8, Holdfast 32-4

Qetjnegartis was inspecting the damage from the prey-creature's aerial attack when the message from Xasdandar arrived. It and Faldprenda had been sent in pursuit of a small party of prey who Qetjnegartis suspected had some connection with the attack.

"Commander Qetjnegartis, respond please."

"Responding. Report."

"Commander, I regret to report that Faldprenda has been slain."

Qetjnegartis instantly focused its attention on this unexpected information. "How?" The most obvious answer would be some sort of an ambush. It prepared to order out a larger force to deal with it.

"It... it was destroyed by an... atmospheric phenomenon, Commander. I have never witnessed anything like it."

"Explain."

"We were pursuing the prey-creatures as you ordered. We encountered a storm and the prey attempted to take cover in it. We followed. But then we encountered a column of air which was spinning at very high speed. Faldprenda's fighting machine was caught in it."

"And this air was able to *destroy* its machine?" That scarcely seemed possible.

"Yes, Commander. It was so strong it lifted it off the ground and to a high altitude before dropping it again. It landed with such force, the machine was shattered in many pieces and Faldprenda was slain. I have recorded images I can send you."

"Do so." Its subordinate complied and Qetjnegartis watched the images with a sense of wonder. It was astonishing, but there was no doubt. "Amazing. There have been sightings of these phenomena by others, but no close encounters with them. We never suspected they could do such damage! We must take precautions to avoid them in the future."

"Yes, Commander."

"And what of the prey you were pursuing?"

"They may have been destroyed by the same phenomenon, Commander. I could find no trace of them once the storm had passed."

"Very well, return to the holdfast. I will dispatch a salvage team to recover the remains of the fighting machine. I am also concerned about this party of prey-creatures. They grow increasingly bold and I dislike their ability to spy upon our activities. There are also many of the non-warriors still at large in these regions. We must be more aggressive in our patrolling and harvesting."

"Yes, Commander."

Qetjnegartis issued the orders, but was disturbed by this senseless loss. The target world held many surprises, some of them deadly. *How many more will we discover to our loss? We had hoped that this place would be the salvation of the Race. Will it be the source of our destruction instead?*

* * * * *

September, 1911, east of Augusta, Arkansas

"Well, that was bloody well amazing, Captain! Do you have things like that around here often?"

Frank Dolfen smiled at the Britisher and nodded. "This time of year? Yeah, I guess we do. Thunderstorms seem to cause 'em. Mostly in the flat lands, though. Kansas, Oklahoma, Iowa, parts of Missouri. Not quite so much down here in Arkansas, where it's not so flat, nor farther east or north. I spent years in the Dakotas and they were pretty rare up there."

"How on Earth do people manage to live in such a country?"

Dolfen shrugged. "I guess they're used to 'em. Most folks have storm cellars - sort of underground bunkers - to shelter in if one comes too close."

"That one definitely came too close!"

"Maybe so, but we were damn lucky it did. Come on, let's get out of here and back to the squadron."

They had found cover in a ravine to let the horses rest, but now they mounted up again and rode northeast toward where he had left the rest of the squadron. For a while he was concerned that the tornado might have rolled over them, the way it did the Martian, but the track of destruction veered off more to the east and was eventually lost to sight. They kept a careful watch to their rear to make certain there was nothing following them. The day was nearly over by the time they encountered the scouts and it was getting dark before he wearily dismounted, turned his horse over to a trooper, and stumbled into his tent. His orderly, Private Gosling, brought him coffee and some stew. He had to admit there were some advantages to being an officer!

"Sounds like ya had quite the adventure t'day, Cap'n!" Gosling, who everyone called 'the Goose', was an old veteran, even older than Dolfen, who himself had recently reached his twenty year mark, and was not quite all there in the head anymore. Dolfen wasn't sure how he'd managed to find his way into the rebuilt 5th Cavalry, but he liked him and he did his job well enough.

"Yeah, damn near rode a twister home tonight."

"Saw the storm off t'the south of us. Looked like a bad one."

"Worst I ever saw. Glad it didn't get any closer to you."

"I remember one I saw when I was stationed down in Texas. We were near Pecos an'..."

"Goose?"

"Sir?"

"Have the officers join me in a half hour."

"Yes, sir. More stew?"

"No, this is fine, thanks." The man went out and Dolfen finished his supper and lay down on his cot for a few minutes. He didn't intend to sleep, but started awake when Gosling shook his shoulder.

"They're here sir."

He sat up, a little embarrassed, and went out under the tent fly. The lieutenants commanding the four troops of the squadron were there along with his aide, Lieutenant Lynnbrooke, and Major Bridges. "Evening, gentlemen, I trust you had a less eventful day than the major and I." This produced a small chuckle. His officers were all very young and seemed to treat him with the sort of automatic respect you gave a grandfather or elderly uncle; it was grating at times. There was also Lieutenant Abernathy, who commanded a battery of artillery which had been attached to the squadron. He didn't know the man well, but the mere fact that he'd managed keep up with the cavalry over sixty miles of dirt roads proved that he was no slouch.

"All right, we've accomplished the first part of our mission. We've observed the effects of the air attack on the Martian fortress. Tomorrow we get on with the rest of it. We will head northwest to hit the White River at Newport, then swing east to Jonesboro, then up to Paragould, and then back to Memphis. Our orders are to scout and lend assistance to any civilians we might find. This includes urging them to head east."

"Sir?" said Lieutenant Lynnbrooke. "We've already had a dozen or so people come in during the day while you were gone. A couple of families from near Beedeville. They're afraid to stay any longer."

"Are they on foot, or are they mounted?"

"Horses and wagons, sir. They have forty or fifty head of cattle, too, and don't want to abandon them."

Dolfen frowned. Escorting the civilians - and the livestock - was part of his job, but he'd hoped to do that on the way back. They were still outbound. "When we're done here, go tell them our route. They might not want to go with us to Newport. If they do, let them know that if we run into trouble they may have to abandon their goods and ride fast. If they don't want to go to Newport, tell them to head east as fast as they can and they should hit army patrols in forty or fifty miles."

"Yes, sir."

They clarified some questions about the departure time and order of march and then dispersed. Dolfen washed some of the dust off himself, pulled a spare hat out of his valise for the next day, and then went to sleep.

The next morning was refreshingly cool and crisp in the aftermath of the storm; a preview of fall. They took to the road - or what passed for a road in these parts. His squadron was a mix of new and old that Dolfen still found strange. A Troop was the usual mounted cavalry that he had spent twenty years with, but B Troop was all mounted on motorcycles, some single bikes and others with sidecars, some of which mounted light machine guns. C Troop was the biggest difference, it consisted of ten armored cars. These were strange-looking vehicles with eight wheels, each supporting an armored cab with a rotating turret on top. Some were armed with new Browning 50-caliber machine guns and a few had a two-inch quick-firing cannon. Just peashooters against a tripod, but still better than rifles. D Troop was also on horseback, but had pack horses to carry more of the 50-calibers and three of the new mortars that were just coming into service. Dolfen had no idea if they would be of much use. Still, the whole force was vastly more powerful than an old-style cavalry squadron. There was also a supply troop with motor trucks carrying food, ammunition, and gasoline. Abernathy's battery was all pulled by trucks and had four three-inch guns. In a fight, those guns might be the best weapons they'd have.

The column mostly stayed to the road, but he had a squad of horsemen scouting a couple of miles ahead and some of the motorcycles providing security on the flanks and in the rear. The bikes were too noisy to be leading the column. The civilians had decided they wanted to stay with the soldiers, so they trundled along just behind the supply trucks. This didn't really slow things down because with the condition of the roads, the motor vehicles had to take it slow anyway. They couldn't risk a broken axle here in enemy country.

The mere fact that they had to consider this 'enemy country' rankled Dolfen in the worst way. This was America, damn it! How dare some invader make parts of it enemy country! *We'll drive them out! We will!*

But there was no doubt that the Martians were here, at least for the moment. Every now and then they'd come across the triangular-shaped holes the enemy tripods made.

And there was the Red Weed.

Dolfen could see a few patches of the damn stuff here and there as they rode. It was a red plant which resembled Earthly lichen and clung to rocks and bare patches of ground. In the winter it only grew very slowly, but in warmer weather it would expand rapidly. Finally, it would enter a period of explosive growth with the patches able to cover acres under a thick mat in a matter of a few days. Then, the stuff would die off just as rapidly, turning brown and crumbling to powder. But during its brief period of life it would choke out the local plants underneath it and worse, it would leave seeds or spores or something which would begin the cycle all over again.

It seemed to appear close to the Martian fortresses. During the siege of Gallup, they had found it frequently and made a point of destroying it by burning. But now, with large regions under the Martians' control, no one was making the effort to get rid of it and it was spreading at a frightening rate. Even if they did drive the enemy out, would they have to deal with this awful stuff forever after?

They headed north until they reached a crossroad which led them to a ford on the Cache River. It wasn't much of a river this time of year, but the land on either side was thickly wooded and the locals had said this would be the best place to get across. They got there around noon and Dolfen called a halt to water the horses. It was a good place to stop; the trees gave them concealment. He posted pickets to keep a watch.

They hadn't been there long before civilians started appearing. Apparently there were dozens of them living in the woodlands. They'd refused to abandon their lands during the disastrous retreat of 1910, but after a year of precarious existence, always on the lookout for Martians, many of them were ready to call it quits before another winter arrived. The appearance of the soldiers and the hope of an escort to safety made up the minds of many of them.

Dolfen looked at these people with renewed anger. They were dirty, their clothes halfway to becoming rags, and there was a scared, hunted look in their eyes. The kids were very quiet, with none of the usual energy you'd expect. Oh yeah, the Martians were going to pay!

What's it like across the river?" asked one woman, clutching a toddler to her. "Will we be safe? Where will we live?"

"You'll be as safe as anyone can be these days," Dolfen told her. "We're building some mighty powerful defenses along the Mississippi. You can live in the camps they've set up until they can resettle you. You're farmers, mostly, right?" She and some of the others nodded. "Good, we sure can use you! They're creating new farms by the thousands across the river. The country needs food. Don't worry, you'll get by fine."

"What about the weed, that red weed? Is it across the river, too? It keeps showing up here, choking out what crops we can plant!"

"No, there's none of it there." *Yet.*

This seemed to satisfy most of them, but one older man asked: "But when can we come back? When are you soldier-boys gonna drive these critters outta here? I've lived here all my life and I don't plan to die anywhere else!"

"The army will be back one of these days. I won't lie to you and say it will be soon. The truth is we took a licking last year and it's gonna take some time to build up our strength so we can beat these devils. But we *will* beat them! Not next week, and maybe not next year, but eventually we will. For the time being we need to get you folks to safety. So pack your stuff up and get ready to go. Those of you without horses can hitch a ride on the trucks." His speech didn't seem to encourage them very much, but they did as he told them.

It took longer than he wanted, but eventually they were on the road again and reached Newport - or what was left of it - before dark. It looked to have been a town of a few thousand before the Martians burned it. It was on the banks of the White River, which while bigger than the Cache, was still only knee deep in most spots during the summer. The ruins were an all-too familiar sight these days. There weren't enough of the Martians to occupy all the vast territories of the American heartland, but there were enough to make periodic sweeps and they routinely burned any structures they found. Single farms and tiny hamlets were sometimes overlooked, but all the bigger towns had been wrecked. And any human unlucky enough to cross the Martians' path would be scooped up and carried back to their larders.

The destruction in Newport looked nearly total, but despite that, they weren't there long before another group of civilians began to emerge from the ruins and gather from the nearby countryside. They were like the earlier group: full of questions, full of worry. It seemed like most wanted to go with them, but others, when they learned the soldiers weren't staying, wandered away, muttering.

They camped there for the night, Dolfen giving strict orders not to let any cook fires or lanterns show. On the relatively flat land, the light would carry for miles and they'd learned, to their cost, that the Martians operated night and day.

But nothing disturbed them and they were up early and on the road not long after dawn. They had well over a hundred civilians and twice that number of cattle with them now. The cattle were a nuisance, but they would be needed to help feed people across the Mississippi, and they shouldn't be left here to feed Martians. They were heading northeast now, toward the town of Jonesboro. It was over thirty miles away and they wouldn't get there in one day. They recrossed the Cache near a little village named Grubbs. The sign at the edge of town was still hanging on a post, but nothing else was left. They camped five miles short of Jonesboro; it wasn't a good day's march for cavalry, but not bad for the traveling circus Dolfen now commanded.

He and his officers gathered around a concealed fire that evening, sharing drinks and stories. As usual, Major Bridges had the most of both. The Britisher had been all over the world and had a seemingly endless supply of stories and tall tales. "I still can't get over how flat this country is," he said for at least the tenth time. "Parts of India and South Africa are pretty flat, but nothing like this!"

"You fought Martians in South Africa, sir?" asked Lieutenant Harvey Brown, commander of A Troop.

"Bless me, no! I was there in 1900, fighting the Boers! The ruddy Dutchmen didn't seem to want the honor of belonging to the Empire. We would have taught them the error of their ways if it hadn't been for the Martians arriving uninvited back home that spring. Threw all our plans into the midden heap, I can tell you! Kitchener was absolutely furious! Have I mentioned I've met the Field Marshal?"

"A few times…"

"Anyway, we had to call off that war, even though the Martians all died quickly enough. We couldn't be sure there weren't more on the way, so we had to bring the army home, just in case, you know. Gave the Boers their independence—for all the good it did them. Most of 'em are dead now, of course—or refugees at Capetown." He paused and took a drink from the bottle being passed around. "I fought the Martians in Afghanistan, of course." He chuckled. "For years the government was worried about the Russians trying to invade India, but when it finally happened it was the bloody Martians, not the Russians! But Afghanistan, as different a place from this as you could imagine; Mountains and more mountains. All up and down! A good thing, too! Their machines aren't too good at handling mountains and we stopped them in their tracks."

"They can do all right in the mountains," said Dolfen quietly. "I saw two regiments of cavalry wiped out trying to stop only six of the bastards at Glorietta Pass."

No one made a reply to that. None of them had been there, but they all knew the story of why the 5th Cavalry had been forced to re-build yet again. Having succeeded in dampening the spirits of everyone, Dolfen turned in. *Gotta watch that, a commander can't afford to be pessimistic - it's contagious.*

He was awakened once during the night by a false alarm from a nervous sentry, but other than that and the arrival of a few more civilians, things were quiet. Gosling had his breakfast waiting for him in the morning, and he pushed his people to get ready to move as soon as possible. The empty, ruined land was getting on his nerves. He waited until they were almost ready to move out before using the radio to send a short message giving their location and situation. Bridges' warning that the Martians could track the radio signals had him worried, too.

They made it to Jonesboro in a couple of hours. It was a bigger place than Newport, but it had been just as thoroughly wrecked. They picked up a few more families who wanted to go, but they didn't linger long. They pushed on northeast, heading for the town of Paragould. With luck, they would get there by the next day and then they would turn back to Memphis.

It was about two o'clock when they spotted the Martians.

A man from B Troop roared up on a motorcycle to give the word: tripods sighted to the southwest. Dolfen took out his field glasses and climbed atop one of the armored cars and swept the horizon to their rear. At first he didn't see them, but then he realized that four tiny specks were not trees. He looked for a few more minutes, but there didn't seem to be any others. *Four, we might be able to take four.* Were they coming this way? Yes, no doubt. Coming fast, too...

"Lynnbrooke! Get on the radio. Tell Colonel Selfridge where we are and what we're facing. We've got a job for his flyboys!"

"Yes, sir!" replied his aide, who dashed off.

"Bugler! Sound Officer's Call." The tones rang down the length of the column and shortly, all of his officers arrived. He looked them over, still standing atop the armored car.

"Well, gentlemen, for the last eight months we've been training and drilling, and organizing. Today we'll find out if all that work was worthwhile. We've got four tripods on our trail, coming fast. We can't outrun them, not with all the civilians. And in any case, we're through running from these bastards. Today we are going to make them run!

Harvey, you will detail one squad to escort the civilians and the extra supply trucks. Head due east toward the river. Forget about Paragould. Push them, you understand?"

"Yes, sir!"

"The rest of your troop will form a skirmish line across our rear, just like we've practiced. We will continue moving east, but slowly. I've sent for the aircraft, but God knows how long it will take them to get here. So we take our time engaging them. Wait for my signal to dismount. Bill, I want your bikes deployed per the plan: one squad with A Troop, another on either flank, and one more in reserve. Got it?"

"Got it, sir," said Lieutenant Bill Calloway, commander of B Troop.

"C and D Troop and Mister Abernathy's guns will maintain a position back near me until I decide how and when to deploy them. If we keep moving, it will probably be at least an hour before they catch up with us. With any luck, that's about when the aircraft will arrive. The key is to hit them with everything at once! Don't use up our men piecemeal!" He reined himself in. They all knew this. He'd been drilling them on it for months. "All right, let's get to it."

His officers dispersed to issue orders to their commands. Dolfen climbed down off the armored car, wincing as his feet touched the ground. He'd broken his leg at Glorietta Pass and it still bothered him at times. He got back on his horse. There were already shouts—and a few screams—from the civilians, but Harvey's troopers soon had them moving east as quickly as they could be made to move. Lieutenant Lynnbrooke returned to tell him that he'd gotten the message sent off and even received a reply. "Colonel Selfridge says to hang on, sir. He's on his way."

"Liar," said Dolfen. "It'll take him at least a half hour to get his crates in the air and another forty minutes to get here. Still, at least he's on the move."

"Yes, sir."

"And we need to get on the move, too." C and D Troop and the artillery started first, taking the same path as the civilians. A and B Troops waited until they were about a half mile ahead before following. The tripods were still six or seven miles behind them, but closing. They were probably the smaller and faster scouts. Well good; they'd be easier to kill.

An hour later there was still no sign of the airplanes, but the Martians had closed to less than three miles from the mounted screen. He'd have to make his move soon, airplanes or no airplanes. He waited a bit longer and then waved to Lieutenant Calloway. "Go to it, Bill!" Calloway waved back and then sent one of his bikers racing out to give the order to the skirmishers.

As soon as he got there, bugles started ringing out and immediately the squad of motorcycles who were with the horsemen roared off directly toward the Martians. They deliberately kicked up as much dust as they could. They closed on the enemy very fast and Dolfen was afraid they would get too close too soon. But they spun about and came racing back the way they'd come.

Meanwhile, three quarters of the cavalry dismounted, the men disappearing into gullies and patches of tall grass. The land was mostly flat, but it was cut up with numerous little creeks and ravines and there were plenty of hiding places for a man. The remaining quarter towed the empty horses back toward Dolfen. With any luck the Martians wouldn't notice all the men now waiting in ambush for them. *Luck. We're gonna need all there is today!*

While this was going on, Lieutenant Abernathy was getting his guns into battery, and D Troop was setting up their mortars and machine guns. The armored cars of C Troop were spreading out into a line facing the oncoming enemy. They were doing it like they were on the drill field and Dolfen looked on in pride and satisfaction. *Now if it just works!*

Abernathy came trotting up. "We're ready, sir. When should I open fire?"

"As soon as you've got even the faintest chance of hitting them, Lieutenant. We need to keep them as busy as possible."

The young lieutenant took a look through his glasses. "All right, sir, I'll open up at thirty-five hundred yards. Normally that would be a waste of ammo, but we might get lucky."

"Get lucky, Lieutenant."

"Yes, sir." The man dashed off. Lieutenant McGuiness came up just as the other man was leaving.

"Ready, sir," he reported.

"Good, have the mortars open up when the bastards are five hundred yards in front of our skirmish line."

"Yes, sir. What about my machine guns?"

Dolfen shook his head. "You can't use them with all of our troops out in front. I'm afraid they'll be our last ditch if they break through."

"I understand, sir." He saluted and went back to his men.

Dolfen looked around. Still no airplanes. Had he taken care of everything? Was there anything left for him to do? Was he going to get his command chewed to pieces yet again?

"Looks like the show's about to begin, old man, eh?" Bridges was there, looking through his field glasses. "Is there anything you'd like me to do, Captain?"

"Stay alive, Major, stay alive."

"Delighted, sir, absolutely delighted."

Four loud booms, so close together that they were almost one, made him jump. Abernathy's guns had opened up. He looked down range and thought he could see a few explosions far beyond the Martians. Yes, a direct hit at this range was very unlikely. After about thirty seconds they fired again, but this time each one in sequence. This was far below their maximum rate of fire, but the gunners were wisely taking their time with each shot.

The Martians continued to close, apparently undismayed by the artillery fire, although they started to zig-zag a bit to throw off the gunners' aim. "The beasties are learning," he heard Bridges say from beside him.

"Yes, damn them."

Closer and closer. The mortars opened fire and explosions started to erupt around the enemy machines. The mortars threw an explosive three-inch bomb high in the air which then fell down on the target. They didn't have nearly the impact of an artillery round, but they had a bigger explosive charge so maybe they'd do some damage. Their one advantage was that they made virtually no smoke when they fired. Maybe the Martians wouldn't know where they were.

The enemy was nearly up to where the line of dismounted troopers were hiding. The motorcycles were gathering to make their sprint. The field guns went to rapid fire and they were now cranking out a round every few seconds. "Hit them," muttered Dolfen. "Hit the damn things!"

He saw what might have been a hit on one of the tripods, but they kept coming, obviously trying to get close enough to the guns to take them out. Just another hundred yards or so...

The motorcycles of B Troop gunned their engines and he could hear them even from three-quarters of a mile away. They leapt toward the Martians just as the cavalry emerged from their hiding places, shooting rifles and throwing bombs. The armored cars of C Troop surged forward, their small guns popping away.

"Nicely done!" shouted Bridges.

Yes, it had been nicely done, exactly as they'd practiced. Everyone was hitting them at the same time, although D Troop had to cease fire with the mortars now that the enemy was mixed in with the men. But was it doing any good? The Martians had halted their advance and were now firing off their heat rays in all directions as they turned to meet the threats coming in all around them. Abernathy's guns kept firing, any misses would fly far beyond the other men before bursting.

Smoke, dust, and flames leapt up all around the tripods, but all four were still there, still fighting. "Come on! Come on!" said Dolfen, it was almost a prayer. His men were dying out there and he was just watching!

Suddenly one of the tripods staggered. It stumbled backward and then toppled, disappearing into the clouds of dust. Got one! A cheer went up along the line, but the other three continued to blast away with their heat rays. Dolfen stared through his field glasses, trying to see, but what he saw was men on foot and men on motorcycles emerging from the smoke, falling back. Two of the armored cars were burning, the others were pulling back...

We've shot our bolt... what the hell do I do now? Try to regroup? Hit them again?

A sudden roar made him flinch and he nearly dropped the glasses. Something passed low overhead. Then another and another. Dolfen looked up in astonishment as wave after wave of aircraft roared past. Dozens of them!

"Selfridge! He made it!"

Indeed he had. The airplanes, like some flock of impossibly large birds, threw themselves at the enemy, machine guns blazing. They were on the Martians before they could react. Dolfen could see the sparks of fifty-caliber bullets hitting the armor. Bombs started exploding around the tripods, making the earlier artillery and mortar fire look like firecrackers. He prayed his men had been able to get clear.

But the Martians recovered immediately and shifted their fire. Airplanes burst into flames and tumbled from the sky as the heat rays washed over them. In moments a dozen blazing wrecks littered the ground. But the rest pressed on and the appearance of the fliers seemed to rally the spirits of the troops. Men were surging forward now instead of retreating.

Plane after plane made its attack, but were they accomplishing anything? Survivors were turning, circling around to attack again, but so many of them had already gone down. And still the tripods were fighting.

Abernathy's guns had ceased fire for fear of hitting the aircraft. Should he order them to open up again? So many planes were being destroyed already, maybe the risk would be...

"I say! Look at that fellow!"

Bridges' cry brought his attention back to the aircraft. A burning plane was diving right at one of the tripods! As Dolfen watched, the machine hit it head on and its bomb exploded. The blast blotted out plane and tripod in a flash and a cloud of smoke. When it cleared, neither one remained.

For a moment, the battle seemed to come to a halt; everyone, human and Martian alike, stunned by what they'd just seen. And then a great cry went up from Dolfen's soldiers. Men rose up and charged, motorcycles and armored cars rumbled forward. Abernathy's guns roared back to life.

And the Martians fled.

The two surviving tripods turned and ran as fast as their spindly legs could carry them. The planes and cycles pursued them for a few miles, but when two more planes were brought down, the rest turned back; after a while the motorcycles did, too. The enemy kept retreating until they were out of sight.

The aircraft regrouped and flew east. One came low and circled several times and waggled its wings. Dolfen guessed that was probably Selfridge and waved back. Then it turned and followed the others.

Dolfen let out a long sigh and ordered the buglers to sound recall. Slowly his men fell back to his position. He was heartened by how many there were. The losses weren't as bad as he'd feared. But he was sure they were bad enough. When they totaled it up they'd lost about forty dead and another dozen wounded. The crazy fliers had lost no less than seventeen of their aircraft and most of their crews died with them. They only pulled five men alive from the wrecks and one of them died within the hour. Damn, this was the part of being an officer that he really hated. All those dead men were acting under his orders. He'd sent them out there to get killed while he stayed safely in the rear. It was the way things worked, he supposed, but he'd never get used to it.

He ordered the artillery to limber up and get moving. The wounded were loaded up on a couple of the ammo trucks. D Troop followed immediately. It took a while to reorganize the others and Dolfen took the opportunity to ride out and inspect the remains of the battle. The one tripod which the plane had struck was just scattered debris, but the other one which had gone down was mostly intact, although its pilot was dead.

Dolfen had standing orders concerning downed tripods: salvage the power units if he could. They were bulky cylindrical objects mounted on the undersides of the tripods. Apparently they were valuable for some reason. He had some of the mechanics from C Troop take a look and they actually got one of the things detached and strapped to an armored car. But the other one would need a crane to get at and there was no time. He fully expected the Martians to come back in greater numbers and he wasn't going to wait for them.

"Okay, great job, everyone. Now let's get the hell out of here."

Chapter Three

October, 1911, Eddystone, Pennsylvania

Colonel Andrew Comstock looked at the behemoth towering over him and whistled.

"God in Heaven," said his aide, Lieutenant Hornbaker.

"Yes," replied Andrew. "If God were going to build himself a chariot, it might look like this."

"Impressive, isn't it?" Andrew turned to see the Baldwin Locomotive Works representative, John Schmidt, smiling broadly. They were standing in Baldwin's new facility in Eddystone, along the Delaware River just south of Philadelphia. With all the demands for war production they had outgrown their factory in the northern part of that city and built the new place here. Production lines were turning out dozens of steam tanks every day, but Andrew wasn't here to see the steam tanks. No, they were here to see something a great deal larger.

"Yes, it certainly is, Mr. Schmidt. But does it work?"

"Of course it works! That's why we invited you here today, Colonel. We've got steam up and we're ready to go."

"Well, by all means then, tell your people to get going."

Schmidt ran off to do that while Andrew continued to stare. They were here to see the tests of the new land ironclad. His thoughts went back to a conversation he'd had with General Hawthorne standing on the banks of this very river four years earlier. They'd been looking at the unfinished battleship *Michigan* and Andrew had quipped that it was a shame they couldn't put wheels on battleships so they could fight the Martians on land. It had just been a joke, but here was his joke made into reality!

Of course, the machine in front of them wasn't a battleship. Andrew had spent some time aboard real battleships and what they had here was only a fraction of the size. It was a little over a hundred feet long and about forty wide. The upper parts did look like a navy warship sitting out of the water like in a drydock. But that image was ruined by the two pairs of enormous caterpillar tracks on which the rest of it was sitting. Each track was about twelve feet wide, and twelve tall and maybe twenty-five feet long. A long angled bracket connected each track to the 'hull' of the vehicle. This was indeed shaped much like the hull of a ship and that was intentional. The only possible way to transport a monster like this would be by water and so the hull was watertight and able to float.

Well, almost. The hull didn't provide enough displacement to actually float, so when in transit, several detachable units would be fixed to the front and sides to provide the additional buoyancy. Or at least that was the theory.

"This thing can actually move, sir?" asked Hornbaker.

"So they claim. I guess we'll find out soon enough."

The upper parts of the vehicle were not finished yet. At the moment there was just a tall smokestack and a temporary control cabin. Assuming this test worked well, they would add the upper works and the armament which would be very formidable indeed. One large turret would mount a twelve-inch naval gun, while another mounted a seven-incher, and four smaller turrets would have five-inch guns. There were also a dozen or so mounts for machine guns. Heavy armor protected all the vulnerable parts and much of it was the metal-asbestos sandwich developed by the metallurgical lab at MIT. Tests had shown it to be extremely resistant to the heat ray, even at short range. Every opening could be sealed off on command to keep out the black dust weapon of the Martians. There was even an ingenious system to produce a cloud of steam around the machine which would reduce the effect of the Martian heat rays. In theory this thing could roll right into a swarm of tripods and smash them all. At least that was the theory. Another theory. The ironclads seemed to abound with theories.

Schmidt had climbed aboard the thing by way of a ladder which could be raised or lowered at need. He reappeared a few minutes later on the deck and waved to Andrew. The smoke coming from the stack thickened and then came billowing out in a steady stream. There was a sound of heavy machinery in motion and then the entire vehicle seemed to shudder. It jerked forward a few inches, stopped, and then lurched into motion, the massive tracks slowly rotating.

"It works!" cried Hornbaker.

"I'll be damned," said Andrew. "It really does." A small mob of workers had gathered and they began cheering.

At first it was moving very slowly, only a couple of feet per minute, but it gradually gained speed until it was moving at about a walking pace. The tracks crunched the gravel underneath them, but only sank a few inches into them. The thick iron plates were so broad they spread the weight over a large area.

"How do they steer it?" shouted Hornbaker.

"Same way as they do the steam tanks," said a nearby worker. "Make the tracks on the outside of the turn go faster. Look! That's what they're doing now."

Sure enough, the ironclad was slowly turning to the left. "If they want to do a really tight turn," said Andrew, "they can reverse the motion of the other tracks."

The huge machine swung around ninety degrees, reversed itself, and did the same thing until it was pointing in the opposite direction.

After that, it halted and the ladder was lowered. Schmidt came to the edge of the deck and waved. "Come aboard!" he shouted.

Andrew eagerly climbed the ladder into the vehicle. The lower level was all hissing and clanking machinery and it was hot as hell, but a man directed him up another ladder to the deck. Schmidt was waiting for him and Andrew stuck out his hand. "Congratulations, sir! It really works!"

Thank you, Colonel. I know it's been a long haul, but we have the measure of the thing now." He directed them over to the control station. "This is just temporary, of course. When we get the upper works finished, there will be something like the bridge of a ship where the commander and helmsman and all will be."

"Huh, I was expecting a ship's wheel," said Andrew. There was just a series of levers.

"Actually there will be a wheel eventually to control the rudder for when it's on the water," explained Schmidt. "These are the controls for the tracks. Would you like to try?"

Andrew smiled sheepishly and then allowed Schmidt to show him which levers to push to set the vehicle in motion. He gingerly slid a pair of them forward a notch and was delighted when they began to move! Another notch and they went a little faster.

"The real breakthrough was when we abandoned the idea of trying to make this like a traditional ship with the steam engine directly moving the tracks," explained the Baldwin man. "Trying to engineer a drive train from the hull down to the track assembly defeated us again and again. Just too much strain and the angles were all wrong. So we decided to put a British-made steam turbine in the main hull and use that to generate electricity. We use that to power Westinghouse electric motors down there in the track assemblies."

"Ingenious," said Andrew. "Uh, we seem to be about to ram that building up ahead." Schmidt laughed and took over the controls to bring them to a safe halt.

"So how long to finish this up? And how soon will you have more?"

"William Cramp & Sons is producing the upper works and gun turrets right now in Philadelphia. They're also building the flotation devices. Once those are done, we can move this up river to their yards and have the upper works and turrets installed. We hope to have this one finished by early next year. We've already started construction of the other five in the first run and they should be much faster to build. We ought to have the first squadron done by the spring."

"Another six months. A lot can happen in six months." He wasn't too happy about that and knew the generals wouldn't be either. "So what about the 'Little Davids'?"

"That's next on the tour, Colonel. Follow me, will you?" They went down through the ironclad and Schmidt led them to another part of the sprawling Baldwin works. Andrew pointed out an area where armored railroad trains were being built.

"Yes," said Schmidt, "we received a large order for those from the government last spring. We're just going into mass-production now."

"They would have been a big help back in 1910," said Andrew grimly. "Could have used one at Glorietta Pass, that's for sure."

They left the train sheds behind and came to another complex of buildings. Sitting outside were a number of huge... *things*. "There they are, Colonel, almost ready to send to the front."

They weren't nearly as big as the land ironclad, but they were still damn big. Four huge wheels, each twice the height of a man, were connected to a central hull which also held a boiler and smoke stack. Projecting above was the mount for a gun turret. The turrets held no guns as of yet, but from the size of the mount you could tell it would be a big one.

"The turrets are the same size and design as the main turret for the land ironclads," explained Schmidt. "It will hold a twelve-inch gun."

"There don't seem to be any other guns, sir," said Hornbaker. "And the boiler looks kind of vulnerable. Will they be adding more armor, sir?"

"No," said Andrew, who was familiar with the project. "These were designed as a fill-in until the land ironclads were ready. They are basically just a way to get a really big gun near the combat. With the range of the twelve-incher, they ought to be able to stay far enough back that the relative lack of armor won't be a liability. Or that's the theory." Turning to Schmidt, he asked: "Can they move?"

"Yes they can, Colonel. We have one with steam up over there." They walked over to one of the Little Davids which had smoke coming out of its stack. "Unlike the land ironclads these are powered directly from the steam engine. Only the rear two wheels have power. The front two are just for steering." He signaled the crew and shortly they had the thing chugging around the yard. While it would certainly be powerful once it had its gun, it seemed a poor substitute for the land ironclads, but Andrew didn't say so aloud. It was certainly far better than nothing.

"This looks good, Mr. Schmidt," said Andrew after they watched for a while. "When can you deliver them?"

"We'll need another few weeks to get them all operational and then the gun needs to be mounted. I understand you'll need to do some firing tests after that."

"Yes, we'll want them moved to Aberdeen for that. As I understand it, these can be disassembled for transport by rail. Correct?"

"Yes, Colonel, although I have to tell you it's a lengthy process both for disassembly and assembly again. It would be far better to put them on barges and ship them by water."

Andrew frowned. "That might be possible to get them down to Aberdeen, but I don't know where they'll be needed after that. You are going to have to train our men in the procedures."

"Yes. And we'll need you to send us the men you plan to use for the crews as soon as possible. Both for these and the land ironclads. They will have a lot to learn both to operate and maintain them."

"I'll talk to my boss. I understand there's some controversy about just where these monsters will fall in our organization charts - or who will be supplying the crews."

Schmidt snorted. "At least the navy doesn't have that problem!"

Yes, that was true. The navy was building its own version of the land ironclads. They were nearly identical to the army's, but apparently they had reduced the armor thickness and eliminated one of the smaller turrets to lighten the load and improve their sea-keeping characteristics. Andrew had heard that the navy was planning to attach them to their naval squadrons and use them to launch raids against Martian held territory that bordered the sea or large rivers.

"Oh, and that reminds me," said Schmidt. "There's one other thing."

"Really? What?"

"Have you decided what you are going to name these? They really ought to have names."

* * * * *

October, 1911, twelve miles west of Quepos, Costa Rica

"Main guns stand by, we're going to try and get a shot at them!"

Lieutenant Commander Drew Harding, gunnery officer aboard the battleship *USS Minnesota*, had been hoping to hear that order for over an hour. The *Minnesota* along with the *Connecticut, Virginia*, and a few cruisers had been patrolling off the west coast of Costa Rica when a scouting destroyer had reported seeing Martian tripods marching around the Gulf of Nicoya, about forty miles to the northwest. They had immediately changed course to intercept.

Drew and the squadron had been on a number of patrols since they arrived in Pacific waters back in July, and while they had seen the depredation of the Martians, this was the first time they'd spotted any live ones. Drew - and every man aboard - was itching to take a crack at them. This was especially true because the other half of the Pacific task force, who they alternated patrols with, had managed to engage the Martians twice and killed a few of them both times. They had made full use of their crowing rights in the bars and fleshpots of Panama City, and Drew and his comrades were heartily sick of it. Time to even the score!

At full speed they had closed the distance quickly, but then the scout reported that the Martians must have spotted their smoke and were now retreating back the way they'd come. It had become a stern chase. Drew was on the forward observation platform, high up on the cage mast. It had the best view on the whole ship and he'd been watching the Martians through a powerful set of binoculars. There looked to be six or eight of them and they were moving along the shoreline with the strange but rapid gait the tripods were capable of. Everyone was worried that they'd turn inland and disappear among the jungles that covered the mountains there. But the tripods didn't do well in thick jungles - or so they'd been told - and this batch seemed to prefer the much better speed possible along the shore. Mile by mile they had overhauled them and now they were nearly in range of the twelve-inch guns of the battleships. The cruisers could have closed the range faster, but the admiral didn't want them to spook the game before the big ships could get close.

And now the order had come to prepare to fire. Reluctantly Drew turned away and headed down the ladder. He enjoyed the status and responsibility of being the ship's gunnery officer, but there was one thing he hated about it: he couldn't see what was going on! In the old days, the gunnery officer would be right there alongside the gunners, directing their fire. They could see the target and see the effect of their shots. But these days, it was all different. Spotters up on the platforms would use precision optical instruments to observe the range, bearing, and speed of the target and pass that information down to a heavily protected compartment in the bowels of the ship. This was the Plotting Room and there, Drew and a team of highly trained officers and ratings, would take that information, add in further data about the course and speed of their own ship, and using an amazingly complicated mechanical calculator, rapidly determine exactly where to point the guns and when to fire them. This was sent to the gunners themselves who fired as directed.

And Drew never got to see a thing.

Information was already coming in when he arrived in the Plotting Room and his team was processing it and setting up shots even though they were still out of range. Before he could sit down, someone handed him a canvas bag which had the anti-dust mask in it. From time to time the Martians would use their toxic black dust weapon. The vessels had been fitted with shutters to try and keep the deadly stuff out, but on the older ships the attempts had not been entirely satisfactory and crews were given the dust masks just in case. Newer ships were being designed with anti-dust features right from the start. Drew looped the strap on the bag over his shoulder and then observed his people at work.

The distance was down to about twenty thousand yards and that was at the very edge of extreme range for the big guns. They really ought to try to close to fifteen thousand if they could. Minutes went by with everyone getting more and more anxious. Would they get a chance? They were setting up another shot when the telephone buzzed. Drew immediately grabbed and said: "Plotting Room."

It was the first officer. "Guns?" he said, using the traditional nickname for the gunnery officer. "The flagship just signaled commence firing. Give 'em hell, Drew!"

"Yes, sir!" He slammed down the phone and turned to his crew. "Stand by to fire! A Turret make ready!" Only the forward turret could be brought to bear with them chasing the enemy. Its two twelve-inch guns were already loaded and they'd been continuously aiming the guns based on the information being sent to them. All they needed was the command to fire.

Drew watched as the latest sightings were fed into the mechanical calculating machine and produced the new aiming directions. This was automatically relayed to the turret. He kept his eyes on the pitch and roll indicator and positioned his hand over the firing button. A green light burned next to it indicating the loaded status of the guns. The button would turn on a similar light in the turret and the commander there would pull the trigger. At just the right moment Drew pressed it.

Almost instantly a strong shudder passed through the ship. He couldn't hear the guns, but he could certainly feel them! A couple of the men gave a cheer before quickly going back to work. Drew picked up a different telephone and waited.

"Two hundred left, three hundred short," said a voice.

"Two hundred left! Three hundred short!" he shouted. His men fed those corrections into the machine. A new firing solution was produced and passed on. A few seconds later the green light went on and after a final check Drew pushed the firing button. Again the ship shuddered as another salvo was sent off.

"A hundred right, a hundred over," reported the lookout.

They had over-corrected. Drew passed on the new data and forty-five seconds later fired again. More corrections, more shots. But were they hitting anything? This went on for about ten minutes and then the order came to cease fire.

"Well?" he said to the observer. "Did we get any hits?"

"Hard to say, sir," came the reply. "A lot of shells fell right in their vicinity, but they've retreated into the jungle and we can't see them now."

"Damn."

A half hour went by and they were released from battle stations. Drew climbed back up to the observation platform and scanned the coastline with his binoculars. The squadron was circling off shore from the point of action. One of the destroyers got as close in as it dared while the rest stood by to support it if the Martians suddenly reappeared.

But they did not and the destroyer couldn't report any conclusive sign of damage to the enemy. The squadron drew off, feeling content with their actions, but disappointed by the results. When Drew came off watch he found his roommate, Hank Coleman, in their compartment. "Hey there, Guns! Get anything today?"

"Who knows? Don't think so. Scared the bastards though."

"Well, we'll get them next time."

"I hope so."

* * * * *

October, 1911, Washington D.C.

Lieutenant General Leonard Wood found the President in his office having a shave. Roosevelt had the odd habit of shaving in the afternoon, after lunch. He said it just seemed like the best time to do it and Wood had never tried to argue the point. He was leaning back in his large desk chair, with a cloth covering him up to his chin and lather on much of his face. His barber was hovering over him, but when Roosevelt caught sight of Wood, he boomed out: "Leonard! Good to see you!" The barber stepped back with a snort of exasperation.

"Mr. President, I nearly cut you! Please stay still!"

"Sorry, sorry. But Leonard, sit down. Tell me what's happening while I stay still."

Wood nodded to Roosevelt's aide, Major Butt, and took a seat where Roosevelt could see him around the barber. "So, good news first or bad, sir?"

"Oh, the good to start! Tony, here, doesn't want me frowning!"

"Very well then. Good news. The lull in Martian attacks has allowed us to really build up our strength along the Mississippi. We're pouring concrete in record amounts and mounting dozens of large guns every month. There are scores of monitors and gunboats on call to move to danger points. We've got reserves on the east shore with large numbers of the steam tanks and armored trains. Many sections we can tentatively call secure from attack, allowing us to shift our mobile forces elsewhere."

"Nothing's ever really secure, Leonard. Funston thought his lines around Albuquerque and Santa Fe were secure and look what happened there."

"True, but we have to make some decisions about what we can live with. We've got over thirteen hundred miles to defend and we have to take some risks. We've fortified our most vital areas to withstand what we calculate as a worst case attack and are now working on less critical areas. I'm particularly pleased with what we've accomplished on the Superior Switch." He got up and walked over to the big wall map and traced his finger on a line from Minneapolis to Lake Superior. "This is what I've been losing sleep over the most for the last year. The line along the river has natural strength, but the gap between it and the lake was wide open to be turned. If the Martians got around the river's headwaters to the north and flanked us, the whole line would have been in danger."

"But they didn't do that," said Roosevelt. "Glad I talked you out of building the line from Davenport to Milwaukee and abandoning the whole state of Wisconsin. We've given up too many states already."

"Yes we have, sir. But the Switch Line is very strong now and I'm no more worried about it than any other section. Currently 1st Army is holding the line from the lake to Davenport, 3rd Army has from Davenport to Memphis, and 4th Army the rest of the way to the Gulf. We've been adding divisions to each army as they arrive, but that's far too much territory for each of them, so I'm planning to split them in half to create three new armies and insert them into the line between the others. Each will have ten to twelve divisions, which is about the proper size."

"Sixty divisions, by God," said Roosevelt. "Over a million men."

"And that doesn't even include all the corps and army assets. Closer to two million right now."

"And all of them sitting on the defensive."

Wood restrained a sigh, knowing where Roosevelt was about to go with this. Fortunately, the barber was finishing up and plunked a hot towel over his face, cutting off anything further. Wood took advantage and plowed on with the news.

"We've got the defenses of St. Louis in good order. Seeing as how it's the largest bastion we still have on the west side of the river, we've put special emphasis there. In addition to regular artillery, we've installed all five of the captured heat rays that Tesla got working for us."

"Mmmph!" said Roosevelt, nodding his head.

"And speaking of Tesla, I've gotten a report from the Ordnance Department, young Comstock - you remember him - and he says that Tesla has really come up with something. A lightning gun of some sort which he thinks has real potential to be an effective weapon. I've given orders to proceed with development. We've also gone into full production of the new small rocket launchers. We'll be getting them to our infantry as soon as possible. We're hoping they will make a real difference. The land ironclads are in their final tests, and the Little Davids will be shipped to the front soon. I haven't decided where I'll station them, but I plan to keep them in reserve for now."

The barber removed the towel and smeared some scented lotion on the President's face.

"In other good news, the British defenses in Canada are shaping up well. They've repulsed a few probes near Montreal and Quebec, and their line from Georgian Bay across to the St. Lawrence is a reality rather than just a line on the map. With luck, they'll secure our northern border."

"Oh, that reminds me Leonard," said Roosevelt, shooing away the barber and rubbing at his chin. "Bryce, asked me the other day if it would be possible for them to buy some of our steam tanks."

"What for? They make their own tanks. Probably better ones than ours."

"Well, he was saying that nearly all their tank production is going out to their regular forces. But the Canadians are raising a lot of provisional units and they don't have enough tanks to supply them, too. I was thinking that it might be a gesture of solidarity and good will. And it would strengthen our northern defenses."

"Hmmm, it might be possible. Production has been expanded enormously. I suppose we could divert some from the Ford plant in Michigan without causing any real problems. I'll have my staff look into it."

"Good! So, any more good news?"

"Not... really. We launched some bombing raids against several Martian fortresses, but the results have been minimal as far as we can tell. I don't think air attacks are going to accomplish much on their own."

"I got a letter from some lieutenant colonel in the Signal Corps the other day claiming exactly the opposite. He says we need more bombers, a lot more."

"What was his name?" asked Wood, scowling.

"Uh, Morgan? No, Mitchell, yes, that was it."

"Damn, I thought so. William Mitchell, he's made a pest of himself to me as well. Always demanding we build more planes - as if we didn't have enough demands on our resources. But blast the man! He had no business writing directly to you! He's a loose cannon."

"He also wrote that the air services ought have their own separate branch of the military."

"Yes, that's a hobby horse of his, too. I think he sees himself as the head of that new branch. Well, if he doesn't behave himself, he's going to find himself the head of some outpost in the Aleutians!"

"He's got spirit," said Roosevelt. "Got to hand him that. We need spirit."

"Yes, that's true. And aircraft have proven themselves useful. Just the other day a group of them helped destroy two tripods that were attacking a cavalry detachment in Arkansas."

"Bully! Well done!" The President shifted himself in his chair and put on his pince-nez glasses. "So what else have you got for me?"

Wood glanced at his notes. "Uh, work continues on the canal defenses. They are firming up. The navy reports that they are seeing more and more Martian scouting forces in the region, both north and south of the canal. They may be preparing for an attack."

"The canal *must* be defended," said Roosevelt sharply.

"And it will be, Theodore, it will be. Our defenses are already very strong and they get stronger every day. My analysts think that the German enclave in Venezuela and the French one in Mexico are proving to be real distractions to the Martians in those areas. They will siphon off strength from any attack on the canal."

"Well, that's good. The French and Germans surely haven't been much help otherwise!"

"We can use any help we can get. And I have to wonder if the French aren't doing more good than any of us suspect."

"What do you mean?"

"Well, I can't think of any other reason why the Martians down in Mexico haven't created more trouble for us in Texas, New Mexico, and Arizona. We are still wide open down there against a serious attack - which I guess brings us to the top of the 'bad news' list."

"Yes," said Roosevelt, nodding. "I'm getting telegrams almost every day from Governor Colquitt in Texas, and messages from their senators and most of their congressmen every week demanding more forces for Texas. I wish we could send more, Leonard."

"I wish we could, too. I'm meeting with General Funston later today. He's come up from Houston to plead his case. Uh... do you want to see him?"

The President frowned and shook his head. "No, you can handle him. I have meetings with the governors of Iowa and Kansas today wanting to know when in hell they can get their states back." He fixed his gaze on Wood. "What should I tell them Leonard?"

Now Wood did sigh. This was the perpetual question: when can we stop being on the defensive and start driving the invader back? "Mr. President, after our defeats last year, our priority has been to establish a secure line of defense for the eastern states..."

"And you just told me we have done so," interrupted Roosevelt.

"And as you just pointed out, sir, nothing is absolutely secure," countered Wood. "If we try to launch an offensive prematurely we risk disaster. Look at what just happened to the Russians: they had a fairly strong line along the Volga River but then tried to attack eastward. The Martians crushed their attack and then followed up with a counteroffensive of their own, and now the Volga's been breached and the Russians are in real trouble. They may lose Moscow before the winter. We can't risk the same thing happening here."

"No, no, of course not. But we can't just sit here forever! The people are demanding action. We've got five million refugees who want to go home."

"My staff *is* making plans, sir."

"I'd like to see them!"

"I'll arrange a presentation. But in brief, nothing will happen until we are certain the Mississippi Line is really secure - and frankly, sir, I'm hoping we can prove that by repulsing some serious Martian attacks and wear *them* down a bit. Once we are confident of our defense, then we can begin our own offensive.

"The whole key is the railroads, of course. The only way to supply our armies across the river is by rail, and as we found out last year to our loss, the railroads are just too damn vulnerable to fast moving Martian raiding forces. This means that any advance we make is going to have to be slow. We will have to push out from our fortified cities, like St. Louis and Memphis, rebuild the railroads for a dozen miles, and then build a heavily fortified outpost to defend the line. Push another dozen miles and do it again."

"Like an old fashioned siege with parallels and communication trenches," grumbled Roosevelt. "Those took a lot of time."

"Yes, sir, exactly like that, I'm afraid. But at the moment we have no choice. The Martian fortresses are too strong to be taken by a sudden rush and as far as we can tell, they aren't dependent on lines of supply like we are. Any attempt to bypass them will just leave our own forces in danger of being cut off and destroyed. No, our strategy will be to slowly approach their fortresses, protecting our own supply lines as we go, and then bring overwhelming force to bear to destroy them. I'm sorry, sir, but this is going to take time."

Roosevelt frowned and tapped his fingers on his desk. "Yes, yes, I can see that," he said after a moment. "But when can we start? Can I at least tell those governors that we'll be starting soon?"

"Not before next spring at the soonest, I'm afraid." *And maybe not even then depending on what the Martians do.* "And of course we need to wait until the next batch of enemy cylinders arrive, which are due in January." Yes, as incredible as it seemed, the dispatch of another wave of cylinders from Mars had now become almost routine. A hundred or so had been launched the previous month. Everyone was assuming they would be like the previous one: reinforcements for the existing Martian forces and not a landing in some new area. But they needed to be sure.

"So the spring, then," said the President. "Well, they won't be happy, but they'll have to accept it, I suppose. Hopefully we can make some real progress before the fall, do you think?"

Before the election you mean. Yes, that was the other thing weighing on the President's mind. There would be an election next year and there was some serious opposition to Roosevelt running for a fourth term - even from within the Republican Party. The Democrats were putting together their most serious threat in twenty years, and if the war continued as it was, there was a real danger that Roosevelt would not be reelected. Wood shuddered at the thought of trying to work with a *President* Nelson Miles! *Well, I probably won't have to - he's sure to fire me right off.*

Wood got up from his chair. "I have to be going, sir. Good luck with those governors."

"Thank you. And good luck to you with Funston. He's not the sort to take no for an answer!"

"Yes, sir, that I know!" Wood left the office, and slipped out a side door of the White House. He'd seen Governors Stubbs and Carroll waiting for their turn with Roosevelt when he'd come in and he didn't want to give them a crack at him. He walked across the street to the newly renamed War & Navy Building. It used to be the State, War, & Navy Building, but the vastly increased demands of the war effort had required more and more space until there just wasn't enough room for all three departments, even in that massive building. Wood had hoped to move the War Department to some location more remote from the center of Washington, but Roosevelt had insisted that the military departments be kept close by and Henry Stimson, the Secretary of War, had agreed, so the State Department's facilities were being moved to a new building under construction a block south. Wood appreciated the extra space for his operations, but they were still too close to Capitol Hill - and be it said, the White House - for comfort.

He trotted up the steps to his office and stopped short when he saw that Funston was already in the outer office. Damn, he wasn't due for another half hour! But it was too late to sneak away for a few moment's relaxation. Funston saw him and Wood had no choice but to go in and greet him. "Good to see you, Freddy! How was your trip?"

"Not too bad, Leonard, not too bad. More than the usual delays on the trains, though. Good God, but there's a lot of military traffic on the roads! Mile after mile of tanks and guns. Why in hell can't some of that be sent my way?"

Wood grimaced. Funston wasn't wasting any time! Well, in his place Wood wouldn't either. "Come into my office and we'll discuss it. I guess you've met my aide, Semancik, here?"

"Yes, and this is Captain Willard Lang, my aide. He's been with me since Albuquerque." They shook hands and then went into Wood's private office. Semancik served them all coffee and then withdrew.

"So, General, what's your situation?" asked Wood.

"I brought a detailed report, but in plain words, my situation stinks. You've given me an absolutely impossible task, General!"

"I know I have, but you're the best I've got, Freddy."

"Don't try to butter me up, Leonard! I learned all about impossible situations when I was a volunteer with the Cuban insurrectionists in '97. But we had it easy compared to this!" Funston was a round-faced, slightly portly man in his late forties with a full beard and a tendency to get red in the face when excited or angry. His face was pretty red right now. "I've got nine divisions of regulars and seven more of Texas Volunteers, and you expect me to defend a line two thousand miles long! You've got sixty divisions on the Mississippi to defend a line barely half that length!"

"And you know perfectly well why that is, General," said Wood softly.

"Because Texas doesn't matter to the stuffed shirts and millionaires back east!"

"I think it would be more fair to say that the east matters more, not that Texas doesn't matter at all."

"Fair?! *Fair!* When the Martians punch through my lines like they were tissue paper - and they will! - what am I supposed to tell my men and the civilians I'm defending? 'Yes, I know it's not fair, but Washington won't let me defend you'!"

"Freddy, calm down. I don't have to tell you the score. If we lose the east, it's the whole shooting match. I have to protect the cities and the factories. There's no choice, damn it!" Anger crept into his voice. Not at Funston, but at the whole situation.

Funston seemed surprise by Wood's outburst and got control of himself. His aide, Captain Lang, stepped into the silence. "We're well aware of the situation, sir. But unless you look at Texas as just a forlorn hope, we are going to need more equipment. Men we've got, but they can't fight Martians with nothing but rifles. If we can't be better supplied perhaps we should face facts and pull everyone back across the Mississippi rather than risk sacrificing them all."

Even Funston looked shocked at the suggestion. Abandon Texas? From a strictly military point of view it did make sense. Eliminate that enormous salient, bring the whole 2nd Army into the main defense line; yes, it would make sense.

But there was no way they could do that.

They'd lost other states, way too many, but they'd lost them after fighting for them. They'd lost a hundred thousand men fighting for those states. But give up the biggest one without a fight? And also give up the last rail connection with the west coast? No, Roosevelt would never agree and the country would go berserk. Funston knew it and he suspected that this Captain Lang knew it, too. The whippersnapper was just baiting him!

We are sending you equipment," growled Wood.

"But not enough," countered Funston. "My regulars don't have half the artillery and tanks as your troops on the Mississippi, and the volunteers have got virtually nothing heavier than a machine gun. As Lang says, with all the refugees, we could field twice the number of volunteer organizations, but we don't even have rifles and machine guns for them!"

Wood nodded. It was true, and he felt guilty about making that promise to Roosevelt about diverting some tanks to the Canadians. And it was also true that Funston's defenses were hopelessly weak against a serious Martian attack. The only really strong part of his line was from Little Rock along the Arkansas River, down to where it joined the Mississippi. And except for Little Rock itself, even that wasn't terribly strong. Which was why he had the 4th Army defending the lower Mississippi line all the way from Memphis down to the Gulf, even though technically Funston's forces were blocking any Martian attack there. Theoretically, he could add 4th Army to Funston's defense, and push them forward, beyond the river. But if - when - Funston's line was breached, then there would be nothing to hold the Mississippi further south. No, he couldn't do it.

But he had to do something. He couldn't hang Funston - and Texas - out to dry.

"All right, Freddy, All right. I've got two new regular divisions, just completing their organization. I was going to send them to 1st Army, but I'll give them to you, instead."

"That would be wonderful, Leonard. But it's still not enough."

Wood held up his hand. "I'll also divert some tanks and artillery your way. There are a dozen train loads heading out to California, but things are still so quiet out there, I'll send them to you instead."

"That's good. I'll tell you I've been damn tempted to grab those trains passing west! Hard to see all that equipment and not get any of it."

"So far you've gotten two or three times as much as we've sent to the west coast. We can't totally ignore them, you know."

"They don't need as much with all those mountains protecting them. Most of my line is stark naked."

"I'm also going to give you another gift. You've probably heard that we're starting production of a small rocket launcher for use by the infantry..."

"I've heard. When can we get some?"

"I'll send you the first thousand that come out of the factories, the very first, Freddy. You have top priority."

"That's good, but what we really need is the ability to produce weapons right there in Texas. Can't anything be done?"

Wood shook his head. "Texas doesn't have the infrastructure for that sort of thing. We can't just pack up and send you a tank factory, Freddy. Well, we could, but it wouldn't do you any good because there are no steel mills or foundries or any of the stuff that you'd need to supply a tank factory. Texas has cattle and cotton and not a whole lot else."

"They've got oil."

"Yes, some. And I know there's the potential for a whole lot more, but you can't build tanks out of oil. It would take years to create the sort of industrial base you'd need. No, we can build the factories here in the east faster and easier and ship the tanks to you. It just makes sense." Funston snorted and frowned, but didn't argue that point.

"Well, if that's the best you can do..."

"Right now, it is. But, let me tell about our future plans. The President wants an offensive as soon as possible and..."

"I bet he does! Everyone does!"

"Yes. And we are drawing up plans for some very deliberate advances starting next spring. We will move along a few routes, heavily fortifying them as we go to protect our lines of communication. I'm going to urge that one of the routes start out along the Arkansas River. As we advance, we will take over the defense of that part of your line. Your forces can then be redeployed to reinforce other areas. That two thousand mile line of yours will shrink and shrink."

Funston considered that and then nodded. "That would help. But if the Martians strike us hard somewhere else, we will be in trouble."

"I know, I know. But we'll have to deal with that when it happens. Sorry, Freddy." Wood got up to signal the meeting was over. The visitors stood, and Wood shook hands with Funston.

"Thank you for your time, General," said Funston.

"Good luck, Freddy."

* * * * *

"The successful launch of the next wave of reinforcements will allow us to resume offensive operations on all fronts. I shall summarize what we have decided to do during the next cycle."

Qetjnegartis observed the image of Coordinator Glangatnar, administrator of the Colonial Conclave, in the communications chamber of the holdfast. This same image was being broadcast to all the other clan commanders on the target world, as well as their chief subordinates.

"Continents Five and Six have been entirely subjugated and will receive no additional reinforcements. Clans in those regions will consolidate and concentrate their efforts on production and resource gathering."

Qetjnegartis reflected that the clans on Continent Five, the south polar continent, had managed to stave off starvation by the unorthodox method of harvesting warm-blooded creatures which lived in the surrounding seas. But that method was so inefficient and labor intensive, that no great increase in their population was proving possible. Little labor was available for resource gathering, and what resources that were there, were buried beneath *telequels* of ice. Continent Five would remain a minor area of operations.

"Continent Six," continued Glangatnar, "is located close to a number of large islands; consideration will be given to developing methods for crossing the oceans to reach those islands. However, this is not a top priority.

The central regions of Continent Two have been secured, although due to the very dense plant growths in those regions, much of the area remains unexplored, although there is no evidence of large prey-creature concentrations and hence, no need for immediate operations. Prey-creatures still control the southern and northern areas and these must be eradicated. The southern area is the most lightly defended and this should be conquered first. Then all forces can be shifted north to take care of the other areas.

"Continent Four is also mostly subdued. Only two fortified regions remain in prey-creature control. However, these are very heavily defended and have the support of powerful sea vessels. Care must be taken in any attack against them. Also, it has been determined that an even more heavily fortified region has been constructed on the narrow isthmus connecting Continent Four to Continent Three. We do not know why this has been done. There is no evidence of any major habitations in that area. We speculate that it has been built specifically to prevent the union of our forces on the two continents. A similar zone is known to exist at the connection between Continents One and Two. Therefore we have decided that this region must be eliminated. The clans on both continents have been directed to cooperate in this endeavor."

Qetjnegartis considered this. Clan Bajantus had not been called upon to join in this operation and it was grateful for that. It would be the responsibility of the clans to the south to carry this out. It did not believe that this fortified zone of the prey-creatures was critical enough to justify such a major operation, but as long as its clan would not have to supply forces it did not really matter.

"Continent One is still a major center of operations The central northern portions have been subdued, except for small groups lurking in out of the way places. But the southern regions are protected by the highest mountains on the planet and so far no attempt to penetrate them have been successful. To the east and southeast are very densely populated regions, and even though their weapons are mostly crude, their vast numbers have slowed our progress. To the west lies a major prey-creature power. We have enjoyed several major successes there recently, but much work remains to be done. It is known that to the west of them lie major habitations and cities with significant power output. We can expect resistance to increase the farther west we go. Operations will be pressed on all of those fronts as much as possible. Half of the new transport capsules are being sent to Continent One.

"On Continent Three a major offensive shall take place," said Glangatnar. "It is here and in regions of Continent One that the most significant resistance has been met. The prey-creatures there have shown the most resilience and ability to adapt. They must be crushed before they adapt further. Clans Bajantus, Mavnaltak, Novmandus and Uxmatrais will all strike eastward and southward. They will each be allotted ten transport in this new wave. Clan Zeejvlapna will provide whatever support it can. Major water barriers exist, but these must be crossed and the populated regions beyond laid waste."

All right, this is what concerned Qetjnegartis. Definite orders to attack, which must be obeyed. And ten capsules! A hundred new clan members! This was good news indeed! It would probably take a tenth of a cycle to get the newcomers organized, but after that a major offensive could be launched.

"One final item," said Glangatnar. "Included with the wave of incoming capsules is an experimental device. Rather than land on this world, it will attempt to go into a stable orbit and become an artificial moon. The capsule will have no crew, but will contain observation equipment which will allow it to provide accurate maps of unoccupied regions and even supply us with intelligence about the movements of the prey-creatures. If the device is successful in achieving orbit, you will be instructed how to receive the information it gathers."

More good news! The lack of accurate data on this world was a serious handicap. Observations from the Homeworld had given a knowledge of the larger geographical features, continents, major rivers, and cities, but smaller features, and the positions of prey-creature armies, could only be learned by actual scouting. If this device worked, it would be a huge help in planning operations.

Glangatnar concluded the conference and the communications link was broken. Qetjnegartis reflected that there was much work to do.

Chapter Four

November, 1911, southeast of Chepillo Island, Panama

Lieutenant Commander Drew Harding couldn't stand it anymore. For six hours he'd been stuck in the plotting room aboard the *Minnesota*, periodically firing salvos at grid coordinates on a map - and not being able to see a damn thing! He stalked around the compartment and it was clear that his people had everything under control. He turned to his second in command, Lieutenant Buckman, and said: "Take over, I'll be right back."

Buckman looked surprised, but nodded and said: "Yes, sir."

Drew climbed up three decks and into a tropical downpour. The rains in this part of the world were incredible and he was soaked to the skin in seconds, but before he was halfway up the mast the rain had stopped and the sun was out again. He reached the observation platform, which was actually a large compartment on top of the lattice mast, and pulled out his binoculars.

He directed them at the Panamanian coast. To the west he could see Panama City and the vast refugee camps which had grown up all around it. Swinging east he could see some of the fortifications the army had built, which stretched clear across the isthmus. As he watched, there was a flash and a billow of smoke. One of the army's big guns had just fired. He looked farther to the east but couldn't see where the shell had landed. There was already so much smoke in that area it just disappeared among the rest.

A loud rumble from behind him told of one of the other ships in the squadron firing. They were all firing slowly and deliberately at a force of Martians which had come up from the southeast. In the past few weeks, the Martians had been getting bolder and bolder, pushing forces through the thick jungle, and getting closer to the canal. They'd been coming from both the north and the south, too. Technically they were coming from east and west, since that was the way the isthmus ran, but the bottom line was that Martian forces from North America and South America were both converging on Panama.

Initially, they had tried to approach along the coasts where the terrain was far easier. But the ships of the fleet had punished them so severely in those attempts they had been forced to stay inland and try to push their way through one of the densest and most inhospitable jungles on the planet. It was slow going and the army and navy had been given plenty of warning. Between the clouds of smoke from where the enemy burned the jungle to the swarms of refugees - the last holdouts -

fleeing in front of them, it was easy to see where they were.

Shelling them while they were further away could be done, but without direct observation it used up a lot of ammunition for questionable results. Aircraft from bases near the canal could do some spotting, but it was still pretty inaccurate. Closer to the canal, the army, working with the navy, had set up a very impressive system for calling down fire on an approaching enemy. The whole area was divided up into grid squares and both the army's fixed guns and the navy's mobile ones could smother any spot on the grid with heavy shells on command. It was a great system - except that Drew still couldn't see anything.

Minnesota let off another salvo shaking the whole ship and surrounding the vessel with a thick cloud of cordite smoke for a few moments until the wind blew it away in a gray cloud that rolled off toward the coast. It blocked his vision and so once again, he couldn't see the results. Damn.

He really ought to get back to the plotting room, but he watched a little while longer. The ships and the forts were still firing and maybe he'd see...

"Wow!"

He gave off a cry when a there was a bright blue flash from inside the smoke cloud. He knew what that meant: the power units on a Martian tripod had exploded. It happened sometimes. After nearly a minute there was a strange crackling rumble that was different from the normal sounds of a bombardment. He didn't think the shell which had caused that had come from Minnesota, but it was still satisfying.

"Commander? Commander Harding?" He turned and saw that it was Seaman Baker, one of his spotters; he was holding a telephone.

"Yes?"

"Uh, it's Lieutenant Buckman, sir. He needs you back in Plot."

"Oh, okay, tell him I'm on my way."

He went down the ladder as quickly as he could, and then down three more decks to the Plotting Room. While he was on the way, the ship's gongs rang and the order to stand down from battle stations was given. Had the Martians been beaten back? He hurried into the compartment and looked around, but all seemed in order. His people were securing their equipment. Cromely spotted him and said: "Oh, there you are sir."

"What's wrong?"

"Oh, nothing, but the captain was just here and wondered where you were."

Shit.

"What did you tell him?"

"Uh, I wasn't sure where you went, so I told him I thought you were in the head. It had been six hours and maybe you had to go."

"What did he say?"

"Nothing."

"Okay, thanks." Drew stayed there and made sure everything was secure until the end of his watch, and then went to the officer's mess room and got his dinner. Most of the other officers were loud and boisterous after the day's gunnery. A few pessimists were grumbling that they'd no doubt spend the next day restocking the ship's magazines from a munitions ship. It was true that they'd used up a lot of shells and powder today. Afterward, he went up on deck to watch the sunset. More clouds were drifting in from the Pacific, but it wasn't raining and there was a pleasant breeze. Panama wasn't bad in the fall and winter.

While he was standing at the rail, a yeoman found him and told him to report to the captain's cabin. *Oh crap...*

He quickly found his way to the holy-of-holies on the ship and rapped on the door. "Come in," came the immediate answer. He went through and saluted Captain Gebhardt.

Gebhardt returned it from behind a table he was sitting at. "Ah, Harding, sit down." Drew plunked down on a chair, back ramrod straight. Was he in trouble?

"Sorry I wasn't in Plot when you were there, sir," he blurted. "I... I needed to get some air."

Gebhardt looked at him with a piercing gaze, bushy eyebrows arching up. "You happy here, son?"

Startled, Drew automatically answered: "Yes, sir!"

The Captain's mouth drew back in a smirk. "But not as happy as you might be, eh? You've done a good job here, Commander. The ship's gunnery has been excellent and your team is well trained and disciplined."

"T-thank you, sir."

"But I've noticed a certain... restlessness about you, son."

"Sorry, sir!"

Gebhardt, shook his head and made a little waving motion with his hand. "It wasn't a criticism, just an observation. But tell me: how is Lieutenant Buckman working out?"

"Sir? Uh, he's a good officer, sir. He knows the job and the men and..."

"Could he take over for you, do you think?"

"Sir? Uh, I suppose he could... but why...?" Drew was getting nervous—more nervous. Was the captain going to fire him? Take the gunnery position away from him? Turn him into the stores officer or something equally awful?

"Calm down," said Gebhardt, obviously noticing Drew's reaction. He picked up a paper from the table and looked it over. "I've noticed that you have a certain... *itch* to close with the enemy. We don't get many chances to do that here, as I'm sure you've noticed. How would you like the chance to do that somewhere else?"

"Sir? I don't understand, sir."

"This," he said holding up the paper, "is an order from the Bureau of Personnel at the Navy Department directing me to give up one of my senior officers and send him to take command of one of the new river monitors that's being built. Unless you have some serious objection, I'm planning to send you."

What?!

"I… uh… but I've never commanded a ship, sir."

"Yes, I know, so does the Bureau, but with the enormous expansion of the fleet we simply don't have enough experienced ship commanders, so we are having to make do. From what I've heard, they will probably give you an executive officer with experience on the rivers but little military experience. He should be able to help you over the rough spots. So do you want this assignment, Commander?

A command of my own! His mouth babbled: "Yes, sir! Uh, what ship, sir?"

"One of the new *Liberation* class ships. The *Santa Fe*. She's finishing up construction in New Orleans right now. Not a sea-going vessel, but heavily armed. And on the rivers you'll get close enough to see the red of their eyes. Satisfied?"

"Yes, sir! Uh, thank you, sir." He could scarcely believe it.

"All right then. Get your bags packed and get yourself to New Orleans. Dismissed."

* * * * *

November, 1911, Memphis, Tennessee

Captain Frank Dolfen led his command across the bridge into Memphis. He was tired and the cold was making his bones ache. He wasn't a young man anymore. He'd hit the twenty year mark in the army last month and that was when he'd hoped to retire. In addition to all the other stuff they'd done, the Martians had wrecked that plan, too. *The bastards really owe me…*

This was their second foray into Martian territory west of the river, but unlike the previous one, they hadn't accomplished much of anything. Last time they'd come back with two kills to their credit - three if you counted the one the tornado got—and a few hundred refugees returned to safety. This time they hadn't seen a single Martian and their tally of refugees could be counted on two hands. The lands over there were getting really empty. On the other hand, he hadn't lost any of his men this time and that was a blessing.

"Good to be back," said Major Bridges. The Britisher was still with the squadron and Dolfen was a bit surprised by that. He was attached to observe and learn what he could about American methods - and give advice about British ones - but Dolfen wasn't sure there was much more for either of them to learn at this point. Oh well, the Limey was a pleasant enough companion on campaign. Sometimes.

"Yeah," replied Dolfen, in no mood to chat at the moment. On the east bank, he turned the column north toward where their camp was located. The massive concrete fortifications to the left blocked out the view of the river. The walls were nearly thirty feet high with a ten foot ditch in front of them, and they were steep enough that - hopefully! - no Martian tripod could climb over them. Large guns on disappearing mounts were placed on platforms at intervals. There were metal gates protected by more guns in rotating turrets every block or so to allow access to the waterfront. The gates were set in recesses in the wall and at right angles so there was no direct line of fire at them. It was an amazing effort and stretched for miles north and south of the city. There were similar fortifications around other river cities like Vicksburg and Baton Rouge. And the workers weren't stopping; they were adding mile after mile of walls spreading north and south of the fortress cities. Dolfen supposed if the war lasted long enough, the walls would stretch the entire length of the Mississippi. The locals were happy to be protected, but they didn't much like the demolition that had been necessary to do it. Whole blocks of buildings had been leveled. But if nothing else, it gave the city the best protection against flooding it had ever had.

After going a few miles north through the city, they were met by a small ambulance train. These took charge of the refugees and Dolfen was happy to tell the officer in charge that there were no wounded to treat. He was even happier when he caught sight of Becca Harding. The nurse was there on that fool horse of hers which had somehow survived all of their earlier adventures. She smiled broadly when she caught sight of him and he couldn't help but smile back. She trotted over to him.

"Welcome back, Frank!"

"Howdy, Becca."

"No casualties?"

"Nary a one. We were lucky."

"Glad you're back safe."

"Me, too. How you been?"

"Oh, about the same. Not too much work these days, although there was a boatload of wounded that came in from Little Rock a week ago."

"Still working with your sharpshooters?"

Becca grimmaced. "Tryin' to. Pretty hopeless."

Dolfen forced himself not to smile. Becca desperately wanted to fight the Martians and the Memphis Lady Sharpshooters organization was about the closest she could get.

"But I've been thinkin'..."

Uh oh...

"'Bout what?"

"Well, when you fellows go out on these long scouting missions, you could use some medical people to go along with you, couldn't you?"

"We do have a couple of medics..."

"Which won't be nearly enough if you get into a serious fight! They weren't near enough after that last fight of yours, I hear. And then there are those civilians you keep picking up. Some of them need medical care, too. Women and kids. What you need is a team with a real doctor and some nurses!"

He couldn't deny it, but Becca was so obviously hinting that she wanted to go along, that he forced his face into complete immobility. "I have no authority to create anything like that," he said stiffly. The last thing he wanted was her out there in the same danger he had to deal with.

"I know that," she said. "But if someone else did, you wouldn't object, would you?"

He felt like he was facing a Martian heat ray. If he said that he did object, she'd get angry. But if he said he didn't...

"Some of the French regiments have women attached to them like that," said Bridges suddenly. Dolfen had forgotten he was even there. "Vivandières they call them, I think. They carry water, tend the wounded, things like that."

"Yes, exactly!" cried Becca.

Dolfen glared at Bridges and said: "Well, I don't know..."

"Couldn't you ask your superiors, Frank?" asked Becca. Her desires were so sincere and deep-felt there was no way he could bring himself to dash them.

"I'll... I'll talk to the colonel."

"Oh, thank you!" she squealed, face bright and smiling. He forced himself to smile, too. Hell, he'd ask Colonel Schumacher and that would be the last anyone would hear of the matter. The 5th's new colonel was a pretty good officer, but he didn't like disruption to the routine. He'd be as happy to have women attached to his command as he would to have an outbreak of hoof-and-mouth disease! It would be all right.

Becca babbled on for a few minutes, but then the ambulance train moved out and she was forced to say goodbye. His troops hadn't stopped when they dropped off the civilians, so he broke into a trot to catch up to the head of the column; Bridges paced him.

"Quite a lassie, that one," said Bridges. "A real spitfire."

"That she is," replied Dolfen, "that she is."

* * * * *

November, 1911, Memphis, Tennessee

Rebecca Harding looked over her shoulder, but Frank was already riding off at a brisk pace and didn't look her way again. That was all right, he had so many responsibilities. But he'd said he would talk to his colonel! She realized it was a long shot that anything would be done and a longer one that she'd be allowed to go even if the idea was approved, but at least it was a chance. She tried not to get her hopes too high, but it was hard not to. She was getting so *bored* with her routine at the hospital. She felt guilty thinking that way; tending the wounded and sick was an important and honorable job. She should be glad she was able to do that much to help in the fight against the Martians.

She thought back to when it seemed like she wouldn't even be allowed to do that much. After fleeing from her home, her mother and father and grandmother killed by the Martians, she'd ended up in Santa Fe and technically the ward of her mother's sister and husband. They'd tried to bundle her off to a school for girls in Connecticut, but she'd escaped into the nurse corps, despite not being of legal age. Well, she was eighteen now and no one could tell her what she had to do.

And there probably wasn't anyone left alive who would even try. Had her aunt and uncle escaped from Santa Fe as she'd urged? She'd had no word from them since the city fell. If they did make it out, they would have had to go south into Texas. Was there any way she could find out about them? Did she even want to? She had no affection for them, but as far as she knew, they were the only family she had left in the world.

No, no one could tell her what she had to do - except for Chief Nurse Chumley, all the doctors, and any officers she met, of course - but there were still plenty of people who could tell her what she couldn't do. She *couldn't* be in the real army, she couldn't take up a weapon, and she couldn't fight Martians. And that's the one thing she really wanted to do!

The lady sharpshooter organization was better than nothing, but only just. It did allow her to do some shooting and even feel a little bit important. The group recently elected officers and NCOs. Mrs. Oswald, the organizer of the group, had been elected captain, of course, but to her surprise, the ladies had elected her to be the company's drill sergeant. She supposed it was an honor. They'd even tried to get her to wear one of their ridiculous uniforms, but she'd begged off.

The little convoy reached the hospital area and the refugees were turned over to the officer in charge of dealing with them. Some of the children were crying and they all wanted to know what was going to happen to them now. *You'll be given a job! These days, everyone has to have a job!*

The huge influx of people from across the river had been a major crisis when it first happened. In that awful spring of 1910, the Martians had broken through the army's defenses along the eastern edge of the Rockies and swept across the Great Plains. Utah, New Mexico, and Idaho had already been lost to the Martians, but now North and South Dakota, Wyoming, Colorado, Nebraska, Kansas, Minnesota, Iowa, most of Missouri, Arkansas, and Oklahoma had been overrun, driving millions from their homes.

They had flooded east to the hoped-for safety behind the Mississippi. At first camps had been set up for them, but it was quickly realized that the loss of the nation's breadbasket, the vast wheat and corn fields, and grazing land from west of the river, was going to create a huge shortage of food unless steps were taken immediately. The obvious solution was to put these displaced farmers to work on new farms. There was still plenty of arable land east of the river, not so good perhaps as the lost lands further west, but good enough. Abandoned land was put back into cultivation and new farmland cut out of the forests. A million acres were planted in time for the 1910 growing season and three million more by 1911. Of course, these were not the modest single-family farms and ranches the refugees came from - and like Becca had grown up on - they were huge plantation-style farms with hundreds of people on each of them working for wages. From what she had heard, the conditions were still pretty grim.

Not as grim as the camps had been at the start, though. She had arrived with the first wave; those who had been driven out of Albuquerque and Santa Fe and a hundred little towns between there and the Mississippi. More and more followed, and many needed medical help. The army nurses and doctors had been overwhelmed. Some of the refugees had been doctors and volunteers had arrived from further east to help, but that first six months had been very bad. A lot of people died. Children died. But bit by bit the refugees were moved out to their new homes.

After the initial shock had worn off and the families settled, most of the young men had joined the army in hopes of taking back their land west of the river. Many of the initial refugee camps were now army camps, filled with those same young men. She had met some of them and they burned to strike back at the invader with a passion that matched her own.

After securing the ambulances and taking care of the horses, Becca checked in with Miss Chumley and was told there were no imme-

diate crises to deal with and she could go back to her normal schedule
- which meant she was free until after dinner. She went back to her
quarters, which were in a barracks-like structure where she had a bed
and a footlocker and not a whole lot else. She lay down on her bunk,
closed her eyes, and dreamed of riding with Frank Dolfen's cavalry out
on patrol against the Martians. She was sure Frank would allow – insist - that she have a rifle. And if the opportunity came along to use it,
well...

And being with Frank would be good, too. Of course, he would
have his duties and she would have hers, but at least she'd see him from
time to time. He was the best friend she had and she liked him a lot.
And he wasn't married and he'd lost his girl to the Martians in the first
days of the war. And he wasn't that much older than her...

"Hey, Becca!"

She opened her eyes and saw that it was Clarissa Forester who
had called her name. Clarissa was one of the other nurses and they saw
a lot of each other. Becca considered her a friend, although lately...

"What?"

"We're having a revival meeting! Come on!"

Becca forced herself not to frown. "No thanks. I'll pass."

Clarissa did frown. "You really ought to come. There'll be music
and a good preacher and it's important."

"Just got back with some refugees and I'm worn out. Leave me
rest."

"Becca, I'm starting to worry about you. I haven't seen you at
church on Sundays, either. How are we going to win this war without
God's help?"

"By killing Martians. And I haven't noticed God killin' any lately. Guess we gotta do it ourselves."

Clarissa's frown became fierce. "Don't talk like that! It's blas-
pheming! God will help us, but we've got to be worthy! If we purge our
sins, God will help us!"

"Go 'way, Clarissa." Becca closed her eyes and rolled over. She
heard Clarissa snort and stalk off.

Revival meetings!

They were becoming very common lately. A religious fervor was
sweeping the country, including the army camps. More and more people
were becoming convinced that the Martian invasion was some sort of
punishment from God for the sins of the world. Becca didn't believe a
word of it. *What sort of sins did Pepe - or me for that matter - commit
to deserve what's happened?* And what sort of god would deal out so
terrible a punishment? When she'd dared to voice such a question a few
months earlier, she'd gotten such a rash of frowns and *Tsk! Tsks!* from
the Bible thumpers, she'd resolved to stay out of such discussions in the

future.

But they were thumping more than Bibles these days. Some were getting downright nasty and blaming the woes of the world - meaning their own woes - on the ones who didn't eagerly join them. Some of the really zealous ones were smashing liquor bottles, dumping beer barrels, busting up poker games, and a few weeks ago a notorious brothel in town had burned down under mysterious circumstances and several people had been badly injured. Naturally, a lot of the soldiers had gotten mad at such high-handed actions, robbing them of their few pleasures, and that there had been fistfights and worse. They'd had to treat some knife wounds in the hospital. Becca was afraid that there was even worse trouble brewing. *There are a lot of angry people out there looking for someone to blame!*

What if they decided to blame her?

She opened her eyes, all hope of sleep vanished. Some of the worst of the thumpers were spouting 'if you're not with God, you're against Him' nonsense, and others were starting to believe them. The last thing she needed was for people like Clarissa to turn against her. Maybe it wouldn't hurt to at least be seen at some of the meetings. And they usually did have pretty good music.

She sat up with a groan and left the barracks.

* * * * *

November, 1911, Washington, D.C.

Leonard Wood was working late - again. He and his new deputy, Colonel Hugh Drum, were seated at a table covered with maps and piles of papers working out the new table of organization for the US Army.

"If we added the 39th Division to the 4th Army, we could push their boundary up to Memphis, sir," said Drum.

"No, no, I don't want the inter-army boundary anywhere near a major fortress. Too much risk that both commanders will overlook a danger because they think the other commander is handling it. We'll put the 39th in 3rd Army and leave the boundary where it is."

"That will make 3rd Army substantially bigger than average, sir."

"So be it. Dickman is doing a good job as an army commander, he can handle things."

"Yes, sir. But it will also leave 4th Army very much below average, just six divisions. And 7th Army is the same."

Wood looked at Drum for a moment. He was damn young for his post, early thirties, already a colonel, and he would probably be a general before his next birthday. The incredible expansion of the army was creating an enormous problem in finding experienced officers to command the new formations. Training schools could turn out captains and lieutenants by the wagon load, but finding capable staff officers - to say nothing of division, corps, and army commanders! - was a daunting challenge. He'd been forced to give up his previous deputy, Doug MacArthur, so he could take command of a new division. He'd probably be a corps commander before long. But at least Drum did have some experience. Fought in Cuba - where his father had been killed—and then later had worked with Fred Funston on his staff before the current war. Still, he'd never had to handle forces of this magnitude - as if anyone in the US Army had!

"We're taking calculated risks here, Hugh. Even with sixty divisions we don't have nearly enough to cover the whole line adequately. More divisions are in the pipeline, but until they are ready, we have to protect the most dangerous areas and pray the other areas don't get hit."

"I understand, sir."

"And we've got eight more divisions which will be ready before spring. I'm keeping them in the east just in case the next wave of cylinders should land there. Probably won't, I know, but we can't ignore the possibility. Once we're sure, we can send them west, and some will go to 4th and 7th Armies."

"What about the two new tank divisions, sir?"

Wood scratched his nose and frowned. Yes, what about them? Major General Samuel Rockenbach was organizing two experimental divisions composed almost entirely of steam tanks at Fort Knox, Kentucky. It was a revolutionary idea originated by an English officer named Fuller which had caught the attention of Roosevelt and Secretary of War Henry Stimson. Instead of infantry regiments with a few battalions of supporting tanks as was the norm in most divisions, these would have tank regiments with just a few battalions of infantry in trucks. Even the artillery would be carried in armored tractors. Wood had his doubts about the utility of the divisions considering the mechanical unreliability of the tanks, but perhaps they could be effective.

"I think we'll keep those in our back pocket for now. Maybe we can use them when we start our offensives."

"Yes, sir."

"Okay, we've got a basic outline here. But we need to find a few corps commanders. Let's start with the XV Corps, I think we'll promote Frederick Foltz and give that to him..."

They worked for another hour and made some good progress. Then, when they were both yawning, Wood sent Drum home to his wife, who was expecting, promising that he'd be going home himself soon. He organized their notes and left them on Semancik's desk, who he'd sent home hours earlier, for him to put into a formal set of orders in the morning. He was about to do the same and surprise his wife by being there before midnight for a change, but his eye caught sight of a stack of letters in the in-basket and couldn't resist paging through them - just to get a jump on tomorrow's work, of course.

He glanced at a few and then took them all back to his desk. These must have arrived from the mail room just before Semancik left because his aide was very good at sorting out the important items from the frivolous - and these clearly hadn't been sorted. Wood had wondered, from time to time, just what he wasn't seeing. A chance to find out. There were a half-dozen requests from rich or important people asking that sons or grandsons or nephews be given safe postings in the army's rear area. There were easily twice that many from rich or important people from the occupied states demanding to know when they could go home - one insisting that the army be careful not to destroy any of his property in the process - and several suggesting that sons or grandsons or nephews deserved promotions or medals. He could see why none of these ever reached his desk. His respect for Semancik - always high - rose another notch.

But then one letter, clearly written in a woman's hand, caught his eye. It asked—begged—for news of her only son, who had been part of 1st Army's V Corps during last year's disaster. She'd heard nothing from him and the Personnel Bureau could only tell her that he was 'missing'. Surely the Chief of Staff could tell her where he was? Wood had just spent part of the evening reorganizing the V Corps, but he knew full well this woman's son wasn't there anymore. He'd almost certainly died with the rest of the corps in North Dakota. He sat and stared at it for a long time. How many other letters like this had Semancik intercepted? He wasn't sure he wanted to know.

Sighing deeply, he paged through the rest of the stack. Here was a letter from that Goddard fellow who had designed the new rocket launchers. He had ideas for larger rockets which could replace conventional heavy artillery. But he didn't think he was getting sufficient support from the Ordnance Department, was there anything Wood could do? Here was another letter from that blasted William Mitchell! Demanding more bombers again, of course. Damn it, hadn't that reprimand for going direct to Roosevelt taught him anything? What was he going to do with him? *Maybe I will send him to the Aleutians!*

Near the bottom of the pile was the weekly plea from Funston for more troops. Or at least he assumed it was weekly. Perhaps they came every day and Semancik filed the rest. But they were all the same: Funston needed more tanks, more heavy artillery, more trained men - especially tank officers, and more supplies. Wood truly wished he could give Freddy what he needed, but he couldn't. Not only was the material needed more urgently on the Mississippi Line, but the hard truth was that even if he sent two or three times as much to Texas, it wouldn't make any difference. Texas was free only because the Martians hadn't decided to conquer it yet. Once they did, it was doomed.

There was an old military maxim: *reinforce success, not defeat.* Every tank and gun he sent there would probably end up wasted. How could he justify it? The war would be won by the deliberate offensives he was now planning - not by trying to hang on to... what did Funston's aide call it? A forlorn hope?

But enough of this. Time to get home. It was nearly midnight - again. He was putting the papers back in order, in hopes Semancik wouldn't notice, when he heard someone in the outer office. Who could it be at this hour? The cleaning staff knew to wait until after he was gone to come in. "Yes?" he called. "Who's there?"

The door opened and a tall young man in a captain's uniform walked in and saluted. "General, I'm George Patton."

Wood looked closer and saw that the right side of his face was scarred and a black eyepatch covered the eye on that side. He'd been a handsome fellow before whatever had caused that. *Heat ray survivor probably...* "What in the world are you doing here, son? It's almost midnight!"

"I've been trying to see you for weeks, sir, but I can't get an appointment. I'd heard you sometimes work late and I thought I'd take a chance to see if I could catch you here without an army of damn clerks and secretaries blocking my path!"

A man with initiative... "All right, so you've caught me. What can I do for you, Captain?"

"I want an assignment, sir. I was wounded at Santa Fe and the goddamn surgeons won't clear me for active duty. *That was a year and a half ago*, sir! I'm fine! I was in tanks, sir, and I when I heard about the new tank divisions I went to see General Rockenbach, but he wouldn't take me without the surgeon's okay. I mean it's true I was down with pneumonia two or three times after I was wounded, but I'm all over that now. Please, sir! I need to get back into the fight against those goddamn..." Patton cut loose with a stream of profanity against the Martians that shocked even an old veteran like Wood.

"Calm down, Captain."

Patton got hold of himself. "Sorry, sir. I just want to fight, sir."

"I can see that, son. I don't suppose you'd accept a light duty assignment..."

"I've been on light duty, sir! You don't think I've just been sitting on my ass all this time, do you?" Despite Patton's impressive size, his voice was surprisingly high-pitched. Right now it was getting very high-pitched.

"No, no, of course not. But you want a combat posting, eh?"

"Yes, sir!"

"And you know tanks..."

"Inside and out!"

Wood looked at the sheaf of papers in his hands and flipped through them until he found the ones he wanted. *Goddard... Mitchell... Funston... maybe I can kill four birds with one stone here.* He stood up from his desk and looked Patton in his eye.

"Then I think I can help you out, Captain. Ever been to Texas?"

Chapter Five

December, 1911, Eddystone, Pennsylvania

"I sure hope this goes better than yesterday, sir," said Lieutenant Jeremiah Hornbaker.

"Amen to that," replied Colonel Andrew Comstock. He glanced over to where Generals Crozier and Hawthorne - his bosses - were talking with John Schmidt of the Baldwin Company. They were all perched atop the USLI-001, the first army land ironclad. No one had agreed on a name for them yet. A cold December wind was flapping the skirts of their greatcoats and a few flakes of snow drifted by. There were still no guns or upper works on the immense vehicle, but everything else had been completed, including a screw-propeller and rudder for when the thing took to the water.

Which it was about to do.

They were parked at the upper end of a concrete ramp which led down into the Delaware River. Waiting for them in the water was a large U-shaped hull, held in position by cables and a pair of small tug boats. If all went well, the USLI-001 would drive down the ramp and into the open end of the 'U' where it would be secured in place. If all the calculations of the engineers were correct, then the land ironclad would transform itself into a sea-going (or at least a river-going) ironclad. It would be able to float. It would then sail under its own power up the river to the William Cramp & Sons shipyard in Philadelphia where the guns and upper works would be installed. There were five more of the ironclads being finished up in the Baldwin works, and if all went well today, they would follow along. Crozier and Hawthorne had come from Washington to see it happen.

But they had also been at the Aberdeen Proving Grounds to see the test firing of the Little David's twelve-inch gun the day before, and as Hornbaker had just reminded him, that had not gone well. Oh, the gun had performed spectacularly, going off with a huge roar and a blast of flame and smoke, and the shell had blown the target to very small pieces. The recoil mechanism on the gun had transferred the force to the vehicle, just as it was designed to do, lifting the front wheels completely off the ground.

That should have warned him.

Several more shots were fired and the generals were very pleased. But then Crozier wanted to see the thing move around a bit and fire some more. All went well until it tried to fire with the turret pointing to the left. This time the recoil lifted the wheels on the left side off the ground - way off the ground. Up and up and three seconds later, the Little David was lying on its side with the gun pointing straight up in the air. Fortunately, no one was seriously hurt. Andrew checked his watch. If they'd gotten the crane out to the firing range as they'd promised, the damn contraption ought to be upright again by now.

Crozier had not been happy. He didn't exactly blame Andrew - there were plenty of people there to blame - but Andrew did feel guilty that he hadn't thought of that potential problem. That was part of his job, after all, to ask the simple questions and find the obvious flaws that the scientists and engineers had overlooked. Up until now he'd been pretty good at that.

Baldwin was already at work designing a set of retractable braces which could be deployed from the sides of the vehicle to prevent that from happening again. But the Little Davids were going to be sent west without waiting for them, with strict instructions to only fire with the turret pointing forward.

Andrew sincerely hoped that today's test would go a lot better.

"All right, I think we are ready!" shouted Schmidt suddenly. "Let's go!" There was a flurry of activity around the controls and the vehicle eased into motion. Smoke billowed out of the stack and Andrew could feel the vibration of the steam turbine down below. It had an entirely different feel to it than the reciprocating engines of other warships he'd been on; just a steady vibration instead of the thump, thump, thump of enormous cylinders.

The USLI-001headed down the ramp at far less than a walking pace. It could go faster, but they were taking this delicate operation slowly. While they waited, several enlisted men began handing out life jackets - just in case, they said. Andrew eyed the gray waters of the Delaware flowing past in the distance. A few chunks of ice were floating on the surface. He was slightly reassured by the lifeboats carried on the auxiliary hull unit up ahead. He sure didn't want to go into the water!

Crozier walked around the upper hull, peering over the railings to look down at the monstrous caterpillar tracks, slowly turning. "Hell of a thing, isn't it?" he remarked to no one in particular.

The forward pair of tracks reached the water and started down in. Another fifty or sixty yards and they'd reach the hull. Andrew wanted to see just how it would be attached and secured. He knew that it had been painstakingly engineered to avoid any possibility of it ripping loose even in rough seas. And yet it had to be easily detachable once the land ironclad reached its destination.

The tracks were nearly submerged when the vehicle suddenly stopped. A Baldwin worker on a telephone shouted for Mr. Schmidt who rushed over and grabbed it away from the man and listened for a moment and then cursed.

"What's wrong, Mr. Schmidt?" asked Crozier.

"Motor Room Number 1 is flooding! A bad leak! Reverse! Put it in reverse!" he shouted to the man at the controls, handing back the phone. Levers were thrown and the ironclad lurched abruptly backward, up the ramp. But they'd only gone a few yards when there was a sharper jolt and they started twisting to one side. There was a muffled screeching sound from up forward.

"It's shorted, sir!" cried the man on the telephone. "Track 1 is out!"

"Keep going! Get us out of the water!"

Andrew ran to the forward railing. Yes, the front track on the left side wasn't turning, it was just being dragged along by the other three. The ironclad pulled itself up the ramp, continuing to twist around a bit, despite attempts to use the other tracks to keep it straight. Finally, they were completely out of the water and Schmidt gave the order to halt.

Workers dashed here and there and disappeared below or arrived on deck to cluster around Schmidt. Through it all, General Crozier stood immobile in the center of the deck, a scowl on his face growing darker by the minute. Finally, Schmidt came over to him, and Andrew edged closer to hear.

"I'm sorry, General, the vibrations of moving must have worked loose some of the seams. Water got into the motor room of the forward left set of tracks. Fortunately, no one was hurt. But we'll have to replace the electric motors before we can try this again."

Crozier remained silent for a very long moment before replying. "This is unacceptable, Mr. Schmidt."

"Yes, sir, I know, and I'm sorry."

"Sorry won't kill any Martians. How long to fix this and how are you going to make sure it doesn't happen again?"

"Probably about a week to pull the motors and replace them. We can inspect the watertight housings at the same time and do what we need to do to make them secure."

Crozier's expression was darker than ever. He swiveled his head around like a gun turret looking for a target. Unfortunately, his gaze came to rest on Andrew. "Comstock!" he snapped.

"Sir!" said Andrew coming to attention.

"We need these things at the front," he said very slowly and very clearly. "I am putting you permanently in charge of seeing that it gets done - soon."

"Yes, sir. Permanently, sir?"

"Permanently, Colonel. You are now formally attached to the 1st Squadron of US Army Land Ironclads until such time as I reassign you. Stay here. Stay with them. Get them ready. Get them into action.

Understood?"

"Yes, sir. Understood."

"Good. Carry on." Crozier turned away.

Andrew looked helplessly at General Hawthorne, his immediate superior—and his father-in-law. The man chewed on his lower lip for a moment and then said: "I'll tell Vickie to send you your things."

* * * * *

Cycle 597, 844.9, Holdfast 32-2

Qetjnegartis sat in its travel chair inside the large underground machine hangar in the second holdfast. Several fighting machines stood nearby, but Qetjnegartis's attention was fixed on a score of much smaller machines arrayed in two rows. Ixmaderna, in its own chair, was speaking: "As you can see, Commander, the small drone fighting machines function very well. Each one has a scaled-down version of the heat ray, which although small, is still completely lethal against the prey-creatures - I tested it on some captives to make sure. It will be less effective against their armored vehicles, but given time or numbers, could also destroy them. They also have a manipulating tentacle which is equipped with a sharp blade to allow it to function as a weapon at close quarters."

"Yes, I see," said Qetjnegartis, "and they are small enough to fit into restricted spaces and dig out the prey-creatures. How vulnerable are they to damage?"

"Obviously we cannot armor them as heavily as our fighting machines, but they should be resistant against the weapons carried by the enemy foot-warriors. The prey-creatures' heavier weapons will be able to destroy the drones, but their small size will make them difficult targets."

"What about their speed and endurance?"

"They are necessarily slower than a fighting machine, but since these are intended for assaults rather than raids or pursuits, that should not be a liability. Their energy storage cells are also much smaller due to their significantly reduced power demands. Fully charged, they should be able to function for thirty rotations of limited action, and perhaps four rotations of intense combat. They also have a charging umbilical which will allow them to replenish their energy from other machines."

"That is all good. But what about controlling them? That will be the key, it seems, since they are not self-directing."

"They have a limited self-directing ability, Commander," said Ixmaderna. "They can be ordered to move in a certain direction or to a certain point, or to simply follow the controller's own machine and they will do so, adapting their movements to the terrain. There is no need for the controller to direct every aspect of the machine's motion."

"Similar to the mining and construction machines, then?"

"Yes, the same principles exactly."

"So basic movement, but not combat?"

"Combat will require a more active participation on the part of the controller, yes, although the cutter-blade can be set to an automatic pattern of movements which create a deadly zone around the machine if the operator's attention is needed elsewhere. But picking targets and firing the heat ray will require direct commands."

"How many drones could one of us control at once?"

"I have been conducting trials, Commander. With practice, an operator can control between five and ten of the drones simultaneously. Interestingly, I have found that our younger members, the buds who matured here, seem the most adept at this."

"That is interesting," agreed Qetjnegartis. "But I am assuming that when fully involved in commanding the drones, the operator would be less able to control its own war machine?"

"That is true, although depending on the tactical situation that might not be a problem. But allow me to demonstrate what we can do."

"Proceed."

Ixmaderna contacted the operators in the two war machines and they activated their drones. The machines, small and large, began to move and went up the ramp leading to the surface. Qetjnegartis and Ixmaderna followed in their travel chairs. On the surface, the drones fanned out and began firing their heat rays at various patches of ground and waving their manipulators around. There was a covering of frozen water on the ground which erupted in gusts of steam where the heat rays touched it. Then the drones repositioned themselves around the controlling machine and assumed different formations, moving precisely and in unison.

"Impressive," said Qetjnegartis. "Actually employing them effectively in combat will require practice, I am thinking."

"Yes, that is certainly true. Perhaps we can find some small group of prey to attack and test out our methods."

"Perhaps. But the Conclave has suggested that we not deploy the drones until we have them in sufficient numbers for a major attack so as not to give away the element of surprise and allow the prey to develop countermeasures."

"It is certainly true that the prey-creatures are adaptable. They have developed many new weapons and methods just in the short time we have been here," said Ixmaderna in agreement. "But perhaps we can improvise some training exercises in the ruins of the two nearby cities.

At least get the drone operators used to moving and working inside the prey-creatures' habitations."

"That is an excellent idea, Ixmaderna," said Qetjnegartis. "Develop a proposal for my review." Holdfast 32-2 had been constructed in the area between the two prey-creature cities which had been overrun during the clan's great offensive almost two local cycles earlier. While much of the useful materials in those places had been salvaged, there were still substantial ruins which remained.

"I shall do so at once, Commander," said Ixmaderna, clearly pleased. "There is one other thing I would like to show you while you are here, Commander, if you have the time. I realize that with four holdfasts to administer, your time is precious."

"It is true that traveling between the holdfasts is time-consuming," said Qetjnegartis. "I hope that someday we can connect our holdfasts with an underground transport system such as we have on the Homeworld."

"It would be a massive undertaking, Commander, but surely worthwhile."

"Yes, but there is no hope we can divert the necessary resources to it while the struggle against the prey-creatures continues. But in answer to your invitation, I can certainly make time for whatever it is you wish to show me."

"That is most kind. Please, follow me." Ixmaderna turned its travel chair and led the way back down the ramp into the underground portions of the holdfast. As they did so, they found themselves following a harvester machine. This was a modification of the basic fighting machine, which was designed to capture and transport prey. While it did have a small heat ray for self-defense, it had additional manipulator arms to seize prey and a large detachable cage for storing them mounted to the rear of the cockpit. The cage on this harvester was only about half full.

"Hunting does not appear to be good," remarked Qetjnegartis.

"Well, it is the local winter," replied Ixmaderna, "and many of the creatures, both intelligent and non-intelligent, spend much time in sheltered locations, rather than venturing out. But you are correct, Commander, large creatures of all kinds are becoming rare in the areas close to the holdfast."

Qetjnegartis paused to watch the harvester being unloaded. It was spending most of its time at the new Holdfast 32-4 and none of the harvesters had been constructed there yet.

"If you please, Commander, move back a bit," said Ixmaderna.

"Why?"

"For your safety. I have received reports from clans on the First Continent that some of the prey have concealed chemical explosives on themselves and then detonated them when they are brought to the holdfasts."

"Indeed?" said Qetjnegartis, hastily backing off its travel chair.

"Yes. The reports state that the prey in the eastern regions of that continent are fighting with a fanaticism and disregard for their own self-preservation unlike anything seen before."

"There have been no incidents of this kind here, have there?"

"No... if one discounts the flying machine which crashed into Hablantar's fighting machine recently..."

Qetjnegartis contemplated that incident. It *could* have been an accidental collision... but perhaps it wasn't. "So what steps are you taking to safeguard against such an incident here?"

"As you can see, the prey-creatures are being stripped of all items they carry and their artificial coverings before being sent to the holding pens." Indeed, a manipulator machine was doing that now and the prey-creatures were making loud noises in apparent fear or protest.

"Why not do that upon capture instead of waiting until they reach the holdfast? Does that not put the harvester as well as the hold-fast at risk?"

"We had been doing that, Commander, but it appears that the prey are not adapted to the low temperatures of their winter season. We did strip them in warmer temperatures, but when we tried that in low-er temperatures, most of the them were dead by the time they reached the holdfast. Perhaps if we constructed heated holding cages we could solve that problem. Oh, pardon me for a moment, Commander, I will be right back." Ixmaderna moved its travel chair forward to converse with the one operating the manipulator and soon returned. "I noticed that one of the females had a young one and directed that they both be sent to my laboratory rather than the usual holding pens," it explained.

"And I assume that is what you wished to show me? Your experiments with the young prey?"

"Yes, indeed, If you'll come with me." It turned its chair and headed into the main corridor which circled the holdfast. Qetjnegar-tis followed. They went down several ramps to the lower levels and eventually reached Ixmaderna's labs. These were quite extensive now and had a number of people working there, Ixmaderna's buds, mostly, and buds of the buds. Four holding pens were located at the far end of the complex. One held five adult prey-creature females and nine of the very young ones. As they watched, the newly captured female and its offspring were deposited in the pen through the hatch in the roof. It was shrieking so loudly it could be heard faintly even through the thick transparency. The other females paid it little heed, except for one which went over to it.

"Due to the complete helplessness of the infant prey-creatures, it is necessary to keep a number of females to feed and care for them."

"The one on the left appears to be carrying an unborn bud," said Qetjnegartis, pointing at one of them. "Am I correct?"

"Yes, and from my observations it will probably give birth quite soon. It is an interesting process. I have a visual recording of another birth if you are interested."

"Perhaps at some other time. This next pen has somewhat older prey."

"Yes, in hopes of training these creatures to obey us, I wished to remove them from the influence of the adults at as young an age as possible to prevent them from learning anything from their parents which might contradict our training. Finding the proper age to do this has proved challenging and is largely a matter of trial and error."

This pen had fifteen of the little creatures. Some were just sitting or lying on the floor, but others were running around and interacting with each other, although the purpose of the interaction was not readily apparent. "What are they doing?"

"I'm not entirely sure," replied Ixmaderna. "They will do this at times, chasing each other, sometimes even striking each other, although not to inflict serious injury, I don't believe. But observe." It touched a control and a row of lights appeared along the rear wall of the pen. The prey immediately noticed and all of them, even the ones who had not been active, got up and ran over with the others. Each one positioned itself directly in front of one of the lights. There was some pushing and shoving but shortly there was one creature in front of each light. Then a small panel slid aside beneath the lights and the creatures grabbed something inside and put it in their mouths.

"You have trained them to respond by feeding them?"

"Yes, it works quite well. It accustoms them to respond to certain signals. This has proved useful in the next stage." It moved to the third pen. "Here we are training them to do more complex tasks in order to be fed. We are combining the visual signals of the lights with audible messages in our language."

"And they are responding to that?"

"Sometimes we use visual signals alone, sometimes audible ones alone, and sometimes together. They respond to the lights very well, the audible ones less so. It is difficult to judge how well their hearing organs receive our speech. Nevertheless, they are responding to our orders - at least in simple ways."

"And in the fourth pen?" asked Qetjnegartis.

"These are the oldest ones and the most advanced. Unfortunately, due to the short time I have been conducting these experiments, these creatures were taken from their parents at a much older stage than I would have wished, so it is impossible to know how much they might have learned from their parents and how that might taint our results. However, they do respond to orders very well. Notice the collars they are wearing. They can deliver a painful electric shock on our command, so we can use both positive and negative reinforcement to their behavior. Their comprehension of spoken commands appears to be growing as the training continues."

Qetjnegartis watched the creatures for a while. They were taking blocks of plastic and arranging them in different ways according to diagrams projected on a screen. Verbal instructions were being given at the same time. At one point, one of them made a mistake and knocked over a nearly complete construction. The bud overseeing the training issued a command and all the creatures twitched in apparent pain. Then, to Qetjnegartis' surprise, all the others struck the one who had made the mistake several times and knocked it to the floor. "What just happened there?"

"We have observed that punishing the whole group for the mistake of an individual results in improved performance for the whole group."

"Interesting. So what is your evaluation of this project, Ixmaderna? Do you believe success is possible? Can these creatures be trained to serve us?"

"All the data so far indicates that it may be possible. But there is still much work to be done and I cannot guarantee the results. There are still too many unknowns."

"Understood. But you shall continue with this project as your duties allow. Now I must go. The next wave of transports from the Homeworld will be arriving soon and I must make plans for the new offensives."

* * * * *

December, 1911, New Orleans, Louisiana

"Standby to launch!"

The cry was repeated down the length of the slipway and the construction teams leapt to their tasks. Drew Harding looked on in satisfaction and no small amount of nervousness as the USS *Santa Fe* - his ship! - was about to take to the water for the first time. Involuntarily, his eyes were drawn to the sleeves of his jacket. They sported a first, too: the three gold bands of a full commander. Along with a ship, he had received a promotion. It had amazed him; in peacetime he would have had to wait until he was well into his thirties to reach such a rank.

But these days...

"Ever seen this done before?"

Drew turned and saw his executive officer standing beside him. Caleb Mackenzie must have been nearly twice Drew's age. He had a wrinkled face, browned by decades of work in the sun, and a perpetual squint, as if warding off light reflecting from the waters. There was no sun to bother him today, and in fact, a light rain was falling. He wore the uniform of a senior grade lieutenant about as naturally as Drew would have worn a pair of lady's knickers. Mackenzie was - as he'd proudly told Drew - a river rat, born and bred. He knew ships and he knew the river, but only the urgent needs of a country at war would have ever put him in the navy.

"Not a sideways launch like this, no. A couple of stern-first launches, though."

"No room for that here."

'Here' was the Ingalls Shipyard on the south bank of the Mississippi, just across from New Orleans. The yard was owned by the huge Bethlehem Shipbuilding Company and was brand new. There were several other new yards along this stretch of the river, but most of them were turning out wooden river barges or similar auxiliary vessels. Only the Ingalls yard was building armored warships. But Mackenzie was correct; despite the width of the river, there was no room to send a new ship rushing backward out into the ship channel. A sideways launch would keep the ship safely close to the shore.

One of the shipyard workers, a foreman named Andy Higgins, dashed up and said: "We're just about ready, sir! You should come up to the platform!" Higgins was even younger than Drew, but in the few weeks he'd been here, it was clear the man was a human dynamo. He'd been an enormous help in learning his way around his ship.

He and Mackenzie followed Higgins up to the bow of the ship, where a wooden platform had been erected for the launching ceremony. A small delegation from the local community was there, holding umbrellas, along with a much larger group of the construction workers and their families clustered around to watch. Drew went up the three steps to the platform, while Mackenzie and Higgins remained behind.

The manager of the shipyard was there, a harried-looking man named Wachman, along with his teenage daughter, who would do the actual christening. He introduced Drew to the other men who were local politicians; councilmen or aldermen or dogcatchers or some such. Drew smiled and shook hands and immediately forgot their names. Wachman made a mercifully brief speech, thanking the workers for their efforts; and the politicians made somewhat longer speeches, cursing the Martians, praising the navy, and reminding everyone to vote for them next November. The rain was much heavier now and turning cold.

Finally, it was Drew's turn and he simply thanked the workers and assured them that their efforts would soon result in dead Martians. They seemed to like that and applauded lustily.

The girl, whose bright dress and flowers were starting to wilt rather badly with the dampness, stepped up holding a bottle. The navy had used a lot of different liquids to christen their ships over the years, ranging from wine to water from lakes or rivers close to whatever state, town, or city the ship was being named after. In recent years Champaign had started to be used. Since no one had wanted to make a thousand mile round trip to get a bottle of water from the Rio Grande, Drew wasn't sure what was in the bottle the girl wielded. But she stepped up and said in a surprisingly strong voice: "I name this ship, *Santa Fe*! May God bless her and all who sail in her!" She whacked the bottle against the bow and it shattered as it was supposed to, but splashed liquid all over her arms, as it wasn't. The crowd cheered and the girl beamed and laughed at the mess.

Shouts rang out all along the length of the ship and the launch crew went to work, knocking away the last of the braces holding it in place. Then with a squeal and rumble, it was moving. It lurched sideways and rushed with frightening speed into the river, throwing up a huge splash of water. Heavy chains were attached to it and these rumbled out after the ship, slowing it down through weight and friction. After a moment, the *Santa Fe* was at rest a few dozen yards from shore. A small tugboat moved in to push it up against a nearby dock.

"Well, it didn't sink," he heard Mackenzie say to Higgins. "A good start."

Drew looked over his command and smiled in satisfaction. The *Liberation* class monitors were basically scaled-down versions of the old *Amphitrite* class. They were two hundred and twelve feet long, fifty-six feet in the beam, which made them considerably shorter than the *Amphitrites* but a little wider, giving them a rather pudgy look. But this allowed them to draw only about eight feet of water so they could go much farther up the tributaries of the Mississippi. Full load displacement would be about three thousand tons.

The ship's small size had allowed its construction to be nearly completed before launching. The superstructure was almost finished so all that was lacking was the mast and the armament. This consisted of four eight-inch guns in a pair of turrets mounted fore and aft, and four four-inch guns mounted singly at the corners of the superstructure. The *Amphitrites* carried ten-inchers, but Drew had been assured that the eights were more than sufficient to destroy a Martian tripod.

The ship's crew, which numbered one hundred and forty, would be arriving in the next few weeks. Aside from Mackenzie, Drew hadn't met any of them. He had no idea how much experience they would have.

So the next few months would be a frenzy of work to get the ship fully operational and the crew trained to work as an efficient team.

He made his farewells to Wachman, his daughter, and the local dignitaries and went down the steps and over to his first officer.

"Well, let's get to work."

* * * * *

December, 1911, northwest of Memphis, Tennessee

"It's no good, sir! We're gonna have to turn back!"

Lieutenant Harvey Brown, Commander of A Troop, practically had to shout into Frank Dolfen's ear to be heard above the howling wind. It was the fourth day after Christmas and the third day since the squadron had set out from Memphis on another scouting mission. The first and second days had been sunny and fairly warm, but by the evening of the second day there were some ominous clouds building to the northwest. A cold wind had been shaking the tents by midnight. In the morning, the first flakes of snow were whipping past and now, by midmorning, the storm had hit with all its fury.

"You think it's that bad?" he shouted back at Brown.

Brown just stared at him, only his eyes visible between his hat brim and a scarf wrapped around his face. It was a stupid question and they both knew it. Yeah, it definitely was that bad. He couldn't see twenty yards and the snow was already six inches deep on the ground. He'd seen some bad storms during his times in the Dakotas and he'd heard the old-timers' tales about the Winter of the Blue Snow in '86-'87. This one wasn't quite that bad, but it was certainly bad enough.

"If it gets much deeper, the vehicles are gonna get stuck!"

That was a fact. The horses and men might be able to push on, but with over half the squadron dependent on trucks and motorcycles... No, there wasn't any choice.

"All right! Pass the word that we're turning around! Make damn sure everyone gets the order, we don't want anyone getting lost!"

"Yes, sir!" Brown waved a gloved hand near his hat by way of a salute and spurred his horse toward the head of the column.

It took a while and there was a great deal of shouting and confusion, but eventually they were all turned around and heading southeast. This put the wind at their backs and everyone felt much better. Dolfen hated like hell to have to abandon the mission - especially since the Martians didn't seem to suspend *their* operations because of the weather. But to keep going wouldn't accomplish anything except probably lose a lot of horses and equipment to no good purpose.

They struggled on for a few more hours until they reached the ruins of Jonesboro, which was near where they'd spent the previous night. Dolfen ordered a halt and they drew up the vehicles in the spaces between the least damaged buildings to create a windbreak. The men and horses clustered in the lee and built fires and pitched tents as best they could.

The wind continued to howl all night.

* * * * *

December, 1911, near Memphis, Tennessee

Rebecca Harding pulled her hat down to conceal her face as Captain Dolfen rode by. She couldn't imagine how he'd react if he discovered she had stowed away on this expedition. He'd be mad as hell, she knew that, but what he might actually *do*, she wasn't sure. She still couldn't quite believe that she was doing this. She'd asked Frank to talk to his colonel about taking nurses along on his scouting missions and he'd *said* that he had done so, but no decisions - or permission - had been forthcoming. Had he really asked, or had he just told her he'd done so to put her off? It hurt to think he'd do something like that. Of course with the army it could take months for even the simplest thing to get done...

But when she heard Frank was heading out again, she had acted on impulse - just like when she and Pepe had gone to find the shooting stars so long ago. She'd asked Miss Chumley for a leave of absence, and since she hadn't taken any time off in over two years, Chumley had granted the request without a problem. She'd found a man's uniform that fit her well enough, packed a medical kit, gotten her horse Ninny, and just sort of tagged along with the two regular medics when the squadron moved out. The medics had discovered that she was a woman the first day, but they just laughed and made no trouble for her—which was probably more luck than she deserved.

So they hadn't turned her in and she had managed to avoid Frank so far. Her original plan - as far as she had one - was that if and when they got into a fight and she had to tend wounded, by that time it would be far too late to send her back so it wouldn't matter if he found her out. And she'd prove she was so useful that he wouldn't get too mad and he'd allow her to stay. Simple, right?

But now, the terrible winter weather had forced them to turn back, and barring any serious cases of frostbite, she'd have no chance to prove her worth. So she had to keep hidden. Fortunately, that same weather made it entirely unremarkable for her to be so bundled up that no one could see who she was. She'd used a blanket to disguise Ninny, too. The snow had finally stopped falling, but the wind was still bitter.

They crested a tiny rise and there was the river laid out in front of them, the city of Memphis on the far shore. It was late afternoon and the sun peeked out for a moment, painting the buildings and the fortress walls a rosy pink. Frank came riding back and he shouted to the men: "Move it along and I'll have you back in camp in time for the new year!"

New Years! It was true, tonight was New Year's Eve. She'd completely forgotten. The Year of Our Lord, Nineteen Twelve. It didn't seem possible.

But what sort of a year would it be?

Chapter Six

Cycle 597, 845.0, Holdfast 32-2

Qetjnegartis watched as Tanbradjus maneuvered its travel chair into the consultation chamber and sealed the door. It had arrived the previous day with the new wave of transport capsules. It was senior-most of the newcomers, indeed, it was senior to all except Qetjnegartis. It said that it had important orders to relay from the clan leaders and the Council of Three Hundred on the Homeworld. Qetjnegartis had been speculating on what those order might be ever since it was informed. *Surely not orders to replace me, or they would have sent someone senior.* They both had the same progenitor, but Tanbradjus was far junior in order of budding. Even so, it was now the second highest member of the Bajantus Clan here on the target world.

"I trust you have recovered from your journey and the revival from hibernation?" asked Qetjnegartis once Tanbradjus was halted.

"Mostly, although this gravity is very irksome! How do you tolerate it?"

"One become used to it quickly. And after a transference or two, one hardly notices the difference."

"Indeed? I hope you are right. My next bud will be ready to detach soon, but I don't relish enduring this for another quarter cycle until I can transfer." It touched the sack on its side with a tendril.

"Hopefully, you won't need to transfer even then."

"Really? I had heard that to avoid the contagions which infest this place it is necessary to transfer on every other budding." Tanbradjus appeared apprehensive; was it that afraid of the local disease organisms?

"Every other, or every third, seems to be the average for a new arrival. But with time, the chance of infection grows less - just as our scientists had hoped. I have only had to transfer once so far. But do not worry, we can test you for infection at frequent intervals and there will be no danger."

"I was not worried."

"Of course not. But come, you spoke of a very urgent matter. What message do you carry that could not be transmitted directly?" Qetjnegartis could not fail to notice that Tanbradjus was not extending a tendril to allow a mental link. Why? What did it have to conceal?

Tanbradjus hesitated before answering. "This chamber is secure? From being overheard, I mean."

"Of course. But what secret do you carry that could be so dire?"

Tanbradjus looked from side to side and its voice sank so far as to be barely audible. "Qetjnegartis, I fear that our leaders have gone mad."

"What?! Why would you say such a thing?"

"Tell, me, why did we - I mean the Race - come to this planet?"

"Why? To avoid extinction, of course. The Homeworld is dying, all recognize that fact. To stay would mean the eventual death of the Race. We will conquer this world and relocate our people here. That was always the plan…" Qetjnegartis focused on Tanbradjus. "Are you saying that this has changed?"

"Yes, the Three Hundred debated this for half a cycle before this last wave was launched. Many objected to the new plan, but the vast majority endorsed it."

"What new plan?"

"There will be no relocation." Tanbradjus quivered in its chair.

"What? Then… then what are we doing here?" Qetjnegartis tried to conceive some logical argument to support this decision, but failed utterly.

"The new plan is that those of us who are here will send resources back to the Homeworld to stave off the long extinction."

"But… but that's…"

"Insane? Yes, just as I said."

"It's not practical!" said Qetjnegartis, not quite daring to use the word *insane*. "The launching guns would need to be impossibly huge to overcome this planet's gravity and we would be firing… *uphill*, outward from the sun, to reach the Homeworld! The payloads we could hope to deliver would be absurdly small!"

"Yes, so the minority argued. But the rest would not listen. The elders are unwilling to leave and they command the rest. The orders I carry - and the orders we must obey - direct us to finish this war with the prey-creatures as quickly as possible…"

"Which we are already directing all our resources to do," interrupted Qetjnegartis.

"Yes, but we must also - simultaneously - begin preparations for the new directive. We must scout out locations for the launching guns we must build and start preparing plans and gathering resources."

Qetjnegartis waved its tendrils in dismay. Tanbradjus was right: this thinking was insane! "Perhaps… perhaps once the Council sees how truly impractical this is, they will reverse their decision…"

"Unlikely, and they have already taken steps which will make re-adoption of the relocation plan more difficult."

"What steps?"

"They are creating new buds to replace those of us who have left to come here."

"Madness!" cried Qetjnegartis, truly shocked. "Even if we could somehow send significant resources home, it would still be vital to reduce the total population!"

"Yes, the opposition made that argument, but the majority simply said that if the dissenters refused to create new buds then the others would be glad to take their allotment. That silenced them."

Qetjnegartis could think of no reply. This was indeed madness. The plan - the plan agreed upon - had been to send people to the target world to carry out the conquest here and prepare the way for the rest of the Race to come also. It would take thousands of cycles to carry out, but each transport which left, each load of people moved, would make the resources left on the Homeworld last all the longer. Calculations indicated they would last long enough to complete the relocation.

But this! This was mass suicide! Even if the new launch guns could be built and loads of resources delivered, it would at best delay the inevitable for a few hundred or a few thousand cycles. Then when the collapse finally became unpreventable, there would be no time and no resources to attempt an evacuation.

"I think that many in the Council were worried about the length of time the original plan would take," continued Tanbradjus.

"All knew it was a long-term project!"

"True, but the worry was that those of us who were here would bud and bud and fill up this world before the transfer could be completed. And..." its voice fell again, "there have been some disturbing rumors about... differences in the buds created on this world."

Qetjnegartis stiffened, but did not reply. Rumors? Ixmaderna had said it was inevitable the other clans would notice the same phenomena. Apparently some had dared to report this home.

"So it is true? The new buds have no loyalty to the Homeworld?"

"Not in the direct fashion such as you and I have but they..."

"Is it true?"

"Yes. Buds created on this world have no instinctive submission to those on the Homeworld. But they do have submission to their progenitors!"

"I was afraid that this was the case. Others at home fear this new development greatly."

"I think they exaggerate the danger..." said Qetjnegartis.

"Do you? And what of our own clan here? Only you and three others remain from the original landing force. You four are your own buds' - and their buds' - only links of loyalty to the Homeworld! If you are killed in this war then there would be an entire growing group who could not be controlled! What of that? Our situation may be extreme compared with most, but the same danger exists with them, too."

"Perhaps, but the situation is what it is and we cannot change it. I will endeavor not to be slain and spare the elders from a crisis - and you from the burden of command."

"I am serious, Qetjnegartis!"

"As am I, Tanbradjus."

They stared at each other in silence for some time, but eventually Qetjnegartis stirred. "Well, no matter how much we might disagree, there is nothing for it but to obey our orders. I will direct Ixmaderna to give some thought to possible locations for a launch gun. It is entirely possible, you realize, that no suitable site might be found in our territory?"

"Yes, in that case we would be expected to assist those clans who do have suitable locations."

"Of course. But of immediate concern is the coming offensive. At least the Council does not see fit to interfere with that!"

No. Indeed they insist it go forward with maximum effort on all fronts."

"The plans are far along. We need wait only for the buds you and the other newcomers bear to detach. This will also give us time to analyze the images being sent down from the orbiting artificial satellite. Those should prove extremely valuable."

"So it was hoped. We must also coordinate our activities with Group 33 to the north."

"Yes, Commander Braxjandar is arrogant and can be difficult to work with, but it is capable and aggressive. It has greater strength than we at the moment and I am hoping that its attacks will draw off the enemy's strength from our front."

"It still seems incredible that these primitive prey-creatures are able to mount so much resistance," said Tanbradjus. "The reports of the first invasion..."

"Were extremely incomplete!" said Qetjnegartis in annoyance. "Has no one on the Homeworld read the reports that we have sent? The prey are intelligent and innovative and very numerous. Their strength is far greater than our initial studies indicated!"

"Calm yourself, Qetjnegartis!" said Tanbradjus. "I am not criticizing your actions. But I fear that the elders do not appreciate the difficulties which you face. Perhaps I do not, either. Please instruct me."

"Very well..."

* * * * *

January, 1912, near Donaldsonville, Louisiana

"Damn," said Commander Drew Harding.

"Don't get your feathers ruffled," said Lieutenant Mackenzie. "Could happen to anyone. Hell, it's happened to me more times than I can count."

Drew was standing at the bow of his ship and staring down at the muddy waters of the Mississippi. "But we were in the channel! This should have been clear!"

Mackenzie chuckled in a fashion that Drew found infuriating. "River's different from the open ocean." He cleared his throat and spat. "Sand bars like this 'un move around all the time. By tomorrow it'll probably be gone—or moved somewhere else. But at least it's just sand. No leaks reported from below."

"Thank God for that. Can we get off?"

"I 'spect so. Put 'er astern and see what happens."

Drew frowned and spun on his heel and walked back to the bridge. *Astern! Hell, I could have figured that out! If Mackenzie's such a damn expert on the river, why didn't he keep us from grounding in the first place?* Drew's relationship with his executive officer had generally been satisfactory, but the man could be really irritating when he wanted. Still, there was no doubt he knew the river, and Drew had to admit if he'd been up on the bridge he might have spotted that sand bar before the *Santa Fe* stuck her bow into it. However, the man didn't know a damn thing about gunnery and Drew took some satisfaction in that.

The bridge of the *Santa Fe* was exactly that, an open platform sitting atop the tiny armored wheelhouse which projected far out to either side so that lookouts could spot things - like sand bars - in the river. There was a wheel and an engine room telegraph - duplicates of the ones in the wheelhouse - and the ship would normally be controlled from here except in bad weather or in combat. Drew nodded to the officer of the watch, Ensign Hinsworth, a very young man with the peculiar first name of Albustus. Alby, as he preferred to be called, was still learning his job and was obviously very nervous that he had the watch when this happened - even though Drew had been there on the bridge, too.

"All back one-third," he ordered.

"Aye aye, sir! All back one-third!" Hinsworth made fluttering motions with his hand at the man at the telegraph until he moved the handles to the proper position. After a moment, a bell rang from the telegraph.

"Engine room answers, all back one-third," said the man.

"Engine room answers, all back one-third, sir!" squeaked Hinsworth.

"Yes, ensign, I heard," said Drew with studied calm. Smoke puffed out from the stack just behind them, and the ship vibrated a bit as the engines went to work.

But the ship didn't move. Drew looked about, trying to convince himself that they were moving, but no, they were still stuck.

"All back two-thirds," he ordered and after another relay of orders and replies, Hinsworth told him they were all back two-thirds. But they still didn't seem to be moving. Drew walked out on the bridge wing for a better look. The water at the stern was boiling now, brown with stirred up mud. He put it at all back full, and even though the ship was vibrating strongly and smoke billowed out of the stack in a thick cloud, they still didn't move. Mackenzie arrived on the bridge and came over to him.

"Got a real suction there, Cap'n. Doesn't want t'let go."

"Any *suggestions*, Lieutenant?" Drew didn't quite snarl at the man.

'Have t'twist 'er loose, I think." He looked out over the river, squinting, checking for other traffic, Drew guessed. "Put the port screw back slow, the starboard ahead full and give 'er full right rudder."

Drew thought about that for a moment and realized what Mackenzie was trying to do; he nodded and gave the order. The engine room slowed the right-side propeller and then ran it in the opposite direction. The helmsman spun the wheel which controlled the rudder. "Hard over, sir," he reported after a moment. The ship had been given an oversized rudder to allow sharp turns in the constricted space of a river. Drew hoped it would do the job now.

The ship was shuddering and the water at the stern was churning, but the boil was off to the right now, instead of dead astern. Between the opposite thrustings of the propellers and the rudder diverting the flow from the right screw, the stern of the *Santa Fe* was being pushed strongly to the left. But was she moving?

Yes!

There was no doubt, the stern was swinging around! Degree by degree, the stern moved left and the bow twisted right. They were pulling free!

"Ease 'er off a bit," said Mackenzie. "Don't want t'run 'er up on the shore once we're loose."

Drew ordered reduced speed on the engines, but before the engine room even answered back, the ship lurched and then swung clear. "Rudder a-midships! All ahead one-third!" cried Drew. Santa Fe slowed, stopped, and then moved forward again as if nothing at all had happened.

"There y'go, Cap'n. Yer gettin' the hang of things."

* * * * *

February, 1912, south of Kansas City, Missouri

"Bloody hell, there's another batch of the blighters!"

Major Bridges' exclamation made Frank Dolfen whip his head around so fast it hurt his neck. "Where?" he demanded.

"Almost due west. Still eight or ten miles off, I'd guess. A lot of them, though."

Dolfen squirmed around on his belly in their hiding place and focused his field glasses to the west. He quickly saw what Bridges was talking about: a cluster of dark shapes on the horizon. Martian tripods. And yeah, there were a lot of them. He tried to count, but at this point they were just silhouettes and they kept moving in front of each other, confusing his count. There had to be at least thirty of them. He watched them for a while until he was sure they were heading for the nearby Martian fortress and not coming for them. Then he rolled over on his back and rubbed his eyes. Bridges kept watching.

"I count forty of them, I think. Mostly the regular ones, but a few of the smaller scouts. And most seem to be carrying stuff on their backs, too."

"Those cages they've been using for captives?"

"No, I don't believe so. They're different."

Groaning, Dolfen rolled back and looked through his glasses again. The Martians were a lot closer now, only three or four miles away. He saw what the Englishman was talking about, but he couldn't figure out what the tripods were carrying. "Cargo of some sort, I guess. I suppose they must need to move stuff from one fortress to another."

"You're probably right, old man. But forty more of the damn things! That's how many we've seen arrive so far?"

"Forty more would be... nearly two hundred." Dolfen whistled. "They must be planning something for sure!"

The 1st Squadron of the 5th Cavalry was a long way from its base in Memphis. Word had come down all the way from 3rd Army Headquarters that things were happening up north. The newly formed 6th Army near St. Louis couldn't get any scouts through a thickening screen of Martian pickets, and bad winter weather had grounded their aircraft for long periods. So they'd asked if 3rd Army could slip someone in from the south to have a look. Dolfen and his men, veterans of several missions into Martian territory, had won the prize. *The reward for a job well done: a tougher job!*

They'd started out at the beginning of the month and traveled well over three hundred miles to reach this position near a newly built Martian fortress. It was now the end of February and they'd been watching the place for over a week. There was no way the armored cars or artillery could make such a journey so they and the supply trucks and half the motorcycles had been left behind. They'd been forced to rely on pack horses just like the old days. But they'd made it undetected and Dolfen now had a half-dozen outposts around the fortress making observations. Still, he was worried about what would happen if they were forced into a fight. Without the armored cars or the artillery they could be in real trouble. They had been issued a few of the new rocket launchers, 'stovepipes' everyone was calling them, but he had no idea if they would be of any use. And with the weather and the distance, he couldn't count on any help from Selfridge or his aircraft. No, they had to avoid a fight if at all possible.

A gust of wind penetrated the thick clump of bushes they were using for cover and Dolfen shivered. It was almost March, but the winter still lingered here in the plains. They didn't dare to build a fire and he was getting chilled to the bone. He glanced at the sun, but there were still several hours until nightfall when their relief would arrive and they could retreat to where the rest of the squadron was waiting in the ruins of the town of La Harpe.

The Martian tripods disappeared inside the walls of their fortress off to the northeast and there was nothing more to see. Sometimes there were tripods walking sentry or out hunting, but today there were none in evidence. Dolfen put away his field glasses, wrapped a blanket around himself, and wished for coffee. He knew it was slightly stupid for the squadron commander to be out scouting in person, but there was still a lot of sergeant in him, and he hated being off in the rear while his men were out in front. Besides, this was still more interesting than doing paperwork.

"I say, old man," said Bridges after a while. "How much longer do you plan to keep us at this lovely exercise?"

"Our orders say to stay here until another unit shows up to take our place - as you well know. The 3rd Cavalry is supposed to be here in two days, but I've got no idea when they'll actually arrive."

"Or *if* they'll arrive, eh? Perhaps you could use the wireless."

"Weekly transmissions only, you know that. The Martians come after us the moment we start sending. I don't want to have to relocate the camp again. So we've got at least two more days."

"Very well."

Dolfen shifted, trying to find a more comfortable position and cursed when something sharp dug into him. He reached around and pulled out a rock. He was about to toss it away when he paused and looked closer. There was a red patch on the rock the size of a dime. Red Weed. *Damn.* He glanced around to make sure there was nothing which could see, lit a match, and toasted it. "You see much of this stuff in India, Major?"

"A bit, but the Martians never got a foothold in India proper. And the locals are very good about getting rid of it when they find it. They think it's some sort of devil weed—which I suppose is true, now that I think on it. But they're very protective about their farmland over there, y'know. They set the children to work rooting it out. It's worse up in the mountains, in Afghanistan and the Western Frontier, though. Fewer people and much rougher land. Still, they're probably better off than any poor blighters still trying to hang on in Siberia. I've heard tell that there are places there where it covers thousands of square miles."

"We can't let that happen here."

"Hard to do anything when there are Martians about, old boy."

"Yeah."

They, and the two troopers they'd brought with them, huddled there shivering until well after nightfall when the relief arrived. Then they stumbled back through the dark to the gully where the horses were kept. At least the hike got Dolfen's blood moving again, although his feet still felt like two blocks of ice. They mounted up and rode back to La Harpe, still keeping a careful watch for the enemy. Unlike them, the Martians had no issues with seeing in the dark.

They made it there without incident and gratefully accepted cups of hot coffee in the warm and cozy headquarters which had been set up in the basement of the ruined courthouse. His aide, Lieutenant Lynnbrooke, was there and Dolfen asked him for the status of the squadron.

"All good, sir. The men are staying out of sight and the pickets all have good positions. They're pretty bored, but I rotate the pickets frequently enough that they don't complain much."

"Good. Any messages on the radio?" While they didn't dare to transmit, they could pick up messages from outside.

"Just the usual traffic and confirmation that the squadron from the 3rd is still on its way and ought to be here to relieve us on time."

"Good, good. Anything else?"

Lynnbrooke hesitated and then said: "Uh, we did pick up a group of refugees today, sir."

"Really? Where are they from? Did you question them about enemy activity?" Dolfen was a bit surprised. They'd encountered no one so far on this trip. The land seemed empty.

"They said they were from Iola. Been hiding there for the last year. They saw one of our pickets and came here to check."

Dolfen nodded. That was only five or six miles west of La Harpe. "Did they say anything else? If they've been here this long, they must have seen something."

"Some of them were pretty sick, sir. I turned them over to... uh, to the medics. Figured we could question them later."

"Were all of them sick?"

"No, but they were worried about the ones who are."

Dolfen frowned. "I want to know if they've seen anything." He got up from his chair with a groan.

"Can't it wait until morning, sir? You must be tired."

"I'm up. It should only take a few minutes."

"But sir..."

"But what?" Dolfen turned to face Lynnbrooke. What was the matter with the man? Couldn't he realize that their safety here depended on having the best information possible?

"Uh... nothing, sir."

Dolfen turned and made his way up out of the basement and then gave his eyes a few moments to adjust to the darkness before making his way across the street to the remains of the town's small library where they'd put their medical section. The stairway down had two sets of blankets rigged to prevent any light from leaking out. As he passed the first one, he heard a child crying and a woman's voice trying to calm it. He paused for a moment. For some reason the voice sounded familiar...

He pulled aside the second curtain and looked around. Yes, there were about a dozen civilians here, and there were two medics, but who was that other soldier? Someone in a greatcoat was kneeling next to the child who was crying. He was a bit smaller than your average trooper and his hair, peeking out from under a cap, was definitely longer than regulation. He turned his head and...

"Becca!"

* * * * *

March, 1912, southeast of La Harpe, Kansas

"So, did *everyone* in the squadron know except for me?"

"Not everyone, I don't think," said Rebecca Harding, trying hard not to smile. She was riding beside Frank Dolfen as the squadron headed south, back to Memphis. The relieving column had arrived the day before and they could go home.

"Well, those two blasted medics knew! And I'll eat my hat if Lynnbrooke didn't know, too! The way he was trying to keep me from going to see the refugees! He knew you were there!"

"Well, I guess there were probably a few..." She shrugged.

"What the devil were you thinking?"

"I was *thinking* that I could be more use here than back at the hospital." She carefully kept her voice level. There was no point in getting into a shouting match.

"Well you're …!" Frank stopped himself in mid-shout. Then he stared at her, snorted, and shook his head. "You're really something, y'know that, girl?"

Now she did smile and quirked an eyebrow.

"Guess it wouldn't do any good for me chew you out, would it?"

"Not one bit. If Miss Chumley can't scare me no more, no way you can, either, Mister Captain, sir."

They rode in silence for a while. There was a warm breeze coming up from the southwest. It would probably bring rain tomorrow, but right now it felt nice. Spring coming at last.

"I don't want you gettin' hurt," said Frank after a while.

"Doin' m'best not to."

"You know what I mean! It's *dangerous* out here!"

"I reckon I'm aware of that. I kinda figured it out when the Martians killed my friend… and my pa… and my ma… and my grandma… and tried to kill me a time or two. I'd a' thought you'd have figured it out when they killed all your friends the day after you found me." She let her voice go cold.

"Becca…"

"Frank?"

He snorted again and looked away. "Never mind."

She stared at him and wondered what he'd been about to say. But he spurred his horse to a trot and went to the head of the column. Blast the man! She had no doubt that he cared for her - just like she cared for him. Why couldn't he say it? *You haven't said it either, girl.* No she hadn't, had she? Why not? And why was she out here? To fight Martians like she'd always said? Or because of Frank? Did she love him? She wasn't sure. She was eighteen and most girls her age were already married or at least betrothed. But that was in a world where the parents arranged such things and good girls didn't go chasing after soldiers. That was in a normal world that hadn't been invaded by Martians. That world didn't exist anymore.

After a while he dropped back and she nudged Ninny up beside his horse. "So I guess you won't let me do this again, huh?"

"I didn't let you do it *this* time, but that didn't stop you."

"But you'll be lookin' for me the next time you go out. What'll you do if you catch me?"

"Damn it! I *did* talk to the colonel and he said he wasn't sending any nurses out here! And he's right! This is no place for women!"

"No place for men neither, but you go."

"I have to! You don't!"

"Yeah, you're ordered out here, so you go. But you can't tell me you don't want to be out here, fighting back. I do, too."

Frank scowled and didn't say anything for a while. But he didn't ride off this time. After a while he said: "Becca?"

"Yes, Frank?"

"You might want to spend more time with those sharpshooters of yours."

She snorted. "Why? What use are they?"

"Because we saw almost two hundred Martian tripods back at that fortress."

"Two hundred!" That was far more than she'd ever seen or what had fought in the big battles in 1910 from what she'd been told. "What are they doing?"

"They didn't tell me. But if they're massing like that, it must be for an attack. Kansas City, maybe even St. Louis. And I can't believe they'll leave Memphis alone for long. There's no need for you to come out here lookin' for a fight." He stared right at her.

"The fight's coming to you."

* * * * *

March, 1912, Washington, D.C.

"Mr. President, I think the lull is over. They're preparing for a major attack," said Leonard Wood.

Theodore Roosevelt walked over to the huge map table and nodded. They were in the large situation room in the bowels of the War and Navy Building, which had become Wood's second home the last few years. Dozens of officers and men bustled about, but they gave the President and his Chief of Staff a little bubble of privacy. "Their new cylinders have arrived and now they go on the offensive again. Just like the last time. Are we ready for them?"

"I believe we are, sir. Our defenses along the Mississippi are very strong and getting stronger every day. But I'm concerned about Kansas City and Little Rock." He grabbed up a pointer and tapped it down near the two fortified cities well beyond the main lines of defense. "The reports from cavalry scouts and aircraft indicate that the main concentrations of the enemy are near to both of those places. They may try to wipe them out before attacking our main lines."

"Can they hold?"

"I don't know. It will all depend on how big a force they throw at them. I wish we could reinforce both those places but..."

"But what?"

"Well, there's a limit to how big a force we can keep supplied out there. And every man we send is one less we have to defend the main line. And... well, to put it bluntly, sir, if they are overrun, there's little hope for any sort of orderly retreat. Those garrisons would probably be annihilated and I don't want to send any more men than I have to into what might be death traps." Wood paused and looked at Roosevelt. "Unless we want to evacuate..."

"Can't do it, Leonard. We just can't do it. I agreed to let you abandon Sioux City and Omaha already, but no more! We've evacuated nearly all the civilians from Kansas City and Little Rock, but we can't abandon the cities themselves. No more than we can abandon Texas. It might make sense militarily, but there's a lot more to it than that."

Like your political future? The thought came to Wood instantly. He was being unfair to Roosevelt, but he couldn't help it. There was still a lingering bitterness about his refusal to allow him to pull back from the Rockies in 1910 because of political considerations. They'd lost a hundred thousand men and nearly the whole war when everything went to hell. But at the same time, Roosevelt was right. The string of defeats, the retreats, and the loss of the whole middle of the country had been a huge blow to the morale of the nation. To give up even more... no, it was time to make a stand!

And politics was important. In spite of the mistakes he'd made, Roosevelt was still the best man to lead the country; of that, Wood had no doubt. The opposition, led by Nelson Miles, was already campaigning fiercely in anticipation of the November election. The main plank of their platform was all that lost ground and the administration's failure to take any of it back. Yes, as cynical as it might seem, politics did matter.

"Well," said Wood, dragging his thoughts back to the problem at hand. "At the very least, Kansas City and Little Rock can act as advanced posts, breakwaters to blunt and disrupt the Martian attacks. Blood them as much as we can."

Roosevelt frowned. "What's the proper military term? A Forlorn Hope?"

Wood sighed. "Yes, I guess that's it. But I'll send them what help we can. Fortunately, we're right at the spring thaw and the rivers will be up. We can send gunboats and monitors to both places. And maybe other boats and barges in case we do need to make a run for it."

Roosevelt turned away suddenly and marched across the room and back again, his hands clasped behind his back. When he returned, he thumped a fist on the edge of the map table, making some of the wooden blocks on it jump. "What else?"

"Assuming they do make it past Kansas City and Little Rock, then we need to think about where they will go next. St. Louis and Memphis are the obvious targets. I plan to send most of our reserves to those areas."

"What about the rest of the line?" asked the President, sweeping his arm to indicate the entire vast stretch of the Mississippi defenses. "Any threats elsewhere?"

"Nothing that we've detected. Of course that could change on short notice considering how fast the damn Martians can move. They did try some probes around Lake Superior when parts of it was frozen during the winter, but they seemed to give up on the idea when we dumped a few tripods through the ice with artillery fire."

Roosevelt laughed. "Yes! They don't like the water—thank God!"

"Oh, and I got a report from Funston—not a demand for more equipment for once—saying that he's gotten word from the French down in Veracruz that the Martians there are using some sort of new machine. No real details other than it is a lot smaller than their tripods. We haven't seen any sign of such a thing around here yet, but I've sent out word to be prepared."

"I suppose it's inevitable that the Martians will invent new weapons just as we have. But what the devil is Funston doing dealing directly with the French? Why didn't this come through our normal liaisons?"

Wood shrugged. "You know Funston. But he is sort of dangling on his own down there. Oh, and the British are reporting activity on their front in Canada. But we are going to have to trust that they can deal with it. As for elsewhere... things on the west coast remain quiet, and we've beaten off every probe they've made toward the canal. General Barry is convinced that a major attack is brewing, but we're already giving him everything he can use and he should be able hold—although the refugee problem is becoming a real crisis."

"Yes, I know, I know..." Roosevelt's brow was creased in worry. He had a lot more than just the military situation to deal with. The international situation, the domestic situation, taxes, war bonds, finances, labor problems, food shortages, the list went on and on and mostly things Wood didn't have to deal with at all. He could see the toll this was taking on the man. Wrinkles on wrinkles and his hair and mustache all gray now with many white strands evident. Just like you? *Take a look in the mirror old man!*

"Those are all the main issues, Mr. President."

"Very good. Well, I have to go. Have to meet with Cortelyou about the damn campaign. Good God, but I hate politics!"

Wood smiled. That was like a fish saying it hated water. "Have a good afternoon, Mr. President."

Roosevelt left accompanied by the ubiquitous Major Butt, his military aide.

"That went pretty well, I thought, sir," said Colonel Drum coming up to Wood. His assistant had watched the whole interchange from a safe distance.

"Yes, I guess it did. But we have a hell of a fight coming up, Hugh. And this one we have to win!"

"Yes, sir." Drum gazed at the map. "St. Louis, sir. We must hold St. Louis."

"We have to hold *everywhere*. Any breach of the Mississippi would be a disaster, but, yes, you are right: St. Louis is the linchpin. We need to form a reserve behind the river at that point."

"Yes, sir. And it's a great location in any case. From there we could quickly reinforce the whole northern half of the line if they do strike elsewhere."

"True. But my gut tells me that the main blow will fall on St. Louis. I want more tanks in that area and I want every one of those Little David machines sent there."

"All of them, sir?"

"Yes, all of them. If we are going to use them, I don't want them wasted in penny-packets. If they hit us there, we'll hit back hard!"

"Very good, sir."

Wood got up, stretched, and walked around the room, looking over people's shoulders and making them nervous. He was tired, but restless. Damn, he'd been cooped up in this tomb for too long! He spun about. "Colonel!"

"Sir?"

"It's about time I made an inspection trip. I've had enough of maps and wooden blocks! I want to see what's really going on out there!"

"Uh, yes, sir," said Drum, startled. "Where do you plan to go?"

He pointed at the map.

"St. Louis."

Chapter Seven

March, 1912, Philadelphia, Pennsylvania

"Lower away!" The cry rang through the dry dock at the William Cramp & Sons shipyard in south Philadelphia. Andrew Comstock looked up at the huge crane and the metal cylinder hanging from it which was almost directly overhead.

"Sure hope they know what they're doing," said Jerry Hornbaker from beside him.

"They build battleships here, Lieutenant. This is nothing new for them," replied Andrew, but privately he echoed his aide's sentiments. Considering how many things had gone wrong so far with this project, it wouldn't really surprise him if the crane failed and the main turret of the land ironclad came crashing down to crush everything.

But inch by inch, the turret, which was close to twenty feet in diameter and ten feet high, came down and down and eventually fit into the circular mounting ring on the deck as neatly as you please. The work crew gave a cheer and then began unfastening the hooks on the end of the chains. The crane drew them up and then swung around to pick up the twelve-inch gun which would fit inside the turret. Another team was already at work inside the turret hooking up the traversing and elevating controls.

"That went well," said a voice. "Starting to look like something at last."

Andrew turned and saw that Brigadier General William Clopton had come aboard without him noticing. Another officer, a major, was with him; he was looking around the ironclad with an inquiring eye.

"Yes, sir, we're making some real progress now."

"About time. I was afraid I was going to get stuck commanding a bunch of very expensive white elephants. Might still happen, I suppose. Oh, by the way, this is Major Harold Stavely, he'll be taking command of this contraption once it's finished. I'll expect you to familiarize him with things."

Andrew shook his hand and said: "Welcome aboard, Major, I'll help you out however I can."

"Thank you, Colonel. I commanded a steam tank company out west, so I have some experience with steam powered vehicles - but nothing on this scale. Quite a thing, isn't it?"

"The other five commanders will be here within the week," said Clopton. "You'll be expected to help all of them, Comstock."

Andrew nodded. "Yes, sir." Clopton had been put in command of the 1st Land Ironclad Squadron and it didn't seem to him that the man was all that happy about it. *Well, you aren't all that happy about being here either, are you?*

He'd only been 'permanently' attached to the squadron for about three months, but it seemed much longer. He was working very long days, pretty much seven days a week. He'd only managed one quick visit to Victoria during that time and he missed her and his son terribly. But they had made progress. The first land ironclad had been repaired and the leaking problem had been solved - they hoped! - by sealing all the seams with electric arc welding. The Baldwin people had felt that just doing it on the four compartments housing the motors for the tracks would be enough, but Andrew had insisted - and General Crozier had gratifyingly backed him up - on welding every single seam which would be under water when the ironclads were afloat. It had taken a month, and they were still working on the last two of the squadron, but the next time they drove out into the river, there hadn't been a drop of leakage. So one problem solved.

The next problem had occurred less than an hour later.

They attached the flotation module without a hitch and the USLI-001 had become a ship. Andrew had been most worried about that, but it had gone as smooth as silk. Then, when they engaged the screw propeller and moved out onto the Delaware for the trip up the river to the shipyard, they discovered that the propeller simply wasn't big enough to move the ship against the current of the river; not with the huge amount of drag created by the caterpillar tracks. They had sat there, chugging away like mad, but all they could do was maintain their position against the flow. They had called for a large tug to help tow them, but by the time it had arrived, the Delaware, which was a tidal river, had shifted its direction and was now helping them upstream instead of pushing them down. So they made it to the dry dock, but it was clear that for any long-distance travel by water, each ironclad was going to need a large ship to tow it.

And those were just the big problems. There were dozens of smaller problems plaguing the unique machines. Andrew had followed John Schmidt, the chief engineer, from top to bottom and front to back into every space, large and tiny, to track down troubles and get them fixed. Andrew had taken a few engineering courses at West Point, which had always emphasized the subject, but they had mostly dealt with civil and military engineering. Now he found himself becoming, if not an expert, at least very familiar with mechanical and electrical engineering. In the last few weeks he was fixing problems on his own without Schmidt's help.

"Another month or so, sir," he said to Clopton. "We should have all six ready to head to the front in another month."

"Well, I hope to God you're right, Colonel. From what I'm hearing, there is going to be a hell of fight out west this spring and I damn well don't intend to miss it!" The general turned away and walked aft, surveying what would be his flagship.

Flagship! You'd think we were in the damn navy!

It *did* seem strange using nautical terms, but there was no denying that the land ironclads were more like ships than vehicles. Each one had a crew of nearly a hundred men and more than half were involved with the boilers, steam turbines, and engines. They'd even recruited some men from the merchant marine with experience in those things to man the engine rooms. The vehicles had a bridge, conning tower, and an observation platform on a tall mast. The gunnery system was an exact copy of that used on navy warships, although the Coast Artillery used a similar system, and they were supplying the gunners.

There were some differences, of course. To avoid wasting space or weight, there were almost no living quarters provided. In the field, the crew would sleep wherever they could on board, or pitch tents on the ground if the ironclad was halted. There was a tiny galley which could provide rudimentary meals in combat, but again, the men were expected to form their own messes most of the time. And each ironclad would have a small fleet of trucks following it to provide supplies, spare parts, and ammunition and rations for the crew.

Just organizing them had forced the army to develop entirely new ways of thinking. Each ironclad was being treated effectively as a battalion and would be commanded by a major or lieutenant colonel. A hundred men was an awfully small battalion, but considering the firepower involved, it wasn't an unreasonable decision. The squadron was treated as the equivalent of a brigade, hence Clopton's exalted rank. Privately, Andrew suspected a bit of one-upmanship with the navy was also involved.

And there was no doubt that a rivalry was developing. The navy was building their own land ironclads and there was competition for funding and resources. Admiral of the Fleet George Dewey, the hero of the Spanish American War, was insisting that the navy ought to have priority, but so far the army was winning that battle, and their ironclads would be in service first. There was even a fight going on over the *names* of the damn things! The army wanted to name them after some of the cities out west they hoped to liberate, but the navy had already grabbed the most prominent ones for a class of river monitors they were building. His old friend, Drew Harding, had just taken command of the *Santa Fe* and there was also a *Denver, Wichita*, and *Salt Lake City*. The army had put its foot down and demanded - and got - Albuquerque for

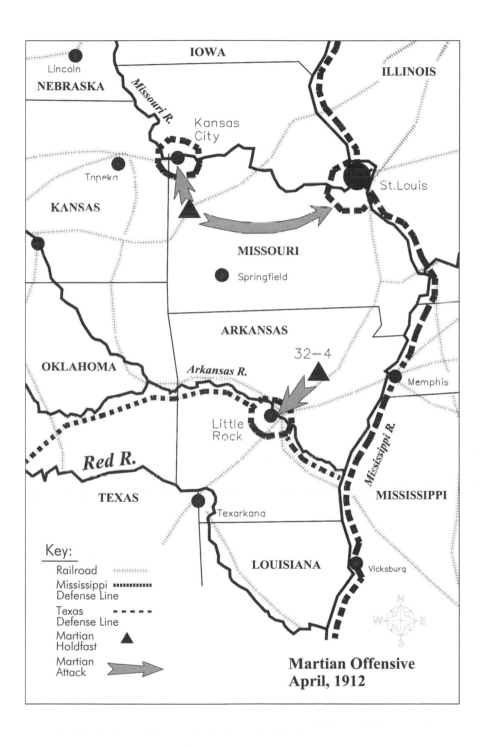

**Martian Offensive
April, 1912**

the USLI-001. But the remaining five were going to be named *Billings, Sioux Falls, Omaha, Tulsa,* and *Springfield.* There would even be a christening ceremony in the coming weeks.

Andrew, accompanied by Stavely and Hornbaker, wandered around inside and outside the newly installed turret, looking over the shoulders of the busy workmen, until they were forced to get out of the way as the gun was swung down through the open top. As he emerged, Lieutenant Hornbaker got his attention and said: "Look, sir, isn't that...?"

"Tesla! What the hell is he doing here?"

There was no mistaking the tall, thin figure of Nikola Tesla. He was standing on the deck and talking in an animated fashion with General Clopton. Andrew hurried over, but as Tesla caught sight of him, he turned his back on Clopton and broke into a huge grin. "Major Comstock! So good to see you again!"

"Good to see you, Doctor, but what brings you here?"

"Ah! I was just explaining to General... uh... General..."

"Clopton," said the general, frowning.

"Yes! General Clopton, here, I have the most marvelous idea for this amazing colossus you've built."

Andrew's heart sank. Something new? They had enough new things to deal with. "But... but, Doctor, aren't you supposed to be working on your new lightning gun?"

"Yes, of course! That's what I'm talking about!"

"You know Doctor Tesla, Colonel?" demanded Clopton, breaking in.

"Uh, yes, sir, we've worked on several different projects in the past..."

"And he's been an enormous help, General! I hope you realize how fortunate you are to have someone like Comstock here!"

Clopton's gaze focused on Andrew. "Indeed?"

"Uh, but, Doctor," said Andrew, "What does your gun have to do with the land ironclads?"

"Why, I want to mount one on them!"

"What?"

"Oh, it's quite simple, really. The construction of the electric cannon has proceeded splendidly, just splendidly, except for the power supply. The army wants the cannon to be mobile, so it needs to be carried on a vehicle of some sort. But no normal vehicle can also carry a generator which can charge the capacitor quickly enough. They are working on some sort of auxiliary vehicle to carry the generator, but it could be many months before such a thing is ready. I don't want to wait!"

No, if Andrew had learned anything about Tesla, it was that he didn't want to wait for anything. "So then you are suggesting..."

"Yes! Exactly! I happened to bump into George Westinghouse last week and he mentioned the electric motors he was providing for the land ironclads. I asked how they were being powered and he said that each one had a steam turbine generator! Exactly what I need! Why in the world didn't you tell me, Major?"

"Well, I didn't think..."

"But it's perfect, can't you see? You could take the silly primitive cannon out of one of the turrets - maybe the one they are trying to put in right now..." He pointed up at the crane.

"Not the twelve-incher!" cried Clopton.

"Well, one of the other ones then, and you could hook it up to the generator and there you would have it! Perfect! I can have the first one delivered here by next week!"

Andrew felt skeptical; Clopton *looked* skeptical. "What is this device you are talking about, Doctor?"

Before Tesla could launch into what was sure to be a long and nearly incomprehensible explanation, Andrew jumped in. "It's a new type of weapon, General, which fires something very much like a lightning bolt. I've seen it demonstrated and it does work - very impressively. I know the high command is eager to get it into action. Perhaps it could be mounted in the turret just forward of the twelve-incher..."

"We can't afford any more delays, Comstock!"

"Well, with *Albuquerque* almost finished up, we'll still have the other five to complete and that will take another few months, sir. That might give us time to install one of the cannons here."

"Yes! Yes!" cried Tesla. "We can certainly do that!"

"We'd need General Crozier's permission..."

"I'll get it! Now, I need to see the generator to work out the power runs!"

Andrew looked at Clopton, who shrugged. They found John Schmidt and sent him and Tesla below. When they were gone, Clopton rounded on him. "You really think this can work? I'm aware of Tesla's reputation; I'm quite an admirer, really, but in person he's a lot more... more..."

"Intense?"

"Yes, surely that, but also, more well, *eccentric*, than I was expecting. So, I ask again: can this contraption of his work?"

"It certainly worked in the test I saw, sir. It doesn't have the range of a conventional gun, but it does have the potential to affect multiple targets at once. It might be a worthwhile tradeoff to lose the forward seven-incher."

"Huh, and the Staff wants to see the thing in action... All right. Get Crozier's go-ahead and then go ahead! But I don't want any delay to prevent us from getting into action!"

"Yes, sir. No, sir, no delays." Clopton turned and left him. Andrew glanced at Hornbaker. "Well, Jerry, we have *another* job to do."

* * * * *

Cycle 597, 845.1, Holdfast 32-4

"So we will attack?" asked Davnitargus.

"Yes," replied Qetjnegartis. "The Colonial Conclave has confirmed the orders and we shall commence the offensive in fifteen local days. But come with me and attend the briefing for our own people." Davnitargus activated its travel chair and fell in beside Qetjnegartis as they moved through the curving corridors of the clan's newest holdfast. Unlike the first holdfast, this one had been constructed without desperate haste and the corridors were properly tiled and leveled—and the roof did not leak! At least so far. As they moved, Qetjnegartis noticed the bud sack on Davnitargus's side. Its bud was going to have its own first bud.

"Your bud progresses well?"

"All appears as expected. It is an interesting experience. But you have gone through this many times, Progenitor."

"Yes, a great many over the long cycles. But only a few times was it for a new being, almost always it was a replacement body for myself."

"This world provides many opportunities not available on the Homeworld."

Qetjnegartis focused more attention on its offspring. Was there some subtle message in its statement? But a moment later it removed all doubt.

"It seems illogical for the others to remain on a dying world rather than come here, does it not? I fear I cannot understand this decision."

"It is not our place to questions the decision of the Council."

"Why not? If the decision clearly is incorrect, why should we not question it?"

"They are older and more experienced and wiser than we, Davnitargus. There may be more factors in their decisions than we know."

"Then why not share those factors with us and let us understand their reasoning? Blind obedience seems... illogical."

Qetjnegartis was becoming alarmed. On the Homeworld, any individual voicing such statements would be facing a quick termination. "Davnitargus... it would be best for you to not say such things."

"Even to you? I realize that those who have come here from the Homeworld are unsettled by the attitude of we young ones, but can I not discuss my concerns with the one who made me? I depend on you for guidance."

"And I am pleased to give it. But you must not speak this way in the hearing of others."

"As you command. I will not speak of this in the presence of those who came from the Homeworld."

Qetjnegartis halted its travel chair. Was this a deliberate prevarication by Davnitargus? Did it mean that it would discuss these matters with the buds created on this world? It had hinted before that there was some secret congress of the younger buds. But there was no opportunity to demand an explanation because at that moment Tanbradjus overtook them in its own travel chair. "Greeting Commander," it said, "We make our final attack plans, do we not?"

"Yes," replied Qetjnegartis. "We were just on our way to the briefing chamber." It glanced at Davnitargus and said: "we will finish our conversation later." It then put its chair in motion and they soon arrived where the other battlegroup commanders were waiting. The strength of the clan had grown significantly in the last half-cycle and could now field no less than twelve battlegroups, ten of which would be committed to this offensive—three hundred fighting machines and nearly that number of the new drones. Qetjnegartis relished having such strength and thought back to when the Clan's survival depended on a mere five machines!

It acknowledged the greetings of its subordinates and then activated a display screen which showed a map of the central portion of Continent Three. "Thanks to the artificial satellite, we now have detailed information on the topography of regions outside our control, as well as intelligence on the location and strength of the enemy forces," it began. "As you can see, the prey-creatures have set up a fortified line along the large river, which had been designated River 3-1." With the detailed maps had come the necessity of giving names or numbers to geographical features. For now, they used the number of the continent, as a prefix, and then numbered the features based on their relative size. It was imprecise, of course, but would suffice for now.

"While the pause in our operations has allowed us to build up our strength, it has also allowed the prey to do the same. This river defense line must be breached before it can be made even more formidable. However, before launching the main assault, there are two enemy fortress-cities west of the river which must be eradicated. One, City 3-20, is in the territory of Group 33 to the north, and the other is in our territory." The display zoomed in on the fortress-city which had so-far resisted all attempts to destroy it. The city was designated 3-118 and it lay along River 3-1.4, being a tributary of the large river.

"At the designated time, we will launch our full strength against 3-118 and destroy all defenders. From there we will move east to prepare for the assault across the river against City 3-37. Once we have a secure hold on the east bank, we can spread out to destroy the enemy's production facilities."

"Commander, will we employ the new drones in this attack?" asked Kantangnar, the leader of Battlegroup 32-4. "I had heard... rumors that they would be withheld."

"It had been proposed to withhold them until the primary attack across the river to achieve maximum surprise, but Group 33 wishes to use them in its attack on City 3-20. Also, Group 31 to our south has already deployed them recently, so the surprise value will soon be lost. Therefore we will use them in the assault on 3-118 to keep our losses to a minimum. Each group will have one of the controller machines and ten of the drones. With this added strength and flexibility, we should be able to overwhelm the defenders very quickly. From there we can move against the main objective along the river.

"Our attack will commence at night to reduce the effectiveness of the prey's weapons. The creatures have begun to use artificial illumination techniques to reduce their disadvantage, but it still exists and we will make use of that. Our main axis of attack will lie along this line..."

Qetjnegartis reviewed the battle plan and its subordinates asked their questions or made suggestions, and the plan was amended as necessary. Finally, all was arranged and it concluded the briefing:

"This stronghold must be destroyed quickly so that our larger operations can proceed. We will have one hundred spare fighting machines held in reserve. Each of our machines carries an emergency transport pod to rescue those whose machines are disabled. Those who are not injured will return to the battle as quickly as possible. There can be no acceptable outcome but complete success. Is this understood?"

"Yes, Commander!"

* * * * *

March, 1912, Memphis, Tennessee

Spring had finally arrived in Memphis. A warm wind from the southwest had driven away the last of the chill and the locals were certain that it would not return. Some of the trees were already in blossom and flowers were opening up in gardens. Becca Harding breathed in the fragrances as she walked up the drive of the huge Oswald estate.

"Jiminy! Willya lookit the size of this place!" exclaimed the man walking next to her. "The cap'in said it was the house of some rich old lady, but he didn't say how rich! Hooee!" He whistled.

"Uh, yeah, the Oswalds seem pretty well heeled," said Becca. She regarded the man. His name was Leonidas Polk Smith, although he went by 'Leo'. He was wearing a not-quite regulation army uniform with sergeant's chevrons on the sleeve. Above the chevrons there was a shoulder patch announcing that he was part of the Memphis Volunteer Militia. With the new Conscription Act, most men not doing absolutely vital jobs were being swept up - or in most cases shamed into enlisting - into the army. But there were some men who did have vital jobs who still wanted to serve. Smith, from what Becca was able to decipher through his thick southern drawl, worked at the local electrical generating plant when he wasn't with his militia company.

"And all the women in this here group of yours, are they rich, too?"

"Most of 'em seem to be. And it's not really my group."

"Heck! Shame I'm already married!" cackled Smith. "But if you ain't in charge, how come I was sent to see you about this company of wimmen?"

"Don't know," she said shrugging. It had come as a surprise to her when Smith had shown up at the hospital with an order signed by the adjutant of Memphis' garrison commander. It simply authorized the integration of the Memphis Women's Volunteer Sharpshooters into the city militia, and named her, Rebecca Harding, as the official liaison! She suspected that Mrs. Oswald, the group's leader, had somehow used her husband's political pull to get this to happen, but why had she been made the liaison instead of Oswald? Theories had swirled in her head, but the leading one was that Frank had been involved somehow. He knew she wanted to be more active in the war, but he didn't want her going out on his scouting missions - he was out there right now, blast him! - so maybe he'd pulled some strings to try and convert the Women Sharpshooters and Quilting Society (as Becca privately referred to it) into something more resembling an actual military unit. Just to please her? Or keep her out of trouble?

Or maybe Frank had nothing to do with it. As he'd warned her, the war seemed to be coming out of its long lull. Rumors were flying through the city and the army camps that a major battle was brewing. Everyone had their own prediction on what would happen: Memphis was the enemy's main target; no, they were going after St. Louis; no, they would attack Vicksburg just like the Yankees did in the Civil War; no they'd surely want New Orleans to block the whole river. It was the major topic of conversation in the mess tent at the hospital. The only thing that was certain was that the high command was putting everyone on alert and making every effort to bolster the city's defenses. Something was surely going to happen and maybe they even wanted the Women's Sharpshooters mobilized.

They reached the front door of the mansion and a colored servant directed them around to the back where they were told Mrs. Oswald was waiting. "We've got a rifle range back there," Becca explained to Smith. They rounded the corner of the house and found Mrs. Oswald waiting - along with about a hundred other women.

Becca's eyes grew wide. They were all wearing the unit's official uniform, buckskin jackets, pantaloons tucked into calf-high boots, and a hat with a feather, and holding their Springfield rifles. At the sight of her, Mrs. Oswald cried: "Oh, there they are! Attention, girls, attention!" The women shuffled into some semblance of formation with only a little bit of laughing and giggling. Oswald had a uniform like the others, but fancier with some gold braid on the collar, cuffs, and hem of the jacket and down the seam of the pantaloons. The feather in her hat was white instead of black like the others, and she had captain's shoulder straps. She also had a sword which she waved about dangerously.

Becca glanced at Smith, who was obviously trying very hard not to laugh. "Uh, here they are." She was amazed at the numbers. The group had over a hundred on its roster, but she'd never managed to get more than thirty to turn up at once.

"The gal with the sword is in charge?" asked Smith.

"Yup. I'll introduce you. C'mon." She led him over to where Oswald was waiting with a huge grin on her face. "Mrs... I mean Captain Oswald, this is Sergeant Smith of the Memphis Militia."

"Oh, Sergeant! So very pleased to meet you!" exclaimed Oswald, stuffing her sword under her arm and extending a gloved hand. To her obvious surprise, Smith grabbed it and shook firmly.

"Pleased to meetcha, ma'am. Captain Carstairs sent me to talk to you 'bout you folks fallin' in with us." He paused and frowned. "But he didn't say nothin' about you havin' rifles." He looked closer. "Hell, those're Springfields! My company's got nothin' but them old Krags!"

"Of course we have rifles!" said Oswald. "Some of the girls are fine shots! How do you expect us to fight without rifles?"

"Fight? The Cap'in jus' said you'd be with us to help out with coffee and rations and tendin' the wounded and all..."

"Certainly not, Sergeant! Wherever did he get such an idea? We are *sharpshooters* and we shall be fighting alongside you!"

"I'll be damned. Don't know nuthin' 'bout that. Well, I was just sent here, along with Miz Harding, to let you know where you're supposed to go if the alarm is sounded."

"And where might that be?" asked Oswald, no longer smiling.

"Oh, down by the river. Our assembly area's at Poplar and Front Streets."

"Near that lovely Riverside Park?"

"Well, t'ain't so lovely anymore, but yessum, that's the area. We're supposed to support a battery of big guns 'long the waterfront. I was supposed to take you and... uh, your NCOs for a tour... If you want."

"I can go with him, Mrs. Oswald," volunteered, Rebecca. "No need for you to go way down there, ma'am."

"Oh, but, Becca, dear, you can't go! Not yet, anyway! We have... well, we have a surprise for you, dear." She turned to Smith. "You can wait for a bit can't you, Sergeant?"

"Uh, for a little spell, but I gotta be gettin' back..."

"Splendid! Now, Becca, all the girls and I are so grateful for all the work you've done that we took a vote and decided that you should be second in command of the Sharpshooters!"

What?! She twitched and took a half-step backwards. She hadn't been expecting anything like this.

"Yes! You shall be our lieutenant! We even had a uniform made for you! Girls?"

To Becca's horror, several of the ladies came forward carrying another of the ridiculous sharpshooter uniforms over which they fussed so much. "I-I don't think... I can't..." she stuttered.

"Oh, don't worry!" said Oswald. "This is our gift to you! Doris, Abigail, take her inside and help her change!"

Becca's immediate impulse was to make a break for it, but she couldn't do that. This was clearly a sincere gesture by the women and she couldn't refuse. So she found herself decked out in the buckskin jacket, pantaloons, and boots and a large hat with a red feather. There were lieutenant's insignia on the shoulders. Then she was paraded back outside so the whole group could applaud. She blushed pink and felt like a complete fool.

Smith was grinning ear to ear and she had to restrain herself from hitting him. "Whooee! Ain't you the sight!" he laughed. "But we got t'get goin' miss. If I show up any later, the Cap'n's gonna think I'm slackin' off!"

"Run along, Becca," said Oswald, fluttering her fingers. "I trust you completely to make the arrangements."

Becca started to turn away, but stopped herself, came to attention, and saluted the way she saw soldiers do. "Yes, ma'am!" The whole company laughed, but then cheered.

Becca spun on her heel and followed the sergeant.

* * * * *

The *Santa Fe* slowly turned left into the mouth of the Arkansas River. Commander Drew Harding closely watched the surface of the river, the banks on either side, and the ship ahead of them. They were part of a small flotilla of supply ships, gunboats, and monitors heading up the Arkansas to Little Rock. Word had come that the Martians were preparing to attack that place, and the high command was sending reinforcements.

"Ya might want t'stay a bit further to the right, Captain," said Mackenzie. "The bend there can throw up quite a sand bar on the left."

Drew nodded and gave the order to the helmsman, and the ship swung a little bit wider in its turn.

"Gonna hafta stay on our toes," continued the first officer. "The Arkansas twists around like a snake most of the way to Little Rock. Lot narrower than the Mississippi, too. Good thing it's at flood right now."

"You've been along this stretch before, I take it."

"A dozen times at least. Not the worst bit of river I've traveled, but she's tricky. And I'm not jokin' about her bein' a snake! Probably ain't a straight stretch more than half a mile long. We're gonna need to relieve the helmsman every hour or so and the lookouts, too."

"What about you, Mr. Mackenzie? How often will you need relief?"

"Oh, I'll manage. Seein' as we're not first in line, we'll have it easier. And you're gettin' pretty good yourself at spotting trouble, you know."

Drew was surprised and pleased at the compliment but did his best to keep it off his face. "I'm sure between the two of us we'll manage."

Santa Fe eased into the channel and followed the other ships upstream. As Mackenzie had said, the Arkansas turned one way and then another, sometimes changing a hundred and eighty degrees and heading back the way they'd come before turning again. It seemed like they traveled two or three miles for every mile closer to Little Rock they got. Several times that day they had to crowd the shore dangerously to let vessels going the other way squeeze by. Most of those vessels were crammed with civilians, people trying to get away from the rumored attack.

After a few hours, Drew felt confident enough of the new routine that he decided to drill the crew on other matters. He was keenly aware of how green most of his men were. He had only a small cadre of experienced sailors, but far too many of the others were raw recruits, or men like Ensign Alby Hinsworth, who had gone through a hasty officers' school. Ever since Santa Fe was launched, he had worked the men ceaselessly to learn their jobs and become an effective team. He was proud of being the ship's captain, but there were times when he missed the veteran crew on the old Minnesota.

"Mr. Mackenzie, I'm going to bring the ship to battle stations. You and the bridge crew will remain at your posts and keep us from crashing into anything."

"All right," replied Mackenzie, "have fun."

Drew sighed, wondering if Mackenzie knew that there really was such a word as sir. He took the ladder down to the small pilothouse and flipped the switch that turned on the battle stations alarm bell. The shrill tone of the bell sent the men scrambling. There was far too much shouting, but at least they were moving. The realization that they were now west of the Mississippi and therefore in enemy country had spread through the ship and possibly some men thought this was the real thing. Well good, if they did, Drew wasn't going to do anything to disabuse them.

His yeoman appeared with Drew's helmet and anti-dust gear, and he dutifully put it all on; he had to set a good example. He waited while reports came from the various locations around the ship. Ensign Hinsworth shouted each one out: *Number Two four-inch, manned and ready! Engine room manned and ready! Number Three four-inch manned and ready! Sick Bay manned and ready! Turret Number One manned and ready! Magazine manned and ready!* On and on until finally: *All Stations manned and ready! The ship is cleared for action, sir!* Hinsworth saluted, banging his elbow against the side of the tiny pilothouse.

Drew returned the salute and checked his pocket watch; four minutes and thirty five seconds. It wouldn't have been bad for a battleship, but for a ship one sixth the size, it wasn't good at all. Still, it was the best they'd done so far.

He then proceeded to run them through as many drills as it was possible to do under the circumstances. Damage control and fire drills sent teams of men to various compartments to fight imaginary fires or plug imaginary leaks. The man overboard drill had them getting one of the ship's boats ready to launch. The casualty drill saw volunteer 'casualties' being taken to the tiny sick bay. The ship didn't rate an actual doctor, but there was a medical orderly trained in basic first aid. For the most part, the drills went pretty well.

But the thing nearest and dearest to Drew's heart - gunnery - couldn't be truly practiced in these circumstances. They could aim the guns, and he had them pick distant objects to act as Martian tripods, and they could bring up ammunition from the magazine and practice loading, but they couldn't actually fire the guns. After the commissioning, he'd had the opportunity to take *Santa Fe* down to a stretch of river where the shoreline was all swamp and no one lived, and shoot off the guns for a while. But it was completely inadequate in Drew's opinion. He was worried that if they did get into a fight, they wouldn't be able to hit a damn thing. He'd asked the captain in charge of this little convoy if once they got closer to Little Rock, they would be allowed to do some target practice. The reply had been evasive and non-committal. They'd have to wait and see.

It was getting on toward the dinner hour but there was one more thing he wanted to practice. Without any advanced warning, he reached over and flipped the Dust Alarm switch. There was a few seconds delay and then a siren began to howl with a shriek that would pierce almost any other noise. The men nearby stiffened and then exploded into action, some of them shouting *Dust! Dust! Dust!* Some pulled out the dust mask from the bag hanging around their necks, while others slammed closed metal shutters to seal off the windows in the pilothouse. The space suddenly became quite dark with only a few beams of light coming though the thick glass in narrow vision slits. If all was going well, then similar precautions were being made throughout the ship. Every hatch and porthole was being sealed to keep out the lethal black dust the Martians occasionally used. Even a few grains of the stuff inhaled was enough to kill a person, and contact with the skin could cause terrible burns.

"Engine room reports dust procedures in effect, sir!" shouted Ensign Hinsworth, his voice muffled by his mask. Yes, that was the real trick in protecting a ship from the dust. The fires for the boilers demanded a large and steady supply of air. Ships had ventilators to suck air down to them, but in a cloud of the black dust, that could be a fatal flaw which would hopelessly contaminate the ship. So the new ships had an air supply system which could channel the incoming air directly into the fires, theoretically destroying the dust before it could do any harm. The air intakes on the decks had filters, but this system took into account the possibility of battle damage destroying them.

Unfortunately, while the system might save the engine room crew from death from the dust, it might also kill them by heat stroke. A normal ship would suck outside air down to the engine room and *then* send it into the fire boxes. The air the crew breathed would be the same temperature as the outside. But under this system, the incoming air went through the fire first to destroy the dust. Some would then leak out for the crew to breathe. But it would be *hot* air - very hot.

The men could stand it for a few minutes, but no longer.

Drew looked out the view slit and saw that they had a relatively straight stretch of river ahead for a mile or so. "Prepare to release steam!"

"Steam lines ready, sir!" shouted Hinsworth.

"Release!"

The ensign threw a lever and a few moments later there was a loud hiss and a cloud of white steam enveloped the ship, released from pipes located all over the superstructure and upper decks. In theory this would destroy dust in the air and scour away any which had fallen on the ship. In an emergency, it could also blunt the effect of enemy heat rays. Drew could see nothing through the view slits. Mackenzie was piloting the ship from up above, but the steam would be blinding him, too. They couldn't sail like this for long.

"Secure steam!"

The hiss died away and the cloud dispersed. "Steam secured!"

"Engine room air to normal!" Hinsworth relayed the order and hopefully there would now be cool air flooding into the engine room. Whether it would also be dust-free, only the test of battle would tell.

Drew waited for a few minutes before he canceled the dust alert and a few minutes longer before letting the men stand down from battle stations. The shutters were swung up and latched, the hatch to the pilothouse propped open, and Drew breathed in the cool spring air. He turned to step outside and was met by a red-faced Mackenzie.

"Ya damn near scalded us to death, you know that?"

"Your dust gear should have protected you. Weren't you wearing yours, Lieutenant?"

The man's face got even redder. "Uh, well, no... it was just a damn drill and..."

"You know the procedures. Next time, wear your gear." Drew stepped past him and climbed up to the bridge, failing to keep a smile from growing on his lips. It was rare for him to get the best of his first officer.

He paced from one end of the bridge to the other, stretching his legs. He heard the off-duty watches being sent to dinner and it looked like the men were in good spirits. The day had gone well. The sun was westering and he thought he could make out the ruins of Pine Bluffs in the distance. They were making good time, despite the twisting river.

Morning should see them at Little Rock.

Chapter Eight

April, 1912, Washington, D.C.

"It's confirmed, sir, they're hitting Kansas City in force." Colonel Hugh Drum met Leonard Wood at the door to the situation room and took his coat as he hurried in.

"When?"

"About an hour ago. I called you as soon as I was sure it wasn't a feint."

Wood rubbed at his eyes and then stared at the map. It was about four in the morning and Drum's call to his house had woken him out of a deep sleep. The map, stretching over thirty feet long, showed the whole Mississippi Line, but Wood's attention was drawn to one blue wood block sitting all alone west of the river. It represented the garrison of Kansas City. As he watched, an enlisted man with a long wooden stick pushed several red blocks up close to the blue one.

"Any estimate on strength?"

"No exact numbers, sir, but General Farnsworth is convinced that this is a major attack."

Wood nodded. Charlies Farnsworth was not one to panic, although after being stuck out on that limb for nearly a year, no man could be blamed for being skittish. But Wood had been sure this was coming for several months, so he had no doubt Farnsworth was right. The long-expected Martian offensive was starting.

And Farnsworth and his 37th Division were likely doomed.

"Any word from Little Rock? They will probably hit there, too."

"Nothing so far, sir," replied Drum. "But there was another message from General Funston just a few minutes ago. He says he can confirm a Martian incursion across the Rio Grande near the town of Hebbronville. That's about ninety miles west of Corpus Christi." Drum pointed to the far corner of the map where a new red block had appeared.

Wood frowned in concern. They didn't need this right now, but he supposed it was inevitable that the southern front couldn't remain quiet forever. It seemed like the French landings around Veracruz had distracted the Martians in Mexico, but perhaps that was coming to an end. "What sort of strength?"

"He isn't sure. It does seem to be localized and they haven't advanced any farther north, but Funston is requesting reinforcements."

"Of course he is. But there's nothing we can send until the situation along the Mississippi becomes clearer."

"Yes, sir. I'll ask him to get more information on the strength of the Martian force down there."

"Do that. But later. Are there any other reports coming in?" He waved his hand to take in the whole defense line.

"Nothing at the moment, sir. Farnsworth *is* requesting reinforcements."

Wood moved to the point on the table closest to Kansas City. There were swarms of blue blocks along the Mississippi, but none in easy supporting distance. In the last few weeks he had sent additional riverine forces up the Missouri, just as he'd sent them up the Arkansas to Little Rock, but there wasn't a great deal more he could do. Anything else he sent would probably be just more lambs to the slaughter. *A forlorn hope, just as Theodore - and Funston's aide - said.* Well, perhaps he could do something...

"Send a message to General Pershing to have the XV Corps send out as much cavalry as it can spare toward Kansas City. Maybe they can create a distraction—or at the least help to cover an evacuation."

"Yes, sir, right away. Uh, what about General Rochenbach's tank divisions, sir? Maybe they could..." He pointed at a blue block at the eastern edge of the table.

Wood looked at it and shook his head. "No, they'd never get there in time. And even if we had them at the front, they're too slow and too prone to breakdowns to send them out on a relief mission. Still... they've completed their training. Have the 1st sent to Cairo and the 2nd to Jackson. We'll keep them in a ready reserve."

"Yes, sir." Drum moved off to one of the multitude of communications stations arrayed around the perimeter of the room. Wood dragged a chair over to the table and sat down, after sending an enlisted man for coffee. God, he was tired. An ache was growing in his head and he firmly told himself it was just the stress on top of lack of sleep and not the damn tumor again.

He stared at the map. Outside, the morning was coming, but no hint of that reached the windowless situation room. Drum circulated between the communications operators and occasionally brought over items of interest. Wood continued to stare. He'd done everything he could to strengthen the defenses, but no line was impregnable. If the Martians hit somewhere that wasn't quite strong enough, got across the river in strength, and spread out to destroy the railroads as they had done out in Colorado and the Dakotas... it could be a disaster of incredible proportions. In his mind's eye he could see raiding forces sweeping through the army's rear areas, destroying supplies, scattering reserves, and then moving on to the cities where the factories were located. Smashing the means of production, interrupting the rail lines which supplied food and raw materials. Splitting the country into smaller and smaller chunks. No, he could not let that happen! Suddenly, just sitting there was intolerable…

"General?"

Drum had come up next to him and startled him out of his dark thoughts. "Yes?"

"A signal from General Duncan in Little Rock, they are under attack."

Wood nodded. Yes, the Kansas City attack wasn't just a lone operation; this was the great offensive, beginning at last. "Send a message to General Dickman at 3rd Army. Have the VII Corps send out its cavalry, same orders as the ones for Pershing."

"Yes, sir," Drum turned away.

"And Hugh?" Drum looked back.

"Sir?"

"Get a train ready. I'm finally going to take that trip to St. Louis."

* * * * *

April, 1912, near Forrest City, Arkansas

"Come on! Keep moving!" shouted Captain Frank Dolfen, 5th United States Cavalry. At times like this, the sergeant in him always came to the fore. He trotted his horse up and down the column urging his men onward. "It's a long way to Little Rock and those boys there need help! Move it!" A few of the men waved at him or made some sort of encouraging remark, but if any of them actually moved any faster, Frank couldn't see it. The main thing, he supposed, was to make sure none of them went any slower.

The word had come shortly after dawn: Little Rock was under attack again and this time the Martians really seemed to mean it. The whole regiment, not just Frank's 1st Squadron, was ordered to move out, and as they trotted across the bridge from Memphis, they were joined by the 9th Cavalry, creating a small brigade. When Dolfen had first reached Memphis after the long retreat, he'd been told that all the cavalry was being formed into an actual division, but up until now, the cavalry had all been used in small groups. This was more like it!

The 9th was a colored regiment and initially there were a few insulting remarks among the 5th, but when Frank heard one, he would stomp on the culprit making it. He'd seen the 9th's brother regiment, the 10th Cavalry, bleed to death at Glorietta Pass; and if anyone ever doubted the bravery of those colored boys, Frank could straighten them out!

They'd ridden hard all day, horsemen, motorcycles, armored cars, trucks, and all, but as night drew on they weren't even halfway to Little Rock. Forty miles was considered about as far as you could expect cavalry to go in a day. They'd gone farther than that, but they still had a long way to go. From time to time flights of aircraft had passed overhead heading west or coming back east. Dolfen wondered if any of them were Selfridge and his boys.

The Englishman, Major Bridges, wasn't with him this time. He'd gone to Washington to consult with the military attaché there and wasn't certain if he'd be back at all. Dolfen found that he missed the man's almost endless chatter.

The remains of Forrest City had disappeared in the darkness to the east when the colonel called a halt. Both regiments formed a defensive laager with the artillery deployed, pickets posted well outside the camp, and a quarter of the men on alert at all times. Once again they were in enemy country and there were too many of them to stay concealed, although campfires were all kept shielded to prevent their light giving them away. The shortest route from Memphis to Little Rock took them uncomfortably close to the Martian fortress. It was only twenty miles or so off to the north and they had encountered some very large patches of the Red Weed. When they moved on in the morning, the fortress would be in their rear. A ticklish situation for sure.

While he was munching on the dinner Private Gosling had provided, one of his sergeants, a man named Burk, came up to him. "Evenin', sir, got a minute?"

"Sure, what's on your mind?"

"It's those crazy new rocket launchers, the stovepipes. sir. We gonna get any more chances to practice with 'em? Ain't like shootin' a rifle! Gonna take more practice to hit anything with 'em!"

Ah, yes, the rocket launchers. A half-dozen had been delivered to the squadron three days ago. The officer who brought them had given a very brief explanation of how to use them. Some of the men had been given the chance to fire off a few rounds and that was it. "'Fraid not. At least not until we get somewhere safer then here. You'll just have to do your best, Sergeant."

"They aren't expectin' us to fire them things from *horseback* are they, sir? Critter won't put up with *that!*"

Dolfen chuckled. "No, I don't expect they will. Better tell the boys to dismount before trying to use the things."

"Yes, sir." Burk nodded and moved off.

After dinner, Colonel Schumacher, who was senior, called all the officers of both regiments together for a conference. "We just picked up a radio signal," he said. "Little Rock has been hammered hard all day, but they are still holding on. We have to get there and relieve some of the pressure on them. We'll sleep now and get on the move again at three."

"It's still at least another sixty miles, sir," said the colonel of the 9th. "We won't get there until dark and the men and horses will be worn out."

"I know, I know," said Schumacher, a tone of irritation in his voice. "But that's what we are going to do. See that your commands are ready, gentlemen!"

Dolfen made his way back to his own unit. Both of the colonels were right, he supposed. Getting there too late to help was pointless. But getting there too tired to fight didn't do any good either. And if they were too exhausted to escape if things went to hell, that was the worst of all. But he had his orders and passed them along to his troop commanders. Then he went to get some sleep.

Private Gosling had his bedroll all laid out, but the man was standing still as stone, looking to the west. Dolfen came up and asked: "What are you looking... oh!"

The western horizon was tinged with a red glow, bright flickers came at intervals like a distant thunderstorm. Dozens of his troopers were looking at it and there wasn't a sound in the camp.

"Looks like them boys in Little Rock are catchin' hell, sir," said Gosling.

"Yeah, it sure does."

* * * * *

Cycle 597, 845.1, near Enemy City 3-118

"Report," ordered Qetjnegartis.

"Commander, the enemy's defensive fire is much reduced," said Kantangnar over the communicator. "I believe that the time has come to launch the main attack."

"Are you sure? The prey-creatures have tried to deceive us before, to lure us into a trap."

"There is no way to be certain, but we have verified the destruction of many of their heavy weapons, and we are pushing our drones very close to their trenches and they are encountering little resistance. The fire from the vessels on the river is much reduced; they may be running short on projectiles."

Qetjnegartis evaluated the situation. So far the attack had gone well. For over a day the clan's battlegroups had probed the enemy; advancing, doing damage, and then pulling back before the prey-creatures could do serious harm in return. Twenty-two fighting machines had been lost, but so far only two pilots had been killed and four wounded.

The other pilots had been rescued, taken to the rear, and given reserve machines so they could return to the fight. Qetjnegartis was determined that losses be kept to an absolute minimum. This was just the first attack in the great offensive, after all. They would need all their strength for the attack across the large river. Over a hundred of the drones had been destroyed, but they did not matter.

Now the enemy's response was faltering. Had the probes done their job? Or was this a ruse to draw them into a killing zone? Qetjnegartis moved its machine forward to one of the hills which ringed the city to the north. It had a commanding view of the battle area. City 3-118 sat on both sides of River 3-1.4. The largest portion of the city was on the far side of the river, but once the northern bank was captured, the southern side would become untenable. On the western end of the city there was a tall hill, very close to the river, which dominated the entire area. The prey-creatures had heavily fortified it, but if it could be captured, their entire defense ought to collapse.

During the previous attack, Qetjnegartis had avoided the northern side specifically because of that hill and the low, swampy ground to the east of it. It had crossed the river, which could be waded with little difficulty, and attacked the city from the south, thinking that their defenses would be weaker there. That had not proved to be the case and the attack had been repulsed.

We shall not be repulsed this time!

The clan had a vastly greater strength now, and while the enemy had improved its defenses somewhat, they could not possibly withstand what Qetjnegartis could now unleash. Still, it was cautious about simply relying on brute force. Victory was certain, but it could not afford heavy losses.

The hill was clearly the key to the enemy defenses. Taken, they could fire down on the prey-creature positions and then roll up the trench lines in both directions. It would not make the mistake of trying to penetrate into the built-up sections of the city immediately, as it had the last time. Once the main defenses ringing the city had been cleared, a more methodical approach could be taken to obliterating the central areas. Yes, the plan was a good one. It activated the communicator.

"Attention all battlegroups. We shall commence the main attack. Groups 32-2 and 32-6, you shall continue to probe along your fronts to distract the enemy. All other groups will converge on Sector Twelve. Groups 32-1, 32-4, 32-5, and 32-7 will attack the tall hill. All other groups will attack the low ground between the hill and the swampy area, penetrate the defense lines, and advance to the river. Avoid unnecessary losses, but press forward and do not stop until you have reached your objectives."

"Commander? Perhaps we should hold back a reserve?" It was Tanbradjus. "In case of emergencies?"

"No, there can be no half-measures now. We will attack and finish this!"

"As you command."

* * * * *

April 1912, Little Rock, Arkansas

"Signal from Captain Gillespie, sir!" shouted Ensign Hinsworth. "He wants us to move upstream of Big Rock Mountain! The Martians are attacking there!"

"Acknowledged," replied Commander Drew Harding. "Helm, bring us about, ahead two-thirds." *Santa Fe* swung around to head upstream, following Captain Gillespie's ship, *Wichita*. The two smaller gunboats, *Evansville* and *Mount Vernon*, did not follow; apparently, they had different orders.

"Good God in Heaven, how much longer is this gonna go on?" Drew glanced at his executive officer. Mackenzie clutched the handrail and his face looked pale despite the smudges of coal and gun smoke on it. "They've been coming agin' an' agin' since yesterday mornin'! When's it gonna stop?"

Drew looked closer; the man was clearly near to the edge. Ever since he'd first met Mackenzie, Drew had been a little jealous of the man's superior knowledge of the rivers and resentful of his lack of military courtesy. He'd been hoping to have the chance to take him down a peg or two. But now, now that it was happening, he was sorry. Mackenzie had never seen combat and had been completely unprepared for the reality. Of course, there was a first time for everyone, and even Drew had never seen a combat like this one. Some men called up the courage to handle it. Other men... well, it looked like Mackenzie was one of the other men. But damnation, he *needed* the man!

"Lieutenant Mackenzie, we've been ordered upstream farther than we've gone so far. Is there any danger we could go aground?" No reaction. He reached over and shook the man's shoulder. "Mackenzie! Will we go aground?"

"Uh... uh, we should be okay," said the man, jerking in surprise. "With all the coal and ammo we've burned up, we're probably drawin' two feet less than when we set out. Should be okay..."

"Good! But could you check the coal bunkers and see how much we've got left?"

"Uh, yeah, yeah, right away... sir." Mackenzie turned and fled below. Drew couldn't help but smile at the sudden use of *sir*, but won-

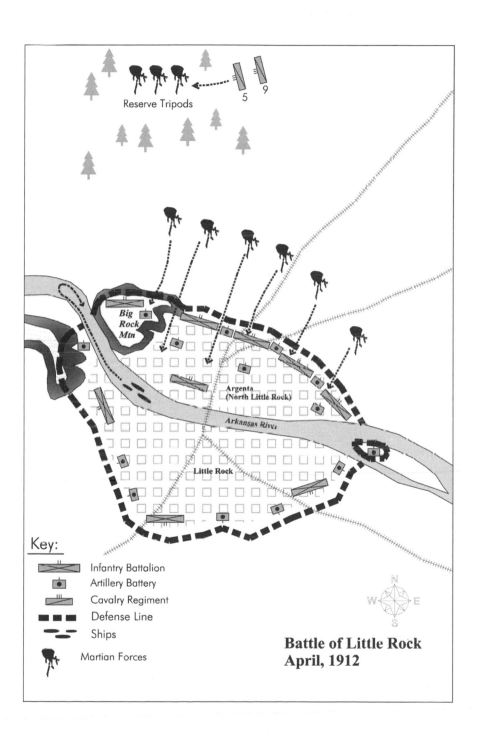

Reserve Tripods

5 9

Big
Rock
Mtn

Argenta
(North Little Rock)

Arkansas River

Little Rock

Key:

Infantry Battalion
Artillery Battery
Cavalry Regiment
Defense Line
Ships
Martian Forces

**Battle of Little Rock
April, 1912**

dered if he'd come back.

"Mister Hinsworth, check the magazines. I want to know what we've got left there, too."

"Aye, aye, sir!" Hinsworth grinned and ran off. At least *he* didn't seem to be having any problems. Apparently, this was all some grand pageant to the kid. The ship completed its turn, heading upstream, and Drew looked at the sun, barely visible behind clouds of smoke; it wasn't quite noon yet.

The Martians had attacked in the dark of early morning the day before. He had been awakened and stumbled up on deck to see the northern sky a mass of red, the buildings of the town silhouetted black against it. The army's guns were already roaring and it wasn't long before the navy had been ordered to join in. They had been tied up along the waterfront, but quickly cast off and moved out into the main channel of the Arkansas. The flotilla was commanded by Captain Ernest Gillespie aboard the *Wichita*, a sister ship of *Santa Fe*. The two monitors, two gunboats, plus a half dozen converted riverboats of various sizes with improvised armor and armaments, completed the force.

At first they had just been firing at coordinates on the map, adding their metal to that of the army batteries. But as dawn came and the day went on, the Martians had become bolder and gotten close enough at times to be fired at directly. Drew thought that *maybe* they had destroyed one of them, but with all the smoke he couldn't be sure.

Night had fallen and by then the city north of the river - which someone told him was actually named Argenta, rather than Little Rock - was almost entirely in flames. Fortunately, the wind was from the southwest so the smoke was blown away and the buildings along the river had remained untouched But the Martian attacks continued. Drew had read stories - and Andrew's letters - about the night attack on Albuquerque, and he was happy to see that the army had learned from it. They now had rockets and artillery rounds which would burst into a bright flare which drifted slowly down by parachute, lighting up the surroundings marvelously. He'd heard that the navy was going to receive similar munitions, but so far none had materialized. *Santa Fe* and some of the other ships mounted powerful searchlights, though, and they had been in use almost constantly. From time to time they'd catch a tripod in their glare and pump off a few rounds, but he didn't think they'd scored any hits.

It had made for a very long night. He'd grabbed a few minutes sleep during a lull just before dawn, but for the most part he was running on coffee and sheer nerves. Now they were into the second day of the battle, and like Mackenzie, he wondered when it would end.

Hinsworth returned and saluted. "Fifteen rounds per gun in the forward turret, twenty in the aft turret, sir! The four-inchers have still got around a hundred per gun."

"Thank you, Ensign," said Drew frowning. He hadn't realized they used up so much of the eight-inch ammunition. They had a supply ship with more tied up at the docks, but there had been no opportunity to replenish. When they went back into action he'd have to...

"We should get a man at the bow with a lead once we're past the cliffs, Captain." Drew turned and was pleased to see Mackenzie was back. "An' we're down to about half of our coal, but nuthin' to worry about yet."

"Thank you, Lieutenant. Send someone forward with the lead."

"Right." Mackenzie left again.

Up ahead on the right was Big Rock Mountain. It wasn't all that much of a mountain as such things went, but it was all alone and reared two hundred and fifty feet above the river, making it look immense. It was some last outlier of the Ozark Mountains, off to the northwest, Drew supposed. The side facing the river was a stone quarry and had been carved into an almost perpendicular cliff. The opposite side, facing the Martians, was the west anchor of the defensive lines north of the river. It was studded with gun emplacements and on top was the main spotting post of all the artillery. If the enemy took it... things could get sticky.

They moved slowly past the mountain against the current, and the man in the bow was shouting out his soundings. It was almost impossible to hear him above the roar of the army's guns, so another man had to keep running back and forth between the bow and the bridge to relay the information. Since *Wichita* was leading the way and drew just as much water as *Santa Fe*, there wasn't much worry about running aground at the moment, but if they were forced to maneuver later on, it was good to have the system set up. Of course, if they came under fire, both the leadsman and the runner would be forced to take cover.

And coming under fire was definitely a possibility.

Wichita, two hundred yards ahead, suddenly fired its forward turret; a few seconds later the rest of her guns fired as well. Drew focused his binoculars in the direction they were shooting and tried to see the targets. The base of the mountain was shrouded in smoke, but he thought he could see some tall shapes moving there. The mountain itself blocked most of their view to the north where the attack would be coming from. They needed to go farther upstream, where the river curved a bit, to get a clear line of fire. He passed the word to the gunnery officer that they'd be going into action shortly.

As they moved, they were passed on their left hand side by one of the converted riverboats, the Arkansas Queen. She was a stern-wheeler and the paddle threw up a huge amount of spray. She'd once been a passenger and cargo hauler, but most of her upper works had been clad in sheet iron. Several modern field guns had been mounted, but she also carried an antique monstrosity on her foredeck which must have been a relic from the Civil War. Someone stuck his head out of the pilothouse and waved to Drew as they passed.

"What the hell's his hurry?" asked Mackenzie, who'd come back to the bridge.

"Guess he wants to get some licks in. Hasn't had much chance so far with all the long range fire we've been doing."

"Damn fool."

The *Wichita* moved ahead another half-mile and then signaled to hold station. Drew turned to Mackenzie. "What do you think, Lieutenant? About a hundred revolutions to hold against the current?"

Mackenzie studied the brown water flowing past. "Yup, about that. Maybe a hundred and five; the currents a bit faster this side of Big Rock." Drew sent the order down to the engine room and carefully judged the distance to the ship ahead to make sure they were maintaining their spacing; the thrust of the propellers balancing the river's current.

"I can see the enemy, sir!" cried Hinsworth, pointing. Drew brought up his binoculars. Yes, there were several dozen tripods moving forward, firing their heat rays against the defenders who couldn't be seen at all amidst the smoke and flames. He studied them in a sort of horrified fascination. They were nightmare things that moved with a gracefulness totally at odds with their appearance.

"Sir, can we open fire, sir?"

There was no use trying to direct fire against specific targets; the situation was changing too fast. "Instruct the guns to commence firing, Ensign. They may choose their own targets."

"Aye, aye, sir!"

"Oh, and Ensign, tell the eight-inch crews to save five rounds per gun."

"Yes, sir!"

Wichita was already firing, and a moment later, Santa Fe joined in. The eight-inchers in the turrets shook the whole ship with deep, throaty roars, while the four-inchers in the casemate mounts made sharper cracks. Thick clouds of dirty smoke rolled away toward the shore to join the smoke already there. Rapid fire was impossible under the circumstances, and the gun-layers had to wait until they had a clear view before firing again.

A strange, almost bell-like sound made Drew turn his head. A new cloud was rolling away from Arkansas Queen; its antique had fired a shot. Not a chance in hell that it had hit anything. He turned back and studied the view through his binoculars. Were they accomplishing anything either? Hard to tell...yes! The smoke cleared for an instant and Drew saw a tripod suddenly topple over, a large chunk of it thrown skyward. "Got one!" he shouted.

"Did we? Did we get it?" asked Mackenzie.

"Sure did!" answered Drew, though in fact it might have been a shot from any one of the ships or even the army guns. No need to tell Mackenzie that, though. The success seemed to pump the man up.

They continued to fire for another ten or fifteen minutes. The forward turret reached its five round limit and ceased fire. The after turret fired a couple more times, but Drew couldn't see any targets now and stopped the fire of all the guns.

"What's happenin'?" asked Mackenzie. "Did we drive 'em off?"

"I don't know..."

"Sir! Sir!" cried Hinsworth. "Up there, sir!"

For a moment, Drew didn't know what the ensign was talking about, and then he saw it: up on top of Big Rock Mountain. Tiny figures were moving, right up to the edge of the cliff. Then, suddenly they were burning! Some dissolved in fire, but others, some of the others tumbled off the cliff, trailing flames all the way to the ground, far below. "Oh God!" groaned Drew.

"Is that...? Are they...?" Mackenzie gasped.

"Yes."

"Merciful God!"

And then there were other figures on top of the cliff. Much bigger ones. Heat rays stabbed out and buildings on the south shore of the Arkansas began to burn.

"Signal... signal from Captain Gillespie, sir," said Hinsworth. The boy's face was ashen. "Martians... the Martians are crossing the river south of Big Rock. We are to follow Wichita down to engage."

"But... but we'll have to sail right beneath those monsters!" cried Mackenzie. "Our guns won't even be able to point at them!"

"No they won't," said Drew grimly. "Helm! Prepare to come about and follow Wichita! Everyone else, get below! Get below and pray!"

* * * * *

Cycle 597, 845.1, near Enemy City 3-118

"The hill is ours, Commander."

"Well done," replied Qetjnegartis. At last, the enemy's defenses were crumbling. It had cost the life of another clan member, three more wounded, and fourteen wrecked fighting machines, but resistance in the city on the north side of the river was all but destroyed. The prey-creatures' large projectile throwers there had been destroyed and the new drones were digging their foot-warriors out of their underground shelters and the above-ground buildings. The drones were proving extreme-ly useful, although losses among them had been heavy. But that is what they existed for: to take losses instead of the large fighting machines and their valuable pilots.

"Continue the advance. Let none escape."

* * * * *

April, 1912, northeast of Little Rock, Arkansas

"Column... *Halt!*"

The command was passed down the long line of horsemen and vehicles. No bugles were used because they were getting close now. Very close. Frank Dolfen got down out of his saddle, more collapsing than climbing. Damn he was tired! It was almost twelve hours since they had set out in the dark of the wee hours. They had stopped from time to time, but not often and not for long. Little Rock was just ahead, just on the other side of a line of ridges.

If there was anything left of Little Rock.

While it was still dark, they could see the red glow ahead; and after dawn, the clouds of smoke. Now they could smell it, too. The smoke clouds were rolling by overhead, and sometimes ash would drift past on the wind. But the fight was still going on; the low rumble of artillery, which had been audible since mid-morning, was now a continuous roar.

With the habits of an old cavalryman, Dolfen looked over his horse before he saw to any comfort for himself. The beast looked to be in fairly good shape - no worse than Dolfen himself - but he doubted it was up to any major exertion - like a battle - without some serious rest. The horse didn't have a name; he'd stopped giving names to his horses years ago. Army duty was hard on horses and they rarely lasted all that long. No point getting attached to them. His tired brain suddenly thought about Becca and that crazy horse of hers. Somehow it had managed to last! *Thank God neither of them are here now!*

Or at least he sure hoped they weren't. He'd looked and looked hard, but he didn't think she'd been able to stow away again. The very short notice they'd been given to get moving made it unlikely she'd manage it, but that girl could be determined.

"So what now, sir?" He turned away from his horse to see Lieu-tenant Bill Calloway of B Troop standing there. "We gonna attack?"

"We didn't come all this way to just watch, Lieutenant. How's your troop?"

"Good, sir. Four of the cycles have conked out, but that ain't bad over a distance like this. The rest are ready to go - unlike your poor critters." He pointed at Dolfen's horse and grinned.

"Yeah, yeah, don't rub it in. Someday you'll run out of gas and then you try and feed your contraption on grass..."

"Scouts coming in, sir," said Calloway suddenly, all levity gone. "Looks like they're in a hurry." Dolfen turned and saw a half-dozen troopers galloping their way, whipping their tired horses.

"Trouble, you think, sir?"

"More than likely," said Dolfen "Better go see." He stiffly walked over to where he saw the colonel and his headquarters group. He got there about the same time the scouts did. The leader, a sergeant from one of the other squadrons, jumped off his horse, saluted, and said breathlessly: "Martians, Colonel! Just up ahead! A whole passel of 'em!"

"Calm down, Sergeant," said Colonel Schumacher. "Where are they, and how many?"

"Just up ahead, sir!" the man turned and pointed. "In a little valley, just the other side of those trees! Not two miles from here! An' there's gotta be at least fifty or sixty of 'em!"

A chill ran through Dolfen. Fifty or sixty? The brigade would be cut to ribbons - or burned to ashes more likely - by a force that size. Hell, the whole 2nd Army had been beaten by a force not much bigger than that back at Albuquerque! They were here to harry the enemy's rear, not take them head on!

"Sixty tripods?" asked Schumacher. "You're sure, Sergeant? Think, man, it's important."

"Sure as shootin', sir! I'm not some green recruit, sir! I counted an' there was at least fifty! You saw 'em, Hadley, didn'tcha?" He turned to one of the other scouts.

"Yes, sir!" said the trooper. "A whole herd of 'em, just like the Sarge said. All standin' there like the regiment on parade!"

"Damnation," muttered Schumacher.

"Hell, Colonel," said Major Urwin. "We can't take on a force like that! It'd be like the Charge of the Light Brigade - only worse!"

"No, no, you're right." He looked over the ground to the south and shook his head. "We'll have to swing to the left, give this batch a wide berth, and come on Little Rock from the east."

"It'll be dark by the time we can do that, sir..."

"Well what else can we do...?"

The command staff began to debate, and then had to do it all over again when the colonel of the 9th arrived with his own staff. Dolfen waited and listened, too tired to do anything else. But as he stood there, something the scout had said tickled an old memory. *Standin' there like the regiment on parade...* Standing there? Why would that many tripods just be standing there? Why weren't they in the fight around Little

Rock? If they were there as a rear guard, why weren't they deployed for battle? It didn't make sense…

Suddenly the memory crystalized and he was back on the rampart of the Martian fortress around Gallup. Lying on his belly on the hard rock with Major Comstock, looking at… *Rows of tripods, standing like they were on parade!*

"Colonel!" The cry was wrenched out of his mouth.

Schumacher turned to him, a look of surprise on his face. "Yes, Captain?"

"Sir! I think… I think things might not be what we think!"

"What do you mean?"

"Sir, let me go take a look! I can be back in twenty minutes and you can all rest in the meantime! Please, sir! If I'm right, we may have caught the bastards with their pants down!"

* * * * *

April, 1912, Little Rock, Arkansas

"Engine room! Give me everything you've got!" Commander Drew Harding shouted into the speaking tube and prayed that he could save his ship.

Santa Fe, which had already been vibrating strongly with the rapid motion of the pistons, took on a new feel, a new tone, as the engines turned the screws faster than they ever had before. Drew looked out the narrow slots in the armored shutters of the pilothouse, trying to gauge their speed. Fifteen, maybe eighteen knots… add in the current of the river and they were surging downstream at twenty-five miles an hour, maybe more.

But it wasn't going to be enough.

In his heart, he knew it wouldn't be enough. The Martians were on the cliffs, and as they passed beneath them, they could fire right down on them. Easy and effective range for their heat rays.

"It…It'll be like shootin' fish in a barrel," whimpered Mackenzie, huddled beside him in the cramped compartment. "We won't have a chance. We can't even shoot back!"

No, they couldn't. They were too close to the cliffs and the guns couldn't elevate enough to hit the Martians on top. "We'll have to try and get past them as quickly as we can."

"Why? Why don't we just stay where we were until…"

"Until what? The defenses of the city are collapsing, Lieutenant! We can't go up river much farther, and sooner or later they'd come and get us. Down river is the only way out. And in any case, this is the navy, mister! We've got our orders and we'll follow them!"

He turned away from the man in disgust and stared out the view slit. A moment later, *Wichita* fired her guns and Drew strained his eyes to see what she was shooting at. The message had said the Martians were crossing the river downstream from Big Rock Mountain; had Captain Gillespie spotted some of them ahead? But no, when the ship fired again, Drew saw explosions blossom out from the face of the cliffs.

"What're they shooting at, sir?" asked Hinsworth." Are they trying to collapse the whole cliff or something?"

That had been Drew's first thought, but no, it would be impossible. The huge mass of the hill looked like the Rock of Gibraltar. But as he watched, the smoke and dust from the explosions was wafted up the cliffside by the southerly breeze. Up and up until it swirled around the Martian tripods at the top. "They're trying to make some cover for us! Well, it can't hurt, I guess."

"Should we fire, too, sir?"

He thought about it. The only guns which could bear were the forward turret and the portside forward casemate gun. If they had to face more Martians downstream, he'd need the turret guns and they only had five rounds left... "Tell the Number One five-incher to join in, Ensign."

"Aye, aye, sir!" Hinsworth dashed away.

But before *Santa Fe* could open up with its single gun, there was more firing from close by. *Arkansas Queen* was shooting, and ironically, its two makeshift mounts using field guns could actually elevate enough to hit the top of the cliffs. A few puffs appeared near the tripods. The chances of three-inch shells doing anything was slim, but maybe they'd get lucky.

Closer and closer, the cliffs loomed up on their left and a half-dozen tripods stood there on top like executioners. One of them turned slightly and its heat ray lashed out to strike *Arkansas Queen*. The ship's improvised armor was pitifully thin and didn't even cover it completely. Almost instantly, fires erupted from a dozen points, and a moment later the ammunition of one of the field guns exploded, blowing the gun and its crew to bits. The ship turned away, toward the southern shore, but there was no escape. The fires spread quickly. A second tripod fired and the ray pierced through to the bowels of the ship and a huge gout of steam billowed up and out as her boiler exploded. Burning from stem to stern, it plowed into a mud bank and lurched to a halt. Drew saw a few men throw themselves into the water, but only a few.

We're next.

He looked toward *Wichita* and saw it engulfed in a steam cloud. Were the Martians using the black dust? He couldn't tell, but it didn't matter, the steam might provide some protection from the heat rays. He reached over and flipped the switch on the dust alarm. The howl of the siren was almost lost amidst the roar of battle, but everyone heard it and took the proper steps. Looking out again, he saw a heat ray strike the water just ahead and sweep toward them.

"Release steam!"

The view out vanished in a white cloud, but an instant later the cloud turned pink, and then a red glare blazed in through the view slits. Drew could feel the heat from it and put on his mask. The helmsman was clutching the wheel, Hinsworth was frozen like a statue, and Mackenzie had slumped to his knees.

Drew looked up and saw that the metal roof of the pilothouse was starting to glow red.

* * * * *

April, 1912, northeast of Little Rock, Arkansas

Captain Frank Dolfen stared through his field glasses and sucked in his breath. Sixty tripods, just as the scout sergeant had said. Dolfen and the sergeant, a man named Findley, had ridden to the edge of the little valley and made their way on foot through a line of trees to where they could see. It was a sight to chill the heart of any man. But the Martian machines were just standing there in three rows, not moving. No, wait, there were a couple of them which were moving. How many? He looked closer and he could only see three of the machines which were moving. They paced around the others, for all the world like sentries guarding a line of horses.

That's exactly what they are!

Yes, this was just like what he and Comstock had seen at Gallup. Tripods in storage, with no Martians inside. He remembered how the ordnance major had babbled on and on about the production capabilities of the Martians and how they could crank out machine after machine. *They have more machines than they have Martians to drive them!*

"Sir? *Sir!*" hissed Findley. "There's another one! Over there!"

Dolfen looked and indeed, a single tripod was quickly approaching from the south. It was carrying something, it looked like a metal egg the size of a man. It walked up to one of the motionless tripods and halted. He squinted through the glasses and could just make out what was happening. The egg opened up and inside was a Martian, a hideous, leathery sack with tentacles. It was lifted up to where a hatch opened in the lower part of the standing tripod. It disappeared inside and the hatch closed. A minute or more passed and then suddenly the tripod came to life. It and the other newly arrived one moved away, heading south, back toward the battle.

"I'll be *damned*," whispered Dolfen.

"What is it, sir?" asked Findley.

"It's an opportunity, Sergeant. The opportunity of a lifetime. Come on! We need to get back to the Colonel!"

* * * * *

Cycle 597, 845.1, inside Enemy City 3-118

Qetjnegartis evaluated the reports and looked on the burning city with satisfaction. Victory. The prey-creature defenses were collapsing. Resistance in the northern half of the city was all but eliminated. War machines were crossing the river into the southern half and it appeared that resistance there was disintegrating. Yes, that was the usual pattern: the prey-creatures would fight tenaciously until the battle began to go against them. At that point, their baser instincts for self-preservation took hold and they would flee to save themselves. Qetjnegartis was determined that this time very few would succeed. It had the forces available to pursue the enemy to complete destruction. It would begin by destroying all the river vessels so that...

"Commander! Commander Qetjnegartis! Respond!"

The communication was so abrupt and so lacking normal protocol that Qetjnegartis paused a moment before replying. "Yes. What is it?"

"Commander! This is Galnandis! Powerful enemy forces have attacked us! They are in among the.... We need assist..." The circuit suddenly went silent.

Galnandis? It had been left with two others to guard... *The reserve fighting machines!*

An enemy force in the rear? A powerful force? How powerful? Scouting reports from yesterday had found nothing for many telequel in any direction. Where had it come from? The artificial satellite, while useful, was in an orbit too low and too erratic to provide useful real-time tactical information. Somehow something had eluded detection and was now attacking.

Qetjnegartis hesitated. The battle here was won, but if a powerful enemy was approaching, and it caught them up against the river and the remainder of the city's garrison... And even if it was not a large force, the reserve fighting machines were vital for the upcoming operations.

"Attention, all battlegroups. A new enemy force is in our rear. All groups halt in place. Groups 32-4, 32-5, and 32-9, move to the machine storage area and report on the situation there. Speed is essential."

* * * * *

April, 1912, northeast of Little Rock, Arkansas

　　"*Charge!*"

　　Frank Dolfen shouted as loudly as he could, waved his arm, and dug his spurs into his mount's flanks. The bugler immediately echoed his command and the 1st Squadron of the 5th US Cavalry surged forward. The other squadrons were doing the same thing, and a tide of horseflesh and machines swept into the west end of the little valley.

　　The 9th was also attacking from the opposite end. In fact, the colored troopers had jumped the gun and attacked a few minutes before the 5th was ready. No matter, it only added to the enemy's confusion. The three sentry tripods had turned one way to meet the first threat, but now they were literally turning in circles as foes came at them from all sides.

　　Colonel Schumacher had been wonderfully quick to understand what Dolfen had told him - and brilliantly decisive in risking his command by believing it. If Dolfen had been wrong, if all sixty of those tripods had been operational, then his regiment would be annihilated in moments.

　　But Dolfen wasn't wrong! The charge thundered forward and the rows of tripods stood there, just as immobile as before. The horses galloped between the standing giants and the troopers whooped at the top of their lungs.

　　Men on horses and men on motorcycles and men in armored cars converged on the three hapless sentries and hammered them with everything they had. Rifles and machine guns, light cannons and stovepipe rockets, bundles of dynamite and sheer human grit hit them, hurt them, and flung them to the ground in mangled wrecks. It was over in what seemed like seconds. It had cost three dozen men and horses turned to ash, and two of the armored cars burned fiercely, spewing black smoke into the sky, but still a bargain price for such a victory.

　　The soldiers shouted and cheered and tossed their hats in the air. Even the horses seemed to be exhilarated by what they'd accomplished. But there was no time to waste. Dolfen nudged his tired horse into motion and found the colonel.

　　"Dolfen!" he cried when he caught sight of him. "You were right! By God you were right!" Colonel Schumacher looked as giddy as his men.

　　"It won't take them long to find out what we've done, sir. We need to get explosives placed and blow these things to hell."

　　"You're right again! You heard him gentlemen! Get your men to work and finish the job!"

Scouts were sent out, the armored cars, along with them, machine guns and mortars formed a defense line facing south, but everyone else got off their horses and their motorbikes and began swarming over the immobile tripods, planting their dynamite bombs where they would do the most good. Fortunately, there was no shortage of explosives. Every man had at least one of the bombs and many had more than one.

Men climbed, or were boosted by their squadmates, up the legs of the machines to where the odd hip joints met the lower bodies of the tripods. The bombs were packed tightly into place anywhere it looked like they might do damage. The trick was going to be setting them off without getting blown up with them. The bombs issued to the troops had a friction igniter to light the fuse, but the fuse only had a ten second delay. Not much time for a man to get down and find cover.

But time was short and these men were used to facing sudden death. Some tried to rig up ropes to pull the pin on the igniters from the ground, but the bolder ones just said to hell with it, pulled the pins and jumped. *Fire in the hole!* they screamed and scattered in all directions.

The first explosion blew two of the legs off one of the machines and it toppled over with a crash. The men, unhurt, whooped and went back to work. Some went on to another machine, while others decided to go back and place more bombs on the relatively unhurt head of the downed tripod to see if they could wreck it some more.

One after another the tripods were felled like trees before lumberjacks. Dolfen looked on in exhausted satisfaction. But then a bugle sounded officers call and he moved over to where the colonel and his staff were clustered around a map.

"Gentlemen," said Colonel Schumacher when everyone was there. All the jubilation was gone from his face. "Our radio has just picked up a signal from the Little Rock garrison commander. The defenses have been breached and the city is going to fall. He's ordered everyone to try and retreat down river. Once we are done here, we will move east and try to link up with what's left of the garrison and cover their..."

For one instant, everything was lit up by a brilliant blue light, and then Dolfen was knocked to the ground and a roar shook the world.

He found himself lying on top of the colonel's adjutant and tried to push himself up. He could see the man with his mouth open, apparently shouting something, but Dolfen couldn't hear anything but a loud ringing in his ears. He twisted around and a huge billowing cloud of smoke was rushing toward him.

But before it reached him, there was another dazzling flash of blue, only slightly dimmed for being inside the smoke cloud, and an instant later another blow slammed him backward onto the unfortunate adjutant again. Smoke and dust swept over the tangled group of officers, choking and blinding them.

As he tried to struggle up, he felt rather than heard a heavy impact nearby. The ringing in his ears slowly faded, only to be replaced by a shrill noise close at hand. The smoke and dust cleared and he could see again. He staggered to his feet, coughed up a mouthful of grit, and tried to spit it out. Colonel Schumacher and some of the officers looked around in a daze, but the others were clustered around... what?

Dolfen moved over to them and discovered the source of the noise. A man was pinned to the ground by the severed leg of one of the tripods. It lay right across his torso and he was screaming, blood coming out of his mouth. Looking around, Dolfen saw bits of metal and wreckage scattered everywhere.

"What the hell happened?!" screamed someone in his ear.

"One of the tripods... two of 'em, must have blown up... Their power gizmos... I saw that happen at Prewitt... didn't think about that..." No he hadn't, had he? "Didn't think it could happen with the ones just standin' there..."

As the smoke cleared away, he saw a scene of devastation. The tripods, those that hadn't been blown completely to pieces, were scattered around the valley, smashed, torn apart, reduced to junk.

The two regiments of cavalry had been reduced to junk, too. Bodies lay among the wreckage; men and horses.

"Oh, God," groaned Dolfen.

Somewhere a bugler was blowing recall and men were picking themselves up off the ground, trying to catch panicked horses, tend to the wounded... what a mess. All the elation of what they had accomplished drained away.

Frank Dolfen limped away to try to find what was left of his squadron.

* * * * *

April, 1912, Little Rock, Arkansas

The heat has almost unbearable and the roof of the pilothouse was cherry-red. Drew Harding was quite certain he was going to die. A loud concussion slammed the ship and he was thrown against the bulkhead. It had been strong but not strong enough to have come from his own ship. *Wichita, that must have been Wichita...*

"Oh, God! Let me out!" screamed Mackenzie. He surged up from his knees and started clawing at the pilothouse hatch. Hinsworth grabbed him to hold him back.

But then the red glare coming through the view slits faded away and the roof changed to a dull red and then back to gray metal. It was still hot as the gates of Hell, but what was happening? Drew went to the speaking tube and shouted: "Secure steam!" The hissing stopped and the white cloud outside dispersed, but the heat...

"Let me out!" shrieked Mackenzie.

"Let him out," gasped Drew.

Hinsworth let the man go and he flung open the hatch and staggered outside. Drew saw Mackenzie grab hold of the railing and then scream and fall back, his hands burned. He slumped to his knees and then screamed again as the hot metal plating of the deck burned through the knees of his trousers. He lurched up and Drew yanked him back into the pilothouse where he collapsed, sobbing. Pulling off his dust mask, Drew and the others went outside, careful to touch nothing. He could feel the heat of the deck through the soles of his shoes, but it didn't get too bad. Cooler air touched his face, and he sucked it greedily into his lungs. He looked up at the cliffs, but to his amazement, the summit was empty. The tripods were gone. Why? What the hell was going on?

"Sir!" cried Hinsworth. "Dead ahead!"

He turned about and saw that the noise he had heard had indeed been the *USS Wichita*. She lay, broken in half, both ends burning, just a few hundred yards ahead. Drew leapt back into the pilothouse and spun the wheel. They were already as far to the south side of the river as they dared, so there was no choice but to steer back into the center, closer to where the Martians had been. But the enemy was gone.

He looked for survivors in the water as they churned past, but there were none. *Wichita* had been battened down just like *Santa Fe*, and there would have been no way for anyone to get out. Only after they were past did he take a good look at his own ship. Good God! The mast and upper works were scorched and blackened and even partially melted in spots. The two wooden launches stored on the after deck were burning, as were some coils of rope. The upper mast with its observation platform was leaning precariously off to starboard, and the bridge railings were twisted all out of shape. The funnel had a hole in its side and the smoke billowed out of that as well as the normal opening on top.

"Sir? Sir, the radio is out," reported Hinsworth.

"Not surprised, the antenna's all melted. Check for damage below, Ensign."

"Aye, aye, sir!"

They were almost past the mountain now, and Drew looked ahead for enemies, but the river banks were strangely deserted. Where were the Martians? He could see some explosions of in the southern part of the city and still hear some artillery fire, so they weren't all gone, but he didn't spot a single one from where he was.

Mackenzie was slumped down on the deck, looking stupidly at his burned hands and whimpering. "Mister Mackenzie, go below and have those looked after. Go on, get below!" The man nearly crawled off.

Once fully beyond Big Rock Mountain, Drew could see tripods off to the north and some others in the southern part of the city, but none seemed to be coming his way. He reduced speed to spare the engines and searched for any sign of organized resistance. The waterfront on the south bank was empty of ships, even though the damage to the docks appeared minimal.

Finally, a couple of miles ahead, he caught sight of a cluster of vessels. He spotted one of the *Olmstead* class gunboats and steered for her. As he got closer, he saw that in addition to the remaining ships of the flotilla, every other ship, boat, or barge that had been at Little Rock - which was still afloat - had gathered near a small island in the river. The island had been fortified and it marked the eastern end of the city's defense lines. There were two forts on either bank and swarms of people, horses, and vehicles were crowded on the shores. Many appeared to be loading on to the ships.

"Looks like they're leaving, sir," said Hinsworth, who had just returned. "Oh, and there's no damage below, but everyone's near passed out from the heat." He looked aft. "Oh, and the flag's all burned up. I'll have another one rigged."

Drew reduced speed even more and pulled up close to the gunboat, it was the *Evansville*, and shouted across to her skipper, Lieutenant Commander Brighton. "What's happening? Our radio's out!"

"General Duncan's ordered a retreat!" Brighton yelled back. "Where's Gillespie?" he gestured up river.

Drew shook his head. "Sunk! I'm low on ammo! Did we save any?"

"*Pelée's* over there," replied Brighton, referring to the munitions ship. "But you're senior now, Harding! What do you want us to do?"

Drew's shoulders sagged. He was suddenly very, very tired and he didn't need anything else piled on him. What to do? He looked around at the barely controlled chaos.

"Load up everyone we can and then cover the retreat!"

Chapter Nine

May, 1912, Philadelphia, Pennsylvania

Colonel Andrew Comstock watched the train chug into the enormous shed of the Broad Street Station. He found that he was both nervous and excited. Victoria and his son were on that train. It had been three months since he'd last been home and he missed them terribly. But as glad as he was to see them, he dreaded telling his wife the news.

The train squealed to a halt and Andrew scanned the cars, looking for Victoria. There she was. He saw her leaning out one of the car windows and waving. He returned the wave and hurried over to where she was. "Hello!" he shouted.

"Andrew!" cried Victoria and then she held up young Arthur, who initially looked very uncertain about this new place he was in, but when he caught sight of him shrieked: *Da! Da!*

A warm glow passed through Andrew that had nothing to do with the spring weather. He stopped just below the window and stood on tip-toe to grasp the hands of his wife and son. "How are you? The trip okay?"

"Yes, fine. So good to see you, love. Can you come in and help with the luggage?"

"Sure! Be right there." He went to the end of the car, up the steps, and inside. He gave his wife and son a quick hug and then got the luggage out of the overhead rack. Before the war there would have been a dozen porters competing for the job, but nearly all of those men were in the army now. Andrew didn't mind carrying the bags at all, except... "Wow, what all did you bring? How long are you planning to stay?"

"Andrew! You've never had to travel with a baby. Almost all of this is for Arthur."

"Oh! Well, no matter, I can manage." He grabbed up the bags and trundled them off the rail car. The platform wasn't terribly crowded, unlike other times he'd been here. New regulations had gone into effect restricting 'unnecessary' civilian travel. It had been done to free up rolling stock for military use, but it was just another example of how the war was changing everyday life. There were still plenty of people, however, because there were always ways around the regulations. Andrew had had no problem getting a pass for Victoria and Arthur.

He lugged the bags down to street level and only had to wait a moment for his driver, who had been circling the block, to spot him and pull over. Being a colonel had its advantages: his own car and driver. The driver popped out and helped him load in the bags and then they were off. Andrew had reserved a room at a nice hotel down on 7th Street, and it was only a short drive on Market Street to get there. He was staying at a boarding house in Eddystone, but it was a dreary place and Eddystone, itself, wasn't much better; so he'd arranged for this hotel instead.

"How's your mother?" he asked.

"Oh, she's fine, fine. Worried about Dad - and you, too, of course." Her father, General Hawthorne, was technically Andrew's boss - or had been. He spent most of his time in Washington these days, unlike when Andrew had first become his aide, before the war. They had never managed to find a house, so Victoria and Arthur were still living in her parent's home at Fort Meyer. He knew Victoria wasn't happy about that, but it was really the only practical thing to do.

"Is everything all right with your dad? You must see him nearly every day now that he's not traveling so much."

"Almost. But we do worry about him. He's sick a lot, though he tries to hide it. He works too hard."

"Everyone's working too hard."

"Like you."

The arrival at the hotel saved him from having to answer that one. They checked in, and his driver helped carry the bags again before he dismissed him. The room was nice enough, and they got settled before taking a stroll. It was a beautiful day, but Andrew noticed his wife wrinkling her nose. "What's wrong?"

"The coal smoke! It's so thick!"

"Really?" he replied, sniffing deeply. "All the new factories, I guess, I hardly notice it anymore."

"I guess it's because there aren't many factories in Washington that I notice it more."

"That's true. But Philadelphia is a huge manufacturing center. And now that you mention it, after one day last winter, the snow was gray, and by the next it had turned black. All the soot from the factories."

Their stroll took them past Independence Hall and there was a large crowd of people gathered in the open space in front of the old building. There was a band and many of the people carried signs and placards. As they got closer, Andrew realized that it was a political rally in support of Presidential-aspirant Nelson Miles.

A banner close to the building had a list of names of cities which had been lost to the Martians. *Salt Lake City, Denver, Bismarck, Omaha, Des Moines, Albuquerque, Santa Fe...* Andrew winced. The list went on and the last two names were in red: *Kansas City* and *Little Rock*. The banner than asked: *How Many More??????*

A speaker on the steps was shouting angrily. "... and Roosevelt has the *gall*, the unmitigated gall to ask the American people to give him another four years! Four terms in office? God in Heaven, Washington himself only wanted two! And Washington won his war! Roosevelt is *losing* this war! How many more cities will the Rough Rider lose? How many more of our precious boys will die? I say no to Roosevelt! He's had his chance! It is time for a change! A time for Nelson Appleton Miles! Miles for President!"

The crowd took up the chant: *Miles! Miles! Miles!*

The band struck up a patriotic march and the crowd cheered and chanted. Andrew steered his family onto 6th Street and away. Victoria looked back with concern on her face. "Do you think Miles will win?" she asked.

"Unless something changes, I'm afraid so," said Andrew. "Most people still don't understand what we are facing in this war. They hear about the defeats and the retreats and the cities lost and they can't accept the fact that it's because the Martians are more advanced than we are, and that we have a lot of catching up to do. They figure it must be because somebody made a mistake."

"So they blame the President? From what you and Dad have said—and from what I saw on the trip to Panama—if it weren't for him we would have *lost* the war!"

"You're right. But people don't listen to reason. And now General Miles comes along and his supporters are all but promising that he'll win the war and win it quickly if they make him President."

"What could he do that President Roosevelt isn't already doing?" snorted Victoria.

"Not much. But the people are tired of the war and I guess they think that any change is better than no change."

"*I'm* tired of the war! But it doesn't mean I'm going to vote against the best man! Not that I *can* vote, of course."

Andrew wasn't going to get drawn into *that* subject again. So he said: "Come, I didn't ask you here to talk politics! Are you hungry? There's a very fine restaurant a few block from here. It's called *Bookbinders* and General Clopton introduced me to it."

"Well, yes, I am hungry, but what about Arthur? He's being very good, but I don't know how long he'd keep that up in a restaurant."

"They have private rooms upstairs. We can get one of those. It's early yet and they should be available."

"All right."

They made their way to the restaurant and Andrew was pleased that it, indeed, was not crowded. The head waiter looked at Arthur doubtfully, but the boy was being on unusually good behavior and they were led upstairs to a cozy room that looked out on Walnut Street. Andrew ordered a bottle of wine and placed their orders. Arthur started getting fussy once they stopped moving, but the little fellow was so worn out by the trip that he soon dozed off in his mother's arms and they settled him down on a side chair.

They sat and held hands across the table and smiled at each other. "Missed you," said Andrew.

"Missed you, too." Victoria's smile faltered. "But where are you off to now?"

Andrew started in surprise. "What do you mean?"

"I *mean* that you obviously aren't coming home any time soon or why would you have sent for us? From your letters I know that the land ironclads are nearly complete and that ought to finish up your need to be here. So if you are not coming home, where are you going?"

Andrew sighed. Yes, Victoria was a smart woman. Too smart sometimes. "Yes, you're right, I have a new assignment and I will be gone for a while longer. I'm sorry."

"Where? What will you be doing? And for how long?"

"You know the old saying that the reward for a job well done is a tougher job?"

"Yes?"

"Well, it appears I did my job here too well. I learned about the land ironclads so well that General Clopton wants me to stay on as his second in command to make sure the darn things keep running properly. I'll be heading west with the squadron in a few days."

"West? You mean to the Mississippi Line?"

Andrew nodded.

"A combat assignment? But... but you're a staff officer!"

"The policy now is to rotate officers between staff and the line. So people don't get stuck in a rut and so each side understands the problems of the other. Clopton went straight to General Crozier and twisted his arm to get me. It's a compliment, really."

"But it will put you in combat."

"Being a staff officer hasn't been too terribly effective at keeping me out of combat so far."

"I know! Oh, Andrew!" She got up out of her chair with tears in her eyes. He automatically stood up and embraced her. At that moment, Arthur decided to wake up and start crying, and a few seconds later the waiter arrived with their food. They sprang apart, Victoria going for the baby, Andrew spinning to face the startled waiter. It took several minutes to get settled again, Victoria with Arthur on her lap and both of them seated again, picking at food they neither really wanted anymore.

"How long do you think?" she said quietly.

"How long until I go? We plan to make the first move down to Newport News next week. That will be the first real test of how the ironclads handle open water. If everything goes well - and I doubt it will - we'll work our way down the coast from harbor to harbor until we get to New Orleans. Then up the river to wherever they need us. If there are any delays at Newport News I might be able to get up to Washington for a day, but I don't know if..."

"I meant, how long until you come home?"

"Oh, well, there's no way to tell. All the brass are hoping that the land ironclads will be the spearhead for the offensives everyone is clamoring for. So they'll probably want us until... until..." He faltered and dropped his eyes.

"Until you win the war? That could be a very long time. Years."

"That's true for any soldier these days, love," He stared at his cooling lobster. "But if things work well, the army will be building more of the ironclads. Maybe they'll send me back here to work up my own squadron. I could be back east for months and months." He looked up and gave her as hopeful a grin as he could manage.

She answered with a tiny smile. "As it happened, I have some news for you, too, Andrew."

"Oh? What?"

In the half-second before she replied, he knew exactly what she was going to say.

"Andrew, I'm expecting again."

* * * *

Cycle 597, 845.1, Holdfast 32-4

Qetjnegartis stared at the image of Commander Braxjandar of Clan Mavnaltak in the communications display and tried to gauge its mood. The clan to the north had also fought a large battle recently and also gained a victory.

"My congratulations on your success, Braxjandar," said Qetjnegartis. "I trust your losses were not excessive."

"Excessive, no. But not inconsequential, either," it replied. "The prey-creatures learn quickly and fight with greater tenacity than ever. Do you not find this to be true?"

"Yes. I fear they are more intelligent than we first gave them credit for."

"All the more reason to crush them quickly and not give them the time to learn more," said Braxjandar. "I propose to attack City 3-4 in six days' time. Can I count on Clan Bajantus to attack City 3-37 at the same time to keep the enemy confused? This was agreed upon."

Qetjnegartis waved its tendrils in the negative. "I am afraid that will not be possible. Despite crushing the enemy at City 3-118, our force of reserve fighting machines was destroyed. It will be at least thirty days before they can be replaced. I cannot launch a major attack without them. Can you delay your assault for that long?"

"Destroyed? How could your entire reserve be destroyed?"

"An enemy raiding force attacked from the rear. Several of the reserve machines had their power supplies explode and the other machines were caught in the explosions. A regrettable setback."

"Did you not have a guard on them?"

"I do not have time to discuss my tactical decisions, Braxjandar! I can attack 3-118 in thirty days! Will you wait or not?"

"I will not, Qetjnegartis! The enemy is off balance and I will not give them time to recover. I will attack as planned. The Colonial Conclave will not be pleased to hear that you have failed to support me properly."

Qetjnegartis held back its anger. The loss of the reserve machines truly rankled and Braxjandar's arrogant attitude was not helping. Still, the opinion of the Conclave could not be ignored. "I and my clan face difficulties you do not. City 3-37 lies on the far side of the great river. Crossing it against the enemy defenses may be very difficult. We do not know the depth of the water, the strength of the current, or the condition of the bottom. Your next objective lies on this side of the river and can be attacked directly. Also, is not Clan Novmandus ordered to assist you from the north?"

Braxjandar waved its tendrils dismissively. "They are proving to be of little help. They have such a vast territory assigned to them, with almost no prey-creatures to contend with, that they are making little effort to construct an effective battle force. Their attention is on building new holdfasts to administer their territory. In time, of course, they may become very powerful, but for the moment all they can do is distract some of the enemy forces to the north. I understand that you have a similar lack of cooperation from the clan to your south."

"That is true, although they do have serious prey-creature forces to contend with, and I have heard that they are also suffering from... internal difficulties."

"Then it would appear that the conquest of this continent has been left to you and I, Qetjnegartis."

It was surprised by this statement. Was this a peace-offering of some sort? Perhaps some gesture in return was wise. "That may well be true. I regret my inability to launch a full-scale assault at this time. But I will agree to send raiding forces north and south along the large river. This may spread alarm and confusion among the prey-creatures. At the very least it will allow me to gather information on the enemy defenses. Perhaps a better attack site will present itself. And I promise that our main attack will commence within thirty days."

"Very well," said Braxjandar. "I will attack on schedule. Perhaps my attack will aid yours, if nothing else."

"So be it," said Qetjnegartis.

* * * * *

May, 1912, St. Louis, Missouri

General Leonard Wood eagerly stepped off the train in the huge expanse of St. Louis' Union Station; Colonel Drum was right behind. Despite the top priority granted his train, it had taken three days to get here. There was a crowd of men in uniform waiting to meet him. Leading the group was John Pershing, commander of 6th Army. Pershing had briefly worked for Wood two years earlier as his assistant chief of staff, but the huge demand for officers with command experience had seen him made a division, corps, and now army commander. 'Black Jack', as he was sometimes called due to his time with a colored regiment, had grown into his new responsibilities well, and Wood was glad to be working with him. He returned his salute and stuck out his hand. "Hello, John, good to see you again."

Pershing took his hand and shook it firmly. "And you, sir. Although you've picked a hell of a time to make an inspection! I've got Martians not thirty miles from this spot!"

"I know, John, I know. That's why I'm here."

Pershing's welcoming expression turned to suspicion. "You're taking command here, sir?"

"Technically I was already in command. Here and everywhere else, John. But do you mean am I relieving you? No. I'm here to observe. And to get the hell out of Washington for a while."

Pershing smiled briefly but still looked wary. Wood could certainly understand the man's uneasiness. No commander wanted the boss looking over his shoulder, but that was just too bad. Wood was very glad that Congress had finally stopped dragging its feet about re-creating the four-star rank and giving it to him. During the Civil War, it had taken them two years to even allow three star ranks, and that had meant a horde of major generals commanding corps and armies and all squabbling over who had seniority. They had been facing the same thing in this war with the lieutenant generals. But now he had four stars on his uniform and there was no doubt who was in charge. Still, they had lieutenant generals at both corps and army level. Perhaps there needed to be a five star rank…

"I see, sir," said Pershing. He turned and gestured to several other officers with him. "This is my own chief of staff, Colonel George Marshall, and you know General Foltz, of course."

"Of course! How are you, Fred?" The commander of XV Corps, which was charged with the defense of St. Louis, Lieutenant General Frederick Foltz, stepped up and shook his hand. "Fred was indispensable helping me sort out that mess in Cuba after the war," said Wood to Pershing. "He was the supervisor of police and captain of the port in Havana, while I was the military governor of the island."

"And now we've got another mess to deal with, sir," said Foltz. "Scouts report I've got a couple of hundred tripods bearing down on me. They could hit us as soon as tomorrow."

"Right, and there's no time to waste. Let's dispense with the formalities and get to work. Take me to your headquarters and brief me on the situation."

Pershing nodded and they all made their way out of the station to the street where a group of staff cars awaited. They chugged off along streets almost devoid of civilian traffic, but crowded with military. "How has the evacuation proceeded?" asked Wood, nodding to the streets.

"Well enough, sir. Nearly all the women and children are gone, but there are still plenty of civilian workers in the factories and maintaining the utilities and other services. Still, the population is less than half of what it was."

"What were you able to save from the Kansas City garrison?" It was a question he'd dreaded to ask, but he needed to know.

"Not much, I'm afraid," said Pershing, frowning deeply. "The reports that made it back are sketchy to say the least. The enemy attacked in overwhelming strength and the defenses collapsed very quickly. Some of the riverine craft have made it back here carrying some survivors. Scouting aircraft report others on foot traveling overland. Whatever has made it out is no longer a usable military force - except for the ships, of course, I've added them to the city's defenses."

"Duncan?"

"No word."

"Damn. Well, hopefully they took some of the bastards with them. From the reports we're getting, the defenders at Little Rock made them pay."

"That's good to know, sir," said Pershing, "but it doesn't help us much here. Forgive me for asking, but can we expect any reinforcements besides yourself, General?"

Wood looked Black Jack in the eyes. "As a matter of fact, yes. I've had the 1st Tank Division sent to Cairo. They're on ships and I can have them sent wherever you like."

Pershing looked surprised. Clearly he hadn't been expecting anything. "That would be wonderful, sir. The steam tanks are the best things we've got to stop the tripods."

"Actually, we may have something better."

"Sir?"

"I'll tell you about it when we're inside." The motorcade had arrived at Foltz's headquarters which was located in the Hotel Jefferson, a fifteen story building which had a good view in most directions from its penthouse ballroom. The elevator took them up.

St. Louis had been identified as a strategic point almost from the start of the war, so plans for its defense had been worked on for years. Since the disaster in 1910, those plans had been put into effect with much greater urgency and had now reached a very sophisticated stage. The penthouse headquarters contained a huge and beautifully made sand table map of the city's defenses with hundreds of small blue flags stuck into it, which Foltz now explained in detail.

"We started with the defenses of the city, itself," he said, using a pointer to trace an egg-shaped oval which fit into a bend in the Mississippi. "A line of concrete walls with emplacements for heavy guns was constructed from the river on the south and then around to meet the river again north of the city, a distance of almost thirty miles. We've also built some substantial works along the waterfront, although we've always assumed we'd have support from the navy to defend that approach."

"Dangerous to make assumptions," muttered Wood, "but for the Martians to attack from the river side would mean they have already gotten across, and that would be a disaster in its own right. Proceed, General."

"Yes, sir. We did not wish to depend solely on a single line of defense, so once this main line was complete, we expanded our defense zones to provide a forward line. As you can see, the Missouri River comes in from the west and then turns to the northeast to join the Mississippi north of the city, forming a rectangular shape with water on three sides. The only landward approach is from the southwest." He traced the river with his pointer.

"To take advantage of this, we've constructed a line from this point on our main line up to the Missouri at the town of St. Charles, giving over two thirds of the main line an outer defense. This new line has a number of concrete forts connected with earthen trenches. We're calling it the Donnelson Line after an engineering officer killed in an accident during construction."

"That looks good, Fred," said Wood. "But it looks like you have an even more extended line further to the southwest." He pointed at the sand table.

"Yes, sir, we do. The Meramec River enters the Mississippi here, about ten miles south of the city, and provides a natural barrier almost halfway to the Missouri. At this time of year, the Meramec is deep enough to get some of the smaller gunboats almost ten miles upstream, so we've built a line of trenches and bunkers along its banks and then the rest of the way to the Missouri here."

"That line has to be what? Forty miles long?" asked Wood.

"About thirty-seven, yes sir. We realize it is far too long to defend with the troops we have, so this will just be a forward outpost line to force the enemy to deploy and reveal his intentions. The 58ᵗʰ Division is holding the position. And we have all the country registered for artillery fire. Our long range guns can hit anywhere along this whole line. We've also dug thousands of pit traps to snare and immobilize their machines. Our intent is to hurt them as much as possible before they can even reach our main defenses."

"Just so long as your troops in the forward line don't get hurt too badly trying to fall back." The 58ᵗʰ was nearly a third of the whole garrison and they couldn't afford to have it destroyed.

Yes, sir, we've given a lot of thought to that. As you can see from our table, there are a multitude of small streams which crisscross the area. We've seen how the enemy tripods have trouble with soft and marshy ground, so we've dammed up a number of these streams creating ponds and small lakes and a lot of flooded ground they will have trouble getting across. Each of our forward units will have designated fall-back routes to the Donnelson Line along dry ground through these areas which are already registered for our artillery. If the Martians follow those routes, they will be hammered by our guns. If they try some other route, they'll get stuck in the mud - and we'll hammer them anyway."

"You are aware that the enemy is now employing a smaller machine in conjunction with the tripods? What provisions have you made to deal with those?"

"Yes, sir. We've gotten reports on those. The men who have seen them are calling them spiders. They will make our trenches and underground bunkers less secure, but the reports also say that they aren't nearly as heavily armored as the big tripods. Rifles, machine guns, and the stovepipes can destroy them. Frankly, sir, our infantry are looking forward to facing something they can fight on more even terms. We'll handle them."

"What about ammunition? Particularly artillery ammunition? How are you supplied?"

"We believe we have a sufficient reserve for seven days of all-out combat, sir. We have eight different main dumps and twenty secondary ones closer to the front to assure rapid resupply to our units. If it goes longer than that..." Foltz shrugged. Yes, it would surely be decided one way or another long before that.

Wood nodded. "I'm impressed, gentlemen, very impressed. Oh, what about the captured heat rays we've sent you? Where are they positioned?"

"Well, General, we were constrained by the fact that the devices require a huge amount of electrical current to work. The local power plants can meet the demand, but obviously we need to get the current from the plant to the device, so we are limited to where we can deploy them. At first we simply picked five locations along the main walls with good lines of fire and then ran power lines to those locations. Later, the engineers realized that the devices themselves were not that large or especially heavy and could be moved quickly with the right equipment. So what they've done is to set up nineteen different locations along the walls and run power lines to each of them. We have the devices themselves on trucks and can move them to whichever locations seem threatened. We can then set up the devices and fire from there."

"That's ingenious, Fred. Good thinking."

"It was the engineers who thought of it, sir, I can't take any credit. But if the Martians get close enough, they are in for one hell of a surprise!"

Wood and many of the others there chuckled. "I sure hope we can give them one, Fred." He turned to face all of the assembled officers. "Gentlemen, you have done an outstanding job, but sometime in the coming days, all of your work will be put to the test. *St. Louis must be held!* At all costs! Not only is it vital to our overall defenses, but all of our future offensive operations depend on our ability to hold on to what we already have." He looked the men over and they seemed properly sobered.

"With this in mind," he continued, "we are giving you every bit of support we can. I've already told General Pershing that the 1st Tank Division has been put at your disposal. I've also alerted II Corps, to your south, to be prepared to take over the southern section of your line on the east bank of the river. So, if necessary, you could cross over the 42nd Division to reinforce your lines here." Foltz's eyebrows went up and many of the others nodded. XV Corps had five division, but only three were in the St. Louis lines. The other two extended the corps' lines north and south along the river.

"That would be excellent, sir," said Foltz. "I'll send General Hotchkiss the word to be ready to move."

"Finally, there will be several ships docking at your wharfs within the next few hours carrying our latest 'secret weapon'. They're called 'Little Davids' and they are a large steam powered vehicle mounting a twelve-inch gun in a rotating turret. Be advised that they are not tanks. Their armor isn't particularly strong and they carry no secondary weapons, so they aren't fit to get in close and mix it up with a bunch of tripods. They are only meant to be a means of moving a very heavy gun to where you might need one. There are six of the beasts and I leave it to you to put them to the best use."

"Thank you, General," said Pershing. "I've put all of 6th Army's reserves on call for XV Corps' use. This is primarily additional artillery, which I'm moving up on the east bank of the river for now." Black Jack looked at Wood. "Sir, I can guarantee you that St. Louis will be held to the last man."

* * * * *

May, 1912, near Montgomery Island, Arkansas

Captain Frank Dolfen looked east and could see the glittering waters of the Mississippi in the far distance. *Thank God, we made it.* The retreat from Little Rock had not been nearly as long as the agonizing trek from Santa Fe two years earlier, but it had been bad enough. For one thing, the Martians had put on a much more aggressive pursuit - although not as aggressive as they might have.

Despite the disastrous explosion among the parked tripods, which had cost the two cavalry regiments five times as many men as the initial attack had, the sudden blow to the enemy seemed to have disorganized them. Precious hours had gone by before any serious response was made, and this allowed the cavalry to put itself back together, slip out to the east to make contact with the survivors of the Little Rock garrison, and retreat down river.

It wasn't until the next day that any real attacks developed. Even then the enemy seemed very cautious, perhaps because of the gunboats in the river. It was clear the Martians didn't like ships and the big guns they carried. Any time the ships pulled within range, the tripods would give ground and try to find cover. The retreating troops huddled close to the river whenever they could. Or maybe the enemy's caution was because they had no reserve tripods to replace losses. Dolfen liked to think that was the reason.

Even so, the Martians had hurt them. The damn things could move so fast they would dart in, blast away at anything they could, and then fall back again before the ships or any of the artillery could find the range. Only a few dozen of the steam tanks had escaped Little Rock, and on the road they broke down at an alarming rate; there were just a handful left now. Infantry - and cavalry - had to do far too much of the fighting and the dying.

Worst of all, their expected support had vanished.

They'd been told that as they fell back down the river, they would run into the forces of General Funston's 2nd Army which had been assigned to defend the south shore of the lower Arkansas. The surviving garrison could join up with them and make a stand somewhere. From what Dolfen had heard, there were supposed to be two infantry divisions stretched out along the south side of the river. That was a hopelessly inadequate force to guard a hundred miles of winding river, but it was still a lot better than nothing - and nothing was what they were finding. The 78th Infantry & 5th Texas Volunteers divisions simply were not there.

They found groups of Texas and Arkansas militia, poorly trained and lightly armed, but when asked where the army units had gone, they could only shrug their shoulders and say *south*. When they found out what was pursuing the Little Rock garrison, most of the militia had melted away. A few had joined in, but only a few.

So the retreat had to continue. There weren't enough of them left, and no good positions to defend, so it was keep running - all the way to the Mississippi. They did get some help; once they were further down river additional gunboats arrived, and when the water was deep enough, their old friend, the monitor *Amphitrite* with its ten-inch guns.

There were also Tom Selfridge's planes, and aircraft from other units as well. During the daylight hours they had planes overhead almost constantly; those gave them warning of approaching Martians and even killed a few of them, too. As a result, the retreat didn't become a rout - not quite.

And now they were here, at the Mississippi. The river was teeming with ships, both military and civilian. Dolfen could see that some were drawn up along the shore and appeared to be loading troops and vehicles.

"So what now d'ya think, Captain?" He turned in his saddle to see Private Gosling alongside. The Goose had managed to stay alive and even provide a few modest comforts during the retreat. If Dolfen had been forced to command his squadron and look out for himself, he would have gone hungry and slept in the mud. With Gosling's help, he'd done neither.

"No one's told me. Looks like they are shifting what's left of us to the east shore." He pointed at the boats.

"It'd sure be nice to put that big stretch o' water 'tween us and them bastards, an' that's the Lord's truth!"

"Amen." Dolfen glanced over his shoulder, looking west, to make sure the Martians weren't going to try and ruin things the way they almost did two years ago, but the horizon was empty. As he looked, he noticed one of his troopers riding past, carrying a strange object. It was a long pole, maybe twelve feet long, and on the end of it was... *What the hell?!*

"Trooper... Private, uh, King, what the devil have you got there? Is that a stovepipe rocket at the end of it?"

"Yes, sir!" grinned the trooper. "Can't fire one of them blamed things from horseback! So I figure I can just ride up to one of them tripods and jam this thing up its... well somewhere it'll hurt, sir!"

"That close and you're like to blow *yourself up!*"

King's smile faded and he shrugged. "Maybe so, sir, but no one can 'spect to live long these days. If I can take one of those devils with me, it'll be worth it."

Dolfen realized that the man was right. Hell, he'd been training his men for months with the idea that they were all expendable if they could hurt the enemy. This wasn't any more dangerous than using the dynamite bombs. Still... *Lancers! Rocket lancers! God help us!*

"Well, be careful how you use it, Private."

"Will do, sir!" King gave him a wave which wasn't quite a salute and moved on.

Dolfen watched him go and shook his head. He had a hell of a lot of brave men in his outfit. It broke his heart to see so many killed, but what else could they do? He sighed. So now what? Gosling's question was a good one. Stay here? Ride a hundred weary miles back to Memphis and rebuild the unit again? He'd lost nearly fifty men and all but two of the armored cars were gone—destroyed or broken down and abandoned. He'd have to...

"Captain! Captain Dolfen!"

He jerked in surprise at the shout. He'd been almost dozing in the saddle. He looked and saw a courier riding up. Now what? "Yeah?" he growled.

"Orders from the Colonel, sir! We are to proceed to the river, where we will be loaded on ships to take us back to Memphis!"

"Well, I'll be damned," he said. Private Gosling was grinning.

"Beats the hell out of riding, sir!"

* * * * *

May, 1912, Near Ozark Island, Arkansas

Commander Drew Harding eased his ship out of the mouth of the Arkansas River into the much broader waters of the Mississippi and breathed a long sigh of relief. They had made it! The retreat from Little Rock had been hell, sheer hell. The army garrison had been a disorganized shambles and so it had been left to the navy to cover the retreat. Mercifully - and inexplicably - the Martians had left them alone for a few precious hours, allowing the boats and barges to get loaded and the armed vessels to replenish their magazines. But from that point afterward, the Martians had come again and again to try and finish the job.

Santa Fe, Olmstead, and the other gunboats had dashed back and forth, like sheepdogs protecting their flock from a pack of wolves. They hadn't saved all of the sheep, but by God, they'd done for some of the wolves! There wasn't any doubt this time that *Santa Fe* had gotten some of the bastards. Drew could still see in his mind the one that had taken two eight-inch shells square in the head. It had been torn to pieces in a glorious explosion.

It had gone on nearly without a pause for days as the footsloggers made their slow and agonizing way down the river. Drew had barely managed a few hours of sleep a day with the attacks coming frequently and Mackenzie useless. He'd pressed young Alby Hinsworth into service as his first officer, and the boy - he was all of five years younger than him - had done an outstanding job.

Speak of the devil, here he was. Hinsworth appeared on the bridge and saluted. "Pardon me, sir, but the radio is working again. Finally got the new antenna rigged."

"Good, good. Signal *Amphitrite* and let them know."

"Aye aye, sir." The lad disappeared again.

The only saving grace during the retreat was when Amphitrite joined them. Captain Jorgensen, the monitor's commander, was the senior by a dozen years, and Drew gladly turned command over to him. With only his own ship to be worried about, the load was merely crushing instead of impossible. Mile by mile they had fought their way along, and now they were here.

So now what? He was so tired he could barely frame the question, let along produce any answers. Well, he could just wait until someone told him...

"Signal from *Amphitrite*, sir!" said Hinsworth, bustling back.

"Sweet Jesus, now what?"

"We are to head to Memphis for repairs and await orders, sir!"

Drew clutched the railing, closed his eyes, and let out his breath. "Thank God. Mr. Hinsworth, you have the con. Carry out our orders, I'm... I'm going to my bunk for a while."

"Aye, aye, sir!"

Chapter Ten

May, 1912, St. Louis, Missouri

It was still dark when Colonel Drum woke him up. The XV Corps staff had put Wood in a ridiculously luxurious suite in the Hotel Jefferson. Despite the clean sheets and tidy appearance, the place had obviously been recently occupied and probably by General Foltz. He'd been tempted to insist that there was no need to displace the corps commander, but he supposed if they hadn't done that for him, they would have felt compelled to do it for Pershing. Protocol; there was no getting away from it, even on the edge of a battle.

"Sorry to wake you, sir," said Drum, "but it's started."

"Where?" asked Wood sitting up and swinging his legs out of bed.

"They are getting reports from all along the outer western perimeter, sir. No major attacks yet, it doesn't seem." Drum handed him a cup of coffee and Wood slurped at it appreciatively.

"Probing us. Their standard tactic. But just on the landward side? Nothing along the rivers?"

"No, sir. At least not yet."

"Good." Not a crisis then. He could at least take time to shave and dress properly. "Tell them I'll be up directly."

"Yes, sir." Drum withdrew and Wood levered himself up and into the bathroom. It was so odd, he thought, as he lathered his face; a critical, perhaps decisive, battle would soon be fought and here he was in a fine hotel, calmly shaving! It didn't seem right, somehow. It was like something out of an earlier age. Wellington at the ball in Brussels on the eve of Waterloo. Something like that.

He shaved, took care of other necessities, and carefully put on his uniform. The elevator - a bloody elevator! - took him up to the command center. He paused in the lobby and peered out a window. There were flashes of artillery in the distance and he thought he could hear a low rumble.

He entered the penthouse and saw that everyone else had preceded him. Pershing and Foltz and all their staffs were clustered around the big sand table and the maps hung on the walls. Unlike his own situation room back in Washington, all the communications people were one floor down and messages had to be sent back and forth by runners. All eyes turned to him as he came through the doors.

"Morning, gentlemen," he said. "A *very* early good morning! So they're here? Show me the situation."

Pershing opened his mouth to say something, but then thought better of it and turned to Foltz. Yes, this was his command and he knew it better than anyone. Pershing looked like he hadn't been out of bed much longer than Wood, while Foltz looked like he hadn't been to bed at all. He stepped forward. "We have reports of the scout tripods all along our lines from the town of Drew, here on the Missouri, down to Fenton, about halfway to the Mississippi." Foltz used a pointer to trace along the defense lines from northwest to southeast. "The reports started first at Drew and then spread down the line, so it appears the bulk of them are following along the west bank of the Missouri. It's just probes so far for the most part. When we send up flares and try to range in the artillery, they pull back out of the light for a while and then try again at another point. They are clearly scouting out our defenses, sir." While the general was talking, a captain on his staff was sticking small red flags on pins into the map.

Wood checked the time and saw that it was after three. It would start getting light in a few hours. "Well, good, if they don't make a major push until daylight, it will be to our advantage. How are you responding?"

"Until they commit themselves, I don't intend to move our reserves beyond their forward staging areas, General. The navy is on alert and getting their ships on station. Naturally, all the men are up and anyone not on the front line is being fed. All the fliers are getting their aircraft ready, and as soon as it's light, they'll go up and get us a better idea of what we're facing."

"Have there been any reports from anywhere else along the Mississippi?" Wood directed this question at Pershing.

"No, sir, nothing."

"All right, then get your 42nd Division ready to cross the river. Drum, send word to II Corps to shift north to fill the gap."

"Yes, sir," said Pershing. "What about the 1st Tank Division? Can I commit them?"

"Where would you want them to go?"

Pershing hesitated. "Until I have a better feel for where the enemy is going to strike, I can't say. But I'd like their transport ships to get as close to here as they can so there will be as little delay as possible once I do know where."

"Makes sense. Drum, see to it."

"Yes, sir."

Wood looked over the map again, wondering if there was anything they'd forgotten. "So we wait."

So they waited.

Reports continued to come in, but they were always the same: Martian tripods spotted but then disappearing again as soon as the artillery opened up on them. "They're trying to spot the location of our guns, sir," said Colonel Drum.

"Yes, no doubt. They did the same thing at Albuquerque and apparently at Little Rock and Kansas City."

"We've kept that in mind, sir," said Foltz, overhearing. "Every one of our forward field gun batteries has at least two alternate firing positions. Just before dawn I'm going to order those that have fired to shift to their secondary sites. If the Martians try to smother them with their black dust, they'll hit a deserted location."

"Excellent, General," said Wood. Foltz really had done a fine job here, but Wood wondered just how much of that was his work and how much it was his staff - or oversight by Pershing? He'd have to make some inquiries. As the war went on, the army was going to get even bigger. He was going to need new army commanders and he was toying with the idea of a command level even higher than the army - a group of armies. If Foltz was capable of greater responsibility than a corps, he wanted to know it.

Orderlies circulated serving coffee, and the hotel's kitchen was able to supply food for those who wanted it. Wood nibbled on a bacon sandwich; he wasn't really hungry, but it helped him appear calm in the eyes of his subordinates. Every hour or so he'd check his watch to discover fifteen minutes had gone by. Dawn, he wanted the dawn.

Around five, the enemy probes started to become more frequent and they spread farther south along the outer line. Assault tripods as well as the scouts were being reported. *Soon, the real attack will come soon.* Wood got up from his chair to stretch and went over to the east-facing windows. Shading his eyes against the glare from inside, he searched the horizon for a hint of the sun...

"General!" Wood turned to see Foltz gesturing to him to come over to the map.

"What's happening?"

"We're getting reports from the 58th of the spider-machines. Here, here, here... and here." He pointed to four locations along the outer perimeter.

"Numbers?"

"Nothing definite yet. A few of the forward outposts have been forced to fall back, but there's no report of huge numbers." Foltz hesitated and glanced at Pershing. "I was just about to order the artillery to reposition, sir. Do you think I should go ahead?"

Wood raised his eyebrows. It was a good question, of course. The appearance of the spiders could presage the main attack, so repositioning the guns would be a smart move. But it would take time, and if the attack came while they were on the move, the 58th might not have its artillery at a critical time. But Foltz shouldn't be asking Wood - or

Pershing for that matter. It was his corps and he should be making the decision. "Do as you think best, General."

Foltz hesitated a moment longer and then nodded and turned to an aide. "Tell General Kuhn to go ahead and move his guns."

The order was sent off and activity slowed again. Wood went back to the window and was pleased to see a faint streak of pink in the eastern sky. Minute by minute the pink crawled up the sky, but it was turning a deeper shade of red instead of shifting to blue. *Red sky at morning, sailor take warning?* They didn't want bad weather, even though rain would cut down the range of the Martian heat rays. They wanted good visibility to...

"I always hated this part the most," said a voice from beside him. He turned and saw Pershing standing there. "The waiting. When you knew there would be a fight today, but you had to wait. I just wanted to get on with it."

"Yes, like that day outside Santiago in '98. Lying there under the Spanish guns for hours! Waiting for someone to give the order to go."

Pershing made a sound which might have been a chuckle. "I was just a lieutenant in the 10th, but I remember you and Roosevelt prowling around like caged lions. And when the word finally came, Roosevelt and his Rough Riders were off like a shot."

"Theodore has always been a man of action." Wood fell silent, thinking of those days.

"And how could any of us have imagined that just fourteen years later we'd be in a war like this?" Pershing shook his head.

"A simpler time. A different world... when the only enemy you had to worry about were other men."

"Yes, sir." Pershing stood there a moment longer, seemingly lost in his own reminiscences, and then moved away, leaving Wood to stare at the growing dawn. *I should send a report to Theodore.* He'd surely know that Wood had slipped out of Washington by now and where he had gone. Hardly a day went by when he didn't stop by Wood's office, although that had dropped off in the last few weeks since the tragic death of his military aide, Major Archie Butt, who had drowned aboard the *RMS Mauretania* when it struck an iceberg and sank the previous month with a great loss of life. Butt had been on a diplomatic mission to England, and Roosevelt was in mourning; his usually dynamic energy damped down. He'd bounce back, of course, he always did. Wood remembered his friend in Cuba where he'd weep over the death of one of his beloved Rough Riders and then the next day be out there leading more of them to their deaths. *A complex man...*

Wood's time as an army surgeon had stripped war of every vestige of glory and romance. When he saw men dying of pneumonia or dysentery on a daily basis, in addition to those mangled in actual combat, it gave him a different perspective on life and death. Yes, he mourned those lost and respected those who soldiered on and risked a death like that, but he'd put it all behind a glass wall to keep the stench of it from driving him mad. If he'd had to mourn each of the hundred thousand men he'd lost in 1910...

Am I going to lose another hundred thousand this week?

It could happen. There were no accurate figures on the losses at Kansas City and Little Rock yet, but they could total thirty or forty thousand. This fight for St. Louis could easily cost another sixty thousand - *even if we win.*

And if we lose...? If they lost, if the Martians got across the river and began to rampage across the east, the deaths would be in the millions. *Well, Leonard, you wanted this job. Now you've got to do it.*

He shook his head to clear out those disturbing thoughts and turned away from the window, back to the map. More messages had arrived and Foltz and his staff were pouring over them. Wood walked over to them. "Something new?"

"Yes, sir," said Foltz, "we've got reports of the spider-machines showing up in the 58th's rear areas. Not a lot of reports, but some. It appears they are slipping through our lines in the dark." Foltz frowned. "Our outpost line isn't continuous, it can't be with so few troops, but it was designed to spot the tripods, not these smaller machines."

"They might not be heavy enough to set off the pit traps we've dug, and they probably aren't as vulnerable to getting stuck in the mud, either," said Pershing. "Damn, some of my officers had suggested stringing barbed wire like the Russians and Japanese did in their war, but I said no because the tripods would just step right over it. Maybe I was wrong. It might stop *these* things. Or at least make them reveal themselves breaking through."

"The tactics keep evolving," nodded Wood.

More reports came in of the spider-machines. Several of the relocating artillery batteries had run into them and one had been routed and the others forced to flee further to the rear, some losing guns in the process. Some of the telegraph and telephone connections to the forward posts were being cut. The 58th was dispatching teams with the stovepipe rocket launchers to try and deal with the intruders. Wood tried to imagine the courage it would take to stalk such things in the dark.

But it wasn't all that dark anymore. The sun was not quite up yet, but there was more than enough light to see by. In addition to the rumble of artillery, he could now hear the drone of aircraft. A half-dozen airfields had been built in and around St. Louis, and with the dawn, the airmen were aloft. Some of the larger, multi-engined craft carried radios, and hopefully they would start sending back good information on the enemy's whereabouts and numbers.

Runners brought in more messages and one was handed to Foltz with special urgency. "Looks like they've stopped their dancing about, sir," he said after reading it. "A force of at least thirty tripods is attacking the outpost at Drew. Our artillery is hitting them, but they are coming on." New red flags were appearing on the sand table. After a few more minutes, another outpost farther south along the line reported the same thing. It looked like the main attack was beginning.

After Wood's brain surgery two years ago, his doctor had absolutely forbidden him to smoke again. He had obeyed, and for the most part he'd been able to resist the urge with no real problem. But nearly all the men around him were smoking like chimneys and suddenly he wanted a cigarette more than he could ever remember. Rather than give in - or stand there fidgeting - he turned and strode away, down the long penthouse ballroom, his hands clasped behind his back.

At the far end of the space was another big table which was covered with a more conventional paper map. This was the artillery plotting area. Between the artillery batteries organic to the infantry divisions, the attached corps and army-level batteries, the heavy guns built into the fortifications, and the weapons on the navy ships, there were close to a thousand artillery pieces arrayed for the defense of St. Louis. They were all coordinated from here. The map showed the artillery positions and the whole area was set out with an overlaid grid. The officers here could direct the fire of any gun to any location within its range. The men were very busy, getting reports on potential targets, receiving specific requests for fire, calculating which guns to use, and issuing the firing instructions. As Wood watched them, he heard the rumbles from outside grow louder. More and more guns, which had stood idle during the early skirmishing, were being committed to the fight.

As he studied their activity, Wood's admiration for the skill of the men grew. He knew the basic principles of what they were doing, but the actual mechanics of making it work were beyond him. These men were experts and he thanked God they were here. The artillery was their best hope to stop these monsters. The sun was fully up now, and though partially obscured by clouds, light was streaming in the eastern windows.

"General?" Wood turned and saw that Pershing was there.

"Yes?"

"Foltz is going to order the 58th to pull back. They've got as many as a hundred and fifty tripods hitting them at six different locations, and if they try to hold any longer, we won't get any of them back."

"All right, carry on." He followed Black Jack over to the sand table. There were a lot more red flags on it now. Foltz looked up as he approached.

"Aircraft are reporting several hundred additional tripods massing in this area, near Manchester, sir." He pointed to the table. "It looks like they are getting ready to do their flying wedge right through the line. My boys can't hold against that."

"No, best get them out of there," agreed Wood.

"Yes, sir, I'll have them fall back to the Donnelson Line northwest of the city. I'm hoping to draw the enemy in that direction. I just hope those damn spiders don't slow up the withdrawal." Wood looked at where Foltz was pointing and nodded. If they could get the Martians to hit the secondary line built between the city walls and the Missouri, perhaps they could get them to expend their strength there. Even if they broke through that - and he was sure they would - they would still have to attack the main defenses around St. Louis, itself. But if their line of attack went farther south, they'd hit the walls on the south side of the city and the defenses to the northwest would be wasted.

"General," said Pershing, "the 42nd is on the move, they'll start crossing the river into the city within the hour, although it will take the better part of the day to get them all here. I'd like to start landing the 1st Tank Division at the city docks as well."

"That's where you want to commit them, then? As a central reserve?"

"Yes, sir," said Pershing. He straightened up from the table, sighed, and rubbed his chin. "I had been thinking about using them in some grand outflanking movement by landing them down river, behind the enemy positions. Pull off a Cannae or an Austerlitz and get my name in the history books. Mighty alluring, but it just won't work. Without the docks and the cranes it would take a full day to land just the tanks, and once they were ashore they'd have to drive for miles through all the flooded ground we've created just to get into action. We'd lose half of them before they got close enough to shoot. No, I've got to play it safe with this."

Wood could fully understand Pershing's frustration. But he was right. To try something bold here might see the whole, very powerful force wasted. "I think you're right, John. We know the Martians are coming here. Let's give them a warm welcome."

Pershing and Foltz continued to issue orders and receive reports. The 58th Division was being hard pressed, but only in a few spots. Most of the troops and guns were falling back along their pre-planned routes, covered by artillery fire from more distant batteries. Air reconnaissance reported that things were very bad in those spots where the Martians were concentrating and losses were heavy there, the enemy advancing faster than the troops could retreat. But the aircraft were also reporting that significant numbers of tripods were blundering into swampy ground and getting stuck when they tried to pursue soldiers who fled off the roads. Artillery was zeroed in on the immobilized Martians, and a number of machines had been destroyed.

The morning dragged by and the blue flags from the forward lines moved back toward the Donnelson Line while several thick concentrations of red flags headed in the same direction. Toward noon, Wood and the other generals were becoming concerned that one large mass of red was drifting eastward toward the southern section of the city walls; but then fire from gunboats on the Meramec River started hitting them from the rear, and more ships on the Mississippi joined in, causing the Martians to veer westward again toward the Donnelson Line where they wanted them to go. They all breathed easier.

Noon came and Wood forced himself to eat something, although he had no appetite at all. As he chewed on a sandwich, he noticed a new officer arrive who almost immediately started arguing with Pershing. He recognized him as General Mason Patrick, the commander of the air forces in the St. Louis area. Wood got up and went over to the pair.

"General, my men are champing at the bit!" said Patrick.

"They're just going to have to champ a bit longer, Mase," replied Pershing. "They are doing a fantastic job with the reconnaissance and artillery spotting, but I'm not going to commit your bombers and attack aircraft until the right moment."

"But dammit, sir, there are hundreds of targets out there right now!"

Wood came up and both men turned to face him. "So, General Patrick, your men want to fight?"

"Yes, sir! We've been training for months, but except for dumping load after load of bombs on dirt mounds, we haven't been allowed to do anything!"

Wood bounced slightly on his heels and clasped his hands behind his back. "General, I can guarantee you that your men will be allowed to fight - and very soon. This battle has barely begun, and we are going to need every man to win it."

"But sir..."

"However, General Pershing is correct: the moment is not quite here. We all know how brave your men are, and the terrible losses they endure when directly attacking the tripods. We can't afford to waste them in random attacks. Use your bombers certainly - from a safe altitude - but the low-level attacks, they are the most effective and the most costly. We must save them for the proper moment: when the enemy is most concentrated and already heavily engaged with our ground forces. Patience, General, patience."

Patrick frowned and chewed on his lip, but eventually he nodded. "I understand, sir. But, sir, what if this 'proper moment' comes

during the night? My boys won't hesitate to fly in the dark if they have
to, but they won't be nearly as effective and I could lose half of them to
accidents. And two of my airfields are up here, behind the Donnelson
Line, and they could be overrun if we wait too long!" he pointed to the
area in the northern bend of the rivers.

"A valid concern," conceded Wood. "But I'm confident we can
hold them through at least one night. The crisis will be tomorrow, General. We'll need your boys tomorrow."

"If you say so, sir." Patrick clearly wasn't happy and Wood could
understand. Holding back the planes was a risk, and he hoped he was
making the right decision. Patrick saluted and left.

"Bit of a firebrand, isn't he?" said Pershing.

"Yes, but that's what we need for that sort of job." He went back
to look at the sand table. The flags representing the 58th Division were
being moved into their fall-back positions in the second line. More flags
were being moved from the docks in St. Louis to the same area. These
were the 42nd Division. It was quite a distance for them, but fortunately
a railroad paralleled the defense line and they were making use of it.
The flags already in the line were for the 19th Division.

They were taking a risk here with this redeployment. The 19th
was holding the entire length of the line. Not knowing just how much
of the 58th would make it back safely, it had been too dangerous to have
the 19th only holding part of the line and praying that the 58th could fill
in the unoccupied sections. So that meant that the 58th would be inter-
mingled with the 19th along the line. And it was the same situation with
the newly arriving 42nd. There was no section reserved for them, either,
and it would have been crazy to put them into a totally new location
in the middle of a battle anyway. All three divisions were going to be
jumbled together and that was a recipe for confusion. But there was no
other real choice. Trying to shuffle troops around so each division had
its own section of the line in the face of the enemy was simply impossible. Each unit would have to dig in and hold where it was. General William Weigel, commander of the 19th Division, was being given tactical
command of the line, although Foltz would be looking over his shoulder
very closely.

More flags began to appear and these were the forces of the 1st
Tank Division. Their ships were at the city wharfs and unloading. They
would head out to form a reserve for the troops holding the Donnelson
Line. Wood hoped they could get there in time. The red flags were getting close. Several other blue flags caught Wood's eye and he leaned forward to see what was written on them. He straightened up and looked
sharply at Pershing.

"You've sent the Little Davids out beyond the walls?" Wood had
assumed the six self-propelled twelve-inch gun vehicles would be kept

as a last reserve.

"It seemed like the proper thing, General. As tall as they are, they aren't tall enough to fire over the city walls, at least not directly. They could fire indirectly, of course, but we have plenty of other heavy guns for that. They seem like ideal long range snipers to pick off tripods with direct fire. And with only one gate in the walls big enough for them to pass through, I felt that having them backing up the Donnelson Line was the best use for them. They can always fall back if they are threatened."

Wood scowled. What Pershing said was true, but they had spent so much time and money on the blasted things, he didn't want to risk losing them unnecessarily. Still, he'd given them to Pershing to use and it was Black Jack's command, so he just nodded and remained silent.

Damn, war was becoming so complicated! Wood had spent most of his career with just the traditional infantry, artillery, and cavalry. Even though he had no formal military training, he had caught on how to use them - and how to lead them - quickly. He'd gone from a contract surgeon to leading an ad hoc infantry formation against Geronimo, to colonel of a regiment of volunteer cavalry, to commanding a brigade, and then a division in Cuba. Each step up had been more complicated, but the cogs of the machine had been mostly the same. But now, now there were airplanes and radios and steam tanks and huge, clanking war machines, and God only knew what else to try and keep track of and coordinate.

But this was the only way they could hope to win.

The afternoon dragged on. The leading elements of the Martian forces reached the Donnelson Line and recoiled, hammered by masses of artillery. This new resistance seemed to surprise the enemy and they drew back, apparently to regroup. "Surely they didn't think the forward line was all we had," said Foltz.

"We have no idea what, or even how, they think," said Wood. "But this is giving us the time to get our forces in place, so let's be thankful."

"Yes, sir, except night's coming. I'd rather not fight these bastards in the dark if we can avoid it."

"I doubt we can avoid it. They know we're not as effective at night, so they'll probably wait. I'd expect them to do the same sort of probing attacks as they did on the first line."

"And they'll probably try to infiltrate those damn spider-machines again, Fred. Better alert your troops to keep a close watch tonight," said Pershing.

"Yes, sir, and this line is held strongly enough we ought to be able to stop them from sneaking through."

Wood nodded and then asked the question he always hated. "Any figures on losses? Ours and theirs?"

Pershing called over his intelligence officer, a colonel named Dowding. He wore spectacles and rummaged through a sheaf of papers. "Reports have been coming in, General, but it's too early to have really good figures."

"I know. But what's your best guess?"

"It seems like the 116th Brigade of the 58th took the brunt of things. Still, their losses don't look too bad. Maybe a thousand men lost, along with a dozen guns or so. The other brigade, the 117th, got off more lightly. Maybe five hundred men and only a few guns. As for Martian losses..." he rummaged some more. "Maybe fifty tripods destroyed. We don't have any good estimates for the spider-machines, I'm sorry, sir."

"Fifty? Out of how many? Do you have any figures on their total force?"

"It's hard to get a good count, since they can move around so quickly. Easy to count the same one twice, you know. But we are estimating a force of around five hundred tripods, sir. No idea on the spiders."

Wood suppressed a shudder. Five hundred tripods? It seemed an enormous force, far larger than the force which had routed the army in 1910. We're a lot stronger now, too. And they'd killed a tenth of this force before they even got to the main defenses... except...

"We've gotten reports that the Martians are recovering the pilots out of wrecked tripods and transferring them to spare machines so they can return to the fight. Your men need to make sure that they destroy the tripods completely and kill the pilots."

"Yes, sir," said Pershing. "We've instructed the men about that and we have teams with every company which have demolition charges - much larger than what the infantry normally carry - to go out and finish off the damaged machines."

"Excellent." He paused. "It will take good men for a job like that."

"Yes, sir, and we've got 'em. Damn good men."

The day drew to a close without a serious attack on the Donnelson Line. It appeared that the Martians were calling up their own reserves and returning to the probing attacks they'd used before. Wood, guessing that they had a few hours before the next round would commence, went down to his own suite and lay down. Despite his exhaustion, it was hard to sleep, but he finally drifted off.

* * * * *

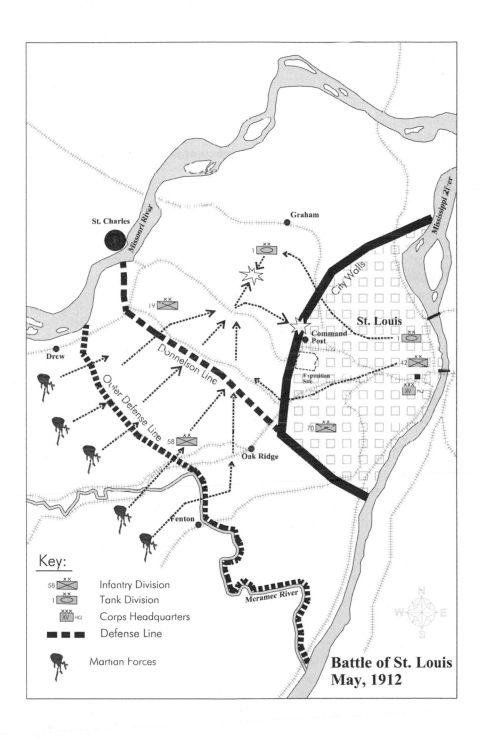

Key:

58 [infantry symbol]   Infantry Division
1 [tank symbol]   Tank Division
XV HQ [corps symbol]   Corps Headquarters
▬ ▬ ▬   Defense Line

[Martian symbol]   Martian Forces

**Battle of St. Louis
May, 1912**

Cycle 597, 845.1, east of Holdfast 32-4

Qetjnegartis halted its fighting machine and looked out at river 3-1. The artificial satellite had provided exact measurements of the feature, but somehow it appeared far larger than expected. Qetjnegartis had not yet seen the planet's oceans, so it knew that there were bodies of water vastly larger than this river, but it had never seen so much water in one place before and it was impressive.

And daunting.

"Forcing a crossing will not be easy, Commander," said Kantangnar, leader of Battlegroup 32-4, which had escorted it here. "Preliminary reconnaissance has shown the river to be deep with a strong current, and a very soft bottom. It is not known if our machines can cross it at all. We have tried to send drones across, all have been lost, either swept away, or hopelessly stuck in the mire."

It used the magnifier in its machine to study the defenses of city 3-37 on the far shore. They were elaborate and formidable, using huge amounts of the cast stone material which was so resistant to the heat rays. There were also very many of the large projectile throwers, both on the shore and on vessels in the river. Some of them were firing the new flares which the prey-creatures were using to provide artificial light. The approach of the battlegroup had not gone unnoticed, despite the darkness.

The prospect of attempting to cross here was not a pleasant one. Losses could be extreme and victory by no means assured. But Group 33 to the north was launching a major attack at this very moment, and Group 32 would have to launch its own assault as soon as possible. Still, there was no absolute necessity to launch the attack at this exact spot...

"We cannot remain here long, Commander," said Kantangnar. "The enemy will concentrate its fire on this location if we do not move."

"Understood. I have seen enough."

Chapter Eleven

May, 1912, St. Louis, Missouri

Wood had managed a few hours sleep, but he still felt very tired, his head full of fog. He yawned as he rolled out of the bed and took the mug of coffee Colonel Drum offered him. Had Drum slept? Probably not. As he drank, he went over to the western window in his room and looked out. The sky was dotted with tiny lights drifting slowly earthward. Star shells the men were calling them, but even from fifteen miles away, they were brighter than any of the true stars in the sky. Wood checked his watch and saw that it was still an hour shy of midnight when the waning moon was due to rise. With the clouds he'd seen at dusk, he doubted the moon would be much help.

There were plenty of other lights out there, too. With the enemy closing in on the main defenses, nearly all the artillery was coming into action and there was a constant flickering of the guns, most in the far distance, but some much closer by. Those nearer flashes tore away the night for an instant, lighting up the landscape and rattling the hotel's windows.

He went back up to the command center to see what was happening. The first thing he noticed was that Fred Foltz wasn't there. "He's gone out to a forward command post," explained Pershing. "With those three divisions mixed together he wants to make sure there are no foul-ups." Wood nodded. It was a good move; the last thing they needed now was the three division commanders arguing over who was in charge.

"So you'll command the rest of the corps from here," said Wood. It was a statement, not a question.

"Seems to make the most sense, sir." Pershing paused and then added. "I think the main attack will start very soon. The front line troops are reporting that more and more of the spider-machines and tripods are massing."

"How are the star shells holding out?"

"We've used a lot, but we've got at least enough for the rest of tonight. If it's not settled by tomorrow night... we may be in trouble."

"I'll have some shipped in from the reserve stocks of 5th Army."

Another hour of anxious waiting proved Pershing correct. The spider-machines began to overwhelm some of the forward strongpoints, despite scores of them being destroyed. Then three groups of tripods, each over a hundred strong, punched their way through the defense lines at different points. This was just what they had done at Albuquerque.

But unlike Albuquerque, the line did not collapse.

There were a dozen concrete forts, each studded with powerful guns, along the line and these served as anchors and rally points to the soldiers in the earthen trenches and bunkers. The troops on each side of the breaches folded back to the nearest fort and continued to fight. The forts were designed to fight in any direction, so their guns blasted away at the Martians moving past them, and many tripods turned to deal with the threat. This gave Foltz time to send his reserve tank battalions forward to counterattack the penetrations. The 1st Tank Division wasn't in position yet, but XV Corps had eight battalions of its own tanks, almost three hundred of them, on hand and they rumbled forward to engage.

Wood stared at the big sand table as red and blue flags were moved around and suddenly couldn't stand it anymore. Maps and models! He needed to see! He found some binoculars and dragged Drum up to the roof of the hotel. The horizon in every direction was a constant blaze of gun flashes. Guns in the city, guns north of the Donnelson Line, guns from the ships on the Mississippi, Missouri, and Meramec, and even a few long range guns from across the river in Illinois were firing as fast as they could. Out there on the open rooftop, the noise was much louder, a constant deep rumble, punctuated by sharp bangs from the closer batteries.

"God Almighty," whispered Drum, staring at the spectacle.

All that firepower was being directed against a few square miles of landscape about fifteen miles off to the west. Wood trained his binoculars that way, hoping to see the results of this incredible onslaught. Surely something was happening! There was smoke and flames and an almost continuous string of explosions, but it was all tiny and far away and impossible to interpret accurately. A westerly wind was coming up and a strong smell of burning was in the air.

Wood watched for a while, but he grew increasingly frustrated. "I need to get closer," he growled.

"I, uh, rather thought you would, General," said Drum. "I've located a secondary command post on the city walls which ought to have a better view. If you want, we can get there in half an hour, sir."

Wood smiled. "You're a good man, Hugh. Get a car ready. I'll tell Pershing what I'm up to."

"Yes, sir."

They went downstairs, Drum to fetch the car and Wood to confer with Pershing. Black Jack didn't seem surprised—or upset—that his senior would finally get out from underfoot. "I'll have any important news relayed to where you'll be, sir," he said. "That post has a full set of telephones."

"Thanks. I'll probably be back here before too long, John. Just need to stretch my legs a bit."

"I completely understand, sir. Be careful out there."

Wood took the elevator down to the sumptuous lobby of the hotel and then out the revolving doors onto the street. Drum was waiting there with a staff car and driver. For some reason the guns were even louder down here and the smell of burning even stronger. They got aboard and the car lurched into motion.

"Gonna have to take a few detours, sir!" shouted the driver. "The streets are fulla trucks 'n tanks 'n guns!"

And so they were. While the bulk of the 42nd Division's fighting formations had already reached the front, the division's logistical train was still moving through the city. Long lines of horse-drawn wagons and motor trucks heading west clogged many of the main streets. And on parallel roads were the tanks and vehicles of the 1st Tank Division, still moving up from the docks. Their driver was forced to take smaller side streets.

At one intersection, they had to wait as a column of steam tanks, smoke belching from their stacks, clanked past. They were mostly the newer Mark IIIs, with the side gun sponsons, but following along were several behemoths which were much larger.

"Good God!" exclaimed the driver. "Lookit those bastards!"

"The Mark IVs," said Wood, nodding. He'd seen drawings of them, but never in the flesh. They looked rather like the Mark IIIs, except they were about twice as large in every dimension. Easily thirty feet long, they sprouted guns from the hull, from side sponsons, and a big cylindrical turret sitting on top. They were so wide they nearly filled the street, and as he watched, a telephone pole was snagged by one of the guns and snapped off like a twig. He could feel the ground shuddering as they lumbered past.

The driver looked at the column nervously and when he saw a slightly longer gap between the tanks, gunned the engine and roared across the street to the other side. Wood gripped the armrest of his seat and winced. "Easy there!" shouted Drum. "Get us there in one piece, will you?"

"Sorry, sir. Thought we was in a hurry!"

They wove their way through back streets and eventually emerged near a large park. It had been the site of the 1904 Louisiana Purchase Exposition and many of the bigger exhibit buildings were still there. Millions of people had attended. Wood had missed the exposition, being in the Philippines at the time, but Roosevelt had come and described it to him several times. It had been a world's fair with all the most advanced technology of the time on display. Now, the park was displaying some of the world's most advanced weaponry. A dozen or more heavy artillery batteries had been sited on the open ground and were in full operation. The flashes of the guns lit up the classical facades of the buildings, and from the looks of things, had broken many of their windows, too.

The new city walls were just beyond the park. A line of concrete, gleaming white in the gun flashes, marched across the western skyline. The walls were a good thirty feet tall with higher towers at intervals. It looked for all the world like some ancient fortification like what Hadrian's Wall or the Great Wall of China must have looked like in their glory. *If only it was just barbarians we were trying to keep out.*

They drove to a spot a few blocks northwest of the park and stopped next to an especially large tower. An officer with the collar disks of the coast artillery was there to meet them. "General Wood!" he shouted above the roar of the guns. "I'm Major Bill Hase, I just received word you were coming!"

"Didn't mean to trouble you, Major. Just wanted to get a closer look. Can you see anything from up there?" He pointed at the tower.

"Hell, yes, sir! Helluva fight going on to the southwest! Come on! Take a look for yourself!" Hase led the way inside the massive concrete tower and up a flight of stairs. Just below the top, he paused at a landing and motioned. "Main command center for this section of the line is in there, sir." Wood peered inside and saw a dimly lit room with narrow view slits and a dozen men; spotters for the artillery, he assumed. "Better view from up top, though."

"Lead on."

They went the rest of the way up onto the roof. Wood was a bit winded after the five-story climb. There were a few men already up there, peering through binoculars and a small telescope. Wood went to the parapet and looked around. The tower was higher than the walls and projected out in front of them a bit so he could look along their length.

The walls were thirty feet high, but only about eight feet thick. Against rifled artillery, they would be breached pretty quickly. But the Martian heat rays had no impact like an artillery round and concrete had proved to be the perfect insulator against the high temperatures of the alien weapons. Eight feet of concrete could defeat the rays almost indefinitely. In front of the wall was a ditch about ten feet deep, although this one was full of water. The experts claimed that a tripod could not climb over the wall. Wood hoped they were right.

The top of the wall had a parapet tall enough for men to shield themselves behind and spots where they could fire out. There were a few machine gun teams at intervals but not many other troops. Wood hoped there were more in reserve somewhere. A few hundred feet to the north there was a broad platform behind the wall on which was mounted a large gun on a disappearing mount. In the loading position, the gun was completely concealed behind the wall. But once loaded and aimed, a counterweight would lift the gun up above the wall for a moment where it would fire. The recoil would drive the gun back down to the loading position. Done properly, it would only be exposed for a few seconds to return fire by the Martians. Wood could make out another platform farther along the wall, and maybe another one beyond that. In the flickering dark it was hard to tell. Walking to the other side of the tower, he could see a similar arrangement going in the opposite direction.

"Quite a set-up you have here, Major."

"Thank you sir. We're the 112th Coast Artillery. I've got six of these twelve inchers under my command."

"The 112th? You were originally stationed at...?"

"Fort DuPont, sir. Well, our guns were mostly at Fort Delaware in the middle of the river, but we lived at DuPont."

"Oh yes, I remember," said Wood. He didn't add that he also remembered the 112th had the worst gunnery scores in the entire army. A report had crossed his desk several years earlier noting how they'd inadvertently fired a dud practice round into downtown Salem, New Jersey. Now that they'd been transferred to St. Louis, he hoped their gunnery had improved.

"I think we can see something from here, General," said Drum gesturing to him from the western edge of the tower. Wood moved over to join him, and Hase offered him a much larger pair of binoculars than what he'd been using. He brought them up to his eyes and focused on an area where there seemed to be a lot of explosions.

Between the larger binoculars, and being five miles closer, he could see quite a lot now. There were clouds of smoke, glowing red from raging fires, billowing up from several areas. Burning villages? Burning supply dump? Burning tanks? All three perhaps. And silhouetted against those clouds he could see tripods, still very small, even with the binoculars, but unmistakable. The light of the drifting flares reflected off others as they moved. Their heat rays stabbed out at intervals and new fires would erupt. From time to time, patches of inky darkness would appear in the midst of the battle, blotting out everything.

"What's that?" asked Drum. "Their black dust weapon?"

"Probably. They like to use it against our artillery and they must be in among some of the batteries behind the defense line by now." Wood didn't like to think what that horrible poison was probably doing to the men and horses out there.

But the Martians were being hit in return. Exploding shells burst around and sometimes on the tripods, obscuring them for a moment - or sometimes obscuring them permanently. Shells had to be raining down on them from almost every direction. Looking to where the Martians were firing their heat rays, he thought he could see small shapes firing back at them. Tanks or maybe field batteries, he couldn't really tell, but whoever it was, they were fighting.

"Looks like they are moving north, across our front, sir," said Drum. He had to shout because the noise here was much louder. "They'll run smack into the 1st Tank Division if they keep going that way."

"Good!" Or he hoped it was good. What if the tanks weren't ready yet? They needed to give them all the support they could. He looked north and south along the wall and then at Major Hase. "Your guns don't seem to be firing, Major."

"No, sir," said the young man, looking frustrated. "We've got orders not to."

"Why not? You've certainly got targets."

"Yes, sir, but we're not really set up to fire a barrage like most of the big guns. We can't lob a shell up in an arc so it comes down right on the bastards. We're designed to fire directly at them—like we would at a ship. And right now if we miss, our shells will fly for miles and probably land right in the midst of friendly troops. We've got orders to wait until they're closer - and for daylight." Hase seemed very eager. "Of course, if you ordered us to shoot…"

"I see," said Wood. Yes, that did make sense, but he shared Hase's frustration that these big guns were out of action. Still, he wasn't going to override whoever had given the order. He said no more and Hase went away disappointed. He watched for a while longer and then went down to the command post to see what he could learn about the big picture. *I should have stayed back at the hotel! What was I doing coming out here?*

The word from headquarters indicated that the eight tank battalions from the XV Corps had hurt the Martians significantly, but they had shot their bolt, taken heavy losses, and the survivors were falling back to join up with the 1st Tank Division, which was still assembling a few miles to the north. Fortunately, the Martians weren't pressing them closely. They still seemed distracted by the forts on their flanks and rear, although they had overrun two of them. It was now after two o'clock and it would start getting light around five. The aircraft could join in the fight then and gunnery would improve. Pershing had no good figures on how badly the Martians had been hurt, but it seemed plain to Wood that the battle was going to be decided, one way or another, in the morning.

They watched from the roof again and the fight was definitely drifting to their right, to the north. It had been off to the southwest, but now the heart of the battle was almost due west. Wood asked Drum to see if there were any similar command posts farther north along the walls in case he wanted to move to follow the action.

But as he continued to watch, it seemed the action had stalled.

There was still a hell of a lot of firing going on, but the Martians were no longer advancing. From what Wood could see, they were milling around in the same general area, shooting their heat rays from time to time and dodging fire, but they had stopped moving north. A trip down to the command post confirmed it. Pershing believed they were regrouping, massing their tripods and spider-machines. "They've pulled away from the forts along the Donnelson Line," he said over the telephone. "They're all assembling in that area near the town of Lackland."

"Regrouping," agreed Wood, "but to do what?"

"I guess we'll find out, sir."

He hung up and went back up to the roof. An hour went by and Drum found some coffee for them. Major Hase pleaded with him again to be allowed to open fire with his big guns, but Wood refused. The chance of a direct hit at this range was slim, and a miss could fly all the way to the Missouri. It would be a fine addition to the 112th's record if they sank a navy warship on the river!

More time passed and finally there was a faint glimmer in the eastern sky that wasn't caused by artillery. The sun was coming at last after what had seemed an endless night. But what sort of day would this new dawn bring?

What are you bastards up to? Wood stared through the binoculars and tried to force them to produce an answer. *They can't stay where they are. Given time, we'll pound them to pieces. If they go south, it will just be back the way they came; a retreat. To the north they'll hit the 1st Tanks and that will draw them further into the pocket with the navy on three sides of them. West will take them to the Missouri. That's no threat, but it could be another direction to retreat. The only other way they can go is...*

"General! Sir!" Drum was pointing. "I think they're moving, sir! It looks like they're... like they're coming..."

"East. Straight for us."

"Yes, sir. General, we better get back to the main command post," said Drum, gesturing toward the stairs.

"I'm staying here."

"But, sir!"

Wood stared right at Drum, the young man's face looked pale in the flickering light. "This is where we stop them, Hugh. I'm done retreating. We will stop them *right here*!"

Drum swallowed and then nodded. "Yes, sir."

Get word to Pershing. Tell him what's happening. Have him concentrate his forces here. Get the 1st Tanks and the Little Davids on the move: hit them in the flank, by God. Get the planes in the air and send every man he's got to the walls."

"Yes, sir!" Drum dashed down the stairs to the command post. Wood turned to Hase, who had been hovering close by.

"Major, you may commence firing."

"Yes, sir! Thank you, sir!" Hase gave a whoop and he too disappeared down the stairs.

Wood went back to the parapet and raised the binoculars once again. Yes, the enemy had stopped their dithering and were on the move again—straight for him. The artillery was shifting its aim to follow them, but for a few minutes, the Martians outdistanced the fire and broke clear of the clouds of smoke and dust which had cloaked them. The growing light in the east was illuminating them better than the star shells now and they were painted in a pink glow. He caught his breath when the Martians crested a slight ridge and almost their whole force was put on display. There were more than he could count easily, several hundred at least, their metal legs bringing them closer and closer.

An old memory suddenly surfaced and he blinked. Years ago, when he was the military governor of Cuba after the war, one of the local officials had taken him on a trip to a remote area of the coast where a strange phenomenon occurred every year. Thousands, millions of land crabs emerged from the jungles to make a trek down to the beaches to lay their eggs. The land was absolutely carpeted with the things, their multiple legs moving with unwavering determination, even if some of their fellows were crushed by passing carts or human feet. They were driven by some irresistible instinct to make the journey no matter what. What Wood was seeing now seemed just like that - an unstoppable wave.

Not this time! This time we are going to stop them!

They were still at least five miles away, but Wood knew the machines could move very fast when they wanted to. They could be here in twenty minutes if they came straight on. But as he continued to watch, he realized that they were not moving all that fast, and then as the light grew, he could see why. At their feet was another swarm of smaller machines. Or so he assumed; at this distance he could see no details, just a mass of moving objects around the larger tripods. The spider-machines. Reports had said that they were slower than the big tripods, and it seemed as though that was true. Well, good! One of the chief strengths of the big tripods was their speed. If these little things slowed them down, it would be a big help - at least on the strategic scale.

Drum rejoined him on the roof top. "I told Pershing and he's directing all his reserves here, sir. He asked me if you'd be coming back to the main headquarters. He seemed a bit put out when I told him you were staying."

"I expect he would be. Well, so be it."

"I found these for you, sir. Please take them." He held out a steel helmet and one of the anti-dust kits. It consisted of a canvas bag holding the hood and mask with breathing filters and a pair of leather gloves to protect the hands. "I didn't bother getting the leggings since you already have your boots. Please, sir, we've seen them using the black dust."

"Very well," said Wood, looping the strap of bag over his neck, exchanging his hat for the helmet, and stuffing the gloves in his pocket. "Did you get a set for yourself?"

"Yes, sir. I have them right..."

A huge roar drowned out whatever else Drum was going to say. A moment later there was another roar and then a third. Wood walked over to the north side of the tower and saw clouds of smoke billowing up around the platforms for the disappearing guns. Hase hadn't wasted any time. He immediately turned and went over to the south side, just in time to see the other three go into action. One by one the big guns rose up on their carriages as the counterweights were released. Their muzzles poked over the top of the wall for a few seconds, then a blast of flame belched out, and the recoils drove them back down into the loading position. Three more crashes of noise left his ears ringing.

Impressive, but are they hitting anything?

He directed his attention back to the enemy, but he couldn't see any notable effect by the twelve-inchers. The other artillery was tracking the movement of the enemy force again and shell bursts were making it hard to see. Hard, but not impossible. A savage grin crossed his face as one of the tripods stumbled and then fell to the ground. *We're hitting them.*

A tap on his shoulder made him look aside and there was Drum again, holding out a small ball of cotton. He pointed to his ears. The roar of the big guns made it perfectly clear what it was for. Wood nodded, took the cotton, ripped it into two pieces and stuffed them into his ears. He picked up the binoculars again and continued to watch the unfolding battle.

The Martians were closing, maybe four miles away now, but they didn't seem to be advancing as quickly as before. Explosions continued to erupt around them, but they were shooting back at things Wood couldn't see. Infantry? Tanks concealed in gullies? He couldn't tell.

Drum tapped him again and pointed up. Aircraft were now overhead in growing swarms. Most of them were the smaller ones and at low altitude, but he spotted a few higher up. They were high enough to catch the sunlight which was not yet touched the dark landscape. There were two distinct groups of the small ones close by and he thought he could make out another group or two off to the north. They were circling, waiting, while others joined up with them; massing their strength before they attacked. Yes, the planes needed to attack *en masse* or they'd just be picked off before they could accomplish anything.

The enemy must have seen the aircraft, but they didn't pause, they kept on coming. Four miles, three miles, the smaller spider-machines were clearly visible now. Hundreds and hundreds of them, although from time to time Wood could see them - or bits of them - flung into the air by the exploding artillery shells.

"Sir? Maybe we should get back to headquarters." Drum had to put his mouth right next to his ear and shout to be heard. Wood just shook his head.

And then the aircraft made their attack. A swarm of at least a hundred swept by almost overhead, the noise of their engines even overpowering that of the guns. Three other groups came in from different directions.

Now the Martians did halt. They quickly formed several tightly-spaced concentric circles facing out in all directions. Wood realized what they were doing and groaned. *No! Break off! You don't have a chance against that!*

But the pilots, those brave, crazy pilots, kept right on going; and then the Martian heat rays lashed out, hundreds of them, and the sky was suddenly full of blazing aircraft and dying fliers. One group after another bore in against their target only to meet the same fate. A few made it through, close enough to fire their machine guns and drop their bombs, and Wood even saw a tripod go down here and there, but it was a feeble accomplishment against such a cost.

The survivors, only a few score of them, pulled out of range and tried to reorganize themselves. Wood prayed that they'd have the sense not to try again. *Damn, what a waste...*

"Sir! Look!" Drum was shaking his shoulder.

Explosions, huge explosions, far larger than artillery would cause, were suddenly erupting in and around the Martian formation! For an instant, Wood thought that perhaps they were from the big disappearing guns along the wall or perhaps some of the railroad guns from across the river, but no, there were far too many of them. He looked up and saw the bombers overhead, just small dots high up in the sky. Bombs!

The wave of explosions marched through the Martian circles and it was too late for them to spread out or avoid them. Tripods were torn apart and flung skyward. One of them blew up in a huge blue flash that left Wood's eyes dazzled. *That hurt them!* A loud rumble shook the tower to its foundation.

It was all over in a just a minute or two. The bombers flew on in a stately fashion and then turned to head back to their bases. As the smoke cleared, Wood could see ragged holes in the enemy formation. He couldn't tell how many machines had been destroyed, but a few dozen at least. Probably a lot of the spider-machines as well. The enemy was trying to reorganize itself, but the artillery, which had paused its fire during the air attack, was finding the range again. The Martians seemed to realize that they couldn't stay there and lurched into motion again.

But they hadn't gone more than a few hundred yards when something tore through them from right to left. In Cuba, Wood had seen rifle fire slicing through tall grass, clipping off stalks. It was just like this now. Several tripods had arms torn away or legs amputated beneath them, and one was shattered completely, its pieces spinning off like pinwheels. "What the hell was that?" he shouted.

"It came from over on the right..." said Drum.

Wood swung his binoculars that way. To the north, there was a bit of high ground and several dark shapes were perched there. As he watched, there was a flash from one of them and a cloud of smoke engulfed it. The smoke billowing up was suddenly turned from gray to white as the first level rays of the dawn touched it. A moment later, the light struck the hulking vehicle which had produced the smoke. *A Little David!*

The newly constructed war machines were there, on the high ground, firing into the massed Martians. And as the last of the night's shadows were swept away, he could see that they weren't alone. Dozens of smaller vehicles, each spewing clouds of black coal smoke, were trundling forward, down the slope, toward the enemy. Smaller puffs of white smoke came from their guns. The 1st Tank Division had arrived!

Once again, the Martians seemed confused by this new attack. They stood there for long moments as the fire tore through them. Machine after machine crashed to the ground. Finally, some sort of decision was made and the large mass split into two, half heading north toward the tanks and the Little Davids, and the other half heading east.

Toward him.

There were still at least a hundred tripods and God knew how many of the spider-machines in the group headed east. They seemed much closer now, no more than three miles away, maybe less. Drum looked from the enemy back to him. "Are you sure you want to stay here, sir?"

He almost answered automatically that he did. But did he? Really? He was the bloody chief of staff of the United States Army! Was he going to get himself killed over some point of honor? Instead, he took a deep breath and walked over to the north side of the tower and looked out.

What he saw surprised him. While he had been watching the battle so single-mindedly, much had happened. The areas behind the walls, which had seemed nearly deserted when they'd arrived, was now teaming with activity. Hundreds of soldiers were marching up or climbing on to the walls. Mortars were being set up behind the walls while machine guns and stovepipe teams took position along the parapet. Field guns were going into battery further back, and a few hundred yards away a crane was lifting something up to one to the towers. A platoon of steam tanks clanked along, looking for some place to deploy. The disappearing guns roared out another salvo and a freshening westerly wind blew the smoke clouds back across the troops. Wood made up his mind.

"I'll stay."

Drum looked exasperated. "Then *please* come down to the command post, sir! It's much better protected!"

"In a bit, in a bit. When they get closer." He went back to the western side of the tower and raised his binoculars again. The Martians were still coming on. The land west of the walls was mostly open, but there were patches of trees, some farms, and a few small clusters of houses. The invaders set them all ablaze as they passed, and the smoke from those fires joined that of the artillery bursts.

Those bursts were coming faster than ever as the word of the assault was spread to the batteries. Now their crews put forth the last of their strength. They'd been working their guns for over a day, but they knew this was the decisive moment and they held nothing back. The roar, which had rarely slackened, now became all encompassing. Geysers of earth and debris shot upward all around the tripods, and he lost sight of the other group which had turned to face the Little Davids and the 1st Tanks. No way to know what was going on over there. No matter, the battle was going to be decided *here!*

Two miles, one mile, the enemy continued to advance. But there were fewer of them now; they were paying for every yard. Wrecked machines littered the ground behind them. And still the artillery hammered the foe. The men at the plotting table back in the Hotel Jefferson were doing their job, calling in fire from every battery and ship within range. Wood suddenly wondered what their orders were for when the enemy got close to the walls? Cease fire? Continue firing despite the chance—hell the certainty—that some shells would land on friendly troops? He wished he'd asked. He instinctively glanced skyward, then looked to his aide.

"Hugh, why don't we go down to the command center?"

"Yes, sir!"

They went down the stairs, Wood giving a backward look at the men who remained behind. What orders did they have? The command center on the floor below was much busier than it had been before. The commanders of some of the newly arrived units had congregated there and they were clearly surprised to find Wood there, too. They snapped to attention when they saw him.

"Carry on, gentlemen. Carry on. We've all got jobs to do so let's do them." The men went back to work. Major Hase was looking out through one of the embrasures with a pair of binoculars in one hand and a field telephone in the other, apparently directing the fire of his big guns. A pair of infantry captains appeared to be arguing about where their men should be posted. Another officer with ordnance tabs was talking excitedly with one of the artillery officers. Other men, the spotters for the artillery, peered through other embrasures, feeding their observations back to those plotters at the Jefferson. Everyone had a task - except Wood.

He moved to one of the view slits, trying not to crowd the spotter, and looked out. The Martians were much closer now, a thousand yards or less. Their bulbous heads reflected the sunlight and their long spindly legs propelled them forward with a gait that simply looked *wrong*. And now their heat rays were firing again - firing at the walls. Blasts of pure heat leapt out from the devices they carried and sprayed across the human defenders.

The men at the embrasures cried out in alarm and began to slam closed the metal shutters. Nothing hit the command center yet, but the observers, and Wood, peered hesitantly through the small but thick quartz vision slit built into the shutters. Theoretically, they would protect a man long enough to duck, but as far as Wood knew, they had never been tested.

The urge to be able to see was irresistible and Wood squinted through the quartz. His field of view was narrow and the smoke was getting thicker, but he could still dimly make out the enemy in the distance. On and on they came. Five hundred yards, four hundred, and the smaller spider-machines - *God they do look like spiders!* - stayed with them, a horrifying mass of legs and waving tendrils.

Now some of the tripods came to an abrupt halt. One fell over completely, even though Wood had seen no shell strike it. The *pit traps*! Out in front of the walls, the men had dug traps to snare the legs of the machine. Skillfully hidden, the enemy hadn't seen them until it was too late.

"Yes!" screamed Major Hase. "Hit the trapped ones! Before they can get free!" Wood glanced aside to see the coast artilleryman shouting into a telephone receiver. He looked back at the Martians, and a moment later, one of them was blasted to fragments as a twelve-inch shell tore through it. After a few seconds, two more were destroyed. *Hit them! Hit them!*

Suddenly, the world turned red.

A blinding red glare filled his vision and a terrible heat seared his face. He flung up his arm, turned away, and ducked down. Around him, men were crying out, but Wood could see nothing but red, despite blinking furiously. Damn! Was he blind?

"General! Are you all right?" He heard Drum next to him and felt him grab his arm and drag him a few feet to one side. Tears were filling his eyes and streaming down his cheeks and he wiped his face with his sleeve. It hurt. He gasped in relief when the red faded and he could see blurry images in front of him. More blinking and wiping and the blur turned into the grainy concrete of the command center's floor. He could see! "General! Are you hurt?"

"I'm... I'm all right."

"Sir, your face is burned!"

Yes, he could feel the pain now. He imagined all the skin around his eyes had been burned. He touched it gingerly, but it didn't seem too bad. "I'm all right."

"I'll send for a medic."

"Later. What's happening?" He looked around and saw several other men who had been injured. The red glow in the vision slits was gone. He went over to the one he'd been looking through and swore. The quartz was cracked and discolored and not transparent at all anymore.

But the battle was going on. He could hear it and feel it. He needed to see it! He reached out to open the metal shutter but jerked his hand back. He could feel the heat radiating off the metal. No, he couldn't open them. He turned toward the door.

"Where are you going, sir?" demanded Drum.

"Up to the roof."

His aide swore a remarkable oath, but didn't try to stop him. Swaying on his feet slightly, he went into the stairwell and nearly collided with a man helping a badly burned soldier down the steps. "You sure about this, sir?" shouted Drum.

He wasn't really, but to stay locked up in that concrete box was intolerable. He went up the steps and then paused just below the opening to the roof. There was the noise of explosions and the shriek of the heat rays and the cries of men, but no blasts of heat were sweeping the rooftop just at the moment. He edged out, crouching low. The men who had been up here were all huddling below the parapet, bobbing up now and again to see. A headless body with a smoldering tunic lay sprawled on the concrete. Working his way to the north wall, Wood popped up to take a look.

The Martians had reached the wall.

Their machines were clustered in front of it and spread out for hundreds of yards to either side of Wood's tower. Some were down in the water-filled ditch, scrabbling and splashing futilely with claws and legs to pull themselves up and over it. Others stood back beyond the ditch, firing their heat rays against the wall or at any human bold enough to show himself above the parapet. Wood saw a ray swinging in his direction and ducked down as it passed. The top of the concrete glowed redly for a moment and he could feel the heat radiating off of it.

He dared to look again. The troops on top of the walls were tossing their dynamite bombs over the parapet and they were exploding among the Martians. One of the tripods had a leg blown off and it topped over into the ditch. Bolder men were rising up to fire off their stovepipe rockets. The disappearing guns still rose up to fire, but Wood wasn't sure what they were aiming at with the enemy so near. The scream of artillery shells was very close now and some were bursting just a few dozen yards beyond the ditch. The mortar crews down below were firing frantically with their tubes pointed almost straight up, trying to drop their bombs just on the other side of the wall.

He had to duck again as another blast of heat swept across the top edge of the tower. Fortunately, the tower was taller than the enemy, and they couldn't hit the men on top—unless they were foolish enough to expose themselves.

He looked again, careful not to touch the hot concrete, and saw a tripod pick up one of the spider-machines and fling it over the wall. It landed among the mortar crews and scrambling up on its metal legs, began firing a small heat ray and lashing out with a razor-tipped tentacle. Men screamed and began to run.

An infantry squad appeared, firing rifles into the horrid thing. It fired back with its ray, but a well-aimed Springfield shot shattered the device and the ray sputtered out. The Martian killing machine advanced on the troops with its red-stained tentacle flashing about in front of it, but then there was a whoosh and a cloud of smoke, and a stovepipe rocket exploded against it, blowing off a leg and tumbling it onto its back. A trooper ran forward, placed a bomb on the machine's belly, and then darted aside. The blast blew the thing to pieces.

But the other Martians had gotten the same idea and more and more of the spiders came flying over the wall. Some landed heavily and were damaged, but most sprang up and attacked. He saw one land among the crew of one of the twelve-inchers and the poor gunners didn't have a chance.

More troops came up to reinforce the line and some of the steam tanks as well. The noise of battle rose to a crescendo and Wood vaguely realized the cotton balls had fallen out of his ears somewhere. The melee behind the walls was mesmerizing. Men died and spiders were crushed. But this wasn't good. If the Martians could clear a section of its defenders, how long until they could rip open a hole they could get through? If the tripods and spiders got loose into the city...

"General! General Wood?" Someone was shaking him. He slumped back behind the wall and saw it was the ordnance officer he had seen earlier. "General! Do I have your permission to fire?"

"What?"

"General, can I open fire?"

"With what? What are you talking about, son?"

"The heat rays, sir! They're set up but I can't use them without an order from headquarters! I can't get through to General Pershing, but I was just told that you were here!"

"What?! You have them here?" A thrill went through him.

"Yes, sir! We've got them hooked up in five locations along this section of wall. But I can't fire them without your orders, sir!"

"Well God in Heaven, fire! Fire the damn things!" The man grinned and ran for the stairs.

Still the battle raged. More and more spiders were making it across the wall and they quickly proved that they could take out a steam tank if given the chance. Reserves in this area were getting used up and the tripods were hammering at the wall with their claws and starting to rip chunks of concrete loose. The artillery fire was slackening, too, out of shells or their crews exhausted.

A sudden commotion from the west parapet of the tower made him jerk his head around. A metal leg had appeared on the edge of the parapet. A second one joined it and they scrabbled to find a hold.

"A spider-machine, sir!" cried Drum. "We need to get out of here!" Drum hauled him up and dragged him toward the stairs. One of the observers grabbed a metal leg and tried to shove it loose, but the machine's tentacle came over the parapet, striking like a scorpion's stinger and skewered the poor devil. Wood stopped resisting Drum. Yes they had to...

The sound of a heat ray pierced the air. There were dozens of them already firing, but this one sounded different somehow. Looking north, Wood saw a ray stab out from one of the towers which had been built so they could enfilade the walls, firing down their length. The ray struck a tripod standing on the edge of the ditch, catching it at the narrow spot where the head met the strangely shaped hip joints. It flared brightly for a moment and burst into molten fragments, and the machine crashed to the ground.

The ray shifted to the next tripod in line.

The Martians did not react at first. Perhaps they thought it was some mistake, an errant shot by one of their own. Perhaps they just didn't believe it. But they hesitated for long fatal seconds as the ray claimed a second tripod and then a third. The ray ceased and Wood knew that it couldn't fire continuously without overheating. Finally, the Martians responded, turning toward where the ray had come from, but still they seemed confused.

"Look, sir!" cried Drum. He was pointing at the spider-machine. It had pulled itself up nearly over the parapet, but it had stopped, frozen in place. Not moving at all. Looking down, Wood saw that all the spiders had stopped moving. Soldiers stared at them for an instant and then attacked. Bombs and stovepipes and steam tank cannons ripped into them.

"Push that thing off!" shouted Wood. A half dozen men sprang into action. They grabbed the spider's legs and with brute strength top plod it off the tower.

The heat ray in the other tower blazed to life again, claiming another victim. The surviving Martians finally fired back, and after a moment there was an explosion in the tower, but not before a fifth tripod crashed to the ground.

There were still a half dozen tripods along this section of wall, and after a few more seconds the spider-machines, the ones which hadn't been wrecked, came back to life; but the tripods were backing away, not renewing the attack. As the wind blew a hole in the smoke, Wood could see out far to the north, and it looked as though the enemy which had turned that way were now heading south. Retreating?

Yes!

The ones in front of him turned and moved away as fast as they could. There were only a handful of the spider-machines with them and they were quickly left behind. Wood walked to the western parapet, stepping around the man who'd been gutted by the spider and looked out, fumbling for his binoculars. He brought them up, but his hands were shaking and he couldn't focus them. He gave up on that and just looked out. All along the walls, the Martians were falling back. At first, the defenders seemed as stunned as the Martians had been when their own heat rays had been turned against them, but they soon went back to work. The 112th's guns claimed at least three more of the tripods before they disappeared. Damn fine shooting.

The enemy drew off to the west and the south, pursued by the remains of the Little Davids and the 1st Tanks. And the artillery and the aircraft. Explosions and airplanes chased the enemy into the distance. Wood couldn't tell how many of the tripods had gotten away, but it wasn't nearly as many as had come in the first place. *We stopped them. They hit us with everything they had and we stopped them.* A wave of relief and exaltation swept through him.

He was very tired, he realized, and he didn't resist when Drum had a medic put some ointment on his burned face and apply some bandages; it was starting to hurt quite a bit now.

"We should get back to headquarters, sir," suggested his aide.

"Yes, yes, we should..."

But he couldn't leave until he'd thanked the men who'd won this victory. He wandered through the command center shaking hands, and then down to the ground level and along the walls, talking to gunners and tank crews and infantrymen. There were wrecked spiders everywhere along with wrecked tanks and a great many casualties. The spiders left a lot more wounded than the big tripods did. Ambulances were arriving near the wall now and doctors, nurses, and medics were working to save those who could be saved. Wood talked with the wounded and thanked the medical people.

It was nearly noon before Drum could stuff him into a staff car and head back to headquarters. On the ride back through the mercifully undamaged streets, Drum was babbling on about the battle, but Wood was trying to decide what to do next. The Martians had been hurt, hurt very badly, he believed. The obvious thing to do was to launch a counterattack. Could that be done? What forces did he have left? What forces could be brought up? What...?

"General? General, we're here."

Wood jerked awake and looked around in confusion. They were outside the Hotel Jefferson. Asleep. He'd fallen asleep. Shaking himself awake, he emerged from the car. There was a swarm of other cars on the streets and a large crowd near the entrance, talking excitedly. Wood slowly made his way through to the doors...

"Well, Leonard, I hope you've had your fun!"

A familiar voice drew him up short and he spun around. The crowd parted to reveal a very familiar figure. Eyes sparkling behind his pince-nez glasses, the mouth was drawn into a grin, exposing those enormous teeth.

"Not very fair to sneak off and direct a battle without me, you know. But well done, Leonard! Bully!"

Wood just gawked for a moment before he could find his voice.

"Roosevelt!"

Chapter Twelve

Cycle 597, 845.1, Holdfast 32-4

Qetjnegartis stared at the communications display and forced its tendrils into immobility. When the alert came from Clan Mavnaltak asking for contact, it had assumed it would be Commander Braxjandar, telling of its latest victory and demanding to know why Qetjnegartis had not launched its own offensive. But it had not been Braxjandar...

"This is truth? Braxjandar is slain? How did this come about?"

Kalfldagvar, one of Braxjandar's subordinates and now, apparently, the leader of Clan Mavnaltak on the target world, waved its tendrils in agitation. "A great calamity, Qetjnegartis. We launched our attack and all seemed to be going well. We crushed the prey-creature's outer defenses as we expected. They fought hard, but they could not stop us. But then there was another line of defenses, much stronger than the first. Their large projectile throwers were in operation in numbers never before encountered. Our losses mounted, but we breached the second line and pushed forward.

"We slew thousands of them, but then we encountered more of the miserable creatures and more of their armored vehicles. There seemed to be no end to the things! At that point we also saw that there was another defensive line constructed of the cast stone material. I... I advised Braxjandar that we should withdraw, but it was convinced that this line of defenses was the last, and if we could pierce them, the enemy would collapse. So we attacked. Braxjandar led it personally."

"And this attacked failed?" asked Qetjnegartis, even though there could be only one possible answer.

"Yes. We took heavy losses just reaching the walls, and then we could not get over them quickly. We began to tear them down. The drones performed well and it looked as though victory could still be achieved but then... then..." Kalfdagvar faltered.

"Then what?"

"Something none of us thought possible! We were suddenly fired upon with heat rays! Our own heat rays! Firing out from the walls! A score of us were destroyed before we even realized what was happening. Braxjandar was among them."

Qetjnegartis was stunned. "How is this possible? Could you have been mistaken? Could it have been some new, primitive weapon of the prey-creatures which just had the appearance of a heat ray?"

"No! Analysis proved that is was identical to our own weapons. We speculate that they have somehow devised a way of using salvaged ray projectors, taken from destroyed war machines. Or at least we hope so. The only other possibility, that they have built these from scratch, is too terrible to contemplate!"

"Even the possibility that they have managed this much is terrible enough, Kalfdagvar! This would indicate a reasoning ability far above anything we credited them with."

"Yes. But in any case, with the loss of Braxjandar and the others, the attack faltered and I had no choice but to order a retreat. Less than fifty of us survived to reach the nearest holdfast."

Fifty! Braxjandar had boasted that its attack would have nearly five hundred fighting machines! Such a loss...

"What will you do now, Kalfdagvar?"

"I have reported this news to the Colonial Conclave. They have ordered that the offensive continue. Obviously it will be some time before my own people can attack in any strength. We shall make what small probes we can to keep the enemy off balance. The Conclave has demanded that Clan Novmandus to our north stir itself to make a major effort and they have agreed. But it is now more urgent than ever that you attack boldly Qetjnegartis. Surely the prey-creatures must have concentrated most of their strength against us to deal such a blow. The opportunity for you to establish a hold across the great river might never be better. You must attack!"

There is no evidence to back up your claim, Kalfdagvar, thought Qetjnegartis. But aloud it said: "We will do what we can. You have our condolences for your losses."

Kalfdagvar appeared to have no interest in condolences, but made no more demands and ended the communications. Qetjnegartis sat there for some time assimilating this new and unexpected information. The situation was very complex—and very dangerous.

Group 31 to the south was in disarray. They had been inadequately supported by their clans on the Homeworld and were now divided by the need to hold what they already had and to assist an offensive against a heavily fortified zone which separated the third continent from the fourth. There would be no help from there. The groups to the far north were only now beginning to render any real assistance.

And Group 33, the Mavnaltak Clan, was defeated. This was entirely unexpected. Up until now, Braxjandar had been the acknowledged leader on this continent. It had produced nothing but victory. Everyone - including Qetjnegartis - had expected this to continue to be the case.

But now, now the hopes for a final victory on the third continent were resting on Qetjnegartis. In some ways it was a very satisfying situation, especially after all of Braxjandar's condescending behavior. But in other ways it was very unsettling. The other clans were now expecting it to produce the victory they wanted.

Can it be done?

The news about the prey making use of captured devices was very alarming, but it made the need for a quick victory all the more vital. If the prey were so clever as to accomplish this, then they must be given no time to accomplish more. The river needed to be crossed and a new holdfast established as quickly as possible. But where? And how?

Qetjnegartis reactivated the communicator and contacted Kantangnar, commanding Battlegroup 32-4. It answered immediately. "Report your situation. Do you continue to advance unopposed?"

"Yes, Commander. Except for a few small garrisons and light scouting forces, we have encountered no significant resistance. We have advanced three hundred telequel south of the confluence of River 3-1.4 with River 3-1, destroying all that we have seen. Unless the situation changes, we could push all the way to the ocean."

"Have you discovered any locations where a crossing of the river might be easily done?"

Kantangnar hesitated for a moment. "None that seem exceptionally favorable, Commander. While it is true that the large cast-stone fortifications are fewer here than to the north, the river grows steadily wider as we progress and much of the land along it is very low-lying and saturated with water. Some areas have proven virtually impassible and we were forced to detour many *telequel* west to get around them. One city on the far shore stands on high ground and was very heavily fortified. Also, the enemy water vessels have been seen in great number and have been following us. Any time we get close to the river they fire upon us, and we have taken some minor damage. Attempting a crossing so far from our holdfasts would be... difficult."

"I understand," said Qetjnegartis. "Very well, continue as you have for as far as you can without putting your force in danger. Report to me regularly."

"Yes, Commander." The connection was closed.

Qetjnegartis considered the situation. Crossing the large river and establishing a strong holdfast on the far side was essential. The crossing itself would be difficult, but it seemed likely that establishing the holdfast would be even more so. The prey-creatures would certainly see the danger such a thing would pose to them and make every effort to prevent that happening. Up until now, every holdfast had been established either in a sparsely populated region or in areas which had been swept clean of prey-creature forces following a major victory. In each case there had been no immediate opposition. The construction machines were much more vulnerable to damage than the war machines, especially in the early stages of construction before the underground areas could be started. If the prey-creatures were to bring up powerful forces, especially their large projectile throwers, building a new holdfast might well prove impossible. Qetjnegartis recalled the siege of the first holdfast and how nearly it had been overrun. If the prey had brought such forces to bear earlier, it probably would not be alive contemplating the problem now.

So yes, we can probably force our way across the river, but then what?

It could see no easy answers. So, as it often did when in need of counsel, Qetjnegartis opened a communications channel to Ixmaderna in its lab in Holdfast 32-2. It was one of only two others who had arrived with the initial landing force and still survived. It was a being of long experience and considerable wisdom. Once the communications link was established, Qetjnegartis explained the problem, including the information from Kalfdagvar.

"I find it most interesting that the prey-creatures have learned how to make use of our technology, even in so simple a way as this," said Ixmaderna.

"You consider using our most potent weapon simple?" asked Qetjnegartis.

"As a device it actually is, Commander. A matter of supplying sufficient power and turning it on. Far less complex than operating one of the fighting machines. Even so, for them to have puzzled out all the particulars so quickly does come as a surprise. Although after working with their young, I suppose it shouldn't have been."

"You consider them intelligent, then?"

"More intelligent than we expected before coming here, surely. Still, it is not as if they constructed a heat ray on their own - or at least so we must hope."

"I find the situation very disturbing. Is there anything we can do to render our technology inoperable in the event it is captured?"

Ixmaderna waved its tendril in contemplation. "Perhaps. It may be possible with certain devices. I shall give it thought."

"And what about the strategic situation? What are your thoughts on that?"

"I see only two possibilities which give a great chance for success with an attack that must be launched soon. One is to somehow arrange for a battle which utterly devastates the enemy without ourselves suffering too great a loss in the process. We would then have the strength to defend the new holdfast before they could assemble a new attack force."

"If I had the power to guarantee such a result, we would not be in the present situation," said Qetjnegartis. "The other possibility?"

"You must force your crossing in an area which is either so isolated that the enemy cannot quickly bring its forces to bear—such as was the case with our first holdfast—or an area which has naturally strong defensive features to give the construction operation protection from attack."

"And an additional factor is that the location cannot be too far from an existing holdfast," said Qetjnegartis. "After what happened to our reserve fighting machines during the attack on city 3-118, I am extremely reluctant to bring the construction machines along with the attack force. But to have to bring them from a holdfast later would take too much time if the distance was great."

"True," said Ixmaderna. "That limits the areas open to you - unless you found the ideal site and built a new holdfast in the vicinity on our side of the river."

"That would take too long. Our attack must come soon. And if the enemy guessed our plans, the ideal site could be fortified before we were ready to attack."

"That is also true. So your area of attack is limited to perhaps two hundred telequel of Holdfast 32-4. Do any locations recommend themselves?"

"No. The principle feature is city 3-37. But it is heavily defended with an outer fortress on the west shore connected by a bridge. Considering what happened to Braxjandar's forces recently, I am extremely reluctant to attack such a fortress."

"Then somewhere to the north or south of it?"

"It is mostly flat, wet country with no dominant features to prevent an enemy counterattack. It would also appear that the tracks of their transportation system are far denser on the east side of the river. This would allow them to assemble their forces quickly. And they can also transport their forces using the rivers. The only easily defensible locale would be..." Qetjnegartis paused.

"Yes?"

"The city itself. It is ringed on all sides with walls and obstructions to deter attack. If we could somehow manage to seize the place without sustaining ruinous losses, we could put those defenses to our own use. Not as effective as our own, but they might suffice until we can build more."

"An interesting idea, Commander. And with the entire city available to salvage, we avoid the danger of picking some unsurveyed spot only to find it completely lacking in necessary resources."

"Yes, that was another danger which concerned me."

"But it comes back to capturing the city. Can you do that?"

"A direct, frontal assault would be extremely costly, perhaps impossible with the river and the enemy water vessels to contend with. And yet clearly the prey-creatures fear exactly such an attack since they have constructed such formidable defenses. Perhaps if we made a feint, a diversionary attack against the section on the west shore to draw in their reserves, and then made a surprise crossing twenty or thirty *telequel* north or south of the city, and then quickly struck the city from the landward side. The defenses are not nearly so strong there. We could take the city, perhaps even capture the bridge across the river intact, and then move in our construction machines. Yes, if we could do this a success might be possible."

"The enemy water vessels could still pose a threat."

"Yes, we would need to establish very strong defenses along the river, north and south of the city to prevent their approach. Give some thought about how best to do that."

"As you command."

"The diversions can be done easily enough, but I am still very uncertain about the river crossing. We shall have to make some trial crossings with just a few machines to see if it can be done at all. Perhaps I will have Kantangnar make some attempts and send another force farther north to do the same. This may also distract the enemy. But it is the drones that worry me most. They will be essential for taking the city, but I fear we will lose great numbers of them to mishap if we try to walk them across the river bottom."

"Yes, that is a great risk," said Ixmaderna. "But an idea comes to me."

"Yes?"

"We have seen that the prey-creatures are capable of making use of our own technology. Perhaps we should make use of theirs."

* * * * *

May, 1912, Memphis, Tennessee

Things were busy again in the hospital. Wounded had started to stream in only a few days after the terrible battle at Little Rock, and the stream hadn't stopped for the two weeks that followed. Even now, nearly a month later, there were still a few new arrivals coming in as the survivors of the battle reached safety. Rebecca Harding looked at their newest patient. He was a middle-aged man with bandages on his hands and knees. His ID disk said his name was Mackenzie and he was with the navy. Probably off one of the gunboats, she thought.

"These burns, sailor?" she asked, pointing to the bandages.

"Yes'm," replied the man. He looked disoriented. She felt his head and it was feverish.

Frowning, she gently cut and peeled away the bandages. The man twitched and moaned as she worked. Yes, as she feared, the burns on his hands had become infected. The ones on his knees looked to be healing, but the hands… Looking closer she saw that the burns weren't actually all that bad, not like many she saw. Over the years she'd seen a lot of burns. These were probably secondary burns, made when the man touched something which was hot rather than as the direct result of a heat ray. Still, he was in danger. She cleaned up the wounds as best she could quickly and then called one of the doctors over to look at him.

The doctor, who looked as exhausted as she felt, examined the patient and just shook his head. "Finish cleaning up the wounds, get fresh sterile bandages on them," he said. "Then make sure he has food and water and rest. We'll just have it let this run its course and hope he can pull through."

Becca nodded and went to work. Sadly, there wasn't much that could be done for an infection like this. Either the man had the strength to fight it off or… he didn't. Becca was glad that this doctor wasn't one of the older ones who still prescribed bromine treatments. They were incredibly painful for the patient and didn't do any good that Becca had ever seen.

She spent nearly an hour using boiled water to clean out the wounds and then carefully covered them with gauze which had also been boiled. The patient cried out from time to time and she had to firmly hold on to his wrists when he tried to jerk away, but he seemed to be in a daze.

As she was finishing up, she heard a voice a few yards off asking: "Excuse me, miss, I'm looking for one of my men, Caleb Mackenzie. I was told he is here." Becca looked up and saw a man three beds down talking to Clarissa Forester. Mackenzie? She double-checked the ID disk and sure enough, it was him.

"Over here, sir," she called. The man's face brightened and he walked over to her. He was quite young, but he wore the uniform of a naval commander.

"Ah, there you are, Mr. Mackenzie!" he said. But when Mackenzie didn't answer, he frowned and looked at Becca. "Is he all right?"

"Uh, he's pretty sick, commander…?"

"Harding, Drew Harding, *USS Santa Fe*. But what's wrong with him? The burns weren't that bad, I didn't think."

"They've become infected. Are you his commandin' officer? When did these happen?" She eyed the man closely. He had the same last name as her…

"At Little Rock. I guess it was three, no, almost four weeks ago now. My ship doesn't have much of a sick bay. No doctor, either. We patched him up as best we could, but there was nothing else we could do for him. The medical services were overwhelmed so we just waited until we got here. But I didn't think… A few days ago it seemed like he was doing fine!"

"Burns are hard to treat. They can get infected days or weeks later, before the skin can finish healin'. I'm sure you did your best, sir."

"But he'll make it, right?"

Becca looked down at the man. No telling how much he was hearing. She got up and led the commander a few yards away. "We're doin' all we can do for him. If he's strong, he should pull through. That's all I can tell you, Commander."

The man frowned and chewed on his lower lip. "I see. Well, if there's anything I can do... Would you be kind enough to keep me informed, Miss...?"

"Uh, Harding, Becca Harding. I'll try to let you know how he's doin'. You said you are on the Santa Fe? Is it docked here at Memphis?"

"Yes, but... Harding? Rebecca Harding?" He was looking at her with a strange expression.

"Yes, that's right."

"Do you, uh, do you know a man named Andrew Comstock?"

"Major Comstock?"

"Well, he's a colonel now, but yes. You know him? You were the girl he met out west in the first days of the war?"

"Yes, that's right! You know him?"

"Yes, I knew him back in Washington when he was just a second lieutenant and I was an ensign. Staff duty, y'know. We've been friends since then and he, uh, he wrote me about you."

"About me?"

"He was curious if we were related, us both having the same last name and all. He, uh, he wrote me that your folks were all killed in the war and you might not have any family left that you knew about. He asked me if I could check into it."

Becca looked at him in shock. A relative? Family? "I... I... did you?"

"I wrote my grandmother, she's the expert on the family history. She's back with most of my other family near Albany. She wrote back, but mostly with questions for me to ask you—not that I ever expected to be able to do it in person! She mentioned a cousin... or was it an uncle? - I'll have to re-read her letter—who moved out west before the Civil War. Colorado, maybe? She said they lost touch with him."

"My grandfather fought in that war and then settled in New Mexico!" said Becca. "Do you think that could be him?"

"Maybe. Can you give me his full name? Any other details?"

"The name sure, it was...."

"Harding! Stop lollygagging! You've got a patient to tend!"

Becca looked and there was Miss Chumley with a stern expression on her face. Commander Harding looked sheepish. "Don't mean to get you in trouble, miss. Maybe you can write down anything you remember and send it to me? The Santa Fe will be docked for repairs for the next few days."

"All right. And thank you!"

"No, thank you - for taking care of Mackenzie. You will let me know if I can help in any way?"

"Yes, sir, certainly." He nodded to her and then left, nodding to Chumley as well as he passed. Becca hastily went back to work on Mackenzie. She got him bandaged up and made sure he had water and that the orderlies would feed him, but her mind was only half on what she was doing. Less than half maybe. The amazing conversation with Commander Harding kept crowding out her other thoughts. Family! She'd pushed the possibility that she still had family left in the world to the far corners of her mind. Her family was dead. And there weren't any more. None. But perhaps there were. And that Commander Harding seemed like a nice man; not like her aunt and uncle. But then he was from her *father's* side of the family, a group she'd never met or knew anything about. Maybe they were different - even if they were from back east. The thought of having *someone* was... exciting. She wished she could tell Frank about it.

Her shift ended but before she could slip off to the mess hall and then her bunk, Miss Chumley intercepted her. "I need to have a word with you, Miss Harding." Her formal tone meant she wasn't happy with something.

"I'm sorry about that, ma'am. The commander was concerned about one of his men and I..."

"That's not what I wanted to talk to you about. It's about that other preoccupation of yours."

"What? You mean the sharpshooters?"

"Yes, exactly. With things quiet here for so long I saw no harm in letting you indulge your interests. You worked hard and well and if that was your idea of fun, so be it. But now things are getting serious again. The rumors are that Memphis may be attacked soon. That will make the influx we had from Little Rock seem like nothing. And yet I've heard you talking about having a position you are supposed to defend with your sharpshooters. Which is it going to be, Rebecca? Are you going to take your gun and go fight, or are you going to stay here and help the wounded? You can't do both."

Becca stared at the woman and didn't know what to say. She'd been afraid that someday it would come to this, but she'd never figured out what she would do when it did. "I... I don't know, ma'am."

"Well, you need to make a decision - and soon. If my best nurse is going to run off and play soldier I need to know *before* the wounded start arriving in truckloads!" She glared at her in her best Chumley fashion and Becca instinctively nodded.

"Yes, ma'am. I'll... I'll let you know tomorrow."

* * * * *

May, 1912, Hampton Roads, Virginia

The *USLI Albuquerque* slipped its moorings and was slowly turned seaward by its towing ship, a freighter called *Monodnock*. Andrew Comstock held onto the railing of the superstructure to steady himself against the motion and looked back. The other five ironclads of the 1st Squadron were also leaving their docks and heading out. The sun was just peeking over the rim of the world to the east, there was a gentle westerly breeze, and it looked like it would be a fine day.

"Finally on our way," said Lieutenant Hornbaker, from beside him.

"I surely hope so, Jerry. And it's certainly about time."

"That it is, sir. I hope there are no more problems."

"Amen."

They had left Philadelphia two week earlier and made it - just barely - to the Norfolk Navy Yard. The voyage was supposed to have taken less than two days, but it ended up taking four. The ironclads with their towing vessels could do eight to ten knots depending on the wind and the seas; maybe two hundred miles a day - in theory. They made it down the Delaware River with no problems, but when they passed Cape Henlopen, at the mouth of Delaware Bay and into the open ocean, they discovered the sea-keeping characteristics of the ironclads with their big flotation modules was about as good as a large rock wrapped in a life jacket. They pitched and rolled, surged and sidled unlike anything ever seen - and the ocean was relatively calm.

The towing vessels struggled to keep their charges under control and on course. Their nice line-ahead formation was soon scattered over twenty miles of ocean and the two escorting destroyers were dashing madly about like overworked sheepdogs trying to keep an eye on everything. By the afternoon of the first day, things were settling down as the crews got used to handling the strange vessels. Then the tow cable on Sioux Falls broke. A few frantic hours followed as the ships tried to get a new cable strung. The others reduced speed to wait for them, and it was well after dark before they were on their way again.

An hour later, Springfield reported a serious leak in one of its floats. A destroyer had to come alongside and lend its pumps to get the flooding under control. It worked, but speed had to be reduced to just a few knots.

By the middle of the second day, all six ironclads were reporting strange and ominous sounds from where the floats were connected to their hulls. Was the motion of the voyage working them loose? If even one of them broke free, an ironclad would be on a quick trip to the bottom. The Baldwin engineers who were aboard scrambled around, inspecting every connection they could get to, and reported no obvious problems. But the naval captain in command reduced speed again and steered the ships as close to the shore as possible. Everyone was on alert and never took off their lifejackets. No one got much sleep that night.

The third day was much the same, although *Tulsa* began leaking, too; fortunately, not badly enough that its own pumps couldn't handle it. General Clopton was getting very annoyed and Andrew could scarcely blame him. He remembered the ordeal of getting the first batch of steam tanks to the front in the first year of the war. This was just like that - except then there had been little risk of drowning.

They finally made it into Chesapeake Bay and the safety of Norfolk. Repairs were made, and Clopton - and Andrew - had insisted on a complete inspection of everything involved with keeping the ironclads afloat; adding an extra week. Then a storm had blown up the coast and they hadn't dared to leave the refuge of the bay.

But it hadn't all been work and frustration. Victoria had taken a train down from Washington and they had a brief reunion and a last night together before saying goodbye again. Her pregnancy was starting to show a little. Would he see her again before the baby came?

Then, just before the storm arrived, came news of a great victory at St. Louis. The Martians had launched a huge attack there and had been stopped cold. Everyone was celebrating and every ship - and ironclad - in the bay had fired a salute. Good news at last!

Finally they were on their way again. Larger ships to do the towing had been found, heavier cables employed, and every flotation module had been triple checked and secured. Maybe this time there would be no mishaps. Their escort was much larger, too. There was now a destroyer assigned to each ironclad and the protected cruiser, *Olympia*, Admiral Dewey's famed flagship from Manila Bay, was leading the squadron, commanded by a commodore. The high command wanted the ironclads at the front and they wanted them there soon. Despite the victory at St. Louis, there were alarming rumors of new threats all along the Mississippi Line.

The squadron moved out into Hampton Roads, and to Andrew's surprise, they started getting salutes from the other ships anchored there. Mostly just horn blasts, but a few actually fired their tiny saluting guns. *Olympia* returned the salutes and many sailors came up on deck to wave.

"Are they only being friendly, or are they expecting us to win the war for them?" wondered Andrew aloud.

"Maybe they're just happy to get our ugly hulks out of their nice harbor," said Hornbaker.

Andrew laughed. "We're certainly a batch of ugly ducklings, aren't we?"

"You can say that again, Colonel."

Andrew turned at the new voice and saw that Lieutenant - junior grade - Jason Broadt along with Major Stavely, the ironclad's commander, had joined them. For the sea voyage, a naval officer had been assigned to each ironclad along with a few ratings to help the poor soldiers keep their contraptions afloat. Broadt seemed like he knew his business, but there was no doubt he considered this duty beneath him.

"Morning, Major, Lieutenant. Everything ship-shape today?"

"So far," replied Broadt. "Which is," he looked back at the docks, "about three miles. Only one thousand eight hundred and forty more to go to reach New Orleans."

"About two weeks, do you think?"

"If we're lucky. And luck isn't something we've had in abundance thus far, Colonel."

"Well, then we are due for a change."

"Two weeks?" said Stavely. "Oh, God..."

Poor Stavely seemed especially prone to seasickness, and even the four day journey from Philadelphia had nearly done him in.

"Maybe our good luck will include some calm seas."

"Let's hope so. Just get me on solid ground and let me fight is all I ask. See you later, Colonel." The two men went on up the ladder to the observation platform.

Andrew refused to let Broadt's cynicism infect him. They were going to make, it and when they went into action, they would make a real difference. The ironclads might look ugly and be cantankerous machines, but they packed enormous firepower and were armored heavily enough that even the Martian heat rays would find them a tough nut to crack. And speaking of firepower...

"Let's go check on how Tesla's people are making out today."

Tesla had gotten General Crozier's permission to replace the forward seven-inch gun on *Albuquerque* with his new lightning cannon, and a team of his people had been working to get it installed for over a month. They couldn't get it done before departure so they had come along.

Andrew, followed by Hornbaker, went down the ladder from the superstructure to the main deck, and then around the huge bulk of the twelve-inch turret to the smaller turret just ahead which now housed Tesla's latest invention. The snout of the device emerged from the front of the turret through the same embrasure the cannon would have normally used. It was a slightly larger version of what he'd seen on Long

Island many months earlier: a long tapering cylinder, like a cannon barrel, with thick rings of a white ceramic material at intervals along its length, until at the end they stopped with a white ball where the muzzle should have been. He wondered how resistant it would be to a heat ray. The steel barrel of a large gun could take high temperatures pretty well, but what about this thing? It would be a shame to see it melted or shattered before it could fire a shot. Perhaps they should keep the turret rotated backward as far as it could go until they were ready to fire. He'd have to mention that to Stavely.

The hatch to the turret was open and he could hear men talking inside. He stuck his head in and saw a multitude of wires and cables and all manner of stuff he could scarcely recognize During the construction of the ironclads he'd become very familiar with the basics of electrical wiring, but Tesla's devices were as far removed from normal electronics as the Martian devices were from human ones. But Tesla's assistants seemed to know what they were doing. Or at least he sure hoped so. They had installed some sort of transformer in the engine room attached to the output of the steam turbine generator and then run thick conduits through the ship up to here. Now they were hooking up the gun to its power supply.

"How are you making out?" he asked the foreman, a very young man named Edwin Armstrong.

"Oh, I think we've got her worried, Colonel," said Armstrong with a grin. "Another few days and we should have it all wired up. D'you think we could do some test firings?"

Andrew jerked in surprise. "Out here? But... but from what Doctor Tesla said, you need to have some of that Martian wire as a target or there's no telling where the lightning will go! Mightn't we hit one of the other ships - or ourselves?"

"I guess that could be a problem. We did bring a few test targets made with the Martian wire, but putting them on a raft or something might not be that good an idea at that. Maybe the next time we're near land?"

"I'll talk to General Clopton, but don't get your hopes up."

"All right, but I don't like the idea of taking this thing into combat without ever having tested it."

"Hopefully we won't go straight into a battle once we get wherever they send us," said Andrew. "Once we're ashore we can run some tests."

"I hope so. We still need to train your men on how to fire this beast."

"Yes, that's true. Well, I'll see what the general says. He's over on the *Olympia* for this stage of the trip."

"Better accommodations?" asked Armstrong with a smirk.

"Better chow, too." They both smiled. The ironclads only had the sketchiest bunk space and galley. For this trip, most of the crews were staying on the towing ships, but Andrew felt duty-bound to stay with the *Albuquerque* - which made him the ranking officer on board. He could deal with the Spartan accommodations and food - he'd certainly survived worse out in New Mexico - and they were scheduled for short stops in Charleston and Key West, so maybe he could at least a get a few decent meals.

"Well, I'll leave you to your work."

They withdrew and went up to the control center on the tall forward mast. Broadt was there and seemed satisfied with the way the vessel - he steadfastly refused to call it a ship - was handling. By mid-morning they rounded Cape Henry and turned south into the Atlantic.

"Well, we are on our way," said Andrew. "Next stop: the war."

Chapter Thirteen

June, 1912, Washington, D.C.

General Leonard Wood bought a copy of the *Washington Post* as he did every morning on his way to his office in the War and Navy Building. It was barely six o'clock, but even at this early hour the streets were bustling with military men, and he was forced to return salute after salute. Not that long ago he could enjoy a few minutes of solitude on this walk from home, but no more.

Matters weren't helped by the fact that he was now being hailed as the 'Hero of St. Louis'. Newsboys shouted at him and total strangers stopped him on the street to shake his hand. No matter that Pershing and Foltz - and the tens of thousands of troops under their command - deserved the real credit. They were still out there, while he was here. It was flattering, of course, but he really didn't need the distraction.

And the total strangers were the least of it. He'd only been back in Washington for three days and he was already getting confidential messages from powerful people suggesting that perhaps he ought to challenge Roosevelt for the nomination at the Republican convention in Chicago next month! Most he hadn't even dignified with a reply, and for the few which he could not avoid answering, he'd made it quite clear that he had no interest. Damn fools! His loyalty to Theodore was absolute and even if it hadn't been, he firmly agreed with Lincoln's advice about changing horses in midstream. They'd started this war with Roosevelt and by God they'd finish it with him!

Or at least he surely hoped so. The victory at St. Louis had given the nation's morale a sharp boost, but would it be enough? While it was true they had inflicted heavy losses on the enemy, they had not retaken any of the lost territory. Many people were still predicting a victory for Nelson Miles in November.

He made it to his office with just another dozen salutes, said good morning to Semancik, and went to his desk to look at the latest dispatches. He had a meeting with the President in only an hour and he wanted to be on top of things. His aide had done his usual excellent job in arranging the dispatches in order of importance, and the first one on the pile was from the intelligence officer at 4th Army headquarters in Vicksburg. It told him exactly what he'd been expecting - and fearing. He read through it twice. "Damn him!" he growled. God damn the man!"

Precisely at seven o'clock he arrived at Roosevelt's office in the White House. The President was having a 'working breakfast' which meant that his desk was piled with dishes as well as paperwork. In spite of warnings from his doctor, he was still eating far too much. The remains of ham, chicken, and sausages as well as rolls and pastries littered plates stacked to each side. A tall pot of coffee sat within easy reach. A servant was trying to clean up, despite Roosevelt snatching a few last morsels before they vanished. Wood's eyebrows rose when he saw the uniformed man standing off to one side.

Roosevelt had a new military aide to replace the unfortunate Archie Butt who had drowned so tragically. The new aide, by coincidence, was also named 'Archie', but he had a far better last name.

It was Roosevelt.

Second Lieutenant Archie Roosevelt snapped to attention when he saw Wood and gave him a parade ground salute. In spite of himself, Wood smiled as he returned it. "At ease, Lieutenant. Good to see you. How'd you like Plattsburg?"

"Very good, sir. They've compressed the course to just ten weeks. No Sundays off now."

"And he passed with flying colors, too!" boomed the elder Roosevelt after swallowing down a last mouthful. "Top of his class!"

"I wouldn't have expected any less," said Wood. The Plattsburg officer training school had been set up prior to the Martian invasion, but it had been expanded and was still turning out junior officers to supply the needs of the huge new armies which were being raised.

"Archie wants a combat assignment, like his brothers, but I thought I'd keep him here for a few months to get adjusted to military life. After that, well, we'll see." He shook his head. "Young Quentin is terribly jealous. He's demanding to go to Plattsburg, too, but fourteen is a bit too young."

Wood nodded, thinking that eighteen had been a bit too young, too, for Archie. Hell, he'd only been seventeen when he left for Plattsburg, and Wood had been forced to give him special permission. But there was no keeping a Roosevelt out of uniform when there was a war to be fought. "Mr. President, we have a very serious matter to discuss - several of them, in fact."

"I gathered as much from your message. So we can't even enjoy the laurels of the victory in St. Louis before the next crisis interferes?"

"I'm afraid not. Still, the victory was crucial. I liked your speech about it very much, by the way. One of your best."

Roosevelt waved that away. "Just words. We need action. What have you got for me, Leonard?"

"Problems. The biggest one comes from down south. I'm afraid that Fred Funston has run amok."

"What do you mean?"

"I mean that he's stripped his defense lines and gone hunting. I've gotten word that the troops we thought were guarding the low-

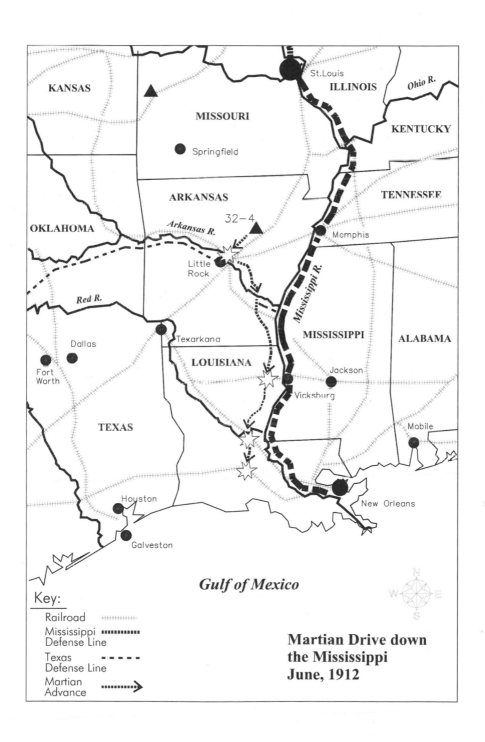

Key:
Railroad
Mississippi Defense Line
Texas Defense Line
Martian Advance

Martian Drive down the Mississippi June, 1912

er Arkansas River have been withdrawn and there's nothing between the Martians and the Gulf of Mexico. They're streaming down the west bank of the Mississippi. They're halfway to Baton Rouge and still moving."

"Thunderation!"

"So far it looks like just a scouting force, but they are burning everything they encounter. If they keep going, we may lose our last rail connection west."

"How did this happen? Where are the troops who were supposed to be guarding that area?"

"That's the mystery, sir. I've managed to piece some of it together, but we are going to have to get the full story from Funston, himself." Wood sighed and took a seat opposite Roosevelt. He waited until the servant left with the breakfast cart before continuing. "I'd been getting some rumors that Funston was massing his forces for some sort of operation. I knew his defeats at Gallup and later at Albuquerque and Santa Fe were really eating at him. He was just itching to hit back somewhere. It appears that he was planning an attack against the Martian fortress near Albuquerque."

"Did he have the sort of strength needed for such an operation?"

"It's hard to say. Perhaps he felt that the fortress there, being in the rear area, would not be so heavily defended. But we'll never know if that was true or not. You recall how back in March, I think it was, we got word of some sort of Martian incursion across the Rio Grande near Corpus Christi?"

"Yes, we were worried that it was a major attack from Mexico. But then nothing much happened and you thought it was just a reconnaissance."

"Well, the word I've now gotten is that the Martians set up some sort of operation down there. It doesn't appear to be construction of a fortress, thank God, but they are up to something. Last month, Funston used those reserves he'd been massing to launch an attack against them. Nothing wrong with that, of course. But the attack failed and rather than inform us and wait for us to send help..."

"Not that we could have sent much," said Roosevelt. Wood shrugged, not disputing the statement.

"Even so, rather than work with us, he stripped out three divisions from the VIII Corps, the ones guarding the lower Arkansas, to reinforce his attack in the south. That was about a week before the enemy hit Little Rock. When our forces retreated along the river, they found nothing there but a few scattered militia companies. The Martians punched through them with ease and are now rampaging south."

"Is the Mississippi Line down there secure?" asked Roosevelt, clearly concerned. "If we stopped them at St. Louis, only to let them across the river further south…"

"As I mentioned, this seems to just be a reconnaissance in force, they've made no attempt to cross. Fortunately, there aren't any bridges below Memphis, just ferries. But that doesn't change the fact that our defenses down that way are very weak. We skimped on building up 4th and 7th Armies because we were depending on Funston's forces to at least delay any drive to the south. I'm afraid we cannot afford to skimp any longer."

Roosevelt drummed his fingers on his desk. "So the counterattack we were hoping to launch from St. Louis will have to be put off."

"Yes, I hate to do it, we have a real opportunity there, but the new divisions are going to have to go south. There's just no choice."

"Blast, and there's no other forces you can draw on? We really bloodied the Martians, and if we could just launch a serious follow-up, maybe we can start driving the devils back."

Wood shook his head. "I'm afraid not. The forces actually at St. Louis are badly battered. Foltz's corps is a shambles, and the 1st Tank Division, just an empty shell. To make matters worse, the enemy is finally stirring himself up north. Our scouts in 1st Army are reporting tripods massing north of the Superior Switch. We don't dare weaken that area at all. A breakthrough there would be a disaster."

"Surely, surely, but what about the 2nd Tank Division? You still have them in reserve, don't you? Couldn't something be done with them?"

"Possibly, but I'm worried about the Memphis area. The force that attacked Little Rock is still out there. The tripods that we've seen going south don't make up a tenth of it, and we need to see where the rest of it is going to strike. Of course, maybe they'll just send some of it north to reinforce what's left of the group that hit St. Louis, but we have no way of knowing for sure. I've ordered out more cavalry patrols and air reconnaissance in hopes of locating them. Until we do, I want to keep the 2nd Tanks in reserve. The navy is sending more ships to the Memphis area, too. And lastly some good news, the new land ironclads are on their way. They ought to be there in a few more weeks. Perhaps if we can clarify the situation, we can find a place to use them where it will do some good."

"Does Memphis have any of the captured heat rays? They really did the job at St. Louis."

Wood shook his head. "Four out of the five we had there were destroyed or damaged. We've captured dozens more, of course, but it will be quite a while before they are ready to be used. For the time being, Memphis will have to depend on the forces already there, and I want the 2nd Tanks available if needed."

Roosevelt frowned and took his pince-nez glasses off his nose, cleaned them with a handkerchief, and put them back in place. "I suppose that's the sensible course of action, but blast I hate to leave the initiative to those bashi-bazouks. I'd much prefer to take some bold action and force them to react to our moves."

"I understand, Theodore, and I share your feelings. But our position is still very precarious. We dare not make a major mistake. If they get across the river in strength, we could be in very serious trouble. We might even lose the war."

"Yes, yes, I suppose you are right. So is that all the bad news?"

"Almost."

"What else do you have?"

Wood got up from his chair and walked over to a window and looked out. The White House gardens were in full bloom, belying the dire situation the country was in. As he watched, young Quentin dashed by, pursued by a pack of boys his own age and several dogs. Wood turned back to face the President.

"We need to decide what to do about Funston."

* * * * *

June, 1912, Memphis, Tennessee

"That should about do it, Commander."

Drew Harding looked over his ship and had to agree with the manager of the Memphis repair yard. *Santa Fe* was back in fighting trim. The damage they'd taken at Little Rock had been repaired. If you knew where to look, you could see the patches and new metal, but he could accept the cosmetic blemishes as long as his ship could fight.

And it looked as though another fight was in the offing. A huge battle had been fought—and won!—up in St. Louis, but the rumors were flying that an attack on Memphis would happen soon. The whole city was stirred up like a nest of bees as last minute preparations were made. The waterfront was crammed with ships, some bringing in supplies, some taking out civilians and wounded; and many were warships, some fresh from the victory at St. Louis, topping off their coal bunkers and magazines. Speaking of which...

"Mr. Hinsworth, how did you make out with the ammunition?" He turned to his newly promoted executive officer.

"Great, sir!" answered the young man with a grin. "The magazines are filled to the brim and I found room for an extra ten rounds per gun for the eight-inchers and twelve for the five!"

"Very good. I don't want to run short like the last time. The loaders understand they are to use the extra rounds first? We don't want them lying around outside the magazines any longer than necessary."

"Yes, sir, I told them."

"Good, good. Well, I have to get over to that big conference, so you are in command, Mr. Hinsworth. Try not to let her sink while I'm away."

"Right, sir," replied Hinsworth, still grinning. The kid was turning into a good exec, and Drew was determined to keep him in that position even in the unlikely event that Mackenzie ever returned. He left the bridge and walked up the gangway to the dock. Making his way around the work gangs, mostly colored men, stripped to the waist in the heat, he reached the gate in the huge concrete walls which ringed the city and passed through. A conference was being held by the local army commander, some general named MacArthur, to coordinate the activities of all the forces which had been massed to defend Memphis.

The conference was in a big hotel on Union Street, and even though it wasn't all that far, it was all uphill. Memphis was built on a string of bluffs along the river which were a good sixty or seventy feet above the water level. Drew was soon sweating like those stevedores under his heavy uniform coat. He was slightly amazed that he was being included in this meeting. MacArthur was a corps commander and the place would probably be swarming with generals. But the senior naval commander in the area, Commodore William Rush, apparently impressed by his performance at Little Rock, had made Drew a squadron commander, in charge of a half-dozen small gunboats, in addition to his own Santa Fe, and he'd been ordered to attend.

He reached the hotel, which was called the Peabody. The entrance had dozens of soldiers and a machine gun stationed there, protected by walls of sandbags. Drew had to present the written order he'd received to get in. From there, he was directed to the ballroom, which was crowded with other officers. Most of them were army, but Drew spotted a cluster of naval uniforms and made his way over to them where he found Rush, who greeted him.

"Morning, Harding. Ready for the circus?"

"Uh, yes, sir. What do you think the general is planning to talk about?"

"God knows. MacArthur has a reputation of being a bit of a showman."

"He's awfully young to be a corps commander, isn't he, sir?" asked one of the other naval officers.

"Yes, just thirty-two. But he's got connection, you know. He was Wood's chief of staff a few years ago, then was promoted to command of the 66th Division, which was the chief unit in the garrison here. Then he was given command of the whole garrison, and two months ago he was given command of the VII Corps when Clarence Edward was promoted and transferred to take command of 4ᵗʰ Army. A lot of promotions going on these days - but then I don't need to tell any of *you* that do I?" He smiled and most of the others did, too. Every one of them was holding a rank they never could have dreamed of just a few years ago.

Drew looked around and saw that some army junior officers were herding people toward the front of the room where there were two large objects - maps he assumed - covered by cloths standing on a raised stage. "Looks like the show is about to begin," said Rush. "Let's find our spots, gentlemen." They trailed along and stood at the rear of the army.

There they waited for a good ten minutes before there was a commotion around one of the side doors. An officer strode through and up the steps to the stage. He was tall, with black hair, a long, slightly curved nose, and a strong jaw. He was immaculately decked out with a Sam Browne belt, polished boots, and the widest set of Jodhpur trousers Drew had ever seen. He moved briskly to the center of the stage as someone shouted out for attention. The army people all instantly snapped to. The Navy people did so a bit more casually.

MacArthur looked over the assembly and stood with feet slightly apart and his hands on his hips. "Stand at ease, gentlemen," he said. "As you all know, we have a great task ahead of us: defending this city. We all know the Martians are coming, and coming soon, but we shall be ready for them and we shall defeat them!" He waved to an aide and the cover was pulled off one of the maps, revealing the city of Memphis and its defenses.

The city, itself, was on the east shore of the Mississippi and protected by the line of massive concrete walls which stretched north and south, eventually disappearing off the edges of the map. A secondary line, which Drew had been informed was not as strong as the main line, formed an arc around the city on the landward sides, meeting the main walls north and south of the city.

MacArthur grabbed a long wooden pointer and started calling out features on the map, but Drew was more interested in the river than the shore defenses. The Mississippi, close to three quarters of a mile wide in this area, came down from the north and then turned almost due east before swinging in a wide arc until it was heading in the exact opposite direction, slightly north of west, before turning south again. The wide loop to the east was where the city was located. He noted with interest that there was a small channel called the Wolf River which sliced northwest from the city to rejoin the Mississippi several miles above the first big turn, creating a sizable island, which was low and swampy. He wasn't sure if the Wolf River was navigable for his ship, but he intended to find out.

MacArthur paused in his lecture and then suddenly slapped the map to the west of the river. "Over here is West Memphis," he said. "My predecessors have regarded this area as expendable, a forlorn hope, an outer work which in the event of a serious attack would be abandoned, its garrison withdrawn over the bridge, which would be demolished after they passed. 'Defense Plan M' they called it. Gentlemen, I feel that plan to be defeatist and I will not endorse it! We will *not* give up any more ground! Not one inch! So forget Defense Plan M!" He had the attention of everyone in the room now and continued.

"Up until now, the West Memphis defenses have been held by a single regiment from the 66th Division along with some artillery and local militia. I plan to reinforce them with two brigades, one taken from the 29th Division and another from the 36th Division, to the north and south of the city."

This created a stir among the army officers and one asked, "Excuse me, sir, but won't that leave the defenses along the river in those areas rather weak?"

"A bit weaker, perhaps," replied MacArthur, "but not weak. The line of concrete walls extends farther and farther along the river every day. As they do, the heavy artillery takes up most of the load and the infantry can sidle north and south, strengthening their positions as they shorten. In the meantime, our friends in the navy can make sure the enemy stay on their side of the river, right, Commodore?" He looked at Rush.

"We'll certainly do our best, General," said Rush.

"Good! But as I was saying, West Memphis and the bridge will be held. Supported by our guns on the river and on the eastern shore, we shall crush the enemy attack and then we shall launch an attack of our own!" He waved to his aide and the man uncovered the second map. It showed a much larger area of Arkansas across the river.

"You've all heard of the big victory at St. Louis. I take nothing away from the brave men who fought there, but a huge opportunity was missed. With the enemy defeated, an immediate counterattack should have been launched. Push them and keep pushing! Kansas City might have been liberated and the enemy driven all the way back to their fortress!" He looked out at the assembled officers, his face stern, eyes blazing. "Gentlemen, we shall not make that same mistake!"

He pointed to West Memphis on the map and then drew a line across it, all the way to...

"Little Rock! That is our objective! Once we have crushed their attack we shall drive the enemy back and liberate Little Rock!"

Silence was the immediate reaction of the men in the room. Drew could only think that MacArthur was getting ahead of himself. Surely their immediate concern was defeating the Martian attack. Plans for the future were fine, but until they had won the immediate battle and then seen what they had left fit for duty, how could they know if such a counterattack was even possible?

One man finally broke the silence, an army officer with two stars on his uniform. "Uh, have you cleared these plans with Washington, sir?"

MacArthur waved his hand in casual dismissal. "Don't worry, Bill, when the time comes I'll make them see what needs to be done. But now, let's get down to brass tacks!" He turned back to the first map and began to lay out the basic plans for the defense of the city. Most of it was meant for the army and had little effect on the navy or Drew. Still, there was an overall plan for utilizing all the artillery in the region, along with the navy ships, which was of the same sort used down in Panama when he was aboard the old Minnesota. A junior officer circulated among the navy officers handing out folders with the details. Drew paged through while the general dealt with non-navy matters. Yes, he could handle this...

The meeting dragged on for another hour, but eventually wrapped up with another declaration of their inevitable victory by MacArthur. Then, to Drew's amazement, a group of newspaper reporters were called in and MacArthur made a prepared statement to them and posed for pictures in front of the maps. Commodore Rush decided they could excuse themselves and they escaped.

"God in Heaven!" said the captain of *Amphitrite*. "What a blowhard!"

Rush snorted, but didn't dispute the statement - or reprimand the man for having made it.

"If nothing else, he's certainly counting unhatched chickens," said another. "Little Rock! Is he serious?"

"I'm sure he is," said Rush. "He was born there, you know."

* * * * *

June, 1912, near Key West, Florida

Andrew grabbed the railing as the Albuquerque rolled sharply to the right. Salt spray lashed his face, only to be immediately washed away by the wind-driven rain. A weird wailing hum filled the air as that wind whipped through the rigging overhead. He was soaked to the skin, despite a rain slicker. He looked around, but the visibility was less than a quarter mile; he could barely make out the dark bulk of the *Monodnock* up ahead. The towing ship had a light on her stern which twinkled fitfully in the gray dimness of the storm. None of the other ships were in sight anywhere. The seas were mountainous, with the tops of the waves far above the main deck of the ironclad. They broke and crashed over the flotation modules, which creaked and groaned loudly enough to be heard over the storm.

"Dear Lord, how much more of this can we take?" shouted Jerry Hornbaker from beside him. "We're gonna break apart!"

Andrew didn't answer. He was wondering the same thing himself. The voyage from Norfolk had been going so well. The sea had been so pleasant that even Major Stavely had managed to throw off his seasickness. They made it past the legendary hazards of Cape Hatteras in a dead calm under sunny skies and paused for two days in Charleston to take on coal. General Clopton had held a wonderful dinner for all the senior officers, both army and navy at the city's best hotel. Then it was back to sea.

They had just rounded the tip of Florida when word reached them of a bad storm which had formed in the northern Gulf and was heading southeast toward them. Some had suggested turning back and going north along the east coast of Florida to try and find a sheltered harbor there, but the commodore in charge had insisted they could make it to the navy anchorage at Key West.

They almost made it.

They ran into the outer edges of the storm during the night and it built steadily in the hours before dawn. Any hope of sleep was long gone, and Andrew had donned his lifejacket and stared out of the pilothouse windows into the shrieking blackness for an eternity. He hadn't seen Stavely all night. Now that it was light, he wasn't sure that being able to see was better than being blind. He'd made it through one storm on that memorable voyage down to Panama with President Roosevelt, but it had been nothing like this.

"The commodore said we should reach Key West this morning!" said Andrew to Hornbaker, shouting to be heard. "But we probably lost time running against the storm. God knows where we are now!" He looked up to the observation platform. Perhaps he could see farther up there. But then the ship rolled again, the platform swung across the sky, and he decided he didn't want to see that badly.

So they clung to the rail as the rain poured down on them. From time to time they'd catch sight of other ships. Usually it would be their escorting destroyer, but sometimes the visibility would improve enough to see farther, and he thought he could see some of the other towing vessels.

Around eight o'clock, Lieutenant Broadt appeared, coming up the ladder from below. He saw them and paused. "Morning! Quite a little blow, ain't it?" The man was actually smiling.

"'Little blow'?!" cried Hornbaker. "Isn't this a hurricane?"

"This? Why, it's scarcely a breeze. A real hurricane and we'd be on the bottom already."

Andrew stared at the man, but then the vessel rolled sharply and even Broadt had to grab the railing. "You're kidding, aren't you?" asked Andrew.

"Well, a bit," admitted the navy man. "Still, this isn't a hurricane. A pretty strong gale, but not a hurricane."

"Are we gonna make it to Key West?" asked Hornbaker. Jerry was looking a bit green. Quite a few of the army crewmen were bent over railings and looking worse. Andrew had discovered the trick on earlier voyages to stare straight out at the horizon when he was feeling queasy - except today there was no horizon.

"We ought to see the lighthouse any time now."

"So we're not in any danger?" demanded Andrew. "The ships are holding up?"

"Can't speak for the others, but this bucket is doing okay. A few leaks, but nothing to worry about. Once we're in the anchorage, we'll be fine."

"And we should be there soon?"

"An hour or two, probably. The approach is going to be a bit tricky, the anchorage was chosen more with coming from the Atlantic in mind, but it should be okay." Broadt, nodded to them and then went up the ladder to the swaying observation platform as if it wasn't moving at all. Andrew and Hornbaker retreated inside the pilot house for a while to escape the rain and spray, but the enclosed space made their nausea worse and they soon went back out into the wind and water.

Suddenly, there was a shout from above and a horn blast from *Monodnock*. They looked around and spotted a dim light off to the north. It appeared and disappeared on a regular rhythm and they assumed it was the lighthouse Broadt had spoken of. And then, bit by bit, a shoreline appeared, although it was just a slightly darker streak of gray in the gloom. It grew more distinct as the blinking light slowly passed to the east.

A few minutes later, Broadt came back down the ladder. He grinned and pointed. "We're here. Told you we'd be all right."

"But where's the anchorage?"

"We'll be rounding the point in a little bit. You can just make out Fort Zachary Taylor over there. Then it's north a few miles and around another point, and we'll be there. Not an enclosed harbor like Charleston, you understand, but a safe anchorage."

He stayed with them as they, oh so slowly, made the turn to the north. The wind and seas seemed worse than ever there and Broadt confirmed that the islands had given them a little shelter which was now lost, but he seemed unconcerned. It was nearly another hour before they saw the second point. Even then they had to claw their way north another mile against wind and waves before they could make their turn. Then, with the weather behind them, they made what seemed like a mad rush into the lee behind the island into the much calmer waters of the anchorage.

The visibility improved a bit and Andrew breathed easier when he spotted three of the other ironclads and their tows and escorts already there. *Monodnock* stopped her engines and dropped anchor. *Albuquerque* followed suit and sat there rolling easily. Signal lamps started blinking, and shortly they received a message that the other ironclads were *Omaha*, *Tulsa*, and *Springfield*.

"I hope *Billings* and *Sioux Falls* are all right," said Andrew.

"They'll be along," said Broadt, and within a half hour, Billings indeed entered the anchorage. Noon came and Andrew was feeling well enough to go down to the galley and get some food. He'd eaten nothing since dinner the previous evening.

But he'd barely started on a sandwich when he heard a faint wailing from outside. It went on and on, and after a few minutes, his curiosity overwhelmed his hunger and he went back out on deck. Broadt was there, and this time there wasn't any trace of good humor on his face. He was leaning into the wind, looking northwest with his head cocked.

Outside, Andrew recognized the sound: a ship's steam whistle. Normally they came in short toots, but this one was continuous. Then, it was abruptly silenced and over the roar of the wind and seas came a low rumble which changed to a screech of metal before fading away.

"That... that surely can't be good," gasped Andrew.

"No," said Broadt, his face grim. "No it can't."

Nor was it. By late afternoon, the storm dwindled and died with amazing swiftness, and a few rays of sun peeked through the shredding clouds. Shortly, a steam launch put off from the *Olympia* and swung by *Albuquerque* to pick up Andrew. General Clopton and the commodore were aboard and the boat chugged out around the point. It didn't take long to see what had made that ominous noise.

The ship towing *Sioux Falls* had lost power just a mile from safety and been thrown up on the shore by the waves. She lay there, her back broken, like a dead leviathan. Amazingly, there had been no loss of life. Even more amazingly, *Sioux Falls* had also survived somehow. With its puny propeller, there had been no hope of fighting the seas, so its commander had turned directly toward shore. The moment its tracks touched bottom, he had jettisoned the flotation modules and lurched onto the shore with only minor damage. The navy men seemed to think it little short of a miracle.

"Miracle or not, it's still stuck here," said Clopton. It was true, the flotation modules had been smashed to bits on the rocks and there wasn't another set this side of Philadelphia. "Well, we aren't going to wait. Can we get going again in the morning, Commodore?"

The naval commander nodded. "Everyone else is in good shape. By morning, the storm should be completely out of our path and we can make a straight run to New Orleans. But for this evening, I'd be pleased if you and your staff could join me for dinner on *Olympia*."

After days of the simple fare offered by *Albuquerque*'s small galley, Andrew was more than willing to accept the invitation. But the launch took them straight back to *Olympia* and he was conscious of his still slightly damp service uniform. He hadn't brought a full dress uniform, but still...

Olympia was an old ship and had been one of the navy's first modern all-steel vessels. As such, she was a transition from the earlier ships. While she mounted her main guns in turrets fore and aft, her secondary guns were in an open gun deck reminiscent of those found on the old wooden ships. The commodore's cabin, along with the other officers', were also on this deck and several of the cabins had been temporarily dismantled to make room for the dinner. White-gloved steward guided Andrew to his chair.

The commodore was naturally at the head of the table with Clopton on his right and *Olympia*'s skipper on his left. The navy officer ran down one side of the table and the army on the other. Andrew sat next to Clopton, but directly across from him was an officer he'd never seen before, and with a start he realized what sort of a uniform he was wearing.

"Oh yes, I almost forgot," said the Commodore. "Let me introduce you all to Major Tom Bridges. He just arrived aboard a few hours ago. Came down from Washington to observe your crazy ironclads. He's British, as you can see, and we've been ordered to extend him every courtesy." Everyone rendered greetings and the tall, red-cheeked, and mustachioed man smiled and nodded to one and all.

"Thank you, sir," he said, his accent very distinct. "I spent a few months observing one of your cavalry units out west. I *thought* I'd be getting some leave back home, but when we found out that your new war machines are going to see action soon, I was ordered here. I look forward to working with you, General Clopton."

Clopton nodded, but didn't look too pleased. "I hope you find your stay enlightening, Major. But I'm afraid there won't be any room on Springfield where I'll have my headquarters. In any case, Comstock here knows more about these contraptions than anyone. You can accompany him."

Andrew was taken back, but Bridges grinned and reached across the table extending his hand. "Splendid! I couldn't be more pleased to serve with you, Colonel!"

There wasn't anything to do but to shake his hand. "Uh, glad to have you with us, Major."

* * * * *

June, 1912, Memphis, Tennessee

Becca Harding peered out over the top of the city wall and across the Mississippi. The sun wasn't quite up yet and there was a thin mist clinging to the river and the shore beyond. The enemy was over there somewhere. Everyone said that they were coming, coming to attack Memphis. The whole city was in a frenzy, with rumors of every sort flying as fast as loose tongues could spread them. Troops were moving into and through the city in large numbers. Even this early in the morning, she could see a column marching across the bridge into West Memphis. Train loads and ship loads of supplies and ammunition were pouring in. And people were leaving, too. The very young and the old were being moved out, by train and by boat. Others were slipping out, by horse or motor car. Becca turned and looked down from the wall and frowned at the campsite of the Memphis Women's Volunteer Sharpshooters.

It was nearly empty.

The word had come down three days ago that all of the local militia units were being mobilized to defend the city. There had been an initial wave of excitement among the women, and grand plans were made and the whole company assembled at the Oswald mansion. They had paraded through the streets to their assigned spot by the river. Becca had felt a thrill of pride to march as their lieutenant, and a surprising number of people came out to wave and give them a cheer.

But it had been a long march, and before they were halfway to their designated spot, Mrs. Oswald had pleaded exhaustion and went back to ride in the carriage which had been following the company, driven by one of her servants. Several other women had soon joined her, and by the time they got to the river, the company had dissolved into a long stream of stragglers - a few even gave up and went home before they got there.

They had pitched camp - fine new canvas tents, also provided by the Oswalds - in the muddy field which had once been a city park, amidst the equipment and supplies of the artillerymen who manned the big guns along the walls, and right next to the other - male - militia unit they were assigned to work with. Sergeant Leo Polk Smith, who she'd met earlier, had strolled over, looking just as amused as before, to make some suggestions on how to arrange things, and he'd been followed by a few dozen of his fellow militiamen. They'd laughed, hooted, and some made some very rude remarks, until one of their officers came over and herded them back where they belonged. That same officer had then posted sentries to make sure they stayed where they belonged.

By that time, many of the women were having second thoughts about the whole thing, and nearly half of them went to sleep in their own homes despite the fact that the tents were what an officer would normally rate with a cot and everything. A number of them had not come back the next morning.

Becca wondered if there would be anyone at all here today.

The artillerymen were up and so were the other militiamen, building fires and boiling coffee. It was an utterly familiar routine to Becca, and she moved to one of the ladders to climb down to ground level to get her own coffee started. A few of the gunners nodded or said good morning. None of them treated her as an officer, but at least they were treating her like a lady. Her hand brushed the lump in her pocket. She still carried the revolver Miss Chumley had given her back at Gallup, almost three years ago.

Even though it wasn't proper work for an officer, she stopped at a pile of shattered lumber which had once been a house before it was demolished to make way for the new walls. The soldiers were using it for firewood and she scooped up an armload. One of the campfires still had a few smoldering embers and she managed to coax it back to life and get a coffee pot hung over it.

By then, there were some moans and groans coming from a few of the tents, so she knew she wouldn't be totally alone. Of course, she wouldn't have been completely alone even if every last sharpshooter had deserted. She looked over to where Ninny was picketed and smiled. She'd managed to spirit her horse away from the hospital after she'd told Miss Chumley that she was leaving to join the sharpshooters full time. It hadn't been an easy decision, and she was wondering if she'd made a mistake. Chumley hadn't been happy, but she had no real means to stop her from leaving as all the nurses were volunteers and Becca had never signed any papers or sworn any oaths. She had told Becca that she could still come back if she wanted to.

A shout from across the way caught her attention. Sergeant Leo Smith was calling his own company together for morning roll call. She had been copying Smith's actions whenever possible in running the sharpshooters, so she got up from the fire and walked down the rows of tents, whacking the poles with a stick. "All right! Up and at 'em, girls! Wake up! Get up! On the street for roll call!"

More moans and groans answered her, but eventually about two dozen women were lined up in front of the tents. It was more than Becca had expected, but still pretty disappointing. The woman who was supposed to be the company first sergeant was among the missing, so she appointed Sarah Halberstam, one the most reliable people in the group, to fill in. She read off the roll, dutifully repeating the names of the absent twice, and then marking them as 'not present'. When she was finished, she saluted Becca and said: "Twenty-five present for duty, Lieutenant."

Becca returned the salute. "Thank you, Sergeant. Get the girls to breakfast. We'll police the camp afterward and then do some drill."

"Yes, m-ma'am." Halberstam, nearly twice her age, looked about as comfortable *ma'aming* her as Becca felt being *ma'amed*, and after a few seconds, they both grinned.

"Takes some gettin' used to, doesn't it?"

"You're doing fine, Becca. It's not easy for any of us, I guess."

"Yeah. But make sure the girls who are still here know how proud I am of 'em, okay?"

"The others will be back. Well, some of them, I'm sure." Halberstam smiled, but she couldn't keep the doubt out of her eyes. She nodded and went back to the rest to get breakfast cooking. At least they had some fresh stuff and weren't depending on hard tack and salted pork.

Becca went back to her own tent and washed her face with some water out of her canteen. Camping out seemed like second nature to her. As a child on the ranch, she'd done it all the time. Then there was the long months during the siege of the Martian fortress at Gallup. But most of the women in the sharpshooters were upper class ladies from Memphis' finest families. They'd lived in nice houses with servants their whole lives. This must seem like a real hardship to most of them. It was hard to blame them for slipping back home at night to sleep in a soft bed.

She was pleased that nearly a dozen of them did return before breakfast was over. They looked a little sheepish, but she decided not to make an issue of it. If she did, they might not come back tomorrow. The fact of the matter was that she had no real authority over them at all. They could walk away any time they wanted to. *Just like I walked away from the hospital.* That was a thought which was intruding more and more lately. She had left a job where she was undeniably doing good to take another job where she might well not do any good at all. Was her obsession about fighting just a childish tantrum? She'd get back to that question - after the battle.

She was just about to order the company to fall in when a carriage clattered up. She recognized it and the driver; they came from the Oswald mansion. Was Theodora coming today? She walked over to the carriage with Sarah Halberstam, but as she got closer, she saw that the driver, an elderly colored man named Moses, was alone.

"Hi, Mo," she said. "What brings you here?"

Moses climbed down from the carriage. The usually jovial man didn't look happy. "Mornin' Miz Becca," he said. "Got a message from

Missus Oswald."

"Oh? What is it?"

"Well, she an' Mister Oswald took out real early this morning, fore it was even light, in their motor car. Took all sorts of bags and boxes with 'em. Wouldn't say where's they were goin', neither. But the Missus told me to tell you that she..." he hesitated as if recalling her exact words. "She has the... ut-most... con-fi-dence in your... ability to command the sharpshooters."

"Oh," said Becca. "I see. I guess... I guess she's not comin' back?"

"Didn't look that way to me, no ma'am," said Mo.

"Oh. Well, thank you for tellin' me, Mo. What are you goin' to do now?"

"Don't rightly know, Miz. They locked the house up tight a'fore they left. 'Cept the servant's quarters, of course. Guess I'll go back there an' see what happens."

"You're welcome to stay and help out here, if you want, Mo."

"Could I?" Mo's expression brightened. "The carriage would be good for haulin' stuff. An' I kin take care of your horse, too, Miz Becca."

"That would be fine, Mo. I can't offer you no pay, but you can eat our chow."

"Thank you, Miz! No pay is fine. I know how to shoot a rifle, too! If you can spare me one, I'll get me a Martian!"

Becca laughed. "I think we can scare one up for you, Mo. Why don't you park the carriage over there."

Mo bobbed his head and got back aboard the vehicle.

Becca looked at Sarah and the older woman was smiling. "Well, looks like you are in charge, Becca. Everyone knew that was the case all along. But now it's official, Lieutenant!"

* * * * *

Cycle 597, 845.2, East of Holdfast 32-4

Qetjnegartis maneuvered its fighting machine between the tall vertical columns of the native vegetation. It was almost completely dark beneath the dense foliage and it had to set the light-amplification on the vision pick-ups to nearly the maximum. The growths were of considerable height, and the main columns of the bigger ones were thick and strong enough to even block a fighting machine. In places where they grew closely together, it was impossible to find a path. Of course, it could simply use the heat ray to burn a way through, but the flames and smoke that would produce would be revealing - and that was to be avoided at all cost.

The long-planned attack was about to be launched and surprise was essential. For the last ten days, a screen of the smaller scouting war machines had spread out from the holdfast, driving back the prey-creature patrols. This would no doubt alert the enemy that something was going to happen soon, but there was no avoiding that, and indeed it could well prove to be an advantage - as long as they did not realize just what was about to happen.

The enemy's air patrols were a more serious problem. Every day in which the atmospheric conditions were not unfavorable, the prey-creature flying machines were in the air, sweeping across the landscape. Fortunately, they did not fly at night. The prey-creatures could not see well in the dark, and while they had started using artificial means of illumination on the battlefield, their flying machines had rarely been encountered after nightfall.

Qetjnegartis had taken advantage of this to move its forces. The areas of dense vegetation, usually an annoying hindrance to movement, were now proving valuable. The growths were tall enough to conceal a fighting machine, and this particular area was now concealing almost two hundred of them. Another area a score of *telequel* to the north held a like number. Over a thousand of the new drones accompanied each group along with the novel... constructs devised by Ixmaderna. A great deal - far too much in Qetjnegartis' judgment - was being staked on the success of these untested things. But there seemed little other choice. The attack must be launched and the river must be crossed.

It reached the main gathering point of the battlegroup commanders. Most of the commanders were older clan members who arrived in the second or third wave of transports, but a few were from the first of the buds to be created here on the target world. Qetjnegartis' own bud, Davnitargus, was in command of Battlegroup 32-8.

"The operation begins tonight," it announced. "Tanbradjus will lead the two battlegroups and the reserve fighting machines which will create the diversionary attack. This is beginning as we speak. We will remain here, out of sight until tomorrow night, when we shall commence the river crossing. Are there any questions?"

"Do you have any estimates on how difficult the physical passage of the river will be, Commander?" asked Gandgenar, commander of Battlegroup 32-12. "Our success will depend much on that."

"You are correct. Unfortunately, we have had no way to test the river bottom in the crossing area for fear that this will give away our intentions. Tests in other locations indicate that the conditions can vary significantly, so we will only know when we make the attempt. This is far from ideal, I know, but there is no other practical alternative. But whatever conditions we encounter, we must make every effort to overcome them and cross the river."

"I understand. We will not fail you, Commander."

There were no other questions. The plan had been worked out in detail, and they had all studied it. "Very well. For now we wait."

* * * * *

June, 1912, near Earle, Arkansas

"They're comin' for sure, Captain! Thick as fleas on a dog's back!"

Captain Frank Dolfen looked at the face of the gasping scout in the light of a lantern.

"You're sure? It's not just another screen of their scouts?"

"No sir. There's enough moonlight to see by and there were swarms of 'em behind the scouts. Couldn't count 'em all, but three or four dozen at least!"

"And coming this way?"

"Coming this way fast, sir! Can't be more'n four or five miles off now!"

Dolfen nodded grimly. They'd been expecting this for days. The 5th Cavalry and two other regiments of the 1st Cavalry Division had been spread out to the west of Memphis to give warning of the impending Martian attack. They'd been skirmishing with the enemy scout machines, on and off, for nearly a week. There had been too many of them to engage in a pitched battle, and they'd been careful enough not allow any ambushes of smaller groups. So the cavalry had been forced back mile by mile until they were less than twenty miles from West Memphis. If this new report was correct, the attack would happen very soon.

"All right," he said, turning to his second in command. "Get the men up and ready to move. Get a messenger off to the colonel and another one straight back to headquarters. Tell them they're coming."

Chapter Fourteen

July, 1912, Memphis, Tennessee

"**H**oly cow! Wouldja lookit that!"

Rebecca Harding stared out from the city walls with hundreds of other people. The dark western sky was lit up with a continuous flickering glow. Closer at hand, artillery was blasting away, adding to the flashes and producing a noise it was hard to hear over. Leo Polk Smith was standing next to her and seemed to think the tremendous display of firepower was some sort of Independence Day celebration come three days early.

She had to admit it was impressive and rivaled, or maybe even exceeded, the one she'd seen back at Gallup. She tried not to think about how that one had ended up. But things were going to be different this time. That time at Gallup, the army had been attacking the Martian stronghold, and just when it seemed like victory was in reach, a new enemy force had arrived by surprise and smashed into the rear area, destroying the artillery and throwing the army into confusion. That couldn't happen this time. The enemy was attacking the defenses of West Memphis across the mile-wide Mississippi. They had attacked the previous night and had been probing and probing all through the day, and now night had fallen again. The guns in the defenses, on the ships in the river, and the long range guns on the eastern shore had hammered back, hopefully hurting the Martians.

Reinforcements had been streaming across the bridge into West Memphis all day. There had been rumors that the Women's Sharpshooters would be ordered across to join them, but Becca refused to believe that. Few people knew they even existed and fewer would deliberately put them in harm's way. She'd always known the sharpshooters would be keep in reserve and never be committed except as an absolute last resort. Before it had gotten dark, she'd seen some ambulances crossing the bridge in the opposite direction as the marching troops. They were bringing back wounded. Maybe she should have stayed at the hospital…

"Do… do you think the Martians will make it over here?"

Rebecca looked and saw that Abigail LaPlace had come up next to her. Abigail was the youngest of the sharpshooters, a few months younger than Becca. She was still amazed that her parents were allowing her to do this.

"Doesn't look like it," said Leo Smith, overhearing. "They've been attackin' all day and don't seem to be makin' much progress."

"Can't tell nothin' from that," said Becca. "They're just probing us. Testin' the strength of the defenses and locating our artillery. They did that at Albuquerque. Then they hit us all at once when it got dark. They might be fixin' to do that same thing here tonight."

Smith jerked his head back, face skeptical in the flickering light. "How d'you know all that?"

"I was there." It wasn't exactly the truth, she'd been further north in Santa Fe, but she had heard what happened from the other soldiers during the retreat. Smith snorted, shook his head, and turned away. He clearly didn't believe her, but she didn't care. She turned back to Abigail. The girl was in uniform and carrying her rifle but...

"Where's your dust mask, Private?"

"I... I left it back in my tent, ma'am."

"If the enemy is close by, never go without carrying it. I gave orders about that."

"Sorry, ma'am. But it's heavy and the Martians are way over there and..."

"That's no excuse. They move fast and they don't always give any warning. We have to always be ready." Becca looked out across the river. "This fight has just begun."

* * * * *

July, 1912, West Memphis, Arkansas

"We will move out in one hour. We'll stay as close to the river as we can until we're past them, then we will turn northwest and head toward Clarkdale. Keep your advanced guard and flankers as close to your column as you safely can. We are to avoid all contact. It shouldn't be too hard, the enemy doesn't like our ships on the river and they've pulled in that flank. Once we reach Clarkdale, we'll send out scouts and see what we can see."

The assembled officers of the 5th Cavalry looked at Colonel Schumacher and listened gravely to his orders. The colonel had to almost shout to be heard above the nearby guns.

"What's our objective, sir?" asked Frank Dolfen. "The men and horses are still pretty tired." They'd been sparring with the Martian scouts for nearly a week and had finally fallen back inside the defenses of West Memphis. They were looking forward to a chance to rest a bit.

"Our objective?" replied Schumacher. He smiled. "Why, Frank, you shouldn't need to ask. The generals are hoping we can pull off the same miracle as we did at Little Rock: find the enemy's reserve tripods and destroy them. They're sending us and the 9th out to the north and the two regiments in the other brigade out to the south with the same mission."

The other officers began murmuring. One of them said: "Hopefully we can avoid blowing ourselves up this time, sir."

"Yes, let's extend every effort to avoiding that. But that is our mission and we will carry it out. Return to your commands and get them ready, gentlemen. That's all."

They all saluted Schumacher and he returned it. Then they dispersed. Frank was just nearing the area where his squadron was camped when the bugles started ringing out down the line sounding the assembly. If it had not been for the roar of the artillery, he was quite sure the bugles would have been answered by the moans and curses of the men, awakened from the first sound sleep they'd had in a week. The fact that they'd been able to sleep only a quarter mile behind the front lines in the middle of a battle showed how tired they were.

Tired or not, they got up. Dolfen passed on the orders to his own officers and in a commendably short time the troops commanders were reporting ready. Normally it would have taken longer in the dark, but there was an almost constant light from the flares and star shells the gunners were sending up. They were mostly a few miles away, but they were so intense they lit up the whole area brighter than a full moon. He hoped it wouldn't give them away to the Martians when they moved out.

There were the inevitable delays getting two regiments ready to move, but in only a little longer than the hour the colonel had given them, they were on their way. The 5th was leading the column, and as 1st Squadron, Frank's men were leading the 5th. He could tell they were tired by the general lack of grumbling, but they were veterans and knew they had a job to do. He was still rather appalled by the number of men in A Troop carrying those damn rocket lances - long poles with stovepipe rockets fixed to the end of them. They were bloody suicide weapons and everyone knew it. Even a few of the motorcycle riders in B Troop were carrying them now, although the bikes with sidecars tended to have the passenger carrying an actual stovepipe launcher if they could get one. The launchers were still in short supply, but the army, in its infinite wisdom, was shipping twenty rockets with each launcher; as if there was any hope that a man would survive long enough to fire more than three or four of the things.

They slowly made their way down streets already packed with troops and wagons. The local commander, General MacArthur, had been pouring troops across the bridge into West Memphis all day. Dolfen had been based in this area for months, and they'd been told that the plan was that West Memphis would not be heavily defended in the event of a major attack; but it sure seemed like MacArthur was planning to hold the place now. Dolfen approved: they'd already given up too much ground. Still, he wondered where all these troops were coming from.

A staff officer had been assigned to show them the route out of town, and at first Dolfen wondered if the young man was lost, because he seemed to be leading them almost due east; but then he saw there was a method to his madness. The east side of West Memphis was protected from flooding by a stout levee, and the top was flat and wide enough for a column of cavalry. He led them up on to it and turned north. This let them pass through the defensive works with no trouble, the river on their right and the Martians - hopefully - well off to their left.

As promised, there were numerous warships on the river firing at the enemy, and their heavy guns did seem to be keeping the Martians away. Dolfen sent his scouts ahead, warning them not to go too far. He was a bit worried about being silhouetted on top of the levee, but a quick look at the ground on either side convinced him this was the only practical route. So they rode north with a grandstand view of the battle to the west.

The artillery was firing at a steady pace, and from time to time there would be a salvo from a ship on the river. He could see explosions where the shells hit and sometimes a tripod would be lit up, but they were too far off to tell if any damage was being done. Every now and then they'd see a heat ray being fired, but it looked as though the enemy was still just probing the defense lines. The main attack was still to come. Dolfen was actually glad to be out of there, now that he thought about it. A city fight was no place for cavalry.

They rode a few miles and got to the place where they were supposed to turn more to the west and head for the town of Clarkdale, but the scouts came back and reported that there was a solid line of enemy tripods blocking the path in that direction. "There's one of them bastards every four or five hundred yards across the line of march," said a sergeant. "No way we'll get past 'em without a fight, sir." Dolfen reported this to Colonel Schumacher.

"There's no point in us getting ourselves into a pitched battle here," he said. "Is the way along the levee still open, Frank?"

"Seems to be, sir. Although it swings in a loop off to the east, following the river."

"Well, so be it. We'll take a wider route up to Gilmore and see if we can get into their rear from there."

"That's gonna take a while. Might be dawn before we get there, sir."

"I know. We'll have to pick up the pace. Get them moving, Captain."

"Yes, sir." He gave the orders and the column lurched into motion again. The levee actually turned away from the direction they wanted to go for a mile or so, but then swung back to the northwest. It was also getting lower and lower and eventually stopped altogether. There was still a dirt road following the river, but it was overgrown and clearly hadn't been used for a while. Frank hoped it wouldn't just lead them into a swamp. Their staff officer had disappeared an hour earlier and he had no one familiar with the area. Except for the remains of one smashed tripod - killed by the navy apparently - they had left the battle behind. While they could still hear it, they were getting no light from the star shells anymore and it was very dark under the trees which lined the road.

It was about one in the morning when by dead reckoning they turned away from the river and headed for Gilmore. They broke out of the trees and found that the moon, just two days past the full, was now overhead and providing enough light to see by. They advanced a mile over abandoned fields and eventually stumbled on a road which appeared to be going the way they wanted. The battle was just a rumble now, and the noise from the motorcycles and armored cars seemed very loud in the warm, still night air.

The land sloped slightly upward away from the Mississippi. Another mile or two and it would flatten out with unobstructed views for miles. Once it was light, maybe they could get some aircraft spotting for them. They'd been a big help during the skirmishing in the previous week, although no attacks had been permitted. Apparently they were saving them for the...

"Captain! Captain Dolfen! Rider coming in!"

The shout wasn't loud, but it still made him flinch. He looked ahead and a man on a horse was galloping down the road as fast as the beast could carry him. Damn, they must have run into another Martian scout. The bastards were being a lot more careful after what had happened at Little Rock. Could they get around it somehow? If they lost the element of surprise...

"Martians! Martians, Captain!" gasped the man. As he reined in his horse, Dolfen saw that it was Sergeant Findley, one of the best scouts in the regiment. "A whole passel of 'em!"

"What? How many? Where?"

"Hundreds! Just the other side of that high ground! Hundreds of them heading east!"

"Get hold of yourself, man! Are you sure?"

"'Course I'm sure! They ain't a mile off and I can see 'em in the moonlight!"

Good God! Another attack force? Where had it come from? And where was it going? "Come on, show me!" The scout turned his horse around and they both headed back the way he'd just come. Dolfen shouted back at Lieutenant Lynnbrooke: "Halt the column! Get the colonel up here!"

Dolfen leaned forward and used one hand to hold his hat on as they galloped to the higher ground. Even before they reached the top, he could see the heads of the tall war machines bobbing along in the distance. The man had been right: there were a lot of them.

A lot of them.

He halted his horse and took in the horrifying sight. More tripods than he'd ever seen at once before. A hundred at least and maybe more, all striding from left to right across his path. Moonlight reflected off their skins like off the water in a flowing stream. The red lights which normally glowed from the middle of their 'faces' were all dark for some reason. Their thin, metal legs were moving with that bizarre, yet rapid gait that always gave him chills. It looked like some metal forest on the march. And all around the machines' legs...

"Are those the spider-machines they've been talking about?" whispered Findley.

"Must be," said Dolfen. They'd heard a lot of stories about them, but this was the first time he'd actually seen them. There looked to be hundreds and hundreds of them moving with the bigger machines.

"Dear Lord! There are more of 'em! Look, sir!" The trooper pointed and Dolfen saw that beyond the horde in front of him, there was another dark and glittering mass on a rise in the ground another mile or so off to the north.

"My God," gasped Dolfen. "This is bad, really bad."

"What's that noise, sir? That other noise?"

Dolfen cocked his head and heard what the man was asking about: a hissing, grinding sound like something big being dragged along the ground. He fumbled out his binoculars and looked. It was hard to see much, even with the moonlight, but after a moment he realized that broad rectangular shapes were being pulled by some of the tripods using cables. At first he couldn't grasp what they were but then it suddenly came to him.

"Boats! Damn, they've got boats!"

"To get across the river?"

"What else? We need to warn headquarters! Come on!" They turned their horses around and galloped back down the hill to where the head of the column had halted. As he'd hoped, Colonel Schumacher was there.

"What have we got, Frank?" he asked.

"Trouble, sir! Big trouble! There's two or three hundred tripods and God knows how many of those spider-machines, and they are all heading toward the river and they've got boats!"

"Boats?"

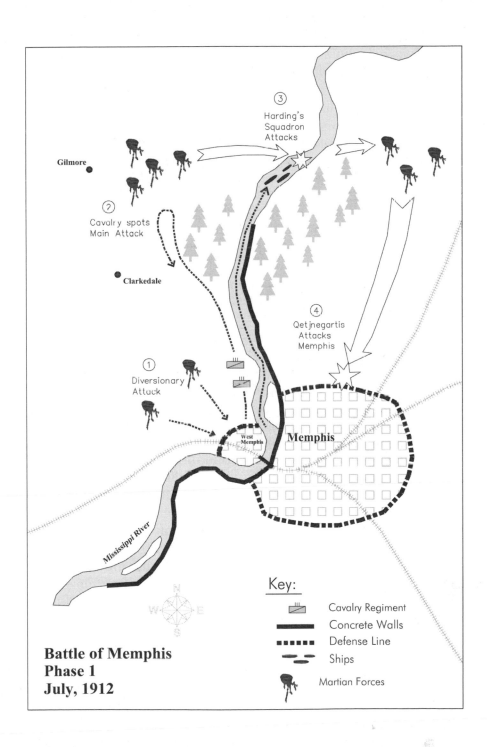

Gilmore

③ Harding's Squadron Attacks

② Cavalry spots Main Attack

Clarkedale

④ Qetjnegartis Attacks Memphis

① Diversionary Attack

West Memphis

Memphis

Mississippi River

Key:

Cavalry Regiment

Concrete Walls

Defense Line

Ships

Martian Forces

**Battle of Memphis
Phase 1
July, 1912**

"Boats or rafts of some kind. They're dragging them along. Sir! They mean to cross the river north of the city!"

"You're right. No other possibility. We need to let MacArthur know. Is there a radio in one of your armored cars?"

"Yes, sir! Right back there."

"Sir," said Schumacher's adjutant, "we transmit this close to them, they'll hear for sure. They'll come after us and we can't fight three hundred tripods!"

"No choice, this can't wait," said the colonel. "Get that message off, Frank. The rest of you, get the column turned around and prepare for a fighting withdrawal!"

* * * * *

Cycle 597, 845.2, West of River 3-1

"Commander, we have intercepted an enemy transmission. It is very close by. Two or three *telequel* to the south."

Qetjnegartis checked its own sensors and saw that it was true. "It is likely that we have been spotted. Tanbradjus 's forces were to have swept this area clear."

"It is a large battle area, Commander," replied the subordinate. "It is difficult to guard every approach and..."

"Enough! We must deal with the reality. Send one group to investigate and make sure no large force is preparing to attack. The rest of us will push on to the river with all speed. We must get across before they can shift forces or their watercraft can interfere."

* * * * *

July, 1912, Memphis, Tennessee

The pounding on his cabin door yanked Drew Harding out of the first sound sleep he'd had in two days. "What? What now?" he snarled.

"Sir! Sir!" came a muffled voice he recognized as belonging to Lieutenant Alby Hinsworth. "Signal from the flag, sir! We need to get moving!"

Not quite awake, Drew sat up and swung his legs out of the bunk. "Move? Where?"

"Up river! There's word the Martians are trying to cross!"

Fully awake now, Drew grabbed his shoes and was grateful he hadn't bothered to undress. "Just us, or the whole—for God's sake open the door so I can talk to you!" The door swung open and Hinsworth looked in. "Just us or the whole squadron?"

"The whole squadron, sir! Commodore Rush wants us up there right away. Engage and report the situation. I've ordered full steam in ten minutes and we're getting ready to raise anchor."

"Good man!" Drew finished with his shoes, grabbed his coat and hat, and went out the door. It was still dark except for the gun flashes on the western shore. "What's the time?"

"A bit after three, sir." Drew was glad Hinsworth wasn't one of those who clung to the traditional navy practice of using 'bells' to tell time. Good, two hours and it would start to get light.

They reached the bridge and a signal rating was there with a scrap of paper. "Sir, *Evansville*, *Vanceberg*, *Manchester*, and *Louisville Star* have all acknowledged the order to move out. No reply from *Dixie Dancer*."

It didn't surprise him. The first three were navy gunboats and the Louisville Star, one of the modified riverboats, had a good skipper. But *Dixie Dancer* was nearly useless, both the ship itself and the man in command. Drew wasn't going to worry about whether they came along or not.

He took up his binoculars and scanned the river for nearby traffic. The commodore had divided his forces into a number of squadrons which he had been rotating into and out of action during the attack so the army would have continuous support. Drew's squadron had been in twice and he'd hoped to be able to rest his men - and himself - for a few more hours before going in again. But it was not to be.

His squadron had been anchored near the eastern shore to keep them out of the way, and as far as he could tell, the route up river was clear. He turned to Hinsworth. "Signal *Evansville* to take the lead, we'll follow and then the rest. Did the commodore say how far north the enemy is?"

"No, sir. Just that they were crossing north of here."

"Well, they can't be crossing along the stretch where they've built the concrete walls. We'd see the flashes from the guns if they were. So they have to be at least ten or twelve miles up river. That gives us a while. Get under way, but don't order battle stations just yet. Tell the galley to feed the men as soon as possible."

"Yes, sir."

The anchor was raised and *Santa Fe* started moving. They slipped in a cable length behind *Evansville* and the engines were put full ahead. Going against the current, they could only do ten or eleven knots. It would be at least an hour or so before they could expect to run into the enemy. Drew rubbed the sleep out of his eyes and gratefully accepted a mug of coffee and a sandwich.

The battle around West Memphis was still going on, but after a half hour, he started seeing flashes from the north - almost dead ahead.

Shortly after that, some of the big guns along the concrete walls on the eastern shore started firing, although he couldn't tell at what.

"Mr. Hinsworth, get the men to battle stations, clear the ship for action."

"Yes, sir!" The alarm gong rang out and the crew hurried to their posts. A rating appeared to hand Drew his life-jacket, helmet, and anti-dust gear. It was a warm, humid night, but he didn't hesitate to put them on. Reports quickly came back that all stations were manned and ready. His crew were veterans now.

The river was in a long shallow curve to the right, and Drew couldn't see that far ahead due to a thick forest on the eastern shore beyond the line of walls. But the flashes of guns flickered above the trees and the sound of explosions could now be heard. As he watched, a star shell burst in the distance and it was followed by a pair of rocket flares. Somewhere around the bend there was fighting.

"Signal *Evansville* to let us catch up. We'll go in in pairs. Have the others do the same. Use the signal light." The orders were given and the leading gunboat slowed to let *Santa Fe* draw abreast of her on the right. *Vanceberg* and *Manchester* were pairing up astern, and to his surprise he saw a shape which had to have been *Dixie Dancer* closing in on *Louisville Star*.

"Shall I send a message to the commodore?" asked Hinsworth.

"Let's wait until we have a better idea what's going on. This could just be a feint to draw our forces away from Memphis."

"Yes, sir."

But minute by minute he became convinced it was no feint. The flashes grew brighter and more numerous, and the roar of explosions even drowned out the rumble from the West Memphis fight, now ten miles astern. Finally, the river straightened out and he could look ahead.

"Good Lord, sir," said Hinsworth. "Look!"

Drew was looking. The river appeared to be filled with dark shapes and the western bank was a mass of flame and smoke. Geysers of water leapt up out of the river, and heat rays stabbed out from the shapes against the shore. He raised his binoculars and the shapes became distinct: tripods. A lot of them. Sweeping his view from shore to shore he saw that there were some tripods already climbing out of the water on the east side. There were no concrete walls here, just trenches. More tripods were wading into the river from the western shore, a seemingly endless horde, their metal skins gleaming in the light of the flares.

"Signal the commodore," said Drew. "Tell him that the enemy is crossing the river in great strength and that we need immediate reinforcements."

"Yes, sir!" said Hinsworth, who dashed away.

The squadron was still advancing at full steam and the range was closing quickly. What to do? Their guns outranged the enemy heat rays, so it would make sense to hang back—at least until reinforcements arrived. Charging right into that mass of tripods would not be a good idea. He turned to a signal rating and said: "Order to squadron. Hold position here and commence firing."

* * * * *

Cycle 597, 845.2, River 3-1

Qetjnegartis stood its machine on the western shore of the river and observed the situation with satisfaction. Despite being discovered by the enemy prior to launching the attack, it was clear that at least some measure of surprise had been achieved. No prey-creature water craft had been waiting and the defenses on the far shore, while substantial, were not proving to be especially formidable. This spot had been chosen because none of the cast stone walls had yet been erected, although there were some not far to the south whose weapons were within range.

Crossing the river itself was proving difficult, but not as bad as feared. A number of fighting machines had become immobilized in the soft bottom, and two had been swept away by the flowing water. But most were crossing with only minor problems. And the vessels Ixmaderna had designed were proving entirely suitable for transporting the drones across the river. Floating vessels had not been used on the Homeworld for many thousands of centuries, since the canals had dried up, but the principle was still understood. A hollow container made of light materials would, along with its cargo, displace a sufficient mass of liquid to balance the pull of gravity. Towed by a fighting machine, the vessel could transport the drones across the water safely.

Some of them had already reached the far shore and were in amongst the defenders there. The prey-creatures were fighting fiercely, but they did not seem to have substantial reserves and had only a few of the armored fighting machines. It appeared as though the feint against the city's outer defenses to the south had been successful in deceiving the enemy about the location of the main attack.

"Commander, enemy water vessels are approaching from the south," communicated a subordinate.

Qetjnegartis turned its attention in that direction and saw that six vessels had appeared from around a bend in the river. They were coming directly toward the crossing, but then turned slightly, slowed, and began firing with their large projectile throwers. Explosions began to erupt in the water, some dangerously close to the fighting machines. But there were only six of the vessels. Surely not a great threat.

"Proceed with the crossing," it commanded. "Ignore those vessels unless they come closer. Get across, destroy the defenders there, and push inland with all speed. We need to strike the defenses around the city before the enemy can redeploy."

Following its own command, Qetjnegartis moved its machine down the bank and into the water.

* * * * *

July, 1912, north of Memphis, Tennessee

"The commodore says that help is on the way. Engage the enemy at your discretion, sir," said Ensign Alby Hinsworth.

"Very well," said Drew Harding. My discretion! Yeah, right! He was engaging the enemy. With long range fire. But he couldn't tell if he was doing anything. There seemed to be a constant flow of Martian tripods moving across the river from west to east. Shells from the squadron were falling among them, but it was impossible to tell if they were scoring many hits. What was evident was the fact that there seemed to be much less resistance on the eastern shore. There wasn't much fire coming from there anymore and the flares were fewer, Drew's ships were firing their own star shells now. Tripods were emerging from the river and moving ashore. They were getting across.

"Sir? Sir?" A rating was holding the intercom phone and calling to him.

"Yes?"

"Sir, the lookout up top says there's something going on you ought to see."

"What is it?"

"He's not sure, but he asks that you come up top."

"Very well. Mr. Hinsworth, you have the con." He went out the bridge hatch and then clambered up the ladder to the observation post on the mast. The observers for the guns worked there.

"Sir!" said the petty officer in charge. "Take a look, sir, they're up to something." He pointed to the very powerful set of binoculars mounted on a pintle. Drew leaned forward and peered through the device.

"What am I looking for, Chief?"

"It looks like the buggers are towing rafts, sir!"

"Rafts? What in the world would they be doing that for?" But looking closer in the erratic light from the star shells he saw what the chief was talking about: dark rectangles were moving behind some of the tripods, which were submerged up to their heads. What were they for? He swung the binoculars over to look at the eastern shore. There were dozens of the things drawn up on the bank. As he watched, another one was pulled up and as it was, a cluster of tiny shapes, just barely visible at this distance, clambered out and moved inland.

"Spider-machines! The damn rafts are full of their spider-machines!"

"That ain't good, sir! Whadda we do?"

"Our job is to keep them from getting across, damn it!"

"Aren't gonna be able to stop them from way back here, sir."

The man looked at him and as they locked eyes, Drew knew what had to be done; and the knowledge chilled him to the bone despite the warm air. Without another word, he went back down the ladder. The forward turret fired just then, the vibration nearly knocking him loose.

Back on the bridge, he looked at the men there. His next action could get them all killed, but there was no choice. No choice at all. The commodore and the reinforcements might take an hour to get here. By then it would be too late for them to do any good. All those tripods and all those spiders would sweep down on the city from the north and...

"Mr. Hinsworth, signal the squadron to advance and engage the enemy closely. Let the commodore know what we are doing. Helm, take us up river, full speed ahead."

To their credit, the men only hesitated for a moment before carrying out their orders. The engine room telegraph rang up full speed and the ship began to vibrate gently. Drew stepped out onto the bridge wing and looked off to the east. There was the faintest glow of dawn in the sky. Good. Hinsworth rejoined him after a few minutes. "All ships acknowledge, sir. No immediate reply from the commodore." Drew looked rearward and saw that the other five ships were following. In ten or fifteen minutes they might all be reduced to flaming wrecks, but they were following, by God. He rested his hands on the rail of his ship and looked up at the mast. An amazing calm filled him.

"Mr. Hinsworth."

"Sir?"

"I think this would be a good time to break out the battle ensign."

"Sir? The... the...?"

"The battle ensign. I know we have one. I think *Santa Fe* should look her best today, don't you? Get it run up, won't you?"

"Uh, yes, sir, right away."

Hinsworth disappeared and returned a few minutes later with two other men hauling a large bundle of cloth. In the days of sailing ships, they carried enormous flags called battle ensigns. They'd be flown during a fight to help identify friend from foe in the smoke and confusion of combat. The navy still carried them, but they were rarely flown anymore except in ceremonies. *Santa Fe's* battle ensign was over twenty feet high and thirty feet long. There was barely enough room to fly it from the cables running up to the observation platform. It took all three men to haul it up. The wind generated by their speed caught the cloth and it billowed out behind them. The red and the blue looked almost black, but the white stripes and stars gleamed dimly in the waning night. Yes, it looked good. Right and proper.

"Ensign, turn on the searchlights and get the machine guns manned. Damage control parties stand ready."

"Yes, sir," gasped Hinsworth. Drew was running the kid ragged. But he got the job done. Beams of light blazed out from the ship and lit up the enemy, who weren't all that far off now. A little over two miles, Drew estimated. Men appeared to man the half-dozen machine guns mounted on the ship. There was one on the end of each bridge wing. The guns had small metal shields to protect the crews, but the men were still terribly exposed. There was nothing for it, however; he was going to need every bit of firepower they had very shortly.

Only their forward guns could shoot at the moment, but they were firing steadily now and it looked as though they were scoring some hits. They'd do better as the range dropped. Hinsworth was back and stood next to him waiting for the next order. Some of his usual bravado appeared to be missing. In fact, he looked scared.

"Mr. Hinsworth."

"Sir?"

"I've been meaning to ask: however did you end up with the name of 'Albustus'?"

"Sir?" The boy seemed startled and then laughed nervously. "Oh, uh, well, I guess it's a family tradition, sir. My father, my grandfather, way on back, all of them were named that. The first one fought in the Revolution, I've been told. He's buried in New Castle, Delaware, right next to George Read who signed the Declaration. Silly name, I guess, but it's tradition."

"Tradition," said Drew, nodding. He looked up at the huge flag. "Tradition. Well, we have some navy traditions to uphold today, Mr. Hinsworth. Let's get to it."

"Yes, sir."

They moved into the armored pilothouse. The shutters were closed, but they left the rear hatch open for the moment. "Course, sir?" asked the helmsman.

"Right into the center of them. If any get in your way, run them down. In fact, aim to run them down."

"Aye, aye, sir!" The man's face took on a wolf-like grin, baring his teeth.

Drew looked through the quartz block in the view slit. The enemy were still moving across the river, seemingly oblivious to the approach of the warships. In the growing light he could see that some of the tripods were almost completely submerged and were moving only slowly. The rafts were being towed by cables, but the current of the river was dragging them downstream, and some of their towing tripods looked to be having trouble controlling them. As he watched, a shell from one of the ships hit the water and exploded very close to a tripod; it must have severed the towing cable because one of the rafts was suddenly drifting loose and slowly spinning down the river toward them. A moment later, another shell hit the raft squarely, ripping it apart and sending spider-machines tumbling off in all directions. They splashed into the water and vanished immediately.

"Can't swim, can you, you bastards?" said Drew, grinning.

But now the enemy was starting to react. Most kept moving toward the eastern bank, but the ones closest to the ships began turning in their direction. Some heat rays stabbed out and he flinched back from the view slit as one swept across *Santa Fe*. But the range was still very long for the Martians and it did no damage.

Not such long range for the humans, though.

The light in the east was growing moment by moment and the searchlights and star shells were barely needed anymore. The gunners aboard the ships were finding the range now and hits were more frequent. A tripod off to the left suddenly blew apart as something tore through it. Another appeared to stumble, disappeared under the water, and didn't reappear.

Drew was briefly tempted to halt the advance and pound the enemy from a safe distance, but no, the bulk of them were still crossing unmolested further upstream. The range was still too long for really accurate shooting against such small targets. They needed to get in there and wreck as many as they could, slow them up, delay them until Commodore Rush arrived with more ships.

The range closed very quickly, as it always did. Ships or objects which seemed to hang in the distance forever without getting any closer were suddenly just here in what seemed an eye-blink. The guns were roaring continuously as their crews slammed shells and powder into the breeches as quickly as they could. The shriek of the heat rays filled the air and the rattle of the fifty-calibers on the bridge wings could be heard through the open hatch. Cordite smoke swept around them and made it very difficult to see. It was impossible for him to assign targets and the gunners were going to have to pick their targets as best they could.

The ship shuddered and that hateful red glow surrounded them. A heat ray was hitting them and he released stream to counter it. The stink of the cordite was joined by a different smell. His ship was on fire.

But the guns in the forward turret roared again and the glow winked out. He looked out port view slit and a tripod, spewing smoke swept by, not two hundred yards away.

"Sir! Dead ahead!" Hinsworth was at the forward slit and shouting to him. He moved up beside him and looked out. The wind was freshening and it blew away the smoke for a moment. Right in front of them was a tripod, but it was submerged hallway up its bulbous head, the glowing red eye in the middle of the face even with the water.

"Ram it! Helm, steer straight for it!"

The Martian seemed to be stuck in the mud for it only made a few jerky attempts to avoid the ship bearing down on it. Suddenly the water just in front of it exploded outward in a billowing cloud of steam. *Its heat ray! It couldn't raise it above the water!* Drew found himself laughing out loud as *Santa Fe,* all three thousand tons of her, slammed into the enemy machine. There was a muffled clang and a slight lurch, but that was all.

Then the red fire was back - some other tripod firing at them - and an instant later an explosion slammed the ship and smoke blotted out everything.

"The forward turret! The forward turret is gone, sir!" cried Hinsworth,

But the aft turret was firing and all the casemate guns as well. They were in the midst of them now. Drew went to the bridge hatch and looked back. *Evansville* was off their port quarter, burning in a dozen spots, but her guns were still firing. A tripod looming next to her suddenly tumbled backward into the water and vanished.

Vanceberg and *Manchester* were following, not hit too badly yet, it didn't seem. But the two converted river boats, *Louisville Star* and *Dixie Dancer*, were both burning from stem to stern a half mile behind. Their improvised armor was just not enough against the Martian weapons. He glanced up and was saddened that the battle ensign was just a few scorched tatters.

Suddenly a rating appeared, climbing up the ladder from below. "Sir! Sir! Message from headquarters!" Drew pulled him into the pilothouse.

"From the commodore?"

"No sir, from General MacArthur's headquarters!" He held out a slip of paper and Drew took it. Read it.

To all commands: Defense Plan M now in effect.

"What the hell?"

"What is it, sir?" asked Hinsworth.

"MacArthur's pulling everything back to Memphis."

Hinsworth looked around. "Bit late for us."

"Yeah." Drew crumpled the paper and threw it away.

The ship lurched again and there was a screech of twisting metal. They'd hit something. Another tripod? No heat ray was raking them just at the moment and he dared to step out on the starboard wing to take a look. There was nothing he could see at first. Smoke was billowing out of the forward turret and the charred bodies of the machine gun crew were sprawled at the end of the wing. A few tripods were in the river not far off, but they were ignoring *Santa Fe* at the moment. Many more were farther off and some were firing at the ships coming on behind. He couldn't see anything they might have hit. Perhaps they'd run down another Martian...

Something moving caught his eye.

A metal bar was hooked over the railing near the bow. It didn't belong there. Another one appeared. Then something the size of a cow heaved itself up and over. It was a metal egg about six or seven feet long, standing on three articulated legs. It had one arm holding something that looked remarkably like a human pistol and another with a long whip-like tentacle. As Drew looked on in horror, another one appeared farther aft. And another. They started scuttling aft.

He retreated into the pilot house and opened his mouth to shout an order he never expected to ever give.

"All hands! Prepare to repel boarders!"

Hinsworth leaned past him through the hatch, paused, looked, and then ran for the machine gun. Drew swung around, saw that the port machine gun was still in action, and the gunner was blasting away at something close at hand. He grabbed the man who had brought up the message and shoved him toward the ladder. "Go below! Have anyone you can find grab a weapon - axes, hammers, anything! - and get up here!"

He stepped out on the starboard wing again. Hinsworth was pouring fire into the spider-machines on the foredeck. One was already down and bullets were tearing through the second. The third one fired the pistol-thing, which was a miniature heat ray, but the flimsy gun shield was able to absorb it just long enough for Hinsworth to swing the gun over and bring it down in a shower of sparks. The boy had a lunatic grin on his face. "I got 'em! I got 'em, sir!"

Drew smiled a crazy smile of his own and stepped toward him...

... just as a metal monster pulled itself up on the bridge railing right behind Hinsworth.

"Alby! Look out!" Drew flung himself forward.

Before the boy could even turn, the long snake-like tentacle with a gleaming blade on the end of it flashed around, slicing Hinsworth's head from his body. Drew's momentum carried him toward the machine gun, but he knew he'd never reach it. The tentacle swung back. He was inside the arc of the deadly blade, but the tentacle slammed into him like a pile driver.

An agonizing pain blasted through his shoulder, and then he was flying through the air. He hit the river and the muddy waters of the Mississippi swallowed him up.

* * * * *

July, 1912, Memphis, Tennessee

"Where'n hell's the commander of those damn lady sharpshooters?!"

For a moment the shout didn't register, but then Becca Harding suddenly jerked awake. That's me! She stood up, the blanket she'd wrapped herself in falling away, and looked down from her perch on the city wall. "Up here!"

"Well, git yerself down here! We've got orders!"

"Coming!" She made her way past some other soldiers who, like her, had decided to camp out on the wall where they could watch the battle, and let herself down an iron ladder attached to the concrete. It was still dark, although she could see the first glimmer of dawn in the east.

The man who had shouted was waiting for her. She saw that he was an officer with the militia so she came to attention and saluted. He didn't bother to return it. "Get your girls up and moving," he said. "They're shifting us to a new position."

"Where, sir?"

"Up on the north side of the city."

"What's happenin', sir?"

"Not sure. Looks like the fight over yonder was just a decoy. The Martians are over the river to the north and headin' this way fast. So get a move on! We'll be pulling out in ten minutes, you be ready to follow." He turned and walked away before she could even respond.

She ran back to her camp and started kicking tent poles and shouting for the girls to get up. The nearby militia company was already falling in. Old Mo came walking over. "What's all the fuss, Missy?"

"Get the horses and the carriage ready! We're movin' right away!"

* * * * *

Cycle 597, 845.2, River 3-1

Qetjnegartis looked back at the river. All six of the enemy vessels had been destroyed; the burning remains of several of them could still be seen. Their reckless charge had done an alarming amount of damage, but they we gone now and the crossing could be completed. But they must move quickly, the black smoke plumes of more vessels could be seen beyond the thick growths of vegetation to the south. They would be here soon, but they would be too late.

"Keep moving. We must strike the city before the prey-creatures can prepare."

* * * * *

July 1912, near Rosedale, Mississippi

"Sorry to wake you, sir, but we just got a signal from General Clopton."

Andrew Comstock squinted at the light streaming in through the door of his tiny cabin. His aide, Lieutenant Hornbaker was standing there, silhouetted by the glare. "Is it important?"

"Looks to be. Memphis is under attack. A major attack. We're to proceed directly there at full speed."

"All right, all right, I'll be up in a minute."

Chapter Fifteen

July, 1912, Washington, D.C.

"Has there been anything more from MacArthur?" asked President Theodore Roosevelt.

"No sir," replied Leonard Wood. "Nothing since that 'Defense Plan M' message an hour ago. I've tried to get hold of him, but his aides just tell me he is 'indisposed'. I've been in touch with Dickman at 3rd Army headquarters, but he can't get through to MacArthur, either. All we know is that the enemy has crossed the river in great strength about fifteen miles north of Memphis."

The early morning light was streaming in the windows of Roosevelt's office in the White House. His son and aide, Archie, came in bearing a tray with a coffee pot and cups. The President filled one and walked over to one of the maps which hung on the walls. "Defense Plan M, that's the one that calls for concentrating everything inside the defensive works around Memphis, is it not?"

"Yes," said Wood, once again amazed by Roosevelt's memory. There were dozens and dozens of different plans for all the sections along the line; Wood, himself couldn't keep them all straight. "In recent weeks, MacArthur was becoming highly critical of it and kept asking for more and more materiel so he could take a more aggressive posture. But now he's fallen back on it."

"And the Martians are across the river, Leonard?" His finger touched a spot north of Memphis on the map. "I thought we had enough troops guarding that area."

"We had hoped that there would be, but we had to make our plans based on calculated risk. We couldn't possibly have enough troops everywhere, so we put what we hoped would be enough to hold until reinforcements arrived. We had the 29th Division in that area, but apparently MacArthur stripped a brigade away to reinforce West Memphis when the Martians made an attack there. What was left couldn't hold long enough."

"And he did that without clearing it with you?" Wood nodded. "Damnation! It's like Funston all over again! This could be our worst nightmare!"

"Well, the worst would be for them to get across and build a fortress on the eastern side. A raid, while bad, would not be a complete disaster so long as we can drive them back across the river."

"And can we?"

"We are certainly going to try. I've ordered Dickman to send everything he can to the Memphis area. The 2nd Tank Division is in Jackson, they will be moving within the hour, although I doubt they'll be able to de-train and get into action before tomorrow." He came over beside Roosevelt and traced his finger along the railroad from Jackson to Memphis. "And Clopton's land ironclads are coming up river. They're somewhere around here, a hundred miles or so from Memphis. I've ordered them directly there."

"Good... good. If we can hit the rapscallions hard, maybe we can drive them back."

"That's what I'm hoping."

Roosevelt frowned. "But what about MacArthur? Why isn't he answering us? Do you think there's something wrong - beyond the obvious, I mean?"

Wood shook his head. "I don't know. When he was head of my staff, he would draw up plans - good plans—but he would act as if they were immutable, like the results were set in stone and were bound to happen just as he'd intended. If anything happened to mess them up, sometimes he would go into a funk. Get all quiet and moody. I was never sure if it was just pique on being forced to change his plans or... or if it was something else. It didn't happen often, but almost always for big things."

"We can hardly afford to have him in a funk right now. He was my military aide for a few months when I first became President and he seemed steady enough then, but that was ten years ago. Do you think he should be replaced?"

"I'm going to order Dickman at 3rd Army to go have a look, but it will take him a while to get there. And I'm sure he'll be reluctant to take any drastic steps in the middle of a battle. MacArthur's got some good subordinates there. Let's hope they can take up the load until... until he's no longer 'indisposed'."

"I suppose you're right. We can't try and fight the battle from here."

"No, battles are fought and won by the men who are there where it's happening."

* * * * *

July, 1912, West Memphis, Arkansas

"Come on! Move it! Move it!" Captain Frank Dolfen stood in his stirrups and tried to see what was holding up the column. All he could see was a solid line of troops and trucks jamming the sole bridge across the Mississippi. It was mid-morning and the battle was still raging.

Battles, he should say, for there were two fights going on now. The first one, which was in its second day, was the fight around West Memphis; but everyone realized it had just been a diversion, a feint to draw strength away from where the real attack would come.

That was the attack he and the 5th had discovered last night. A huge force of tripods, pulling boats and swarms of the spider-machines all heading for a crossing point north of the city. They had sent the warning back by radio and that had drawn a dozen of the tripods down on them. Both regiments of cavalry had beat a hasty retreat back to the defenses of West Memphis. Dolfen didn't think they'd gotten hurt too badly, and somehow he'd managed to get his own squadron to safety more or less intact. The rest of the regiment had been more badly scattered.

They had barely been given time to catch their breath before the word reached them that the enemy had gotten across the river and was threatening Memphis from the north. The cavalry had been ordered to cross the bridge and get up there to do what it could. Unfortunately several brigades of infantry along with battalions of steam tanks and batteries of guns had been given the same order and there was only the one bridge.

Somehow, Dolfen had gotten 1st Squadron reformed and up to the approaches to the bridge ahead of most of the other troops, but it had still been a colossal traffic jam; and now, three hours after dawn, they were just starting to cross.

The column lurched into motion and they made it about halfway across before halting again. From the bridge, he could look to the north. There was a lot of smoke in that direction, but it still seemed pretty far off. Maybe the enemy wasn't in the city yet. The noise of the guns was all around and he couldn't tell if there was any noise coming from the north. In truth, ever since that explosion at Little Rock, his hearing wasn't as good as it used to be. And where was Becca in all this? Was she with her sharpshooters or back at the hospital? The hospital was on the north side of the city. He couldn't believe that in the midst of all that was happening, he was worrying about that girl - but he was.

There were dozens of boats, big and small, in the river below him. Some were heading north, but others were going south. He noted one coming down river which had smoke drifting off it from a dozen wounds. A navy warship, and it had clearly gotten the worst of a fight. The river was filled with floating wreckage, bits of wood, boxes, life rings... bodies. Yes, there were a few floating bodies, too.

"Navy couldn't stop 'em, I guess," said Lieutenant Lynnebrook.

"But it looks like they tried."

They started moving again, and to Dolfen's amazement, they actually reached the other side where provost officers shouted at them to keep going. Dolfen had lost all contact with Colonel Schumacher so he just picked a street going north and urged his men along it. They were all tired, but there was no stopping now. The Martians were trying to break into the city.

And they were going to stop them.

* * * * *

July, 1912, somewhere along the Mississippi

Drew Harding's feet touched something solid and he opened his eyes. Bright sunshine dazzled him, but he saw something large and dark stretching out before him. After a moment he realized it was the river bank. With the sun in his eyes, as it was, it had to be the east shore. Thank God. The last he remembered, he was trying to reach the east shore. That was after... after...

After the *USS Santa Fe* blew up and sank.

My ship. I lost my ship.

The thought was numbing. Every captain's nightmare.

Those spider-machines. It had been them. Not even one of the tripods. They had collided with something, he remembered that. It must have been one of the rafts full of the spiders. They hadn't seen it in all the smoke and confusion. And then the things were everywhere. With *Santa Fe's* low freeboard, they could climb aboard easily. They'd killed poor Alby and knocked Drew into the river. Hurt his shoulder. It was so painful, he couldn't use the arm at all; he'd have gone right to the bottom if he hadn't been wearing a life jacket. He'd bumped into some piece of drifting wreckage and clung to it.

When he looked back at his ship, he'd seen that the spiders had small heat rays and they were burning their way inside. The current took him farther and farther away, so he couldn't see much more, but then the ship exploded. One of the things must have gotten into the magazine. She broke in half and went down.

Then the river took him around the bend and out of sight of the fighting. He was nearly run down by the arrival of the rest of Commodore Rush's command surging up the river at full speed. He'd shouted and tried to wave with his good arm, but no one had seen him. Or they hadn't tried to help if they had.

He had kicked his legs and paddled as best he could toward the eastern shore, but he never seemed to get any closer. He kept trying until he was exhausted. At last he saw what he thought was the entrance to the Wolf River, that little channel which cut off the swampy island he'd been curious about earlier. He'd used his last strength trying to get into that, and looking around now, it seemed like he'd succeeded.

His feet touched the bottom again and he tried to stand. But there was no strength in his legs. All he could manage was to use his legs to push himself the rest of the way to shore. He abandoned the faithful bit of flotsam and dragged his sodden body up out of the water and collapsed on the muddy bank. The pain in his shoulder, which had subsided to a dull ache, returned full force and he groaned.

After hours in the water, he was chilled to the bone, but the bright morning sunshine beat down on his dark uniform, warming him. He tried dragging himself farther up the bank but made little progress. Then he heard some shouts and strong hands grabbed him and turned him over.

"Yeah, he's alive! Navy guy—an officer, too! Get the stretcher!"

* * * * *

July, 1912, Memphis, Tennessee

"Becca! What are you doing here?"

Becca Harding turned at the sound of the familiar voice. There was Miss Chumley, the chief nurse of the hospital. In spite of the cloud they'd parted under when she'd told her she was choosing the sharp-shooters over her nursing duties, she smiled when she saw the woman. Chumley had been very kind to her over the years and she still thought of her as a friend.

"Hello, ma'am. We were pulled out of our position along the river and sent up to the northern defenses. They shifted us around two or three times and then an officer told us to come back here an' guard the hospital. I'm sorta surprised you're all still here."

"We've been told to be ready to evacuate twice now, but we've gotten no orders to do anything. I've been getting the ambulances ready, just in case."

"Well, you've got thirty armed sharpshooters to make sure no one troubles you, ma'am." Her girls were marching up behind her; tired, but still enthusiastic, now that things were actually happening.

"Good, good. I hope we don't need you, but you remember the chaos when we pulled out of Gallup and again at Santa Fe. Pray God we won't have to do that again, but if we do, I'll be glad to have you around, Becca."

Yes, those had been real messes. At Gallup she'd been forced to draw her pistol to keep some men from stealing a wagon she needed to transport the wounded.

Chumley gave her an odd look. "And if you do have a spare moment, I'm sure we can find some work at your old job, Becca. We've gotten quite a lot of wounded here from the fight across the river. They're not sending us any more from there, but now we're starting to get men coming down from the north." She looked in that direction where the rumble of artillery was getting louder by the minute.

"Uh, we'll see, ma'am. I'm in charge of the sharpshooters now and I have responsibilities." For a moment she thought Chumley was going to remind her of the responsibilities here that she'd abandoned, but the older woman refrained and just nodded.

"I understand. Well, I'm glad you're here, Becca. I have to get back to work." Chumley turned and walked quickly back to one of the tents.

Becca had been leading Ninny, and when Moses came up with the wagon, she turned the horse over to him. She had organized her girls into four squads and she put one on sentry while the other three set up a camp in an open area. While she was getting things organized, she saw Sam Jones come up. The strange, quirky man who had been rescued from the Martian fortress at Gallup was still hanging around the hospital as an orderly. He'd clearly been in the infantry before that, but he'd refused to go back to his unit and was technically a deserter. But no one at the hospital had wanted to make an issue of it and so here he was.

"Hi, Sam," she said.

"Hi, Miss Becca. Looks like you might get that fight you've been lookin' for so long." He nodded his head in the direction of the gunfire. The man seemed nervous.

"Yeah, it seems so. What are you gonna do, Sam?"

He didn't answer, but his eyes took on that same look as they had when she's first seen him; a wild animal fear. As near as she could guess, he'd been captured and held with some of his comrades in a cage while the Martians ate them one by one. The attack on the fortress at Gallup, which had come oh, so close to victory, had managed to free him, but he was in mortal terror of ending up like that again. "I'll... I'll do what I have to," he said, finally.

"Well, take care of yourself, Sam."

"You, too." He turned and left, looking back at her once as he walked away.

"Was that Sam Jones?" asked Sarah Halberstam, coming up behind her.

"Yup."

"Is he going to be joining up with us?"

"Nope."

"Too bad, he worked so well with us, teaching us the drill."

Becca didn't answer, but Sarah stood in front of her, face worried. "Becca, what are we going to do if the Martians break into the city?"

She shrugged. "Fight."

"How? These rifles won't hurt one of those tripods and you know it. And we don't have any of the dynamite bombs or those stovepipe rocket-things like the real soldiers do. If a tripod comes walking up, what are we supposed to do?"

"I've heard that the spider-machines aren't as tough. That rifles can hurt them. Maybe we can deal with them while the other soldiers take care of the tripods."

"None of the other soldiers are even around!" It was true, they'd gotten separated from the militia company they'd been attached to.

"Then we help evacuate the wounded!" said Becca, growing annoyed. "We do what we *can*, Sarah. If that's not good enough for you, then maybe you should go home!" She immediately regretted her words. Sarah had been one of the most dedicated women in the group, making almost every meeting. "Sorry, sorry, I shouldn't have said that to you."

"It's all right, Becca," said Sarah, nodding. "All of us, all of us who are still here anyway, want to do something to help. But you're the one who made this all real, showed us how to do something that matters." She reached out and squeezed her arm. "Don't worry, we'll make you proud."

Becca blinked, sniffed, and then nodded. "I know you will."

* * * * *

Cycle 597, 845.2, East of River 3-1

Finally across the river! Qetjnegartis felt a distinct sensation of relief. The enormous body of water, which had posed such a strategic puzzle for so long, was behind them at last.

The challenge now is to stay here.

Yes, that was the next task. They were across the river and had done so with only moderate losses. Forty-seven fighting machines and two hundred and thirty drones had been destroyed or crippled or lost in the river while smashing through the defenses along the river bank or dealing with the group of water vessels which had attacked in the midst of the crossing. But it could have been far worse. A much more powerful water force had arrived, but only after the crossing was complete. Qetjnegartis had not tarried to fight those when there was no need. It had ordered its forces away from the river, southeast to strike the city, away from any interference from the river craft.

A large area of very dense vegetation lay off to the west along the river, and many of the prey-creatures who had held the defenses had fled there, but it was so dense it seemed unlikely that the enemy's armored gun vehicles could operate there. So the right flank was secure. To the east and south, the country was far more open, with crop lands and small habitation centers and roadways. They would have to be wary of possible attacks from those directions. The plan was to penetrate into the city as quickly as possible and use the enemy's own defenses to guard the rear.

The city was about ten *telequel* away and Qetjnegartis had dispatched a force of the fast fighting machines to scout ahead. They were reporting only a scattering of enemy forces, which they were destroying or driving off with ease. The main force with the slower-moving drones was following as quickly as possible. Qetjnegartis would have preferred to probe the enemy defense lines and then launch the main attack after nightfall, but there was no time for that. The attack must be made immediately.

As they got closer to the city, the projectiles from the prey-creatures' long range weapons started to fall more frequently. It appeared that the diversion and sudden crossing of the river had achieved the surprise that had been hoped for, but that surprise was now wearing off. The enemy was reorganizing and responding more forcefully. Some of the fire was coming from the vessels on the river, even though they had no direct line of sight. So far, most of the projectiles were doing no damage, but it expected that to change once they got closer to the defensive lines. Reports from the failed attack at City 3-4 indicated that the prey-creatures were becoming increasingly sophisticated and had devised a system where they could direct fire from widely separated weapons against a specific target many *telequel* away.

Images sent from the artificial satellite showed that the defenses on the landward side, while not as formidable as the cast-stone walls along the river, still could not be discounted. There were several small fortresses, which were made from the cast stone and mounted large weapons, and these were linked by trenches where the foot-warriors and the smaller projectile throwers could take refuge.

Tanbradjus reported that although it was continuing the diversionary attack, there was clear evidence that the enemy was moving forces eastward, back across the river into the city. Those forces would no doubt be moving to reinforce the northern defense lines.

"Commander, we are crossing one of the prey-creatures' transport tracks and a strange vehicle is approaching along it." The communication was from Battlegroup 32-6, on the left flank.

"Relay an image."

The subordinate did so and Qetjnegartis saw what at first appeared to be one of the steam powered transport engines towing a string of other vehicles, as was normal. But on closer examination it realized that all the vehicles were armored and many of them mounted weapons. Indeed, they began firing almost at once. The battlegroup responded immediately and the strange vehicle was quickly reduced to wreckage, but not before it had destroyed a fighting machine. The operator was rescued, but as there were no reserve machines available, it had to be kept in a transport pod in hopes that it would survive the battle. There was no chance of sending it to the rear, as there was no rear in this fight.

Some of the habitation centers they passed had prey-creature warriors inside them. These fired their small weapons, even though they had little hope of doing any damage. Qetjnegartis ordered that the structures be set afire from a distance and that no attempt be made to destroy every last creature. They could not afford the time. Soon, hundreds of burning structures marked their passage. Clumps of vegetation were similarly dealt with. The scouts had discovered and mapped areas where the ground was especially soft and these places were avoided.

Shortly after the encounter with the armored transport machine, Battlegroup 32-4 discovered a base for the prey-creatures' flying machines. Over fifty of the machines were lined up on the ground or preparing to take to the air. On the ground, the flimsy devices were completely defenseless and all were destroyed in moments. That was very good, although other flying machines were already in the air overhead, and there would certainly be more arriving if past battles were any indication. They needed to press on to the city before they did.

The pace of the drones slowed their progress and the sun was far up in the sky by the time the outer line of the city's defenses came into view. The scouts had done their jobs well and most of the heavy weapons positions had been plotted. Only two of the cast stone forts were on the northern side, and Qetjnegartis decided that the easternmost one could be ignored.

"Battlegroups 32-9 and 32-11, you shall engage the other fort and keep it occupied. Battlegroup 32-4, you shall protect our right flank. All other battlegroups will concentrate and strike in the area to the west of the fort. Any machine becoming immobilized or disabled shall be left behind, your orders are to press into the city as quickly as possible. Use the eradicator against the heavy weapons positions. Battlegroup 32-14 shall bring up the rear and assist those in need of help. Take up your positions and commence the attack on my command."

The components of the force moved into their spots quickly and precisely, with only the smallest amount of confusion with the drones. Not every drone operator was fully proficient yet, and it was as Ixmaderna had once said: the younger operators seemed to be the best at this. Even so, soon all was ready and Qetjnegartis gave the order to attack.

The battlegroups sent to engage the fort quickly had it so blanketed with the eradicator dust that almost no fire was coming from it, and they had only lost two machines in the process. A force of drones was sent to see if it could be silenced permanently. All the others, with Qetjnegartis following along, pressed ahead against the defensive lines. Projectiles fell all around them like one of the local precipitation storms, and a number of fighting machines and drones were destroyed. But the rest kept moving.

As it had feared, once they were within a *telequel* of the enemy positions, they began to encounter the pit traps set to snare the legs of the fighting machines. Most were cleverly hidden and constructed so that a drone or, presumably the prey-creatures themselves, could cross without triggering them. But when a fighting machine put its weight down on one, its leg would crash through and be caught. Qetjnegartis could not see any easy way of dealing with these, or at least none that would not delay an advance just as much as the traps themselves.

As it had ordered, those which became immobilized were left to fend for themselves, even though they became excellent targets for the enemy weapons. Assigning others to assist would just make both easy targets. The surest way to help them would be to destroy the prey-creature weapons as quickly as possible. This the attacking force did, moving forward and opening fire with their heat rays. Eradicator projectiles were fired against known weapon positions.

There were more traps immediately in front of the enemy trenches and a ditch filled with water. A score or more machines became trapped or mired in the mud at the bottom of the ditch, but the rest pulled themselves up and over, sweeping the defenses with their heat rays. A number of fully enclosed bunkers held out for a while, but those in the trenches were annihilated.

But not before they did considerable damage. The explosive bombs which the prey had been using for some time destroyed or damaged a number of machines, but perhaps more alarming was a new weapon, first encountered in small numbers at City 3-118 and in larger numbers by Clan Mavnaltak at City 3-4. It was a small device, small enough that it could be carried by a single prey-creature. It appeared to fire some sort of rocket-propelled projectile which could explode with a force similar to those fired by the much larger weapons the enemy used. A single shot could rarely do serious damage to a fighting machine, but multiple hits were capable of bringing one down; and even a single shot proved sufficient to destroy the drones.

To Qetjnegartis' relief, there were none of the armored gun vehicles waiting in reserve as was so often the case. The prey had learned that the best response to an assault was to mass all of their vehicles for an immediate counterattack. But there were none here now, another success for the diversionary attack.

A half *telequel* of open ground lay ahead, between the defenses and the structures of the city. A few weapon positions and some fleeting prey could be seen, but little else.

"Continue the advance," commanded Qetjnegartis. "Drive through the city to the bridge over the river. Destroy everything you can, but do not delay your progress. We must move quickly."

* * * * *

July, 1912, Memphis, Tennessee

"Rebecca, we've finally been given orders to evacuate. Can you and your girls help?"

Becca Harding had been staring north. The hospital had been built on the northern outskirts of Memphis and about a mile south of the defense lines. A stand of trees blocked a direct view to the north, but the sounds of fighting had been growing louder for the past hour, and clouds of black smoke had been billowing up above the trees for a while. The Martians were clearly there and getting closer. She turned and saw that it was Miss Chumley who has spoken.

"Well it's certainly about time! Those monsters could be here in five minutes!"

"I know, I know," replied Chumley. "We're loading the wounded into ambulances and wagons, but we could use some help."

"All right, you've got it. Sarah! Get the girls! We've got a job to do!" Sarah Halberstam, who was acting as her company sergeant, immediately rounded up the sharpshooters who had been watching the smoke just like everyone else. She brought them over to Becca. "Ladies, the hospital is being evacuated. We need to help load the wounded. And we'll probably be pulling out along with them, so keep all your gear handy. There's not much time, so move it!"

Rather than being annoyed or sullen, as Becca had feared, the women looked relieved and happy to have an actual task to do. They'd been ordered here, there, and everywhere with no apparent purpose so many times that a clear job was welcome. They stacked their rifles and went inside the hospital tents and buildings and started hauling out the wounded men on stretchers. It usually took four of them for each stretcher, but they did it and loaded the men into the ambulances.

It quickly became apparent that there weren't going to be enough vehicles for all the patients. They pulled aside those who were able to walk and made them do so, marching alongside the wagons. Becca spotted Moses with his wagon and waved to him. "Mo! We're gonna need you here!" The man jogged over to her.

"Yes, Miz Becca?"

"Dump all the junk you've got in the back! I need you to carry some wounded!"

"But that's all the ladies' things!" he protested. "Your tent, too."

"Dump it! There's more important things to carry."

Moses nodded. "I reckon you're right, miz." He pointed off to a column of smoke in the distance. "I'm guessin' that's the Oswald place. Nuthin' to go back to anyways. Only people matter now."

"That's right, only people." She hesitated. "When you go, take Ninny along with you."

Moses stared at her. "You sure 'bout that, Miz Becca?"

"Yeah. He's people, too. Keep him safe, will you?"

"Do my level best, Miz."

"Good. Take the wagon over there and load it up."

"Yes'm. Uh, where am I takin' 'em?"

"Just follow the others. Do what they tell you." Moses nodded and went back to his rig. Ninny was tied nearby and the man retied his lead to the back of the wagon. Becca wondered if she'd ever see him again. But he had no business here...

A sudden roar off to her left made her spin around. While she'd been working, an army field battery had unlimbered on some open ground just a hundred yards away and was now firing at something. She couldn't see what, but the noise of battle was closer than ever. They didn't have much time left.

While she was searching through the camp, looking for anyone who might have been missed, she saw a horse-drawn ambulance coming up from the west. She ran over to it. "The hospital's being evacuated! You have any room for more?"

"Yeah," said the driver. "Only carrying one guy. Where they taking the wounded now?"

"Not sure. Railroad depot, probably. Just head south into town as soon as we get you loaded. Sarah! We got room for a couple more here!" She went around to the back and opened the door. As the driver had said, there was just a single occupant; a young man with his arm in a sling and a grotesque lump on his shoulder. No, that was his shoulder. It had been dislocated and needed to be popped back into its socket. She could do that, but there was no time. "Sorry, but you have to move over, we need to get more people in here."

"R-Rebecca?"

She twitched and looked closer. Did she know this fellow? His face did look familiar, even twisted in pain and covered with dirt. Suddenly she recognized him. "Commander Harding! What are you doing here?"

"Don't know, 'cause I don't know where here is."

"You're at the general military hospital, but we're evacuating. How did you get here?"

"Lost my ship. Ended up in the river. Crawled ashore. After that, I don't know."

"Oh." She didn't know what else to say. Her girls were there with another stretcher. "Well, no time to talk now. We'll get you to someplace they can fix you up." She stood aside while the ambulance was filled up and then it lurched away.

"I think that's all, Becca." She turned and saw Sarah Halberstam. "They're all on their way, all the patients and staff are gone."

"Good. Let's grab our stuff and get along after them. We'll escort them all the way to..."

"Look! Oh God, look!"

Becca spun around and immediately saw what had caused the shout. Beyond the trees was a Martian tripod. No, two of them. Three. Maybe more. Still a quarter mile off, but heading this way. "Come on!" she shouted. "Move!" She led the way toward where their rifles and backpacks were stacked.

There was a mad scramble to grab all their stuff. Becca had left hers to the side so she had it immediately, but the others took precious seconds. She ran a few dozen steps to the south, looking for the best route of escape. The outskirts of the city started just beyond the hospital, but they were all low wooden houses. Not much cover, they'd have to...

The artillery battery off to the left roared again, and an odd, metallic sound made her look back. They'd hit one of the tripods! The closest one was staggering around, smoke pouring from its head, and then it fell with a crash, disappearing behind the trees. *That's gonna make them mad...* "Come on! *Move!*" she screamed.

The women came running and she let half of them pass before following along. "Just keep going! Straight for the town!"

A strange *wumpf* sound had her looking back again. Something flew from one of the tripods and soared over toward the guns where it burst in an inky black cloud. It spread out and the wind blew it in her direction. An icy chill spread through her despite the July heat.

"Dust! Black dust! Get your masks and gloves on!" She instantly tore open the canvas bag hanging from her neck. She pulled out the mask and hood, threw away her hat and pulled the apparatus over her head. The hood covered her head completely and extended down around her neck with a cinch-cord to close it tight around her collar. There were two round eye pieces to see through and a bulky filter to allow her to breathe. Two leather gloves, almost like a cavalryman's long gauntlets, completed the outfit. She looked down to make sure her trousers were tucked into her boots.

Then she looked up and the black dust was nearly upon them. A large hospital tent stood a dozen yards away. It would not provide complete protection, but it was better than nothing. "The tent! Get inside! Hurry!" She started pushing the women toward it.

"Abigail! Come on!" Sarah Halberstam suddenly looked back and shouted.

Becca turned and there was Abigail LaPlace standing frozen, hands clutching the unopened bag holding her dust gear, looking at the cloud of death sweeping toward her. She shoved Sarah toward shelter and leapt back to grab Abigail. The girl was as rigid as a statue; Becca hauled her to the tent.

But it was too late.

The dust, like some swarm of tiny locusts, swirled around them, so thickly she could barely see the tent only a few paces away. With one last surge she dragged them both through the flaps inside where the others were clustered. Abigail was screaming and fell to the ground.

Becca had seen dust victims before, but never like this. Anyone caught fully in a cloud with no protection never reached the hospital. Abigail had the dust all over her. On her clothes, in her hair, on her face, and hands. Tiny black specks like coal dust. She lay on the ground thrashing and shrieking, her eyes squeezed shut. Her hands came up and started to tear at her face.

Becca fell to her knees and grabbed Abigail's wrists, trying to keep her from hurting herself. But it was no use, the dust was starting to eat into the skin. Her screams were interrupted by gasping coughs, and foam, flecked with red and black, started spitting out of her mouth. Becca could hear more screams, muffled by dust masks and realized it was the other women.

"Do something!" shouted one of them.

But there was nothing that could be done. The horror went on for what seemed an eternity, but which probably wasn't more than a minute, until the girl suddenly went stiff and then collapsed. Not screaming, not breathing, her face a terrible mass of black and red.

Shaking, Becca stood up. The others were crying and sobbing and one of them was clawing at the tie holding her mask. "Leave that on!" she shouted. But the woman lifted it up far enough to vomit, before tugging it back into place. Becca grabbed a blanket off a cot and threw it over Abigail.

The shriek of a heat ray and a red light glowing through the tent's canvas reminded her where they were. "Come on! We can't stay here! Grab your stuff and let's go!"

"You've got dust all over you, Becca!" said someone, it sounded like Sarah.

"I know. I'll deal with that later! Come on!" She peered out of the tent and the black cloud was gone, blown along with the westerly breeze. There was dust all over the ground, but there was no choice. She hustled them out of the tent and saw a tripod not two hundred yards away. Its heat ray was sweeping across the first row of tents and shacks on the edge of the hospital, sending them up in flames. Becca turned in the opposite direction and they fled into the town.

* * * * *

July, 1912, Memphis, Tennessee

"Looks like a helluva mess ahead, Captain!" Lieutenant Lynnbrooke turned in his saddle and looked back at Frank Dolfen. "Not sure we can get through here!"

Dolfen stood up in his stirrups and saw what his aide was talking about. The street ahead was jammed with wagons, trucks, and people on foot, all heading south. They might be able to get the horses and motorcycles through on the sidewalks, but the armored cars would never make it. They'd have to take a different route…

Wait a minute…

Squinting, he saw that some of the vehicles in the oncoming column had large red crosses on the side. Ambulances! Having no definite orders beyond heading north and engaging whatever enemy he found, he'd been deliberately leading his squadron in the direction of Becca's hospital in hopes that she might be there. He'd led them over to Ayres Street which went to the hospital, but it now looked as though the hospital was coming to him. He realized it was ridiculous to be worrying about one girl in all this madness, but he couldn't help it.

"Lynnbrooke! Take the squadron west a block or two and find a route north. I'll rejoin you up ahead."

"But…"

"Do it!" He spurred his horse onto the sidewalk and pushed his way through the people fleeing the other way. Some were walking wounded, and others were stragglers of one sort or another. There were also an alarming number of civilians. The city was supposed to have been mostly evacuated, but clearly a lot of folks had stayed behind - until the Martians arrived. But Frank wasn't paying much attention to them. He was scanning the hospital vehicles for any familiar face.

Amazingly, he found one.

There was Nurse Chumley, perched on one of the wagons. He'd met her a number of times when he'd visited Becca. At first, she'd made no secret of her disapproval of any soldier showing interest in one of her girls. That had changed a bit after he was made an officer, but she had remained a snappy old biddy. But she was there now and Frank was glad. He ruthless turned his horse across the traffic and pulled up beside the wagon. "Chumley! Where's Rebecca?"

The woman acted as though he'd grown up out of the ground. "Who…? Oh, Captain Dolfen! What are you doing here?"

"Comin' t'give the Martians a warm welcome. But is Rebecca with you?"

"She's with her sharpshooters," she said and Frank's heart fell. She could be anywhere then… "But they helped us evacuate. She ought to be bringing up the rear." She jerked her head backward.

"Thanks! Thanks a lot!" He turned his horse again.

"Be careful! Those devils aren't far behind!"

Yes, that was for sure. He could see smoke and flames ahead and not nearly far enough away. He couldn't see any of the tripods yet, but where there was smoke and flames, there were usually Martians. He reached the end of the block and looked west and he was gratified to see Lynnbrooke on the next street over urging along the squadron. Lynnbrooke spotted him, but Dolfen just waved him on.

He kept forcing his way through the people headed the other direction and saw that he was nearing the end of the line of wagons and ambulances. If Becca was bringing up the rear she ought to be around here somewhere. But all the people on foot he could see were walking wounded, retreating soldiers, or civilians. Did Becca still have that fool horse with her? She'd be easier to spot if she were mounted, but he didn't see any riders ahead.

A trooper caught up with him. "Captain! Lieutenant Lynnbrooke says that he can see Martians ahead! Do you want to halt and deploy?" Dolfen stared ahead and yes, now he could make out tall shapes, dimly through the smoke. Maybe a half mile ahead. But where was Becca? Could he have missed her in the crowd? Maybe just her, but there were supposed to be a group of them. Women in silly uniforms with rifles, he couldn't have missed seeing all of them. So were they still up ahead? Closer to the Martians? Maybe there had been stragglers with the wounded that they were helping. Damn, he couldn't just keep marching right toward the bastards, his command would be slaughtered. They'd have to deploy and hope Becca could get here ahead of the enemy. *If she's even out there. She might have taken some other street and I've missed her completely.*

"Yes. I'll come." He turned down a side street and made it over to where Lynnbrooke had the squadron. He signaled a halt as soon as he saw Dolfen coming. The squadron was still in pretty good order and the officers gathered quickly.

"All right," he told them, "we are going to set up a blocking position here, along this cross street." He spotted the street sign. "Along Jackson Avenue. We'll take position here and the next two main intersection to the east. This one… Manassas, the next one over is Ayres, and I don't know what the next one over is, but you can see that big red shop sign on the corner. The armored cars will wait in ambush along Jackson. You can pop out and fire down the streets at the tripods when they get closer and then scoot on across behind the buildings before you become a sitting duck. Understood?" Lieutenant Buckman, commander of the armored car troop nodded.

"A and B Troops will dismount three sections each and get them into the buildings on each side of the streets farther up the block. The rest will stay mounted and get into these alleys between the buildings, so that they'll be ready to come out and hit them while they're busy with the armored cars and the dismounted troopers. Gregory," he turned and looked at Lieutenant McGuiness, the commander of D Troop, "get your heavy machine guns set up inside buildings where they can support everyone else. As for your mortars, I leave that to you." He swept his gaze across everyone.

"We haven't got much time, but scout out routes to fall back along. We aren't going to be able to hold here very long, I don't think, and we will have to fall back from position to position. Our mission is to hurt and delay these bastards as long as we can without getting shot all to hell. There are reinforcements coming, we just need to buy time for them to come up.

"One last thing: the Martians have got those spider-machines with them, so be on alert. *But...* there are still people trying to get away out there! Be certain you don't kill any of 'em by mistake! Questions?" There weren't any and Dolfen nodded. "Okay, let's get to it."

His officers ran back to their men, and in moments the squadron was in motion. Horsemen, their mount's hooves clattering on the cobblestones, trotted off to take up positions. Some dismounted and had their horses taken to sheltered areas in the block south of them. Motorcycles, their engine roars echoing off the surrounding buildings, did the same, although there was no way to take the bikes to the rear; they were parked in alleys or on sidewalks. Troops scrambled into the buildings, all carrying bombs and some - not enough - with the new stovepipe rocket launchers. The armored cars formed three groups, near each of the intersections, ready to dart out at the right moment. The machine gun crews, straining under their heavy loads - the fifty-caliber Brownings weighed a hundred pounds even without their tripods or ammunition - as they lugged them into position. Dolfen didn't know how the mortars were going to be placed or directed, but he left that to McGuiness.

It was all done very efficiently and he was proud of his men, especially since this urban setting wasn't one they had trained for. But damn it, where was Becca? He pulled out his binoculars and looked down the street. The Martians were about four blocks away, at least four or five of them on Ayres Street; and from the smoke, at least that many on the parallel streets. Their heat rays were in almost constant use, blasting the buildings along the streets as they advanced. Most of the smoke was rolling to the east, but the smell of burning was heavy in the air.

Artillery fire was coming down around them intermittently, although he had no idea where it was coming from or who was directing it. There were aircraft circling far overhead, so maybe they were the ones calling it in. And speaking of aircraft, where the hell were Selfridge and his boys? He knew that several hundred aircraft had been assembled around Memphis to help in the defense. They would surely be a help now.

"Sir? Captain?" It was Lynnbrooke. "We're about ready, but our flanks are wide open. We're blocking three streets, but it looks like they're coming down every one of them from the north. They'll move right past us on the east and west, sir."

"I know, I know, but there's nothing we can do. There are more troops moving up from the bridge, we'll just have to hope they can fill in on our flanks. In any case we need to be ready to fall back on a moment's notice. We might be in a city, but we're still cavalry."

"Yes, sir."

The enemy drew closer and Dolfen cursed when he realized that they were simply setting fire to every building they passed whether there were any humans in evidence or not. His troops in the buildings here would have to evacuate or fry - and before they could hope to do anything to the Martians. *Unless we give them something else to worry about...*

The only thing he had to work with were the armored cars. Their guns, though small, had a range comparable to the heat rays. If they started shooting, maybe they could draw the Martians close enough for the others to strike. He ran over to where Lieutenant Buckman was standing atop his command vehicle. "Change of plans! We need to sucker them in to let the boys get a crack at them."

"And you want us to be the suckers, sir?"

"That's right. Move into the intersection, fire a couple of shots, and then run south to the next street. Take cover and then do it again. No more than three blocks, though. Got it?"

"Yes, sir, got it. Give me a minute to get it set up." Buckman sent a pair of runners off to relay the order to the more distant squads while he instructed the one that was with him. While this was being done, Dolfen peered down Ayers Street with his binoculars. The tripods were just two blocks away now and still burning everything along their path. If the armored cars weren't able to grab their attention and get them to chase them, he was going to have to pull his men out and... *wait!*

A sudden motion at the end of the block, caught his eye. A group of men were running down the sidewalk toward him. No, not men—

women! It was Becca's sharpshooters, desperately trying to stay ahead of the pursuing enemy. Not that the Martians seemed to be chasing them in particular, but they'd be just as dead if they caught up.

And they were catching up.

The women were stumbling along, some supporting others, some had their dust masks on and others did not. But they were clearly exhausted and not moving nearly fast enough. He couldn't spot Becca among them, but she had to be there. *Come on girl, move!*

"Ready, sir!" shouted Buckman.

He looked back at the waiting armored cars and cursed. If he sent them out now and the plan worked, the Martians would increase their speed and walk into the trap he'd set - and Becca and the women would be caught right in the middle of it. But if he waited... the women and his men might all get fried anyway.

"Wait!" he commanded Buckman, holding up his hand. Then he ran out into the middle of the street, waving his hat and screaming at the women to hurry. They saw him and they did hurry up, Dolfen waited until they were halfway down the block, but he could wait no longer. He jumped back and told Buckman to go.

The gas engines of the armored cars roared and the balky machines lurched out into the open. The sharp crack of their two-inch guns seemed very loud despite all the other noise. They fired off three rounds apiece in just a few seconds and then they gunned their engines and raced south down the street, their turrets swiveling around to fire a few more parting shots.

Looking the other way, he was amazed to see the leading tripod stagger and come to a halt. A lucky shot hit something important? Another tripod maneuvered past it, but valuable seconds were gained. The armored cars made it down to the next intersection and the women made a last sprint to where Dolfen waited for them. "Quick! Get around the corner here!"

The women, about twenty of them, turned the corner and collapsed on the ground. He still didn't see Becca, but a number of them were wearing their dust gear and their faces were hidden. The shriek of a heat ray brought his attention back to the fight. He peered around the corner and grinned savagely. The plan was working, the fire from the armored cars had caught the Martians' attention and they were advancing down the street, firing back at them and no longer blasting the buildings indiscriminately. Just a little bit farther and...

A bugle rang out, its shrill tones audible above the roar of battle. Immediately, rifle fire and machine gun fire and stovepipe fire blasted out from the buildings along the street. Bullets sparked off the tripod's armor and the smoke trails of the rockets ended in small explosions, ripping at the machines.

The Martians, four or five of them, halted in mid-block and swung their rays across the buildings on either side; brick facades crumbled and flames erupted from the windows and burst through the roofs. Dolfen hoped his boys had the sense to get out before they burned.

But while the enemy was firing into the buildings, more troopers, men on foot, on motorcycles, and on horseback were emerging from the alleys between the buildings. Some were flinging dynamite bombs, others were firing stovepipes, and as he watched, half a dozen of those madmen with the rocket-lances galloped out around the legs of the enemy.

Explosions staggered the metal giants. Arms and legs were torn off, the lead machine crashing to the ground in a cloud of smoke. As Dolfen watched in wonder, a mounted trooper drove his lance into the knee joint of one of the tripods. The explosion blew the man off his horse, but it also blew the leg off the Martian. It swayed to one side, tried to regain its balance, and then toppled over right into the front of one of the burning buildings. The wall gave way and the machine crashed through, into an inferno, its remaining legs thrashing wildly.

"That's it! Burn you bastard!"

And then it was over, the remaining Martians retreated as quickly as they could, one limping noticeably.

"By God! By God, Captain! Did you see that?" Lynnbrooke had come up beside him and was pointing and almost dancing.

"I did, Lieutenant. But I hope the boys on the other streets did as well." He looked over the rooftops, but couldn't see much. At least no Martians were turning the corners at the other intersections—yet. "But we can't stay here celebrating. Look, they're regrouping and I think there are some of those spider-machines with them now. We can't stay here. Pass the word for the men to fall back four blocks south."

"Yes, sir!" Lynnbrooke dashed off. Private Gosling trotted up holding Dolfen's horse.

"We movin', Captain?"

"Yup. But we need to help these women, they're spent. Round up some more horses, or a truck if you can find one." He pointed to where the sharpshooters were huddled. Damn it, he still didn't see Becca! Had she made it...?

"Frank?" A muffled voice drew his attention to one of them. One of the women came forward. She was wearing her mask, but the height and build were about right.

"Becca?" He moved toward her, his hands out.

"Don't touch me!"

That wasn't the greeting he'd been hoping for. "Are... Becca, are you all right?"

"I'm covered with the black dust! Don't touch me!"

Instinctively he backed off, but a dagger of fear pierced him. Dust! An uglier death was hard to imagine. But wait, she clearly wasn't dying... "Did you get any on you?"

"Not so far, but it's all over me." He looked closer and yes, he could see black specks on her leather jacket and skirt. Not a lot, but it only took one. "I can't ride a horse, I'd kill the poor beast." She pointed at where Golsing was bringing up some horses.

"Well, we can't stay here! They're coming back."

"I know, I can walk. Let's go."

The men of the squadron - a gratifying number of them, too - were emerging from the alleys and heading south. The other women were loaded on horses or put behind some of the motorcycle riders. Frank remained on foot and motioned Becca to move. "Let's get out of here."

Chapter Sixteen

July, 1912, South of Memphis, Tennessee

"Looks like a hell of a fight going on, Colonel." Andrew Comstock glanced at his aide, Lieutenant Jerry Hornbaker, and then back at what he was referring to. The whole sky to the north was a mass of black smoke. Memphis was burning. The view from *USLI Albuquerque*'s observation platform was both exhilarating and daunting. The city was obviously in trouble.

But there was clearly a battle still in progress. The rumble of artillery could be heard clearly even from ten miles away. Ten miles; they had sailed all the way from Philadelphia, survived storms and river sand bars, and now here they were, only ten miles from Memphis. The five remaining units in the army's 1st Land Ironclad Squadron would soon enter combat for the first time.

He hoped.

The ironclads were still being towed, as their tiny propellers would have made little headway against the flow of the Mississippi. They had made it to New Orleans with no further mishaps, but then there had been an infuriating delay to find new towing ships since the vessels which had brought them from Philadelphia drew far too much water for the river. The ironclads themselves also drew too much water, but anytime they encountered a sand bar or mud bank, they could simply engage the caterpillar tracks and drive right over it. He'd lost count of the number of times they'd had to do that. But the towing ships couldn't do it so they had to be powerful enough to do the job, but with a shallow enough draft to avoid getting stuck. The vessels had finally been found and they set out, but it was slow going, maybe five miles per hour at most.

So, another two hours to Memphis. But what would they do when they got there? Where was the fight actually taking place? And would they be able to get from the river to the fight? He looked to the eastern shore and eyed the imposing concrete walls marching northward. They looked to be at least thirty feet high and with a ditch in front of them. There were gates at intervals, but there was no way a land ironclad could fit through them. If the fight was inside the city, they might be stuck on the wrong side of the walls. At least there were no cliffs along the shores like there had been at Vicksburg.

"It appears we are in for a bit of a party, eh, Colonel?"

The Englishman, Major Bridges, had climbed up into the observation platform and now crowded out Hornbaker from the viewport.

Andrew hadn't been happy being made host for the man, and he found that he didn't like him at all. He was older, far more experienced in the ways of the world, and not shy about reminding everyone of the fact. He talked too much and too loudly, and laughed at his own jokes. The enforced close conditions of the ironclad didn't help matters. He wished that Bridges would have gone with Clopton, but Andrew got the impression that Clopton didn't like him, either.

"Yes," said Andrew shortly.

If Bridges sensed Andrew's dislike, he made no sign. "Any word from the general about what he plans to do?"

Clopton had made his flagship on the *Springfield* but ordered Andrew to remain with the *Albuquerque*. After what had happened to *Sioux Falls* in the storm, the general decided that it was too risky to put the commander and his second in command on the same ironclad. It was sensible, but it made consultation difficult.

"I imagine he'll keep his plans to himself until he finds out what the situation is. We've gotten damn little information from the people in Memphis."

"That's his prerogative, of course. Wellington - and Good God Kitchener! - always played their cards very close to the vest. A bit hard on their subordinates, of course."

"I'll be sure to mention that to the general next I see him," muttered Andrew. He mentally chided himself for being snippy, but the man just brought that out in him. And, of course, Bridges was right: a commander did need to confide his plans with the men who would carry out the orders he gave. How else could they act intelligently? And that was especially true for the second in command. What the hell would Andrew do if Clopton suddenly dropped dead?

Bridges looked to be about to say something else when Major Stavely joined them in the already crowded platform. He saluted Andrew. "Sir, the engineers who came with the Tesla cannon are asking if they should start charging up their capacitors? I wasn't sure what to tell them."

Yes, there was the new experimental lightning gun in the forward turret. They had managed to test it exactly once two days earlier. They had sent a boat ahead with one of the special targets and dropped it in the river, and then they'd fired at it when it drifted past. The gun had worked, sending out a spectacular lightning bolt to vaporize the target, light up a large patch of the river, and kill a few thousand fish which came floating to the surface. The rest of the vessels in the convoy had all signaled their approval with their steam whistles. It was true that the capacitors took several minutes to charge up, but there was no need to do it hours early as far as Andrew knew. Perhaps the engineers were getting anxious about the coming fight, too.

He looked at Stavely. The man was the commander of the iron-clad and theoretically it was his decision. He could understand why he might defer to Andrew on the question this experimental weapon—Andrew had been the liaison with Tesla after all—but he seemed to defer to Andrew in an awful lot of other matters, too. Was he that intimidated by Andrew's rank? That might be possible, he supposed, because for once a junior officer wasn't years older than him. Stavely didn't appear any older at all.

"I'd advise them to wait a bit longer, Major. We're still at least a couple of hours away from the battle."

"Very good, sir." He saluted again and left.

"The waiting is always the worst, isn't it?" said Bridges.

"Yes," replied Andrew. "The waiting is the worst—except for what comes after."

* * * * *

July, 1912, Memphis, Tennessee

The ambulance wagon rocked and swayed and rumbled its way down the street. Every jolt seemed to go directly into Drew Harding's shoulder. He'd never experienced this kind of pain in his life. A dislocated shoulder; he'd heard someone say that. Not all that serious and not all that hard to fix if he remembered correctly. Damnation, how much longer to get to a hospital?

And was there even any hospital to go to? The sounds of combat were growing louder behind him, not fainter. Were the Martians catching up? *Maybe it would be better if they did catch me...*

The pain in his shoulder was replaced by one in his heart, in his gut. He'd lost his ship. How many of his crew had survived? Surely some must have. Surely. Hinsworth hadn't. The crew in the forward turret hadn't. The machine gunners out on the wings... The image of the exploding Santa Fe was burned into his memory as if by a heat ray. It was entirely possible that no one had escaped. No one but him. How did you explain that to a board of inquiry? How did you explain it to the wives and parents of the men who died?

I should have just drowned...

No chance of that now, although the damned wagon might shake him to death, he supposed. His strength was slowly returning after the long time in the water and the death-like lethargy was leaving. Where were they? Somewhere in Memphis, but where? He supposed he ought to check in with someone, let them know he was alive; get word to Commodore Rush somehow. There was a little sliding hatch between the main compartment and the driver up front. Maybe he could ask where they were going.

Wincing with the pain, he slowly turned around, but couldn't reach the hatch. He'd have to stand up. He pushed himself up and reached for the wooden knob on the hatch. But just then the wagon hit some especially bad bump and he lost his balance. He twisted so as not to land on one of the other wounded men and ended up falling all the way to the floor of the ambulance. A terrible pain shot through his shoulder, but at the same time there was a loud pop, which went all the way through him. He lay there, gritting his teeth and drenched with sweat, but as the pain subsided, he realized that something had happened. His shoulder was back where it belonged! And the pain was not nearly as bad as it had been. It still hurt, but nothing like before. He struggled upright.

"You okay back there?" Drew looked up and saw that the little hatch he'd been trying to reach was now open the driver was looking through it.

"Yeah, yeah, fine. Where are we?"

"Stuck. Streets ahead are jammed with troops and tanks. We might be here a while, so relax." The hatch slid shut again.

Drew sat there for a minute or two and then got up and shuffled between the stretchers to the back of the wagon and looked out. The rear of the wagon was facing north and the whole sky was covered with black clouds of smoke. It looked like the city was on fire. Closer at hand, it was like the driver had said: the streets were packed with troops and tanks and artillery, trying to get to the fighting.

He flexed his arm and winced. It still hurt and didn't seem like there was any strength in it, but at least he could move around without the agonizing pain like before. He lowered himself down to the street and looked south, the way the ambulance was trying to go, and saw that there was little hope in getting through any time soon. What to do? He was still very tired, but somehow waiting in the ambulance was intolerable. Looking closer, he recognized where he was. That was Union Street up ahead and that meant that the tall building a few blocks west must be the hotel where MacArthur had his headquarters.

Making up his mind, he abandoned the ambulance and slowly made his way through the crowds of soldiers. The intersection at Union Street was filled with clanking, smoking steam tanks, and he was obliged to move down an alley between buildings to reach the next block. The rumbles from the north were getting louder. If the Martians arrived before the mob could get itself sorted out, it was going to be a slaughter.

He reached the hotel and saw that the chaos on the streets extended into the building as well. Or perhaps he had it backward; maybe the chaos in the hotel had spilled out onto the streets. Men were clustered around the front doors and being held back by a half-dozen sentries. Men emerged and made their way through the crowd to dash away on whatever mission they had, but no one seemed to be getting in. Drew looked down at himself. Someone had taken off his waterlogged tunic when they'd found him on the shore, and without that, his navy service dress had no rank insignia of any kind. They'd never let him in.

He stood there trying to decide what to do when one of the army officers at the edge of the crowd turned away and stomped in his direction, a look of disgust on his face. As he came up to Drew, he reached out to seize the man's arm. "What's going on?" he demanded.

The man, a major, pulled loose, but then paused to stare at Drew in puzzlement. "Who are you?"

"Commander Harding, US Navy. What's happening?"

The man shrugged. "I don't know! They're not letting anyone into headquarters and there aren't any orders coming out! Nothing since that 'Defense Plan M' message last night!"

"Yeah, I got that one. But what you mean there aren't any orders? What's MacArthur doing?"

"Nothing, apparently. Someone said he's down in the basement and won't see anyone!"

"What? So who's in command?"

The man shrugged. "No one, I guess."

* * * * *

Cycle 597, 845.2, City 3-37

Qetjnegartis considered the situation. The plan appeared to be succeeding. They had broken through the defenses of the city on a wide front from the north. Two of the fortresses which were part of that line had been overrun and a third would soon fall. The main attacking force was driving through the northern parts of the city causing great destruction. Prey-creature resistance had been tenacious in spots and almost non-existent in others. A number of war machines had been lost and quite a few of the transport pods were now in use with rescued pilots. It might become necessary to set up some secure zone where they could be placed to avoid carrying them along into combat.

The most advanced elements were nearing the center of the city and resistance was stiffening. Enemy reinforcements were crossing the bridge from the western shore despite Tanbradjus's efforts to keep them occupied with the diversionary attack. But reports indicated that most of these forces were disorganized and not yet deployed for battle. If they could be struck before they were ready, they might be destroyed in detail.

"All units continue the advance," it commanded. "Drive through to the bridge and secure it. Victory is in our grasp."

* * * * *

July, 1912, Memphis, Tennessee

"They're pushing through down that street on the left, Captain!" shouted Lieutenant Lynnbrooke. "If we don't pull back, they're gonna flank us!"

Frank Dolfen looked to his left and saw a steam tank at the next intersection on fire and infantry fleeing past it. Damn. After falling back twice, they'd found a good position which looked like they might be able to hold a while. The Martians had tried to break through twice, but three wrecked tripods were now forming a nice roadblock. The spider-machines were forcing their way through the wreckage, but the small machines were nowhere near as hard to kill as the big ones, and a dozen or more of them lay wrecked just beyond their larger brethren. The buildings here were mostly brick and concrete, and while they still had stuff inside which would burn, they were providing better defensive positions than before.

But if the Martians got past them on the left and curved in from behind, they were cooked. "All right, spread the word to pull back. We can move before they hit us again." Lynnbrooke ran to obey and soon the squadron was starting to move. He wasn't sure how many men he had left now. Half the armored cars had been lost and most of the men were on foot; horses run off and motorcycles abandoned. But they were still a cohesive combat force and they were fighting hard.

They weren't alone anymore, either. Fresh troops had come up and they only had to try and defend one street instead of three. But the boys on their left were getting pushed back and there was no choice but to retreat. He looked around and spotted Becca and her girls and waved to them to join the withdrawal. They were fighting hard, too. Or at least as hard as the men would let them. There was a natural instinct to protect them, so the women kept getting pushed back toward the rear and into areas where they would be safer. The women didn't seem to be all that upset about it, except for Becca who was constantly coming forward to take some pot shots with her Springfield. He thought he'd seen her take down one of the spiders with a great shot.

He was still terrified about the black dust on her. It was an incredibly ghastly way to die and it would only take a single inhaled grain to kill her. Sooner or later she had to get out of the dust gear, and unless she was very careful - and lucky - she would get some of the dust on her or in her. -

But there was no time to worry about that now. They had to pull back and do it quickly. He herded the women across the street, onto the next block, and moved them down the sidewalk. One of the buildings was already on fire and they had to detour into the street to get around it. He looked back just in time to see one of the men in the rearguard be incinerated by a heat ray that came from off to the left. Yes, they'd pulled out just in time. Well, almost in time.

As they moved, the block was shaken by several explosions and debris rained down around them. It wasn't the Martians, it was 'friendly' artillery. Batteries from all over the Memphis area were being trained on the invaders, and some had either bad aim or bad spotters. Errant rounds kept falling among the troops. It was to be expected, and losing the occasional man was far, far better than having no artillery support. The big guns probably killed more of the enemy than any other weapon. Without them, they would have been overrun long ago.

They reached the end of the block and Dolfen was met by a major with engineer tabs. "Captain, pull back another block. We're going to bring down these buildings here to form a roadblock." He pointed at several tall buildings just to the south.

"All right, but they're coming down on the flanks." Dolfen pointed to the next street over.

"I know, but we've got teams over there, too. All along this line actually. We're gonna try to hold them here for a while."

"Sounds good, sir. We'll pull back." He waved to Lynnbrooke and got the men moving again. Looking back north, he saw that the Martians were now getting past the tangle of wrecked machines. It wouldn't be long before they were here. "Come on! I know you're tired, but keep moving!"

They made it to the next intersection and he was heartened to find three steam tanks waiting there, just out of sight around the corner. Some of the heavy stuff from across the river was finally getting through. He deployed his troopers into the buildings on either side of the street and put the armored cars in ambush just like the tanks. Becca and her sharpshooters slumped down on the sidewalk across from them.

He found a spot where he could see around the corner in relative safety. The enemy was coming on again. A half dozen of the tripods and a swarm of the spiders were at the end of the block, spraying the buildings on each side with their heat rays. The two buildings the major had pointed out were already in flames. He hoped the explosives and the detonator wires were somewhere they wouldn't burn.

Artillery fire started falling around the tripods and that got them moving forward. The spiders came first and then one tripod with the others following at intervals. He spotted the engineer on the other side, peering intently down the street. He slowly raised his hand.

The spiders and the lead tripod reached the buildings and Dolfen braced himself for the explosion, but it didn't come. Had it misfired? No, the major still had his hand raised. What was he waiting for? *Come on! Do it!*

But he waited a little longer, until the second tripod was between the buildings. Then he dropped his hand. Dust and smoke erupted from the base of both buildings almost simultaneously. The structures were five or six stories tall and they slowly bowed in toward the street. Then they were falling and disintegrated in a huge cloud of dust which enveloped everything, including the tripod in the lead. More explosions rumbled in the distance and he saw other dust clouds billowing up on the blocks to the north and south.

Moments later, the steam tanks started to move and they clattered, squeaked, and groaned their way around the corner to face down the street. The smoke and dust slowly cleared, and as soon as the lead tripod became visible the tanks opened fire. Two of the armored cars managed to find a spot where they could get a clear shot and joined in as well. Beyond the tripod, the street was blocked with a mound of rubble thirty feet high. Dolfen hoped that there was another tripod underneath it.

He ducked back behind cover as a heat ray swept across the steam tanks. Their armor started to glow red, but they fired off another volley of shots and the ray abruptly blinked out. Daring to look, he saw that the Martian machine had toppled backward against the piled rubble, a gaping hole in the front of the head.

A dozen or so of the spider-machines were in the street, but they were motionless. He'd seen that happen several times before that day. The spiders would be moving and firing and then suddenly freeze in place. Sometimes for just a few seconds and sometimes for longer. His troopers in the buildings wasted no time in taking advantage. Fire ripped at the spiders, puncturing bodies or blasting off limbs. A few shots from the tanks completed the destruction.

After a minute or two, a tripod's head appeared above the mound of rubble and it seemed to be trying to climb over the obstruction. But when a four-inch round from one of the tanks caromed off its armor, the thing disappeared again. Artillery continued to fall, and when some aircraft—finally!—appeared, their attacks and the answering heat rays looked to be several blocks further north.

"Have they given up, do you think, sir?" asked Lynnbrooke.

"I doubt it. But it may be a while before they attack again. Make sure the men take the opportunity to resupply with ammo. See if you can scrounge up any more bombs or stovepipe rockets. We're nearly out."

"Yes, sir." Lynnbrooke moved off. Dolfen pulled out a handkerchief and mopped his face.

"Frank? Frank?"

He turned and saw that Becca had come up behind him. "Are you all right?"

"Frank, can you help me take off this mask?" her hand came up to touch her dust mask.

"Becca, you've still got dust on you! You could die."

"I will die unless I get this damn thing off! I'm melting in here and I've got to have some water." She was swaying on her feet and grabbed a lamp post to keep from falling. Yeah, it was hot as blazes today and it must have been absolute hell under that mask. She had to take it off sooner or later. "Frank, please."

"All right, all right. Come over here. Let's take this real slow and careful." He moved her into the doorway of a tobacco shop and looked her over. There were still some dust specks on her, but not nearly as many as when he first saw her. The ridiculous buckskin uniform she had complained to him about was finally proving its worth. The smooth, tanned leather provided little for the grains of dust to cling too. Unlike the wool uniforms the soldiers wore where the dust grains would get caught in the weave.

He was already wearing his gauntlets, so his hands were protected. He took his handkerchief and started brushing away the grains he could see, being careful to stand upwind of her. Shoulders, back, front...

"The mask, Frank, get the *mask* off!"

"Uh... right, right..." There wasn't much dust that he could find on the mask. It was a rubberized canvas material that was as smooth as the buckskin. He dislodged a few grains from the edges of the round eyepieces. He could see her eyes dimly through the glass, which was partially fogged up with moisture. He worked his way down to the neck area and grimaced. Where the cinch cord pulled the bottom tight around her neck were creases and folds that had caught a lot of the dust. "Hold still, this is gonna be tricky."

He brushed away as much as he could with the neck tight. Then he very carefully loosened the cord...

"Captain, I've got the men resting and..." It was Lynnbrooke.

"Lieutenant, are the Martians hitting us again?" He asked without looking away.

"Uh, no, sir, not yet."

"Then you can handle things for the moment. Leave us be."

"Uh, right, sir."

He loosened the cord and pulled the bottom of the mask out a little, revealing more grains of dust. He brushed them off and then repeated the process until he had the bottom as loose as it would go. "Ready?"

"More than ready! Do it!"

Okay, how best to do this? Slow or fast? Fast might dislodge any hidden dust, so slow. "Don't move and don't breathe." He grasped the top of the mask and slowly lifted it upward. Inch by inch he pulled it over her head. Every moment he expected her to start screaming as some grain he'd missed fell on her bare skin. But she didn't and finally the mask was clear. He moved it aside and tossed it away.

"Thank God!" gasped Becca. She started to reach for her canteen.

"Don't move, dammit!" snapped Dolfen. "I need to check around your collar."

"Well, hurry!" she snapped back.

"Yeah, yeah..." He looked closely around the collar of the jacket, but he didn't find anything. She reached for the canteen again, but he slapped her arm back. "Wait!" He inspected the canteen and frowned when he saw a few grains of dust on its cover. "Here, take mine." He gave her his own canteen and she gulped it down. Her face was a bright rosy red, covered with sweat, and beautiful.

"Oh... oh that's good," she gasped. "Thank you, Frank." She looked intently into his eyes. "Thank you, Frank."

He found himself blushing. "Uh, you're... you're welcome. But you've still got dust on you from the waist down. You need to be careful."

"I will be."

"And let me find you a helmet and another dust mask. They could use it again." It only took a short search to find what he was looking for. There was discarded equipment all over the place. He found her a spare canteen and a rations pack as well.

He had just gotten her settled back with the other women when Lynnbrooke reported that the Martians looked to be forming for another attack.

"They're coming again?" asked one of the women, her face twisted in dismay.

"Yeah, ma'am, this ain't over yet."

* * * * *

Cycle 597, 845.2, City 3-37

"Resistance has stiffened, commander. The direct routes to the bridge are blocked by fallen buildings and the prey-creatures are well dug-in among the ruins. It will take much time to fight our way through. Heavy losses are to be expected."

Qetjnegartis regarded the tactical display in his fighting machine and had to agree with the report of its subordinate. The attack had lost momentum and the enemy had managed to assemble enough force to block the direct route to the vital bridge. Perhaps they could just smash their way through, but at what cost? They had to have enough force left to hold the city once they took it. Reports from the battlegroups pushing along the eastern line of defenses indicated that a new enemy force was assembling in that area, and if it attacked while the bulk of Qetjnegartis' forces were still engaged in the city, the situation could become very precarious. They needed to finish things here as quickly as possible so they could redeploy to meet the new threat. But how?

An indicator light on its control panel notified it that Ixmaderna wished to communicate. This was hardly an opportune time, but Ixmaderna was well aware of the current situation; it would only try to communicate if it was an urgent matter. Qetjnegartis opened the channel. "Yes?"

"Commander, as you have directed, I have analyzed the images taken by the artificial satellite taken when it passed over your location a short time ago. I can transfer the data whenever you wish."

"Excellent, do so at once."

"Transmission commencing."

The data arrived and immediately the tactical display was updated. The images from the satellite were very detailed and Ixmaderna had been able to interpret them to give at least an approximation of the location of the prey-creature forces. The satellite only passed over any given location on the planet about once per local day. It was fortunate that it had passed over City 3-37 when it did.

Qetjnegartis studied the information and saw that the enemy's forces were still moving across the bridge from the fortified area west of the river. But as they arrived they were being fed directly into the areas under direct attack by the clan's forces. As its subordinate had reported, the direct routes to the bridge were filled with foot-warriors and machines. But to the east...

To the east, their line ended at about the same point as Qetjnegartis'. There was a gap of nearly three *telequel* between the end of the prey's line and the defensive structures guarding the eastern approach to the city. If it were to use the superior mobility of the war machines and suddenly shift the route of attack... Yes.

"Attention, all units. Battlegroups 2, 10, and 14 will maintain the pressure on our current front. Seventy-five percent of the remaining drones will assist. All other groups will immediately disengage and move east to the coordinates shown on your tactical map. From that point we will turn south and then west to outflank the enemy, surround them, and drive to the bridge. Speed is essential. Commence immediately."

* * * * *

July, 1912, Memphis, Tennessee

"Well, we're here. Now what the hell do we do?" Andrew Comstock was speaking rhetorically, but naturally Major Bridges felt compelled to answer. He always felt compelled to answer.

"Bit of a sticky wicket, eh, old chap?" He pointed to the burning city. "The battle is over there, and you're on the wrong side of the wall. A pity there's no gate big enough to let you through."

"They didn't know about the ironclads when they built the walls, Major."

"There looks to be a big gate at the end of the bridge, there, but I'm damned if I can see any way for us to get up to it."

"No. I don't think it would be wide enough even if we could."

The 1ˢᵗ Land Ironclad Squadron had finally arrived at Memphis only to find an unholy mess inside the city and on the river as well. Dozens of ships and hundreds of smaller craft were clustered in the vicinity of the bridge that crossed the Mississippi. The bridge itself was crammed with men and vehicles, but they didn't seem to be moving at all. A few of the warships were lobbing shells into the city, but most of them were silent. In fact, many were tied up alongside other vessel, apparently replenishing their ammunition. If they'd been fighting for the last day, they were probably out.

The smoke from the city was a dense cloud drifting eastward and flames could be seen shooting skyward in many places. The land sloped up steadily from the river and it was possible to see things over the wall. What Andrew could see didn't look good.

"Sir," said Jerry Hornbaker. "General Clopton wants us to come alongside *Springfield* to confer with you. I've ordered our tow to bring us over there."

The squadron was loitering just south of the bridge, not wanting to get caught in the jam of vessels ahead. They slowly brought *Albuquerque* over next to the flagship. Clopton was on the bridge with a speaking trumpet. "What do you think?" he called over.

Andrew had his own trumpet. "The fight is over there, sir." He pointed to the city.

"How do we get there, Colonel?"

"Sir, those walls are only six or eight feet thick. Enough to stop a heat ray, but not a twelve-incher! I suggest we take the direct ap-

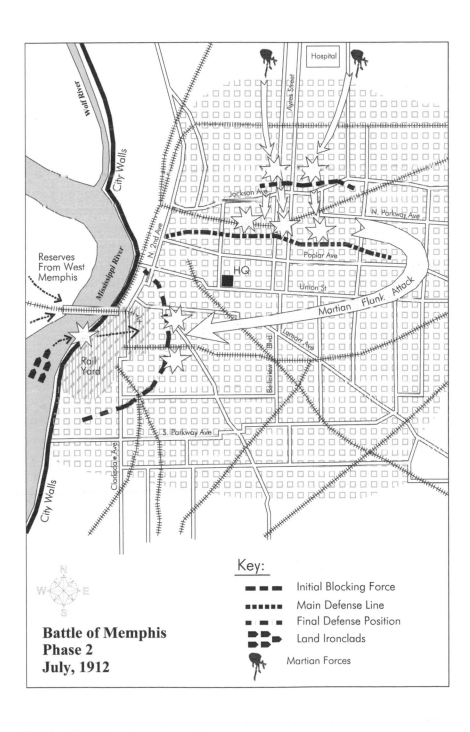

Key:

▬ ▬ ▬   Initial Blocking Force

■■■■■   Main Defense Line

■ ■ ■   Final Defense Position

◀▶◀▶   Land Ironclads

🐙   Martian Forces

Battle of Memphis
Phase 2
July, 1912

proach!"

Clopton was silent for a moment; surprised perhaps. But then he nodded vigorously. "Let's do it! The squadron will form line on the right! Let's get ashore!"

* * * * *

July, 1912, Memphis, Tennessee

Becca Harding opened the bolt of her rifle and pulled a five-round stripper clip of ammunition out of her cartridge belt. She fit the clip in place and pressed the cartridges down into the magazine. She flicked away the empty clip and closed the bolt, loading a round into the breech. She'd done this what seemed like a thousand times in the last few hours. Only a couple of the other women were firing their weapons, but the rest were happy to keep Becca supplied with ammo from their own belts. She'd had to swap rifles a few times when hers got so hot the grease started dripping out of the stock.

She leaned around the corner of the building she was hiding behind, spotted one of the damn spider-machines, took aim, and fired. The bullet hit it, causing a visible spark, but not affecting it in any other way that she could see. It swung its small heat ray in her direction and she dodged back. The ray swept across where she'd just been and the edges of the brick glowed redly for a moment. Cursing under her breath, she worked the bolt, loading another round, and tried to decide if she dared risk another shot. Sometimes the machines kept their weapon trained on the same spot, waiting for an unwary shooter to try again. She'd almost been killed several times that way, but so far she'd been lucky.

"Becca," called Sarah Halberstam. "The soldiers are waving us back again!"

All right, that decided the issue, she wouldn't chance it again. She turned and trudged along the alley, herding the women in front of her. She glanced back over her shoulder to make sure the spider wasn't following. They made it through to the next street unharmed and followed a corporal's direction to the new position.

Fall back, fall back. For the last two hours they'd been chased from one location to the next. They'd hoped that they could hold the strong position they'd built behind the collapsed buildings where Frank had helped her out of her mask. At first it seemed like the Martians had given up. They'd only probed half-heartedly with a few tripods and some spider-machines, which they'd beaten back easily. But then the word came that more Martians were attacking from the east, getting in behind the defenders; slaughtering them.

They had to retreat or risk being slaughtered, too. So the line bent back, swinging away from the Martians and toward the river. The Mississippi was at their backs now, only a few blocks away. She wasn't sure where Frank was; at first he'd hovered around her and the other women like some mother hen until she'd tartly told him to go take care of his own company. This one was hers. So he had and she had hardly seen him since. She hoped he was all right. Maybe she should have kept her mouth shut…

She and the others moved through another block of buildings and out onto a very wide street. In her fatigue, she stumbled over a set of railroad tracks and then looked around in surprise. The bridge across the Mississippi had been primarily for railroad traffic and there were several rail yards at its eastern end. In all the confused movements and retreats she'd lost track of where she was and didn't realize they were on the edge of those yards.

There were large sheds and engine houses and lots and lots of box cars and flat cars, some of them piled with supplies, lined up on sidings. There were also great crowds of troops and steam tanks and horses and guns all jammed up around the large set of gates leading to the bridge. She'd heard Frank say that a lot of the garrison's troops and equipment had been sent across the river to West Memphis because it seemed like the main enemy attack was going to be there. When the attack had really come from the north, they had to try and bring all those troops back across the river. She and the others had been fighting alongside many of those troops for the last few hours, but she knew from personal experience during the long retreat from Santa Fe in 1910 how long it could take to squeeze an army through a narrow choke point. It appeared as though an awful lot of those troops were still stuck on the bridge or on the far shore.

But at the moment it didn't look like these troops were trying to get through to the battle anymore. The battle was coming to them and they were trying to get themselves sorted out into some kind of combat formation. Officers were shouting directions and Becca finally spotted Frank. He talked briefly with one of those officers and then waved to his men to follow him. They were nearly all on foot; all the armored cars and most of the motorcycles and horses were gone. They were infantry now. As she and her girls followed along, she wondered what had become of Moses and Ninny. Had they found some refuge or had they been caught up in the fighting? Her horse had survived so much since that fateful trip down to see where the shooting stars had landed, it would be a shame for him to get killed now. *It would be a shame for you to get killed now, kid! Keep your mind on your business!*

Frank led them over to a position by some large piles of coal, stacked railroad ties, and gondola cars sitting on the tracks. They were south of the bridge now with their backs to the tall concrete walls lining the river. She saw some of the gunners on one of the platforms with a big disappearing gun. They had turned the weapon as far as it could, but it was just facing along the wall's length. It wouldn't turn far enough to shoot to the rear.

They found cover in and around the gondola cars and behind the stacks of ties. They were very conscious of the fact that the coal and the ties would burn very nicely when touched by a heat ray. But the cars were mostly metal and that would help. The cavalrymen's sole remaining machine gun was set up along with a pair of mortars. Becca found a spot under one of the cars where she had a good view to the east. Well, not a good view, but a clear line of fire extending a hundred yards or so. She scrounged a half-dozen clips of ammo from the other girls, who were mostly sheltered behind the big metal wheels of the cars, and tucked them into her belt pouches. Sarah Halberstam lay down under the car beside her. Frank came by, appearing very harried. He just looked over their position, nodded, and moved on.

Several of the steam tanks chugged up on their left and infantry clustered around and behind them. A squad of men came up, apparently thinking about occupying the spot Becca and her girls were in, looked at them in confusion, and then moved off to find a spot somewhere else. She had no idea what unit they belonged to, everything was all mixed up.

"How are the others holding up?" she asked Sarah.

"They're scared, Becca. Worn out and scared to death." She paused and then added: "So am I."

"Yeah, yeah, me, too."

"Really? You don't look it. You never look scared; you look angry."

Becca shrugged. "The mad hides the scared, I guess."

Sarah nodded and then looked around. "Well, I guess our retreating is over. Nowhere left to run from here."

"No, I reckon that's true." And it was; their backs were literally to the wall. "So we have to stop them."

"You think we can?"

"We can try."

Sarah smiled. "We did our best. So did you, Becca. You've done a great job. As the soldiers would say: it's been an honor serving under your command today, sir."

Becca blinked, her throat tight. "I... we *are* soldiers, Sarah."

"Yes, I guess we are, aren't we? - thanks to you."

"Not sure if that's a compliment, considerin' the circumstances."

Sarah laughed. "Well, it was meant to be. This is our home, Becca. We all ought to be willing to fight to defend it. You showed us how."

She held out her hand and Becca leaned over and grasped it.

"Well, those monsters don't care that we're women. Let's show them what humans can do!"

"Yes... Oh God, here they come!"

The firing, which had died down a bit, suddenly rose to a high tempo again and the noise of the heat rays pierced the roar. Through the smoke she could see the dark shapes of the tripods stalking forward. She didn't waste her ammunition shooting at them, instead she squinted through her sights, looking for the spider-machines.

Cannons were firing and she saw one of the tripods fall, but then heat rays were sweeping across the area. Shooting down from above, they couldn't quite reach Becca where she was under the gondola, but the ground just in front of her blazed red, the far metal rail of the track turned a dull orange and the gravel gleamed like hot coals. She ducked her head to shield her face from the blast of scalding air which roiled around her. But then it moved on. Screams and an explosion came from her left where the steam tanks had been.

She looked up again, her eyes watering from the heat and the smoke. As she'd feared, the piles of coal were burning and she couldn't see more than a few dozen yards now. A puff of wind from the west blew some of it away, but it was still bad.

The air shook as artillery fell much too close for comfort. Stones rattled down around them, banging off the top and sides of the gondola. *This is it. Can't hold nothing back now!*

Squinting and coughing, she peered ahead looking for a target. Any target.

A shape materialized a little to her left and she swung the rifle toward it. A squat horror with multiple legs and arms was scuttling toward her. She aimed and fired and hit it. She worked the bolt and fired again. She thought Sarah was firing, too, but the noise had grown so great it was all mingled in one all-encompassing roar. She emptied the magazine and loaded in another clip. She fired again. The spider-machines had a small glowing red 'eye', just like the larger ones. She aimed at that and squeezed the trigger. The eye shattered and went out. The spider halted and seemed to turn from side to side as if blinded. Becca chambered another round and sent it through the hole where the eye had been. A few sparks shot out and the spider slowly leaned to one side and fell over.

"We got it! We got it!" screamed Sarah Halberstam, her voice just barely audible in the bedlam.

But then her scream became a wordless shriek and Becca turned and saw that the woman was on fire. A second spider had emerged from the smoke and turned its heat ray on Sarah. The small ray devices carried by the spiders weren't powerful enough to reduce a person to ashes, but they were still deadly. Sarah's clothes were burning and she rolled toward Becca trying to put out the flames. The spider was twenty yards away and followed her with the ray. Becca grabbed the woman and dragged her behind the wheel of the gondola, out of the line of fire for the moment. She beat on Sarah's clothes with her leather-gloved hands to try and put out the flames. She was still screaming and thrashing almost uncontrollably. Her left shoulder was a blackened ruin.

At last the fire was out and Sarah collapsed in her arms, moaning. Becca peered around the wheel and saw the spider moving forward, around the end of the car. In a moment it would have a clear line on them. She grabbed her rifle and worked the bolt, but the magazine was empty. She fumbled for a clip, but each pouch on her belt that her frantic fingers came to was empty, too. The spider was coming…

A massive rumble shook the earth beneath her and a loud explosion echoed across the rail yard. It came from the west and she tore her eyes away from the spider-machine for an instant to look that way. But all she could see were burning vehicles, dead men and…

…the city walls.

A cloud of smoke was rising up from just beyond a stretch of them, just to the right of the big disappearing gun. What was that? Some new Martian attack? The final blow? But when she jerked her head back to look at the spider-machine, it seemed to be as transfixed by this new development as she was.

Another series of explosions made her look at the walls again and new clouds were rising up and then… then a whole long section of the wall seemed to be leaning, leaning away, leaning outward. With a roar of shattering concrete they crumbled to pieces and fell in a huge swirling cloud of dust. What was happening?

She sat there, frozen, cradling Sarah Halberstam and her useless rifle in her arms, watching the dust. A dark form began to take shape within the cloud. At first all she could see was a dark mass atop long rods, and for an instant she was sure it was a tripod. But no, the shape on top was square, not round like a Martian machine, and it was perched on something even larger…

As she stared in astonishment, a huge green shape emerged from the cloud. It was bristling with guns and from a pole on the top flew the Stars and Stripes. In white letters across the prow was written the word:

Albuquerque.

* * * * *

July, 1912, Memphis, Tennessee

Colonel Andrew Comstock whooped in delight as the section of city wall toppled outward into the ditch, disappearing in a cloud of dust.

"That did it, Major! Let's get moving!"

"Yes, sir!" said Major Stavely. "Driver! Full speed! Steer for the hole! All guns prepare to fire!"

The *Albuquerque* lurched into motion and rumbled its way up the bank and toward the gap in the walls. Andrew hoped they hadn't killed anyone in making that gap, but he supposed it was possible. Anyone looking out should have immediately understood what was going to happen and gotten the hell out of the way. But with the battle raging, maybe they hadn't looked out. Or were too confused to understand.

But there hadn't been any choice, none at all.

They had to get into the city where the battle was and the only way to do that wouldn't include a thirty mile detour was to go through the walls. Against a fortification built to withstand an attack by humans it would have been hopeless. Walls thirty feet high would have also been thirty feet thick to resist the impact of rifled artillery. It would have taken them days to blast their way through. But the Martian heat rays had no impact when they struck. They burned or melted their way through objects, but concrete was the ideal material to resist the rays. Walls a mere six or eight feet thick had proved perfectly able to resist the rays. In the rush to build as many walls as possible, they were made as thin as practical to save time and materials. Which also meant they were vulnerable to heavy artillery.

The land ironclads had plenty of that.

They had turned toward the river bank, and when their tracks had touched ground they jettisoned their flotation modules and hauled themselves ashore. They had to crush or shove aside some wooden piers and a few small boats along the waterfront, but that didn't hinder them in the slightest. Some sheds and other buildings had to go, too. People were gathering all around waving. Whether in welcome of the ironclads or in protest of the property damage Andrew wasn't sure. The city walls, just ahead, had thick concrete platforms to mount the big disappearing guns built at intervals, and they didn't want to try and blast through there. Fortunately, the walls projected out at those points and they were easy to spot. Clopton directed the squadron to concentrate on a single one hundred yard section of wall about a quarter mile south of the bridge.

The first salvo, five twelve-inch, four seven-inch and ten five-inch shells, exploded all along the base of the wall. This close, they could aim very precisely. Huge chunks of concrete were gouged out and flew off in all directions. A couple of the twelve-inchers had punched all the way through. The five-inch guns got off a few more shots before the big guns were reloaded, but then they all fired off again.

The next salvo had brought the whole section of wall down, exactly as they had hoped. Not only did it open a gap in the wall, but the debris had nearly filled the ditch which lay in front of it. The path was now clear.

Albuquerque led the way with the others following close behind. The gap was probably wide enough to go two abreast, but they were going single file. None of them knew exactly what they'd be facing on the other side, but the smoke and flames and noise indicated that the fighting was very close. They had to be ready for anything as they drove into the cloud of dust.

The ironclad's huge tracks crunched over the rubble in the ditch and then climbed up over the broken-off stub of the walls. Andrew had to steady himself as the machine pitched and jerked over the uneven ground. The other people on the bridge, Stavely, Hornbaker, several enlisted men, and the inevitable Major Bridges did so as well.

Up, over, and through. The wind pulled the dust away like a curtain and they were in Memphis.

They were in what looked to be the rail yards. Tracks filled with cars, sheds, engine houses, mounds of coal, water towers, control towers, and all manner of other things covering several hundred acres. Most of the things seemed to be on fire. The open spaces were crammed with troops and steam tanks, wagons and horses. Many of them were on fire, too.

On the far side of the yards were what they had come for: Martian tripods.

A dozen at least were in sight, and from the heat rays emerging from the smoke in the distance, there were surely more coming. But the nearer ones were motionless, not moving, not firing. Why?

"I think we surprised the blighters," said Bridges.

"I think you're right! Well, let's take advantage of it! Major Stavely, fire at will!"

"Yes, sir! All guns, commence firing!"

The main turret swung slightly to the left, steadied, and then fired. A gout of flame and a cloud of black cordite smoke erupted from the end of the barrel. In the instant before the smoke hid the view, Andrew saw a tripod simply disintegrate; head blown to flinders, arms and legs flying off in all directions. A moment later, the five-inchers joined in, although he wasn't sure what they were firing at.

Albuquerque continued to move forward, clearing the way for the others to follow. *Tulsa* was behind them and swung out to the right, *Omaha* was next and would go left. By the time the twelve-incher was reloaded, the view had cleared enough to pick a new target; and a moment later, another tripod was annihilated. Hornbaker was shouting like it was a football game.

But now the enemy was beginning to react. Heat rays stabbed out to hit the ironclads and Andrew tensed. The forward armor ought to be able to stand up to them, but would it? The bridge shutters had been lowered and the steam lines pressurized if a defensive cloud needed to be released.

A ray blazed around the bow and another played along the main turret. But there were no explosions, no sudden alarms, and a moment later the guns roared out again and claimed the attackers. "No damage reported!" cried Stavely jubilantly.

"Looks like you've gotten their attention, though, old chap," said Bridges, pointing.

Andrew looked through the thick quartz view block and saw what the Britisher was talking about. Six tripods were moving into position in front of them. "Major Stavely, I think we have a target for Professor Tesla's cannon! Tell them to get ready!

"Yes, sir!"

* * * * *

Cycle 597, 845.2, City 3-37

Qetjnegartis absorbed the status reports and was pleased. Victory was within its grasp. The flanking movement had succeeded perfectly. The prey-creature defenses had been thrown into confusion and they had retreated in disarray back toward the vital bridge. Now they were penned into a narrow space with the clan's fighting machines closing in from three sides. Once they were destroyed, the enemy on the bridge could be similarly disposed of. There were still the dangerous water vessels on the river, but the enemy's own defensive walls would provide cover for the war machines and they could be destroyed or driven off by heat ray fire from the shores. Other battlegroups could be sent to the eastern perimeter to deal with the new enemy force assembling there.

Losses had been heavy, but not so crippling that the city could not be held. Once a link-up with Tanbradjus' forces on the western shore was made, construction machines could be moved into the city and a proper holdfast constructed. The base on the eastern shore would be secured. Raiding parties could be sent out to disrupt the prey-creatures' transportation systems and the manufacturing facilities which surely must exist in the east. The way would be opened for the final conquest of this continent. Success. The Colonial Conclave and the elders back on the Homeworld would be pleased...

"Commander! Commander Qetjnegartis! Respond!"

It was Davnitargus, commander of battlegroup 32-8. It sounded very agitated. What could be wrong? "This is Qetjnegartis. What do you want?"

"Commander, we have reached the bridge, but are under attack by... by..."

"By what?"

"I do not know! War machines of some sort. Huge war machines! Much larger than ours! The heat rays seem to have little effect on them!"

"Relay an image."

The image was difficult to interpret. Smoke obscured much of the details, but it could see a very large object... no, several very large objects. They were somewhat similar to the armored gun vehicles the prey-creatures used, but much larger. Projectile throwers in rotating cylinders studded their surface. Other objects of unknown purpose projected above. As Qetjnegartis watched, a war machine's heat ray struck the forward surface with seemingly no effect until the war machine was destroyed by a single shot from one of the enemy weapons.

"Davnitagus, concentrate your forces against a single enemy and destroy it. I will be on the scene shortly."

"Understood," said the bud.

Qetjnegartis was not far off. It had followed along behind the main advance, coordinating activity rather than directly engaging in combat. Now it set its machine in motion and quickly came forward to a spot with a clear view. The tall buildings ended on the edge of a large open space filled with burning structures, prey-creatures, war machines, and the newly arrived devices.

Just as it halted, six of the war machines opened fire on the leading vehicle. The heat rays struck various locations on the thing with no immediate effect, but then all six rays converged on a single point at the front. The metal quickly turned bright yellow and started to melt. *Yes, this is the proper way to deal...*

A blindingly bright light sprang from one of the cylinders. It wasn't a beam of energy, like a heat ray, but a jagged, twisting blast like a static charge jumping from point to point. It leapt out and connected to the nearest fighting machine, but then jumped to the next and the next until all six were connected. The bolt writhed and twisted, and all the fighting machines jerked spasmodically as they sent out showers of sparks and gouts of smoke. After, a moment the bolt vanished and the six machines collapsed to the ground.

"Commander!" said Davnitargus over the communicator. "Did you see that?"

"Yes, I saw."

"What was that?"

"I don't know." It tried to formulate a more useful response but nothing came.

"What are you orders?"

Even as it tried to reach a decision, the enemy giants came forward. There were five of them, and their weapons smashed machine after machine.

"Commander?"

"Fall back. We must fall back and regroup so we can concentrate and destroy these things."

"Yes, Commander, at once."

* * * * *

July, 1912, Memphis, Tennessee

Rebecca stared in wonder at the enormous machines. They were like ships mounted on big caterpillar tracks like the steam tanks used. They had guns, big guns, all over them. And they were olive drab and they flew the American flag.

"They're ours," she whispered. "They're ours, Sarah." She looked down at the woman in her arms. Her eyes were closed, but she stirred, moaned, and her eyes fluttered open.

"Look, Sarah, they're ours. And they're killing the Martians. Look!" As she sat there, soldiers were coming forward, shouting, faces twisted with some terrible combination of fear, joy, and anger. One of them ran up to the still frozen spider-machine, strapped a bomb to it, pulled the fuse, and ran off. He obviously hadn't even seen her there, only twenty feet away. She twisted around to shield Sarah as much as she could. The bomb exploded wrecking the spider. Some bit of shrapnel stung her cheek.

One of the colossal machines rolled by, not a hundred feet away, its massive tracks crushing everything under them. "Look, Sarah, can you see it? Can you see?"

Sarah Halberstam jerked her head in a tiny nod. Her mouth shaped *I see it, Becca*, but made no sound she could hear. They watched the behemoth pass by, its guns shaking the ground. Becca turned her head to try and see what was happening, but the gondola blocked her view. More troops streamed past. She couldn't keep sitting there. She needed to see what was happening and get medical help for Sarah. God only knew where the hospital people were now.

"Sarah? Sarah, we need to get you some help. Can you move?"

But Sarah Halberstam didn't move. Becca shook her gently, but she didn't move.

Her lips were quivering as she closed the woman's eyes and gently moved her aside so she could get up. She pulled her under the gondola car where hopefully nothing would disturb her.

She rubbed away her tears, grabbed her rifle, and went in search of ammunition.

* * * * *

July, 1912, Memphis, Tennessee

"Major, there are men on the ground in front of us. What should I do?" The driver of *Albuquerque* looked toward his commander, seeking guidance.

Andrew looked forward as well as he could through the narrow view slit. The rail yards were a mass of train cars, steam tanks, men, artillery limbers, and horses. And there were men on the ground. Dead? Wounded? Stavely turned to look at him. "Colonel?"

He swallowed. "We have to pursue, Major, we can't let the enemy regroup. Keep going."

"When I was commanding a company of steam tanks, sometimes we had to..." Stavely grimaced, nodded, and turned back to the driver. "Keep going, Sergeant."

The man didn't look happy, but he said: "Yes, sir."

The ironclad continued to move at its top speed of about five miles an hour. Mercifully, it was impossible to see the ground directly in front of the machine, nor see what its huge tracks were rolling over. There were definitely crunching sounds coming from below, but Andrew told himself it was from empty wagons and rail cars and not human bones. *No choice. No choice.*

"Bloody sad thing, Colonel, but war is hell, as your General Sherman would say," said Major Bridges.

The enemy was retreating. Tesla's lightning cannon had worked beyond anything Andrew had hoped for. Six Martians destroyed with a single shot! Granted, it would be ten minutes before they could fire it again, but the Martians didn't know that. And it was clear that they had been shocked by what had happened. Just moments after it fired, the surviving tripods started falling back. General Clopton had ordered a pursuit and that is what they would do.

Beyond the rail yards, the larger buildings of the city took over, creating narrow canyons on either side of the streets. The bigger avenues were just wide enough for an ironclad to move along. Well, almost wide enough; the ironclad was snapping off lamp posts and electrical poles and projecting signs as it moved. Andrew wasn't sure if they could actually smash their way through a block of buildings, and hopefully they wouldn't have to find out. *Albuquerque* steered into one of the streets, while the four others each took parallel routes. The remains of the other army troops in the area were rallying and following along.

Most of the Martians, able to move much faster, had already retreated a half mile or more, but some of the spider-machines had been left behind. The ironclads had a dozen heavy machine guns able to shoot from armored mounts along the lower hull, and these were firing busily at them. Oddly, most that Andrew could catch sight of were just standing frozen as the bullets tore them apart. Some of them were simply crushed as the ironclad rolled over them.

Up ahead there was a crippled tripod, one of its legs blown off, trying to drag itself along with its arms and other legs. As the *Albuquerque* approached, it propped itself up and fired its heat ray. But the front of the ironclads were very heavily armored with the steel-asbestos sandwiches developed by the MIT engineers. The shoes on the caterpillar tracks were solid steel six inches thick and continually rotating to prevent a heat ray from being able to burn its way through. For a short exposure, there wasn't a thing the Martian could do.

"Run it down," Andrew said with grim satisfaction.

There was slight lurch and they crushed the thing flat. Only after they'd done it did Andrew wonder what would have happened if the tripod's power cells had exploded with them sitting on top of it. *Need to be careful about that...*

"Colonel, there are a bunch of them gathered up ahead. Seven or eight blocks away, there. Do you see?" Stavely pointed. Andrew squinted, pulled out his binoculars, cursed at the fuzzy image, and stepped out onto the bridge wing to get a clear view. Yes, three-quarters of a mile ahead there was a cluster of tripods milling about. A dozen or more of them.

"Do they think they're out of our range?" asked Stavely who had followed along.

"Let's enlighten them with the twelve-incher, Major. Give them a shot and tell the crew to make the next one armor piercing."

"My pleasure, Colonel!" said Stavely with a grin.

A moment later the big gun roared out, half-deafening Andrew. Through his binoculars he saw the shell burst among the tripods and at least one went down. Now, if the gunners could just reload before they had the sense to disperse. A well-drilled crew ought to be able to reload and fire in less than a minute, even with the thousand pound shells the big gun fired. He counted silently and had only reached fifty-two when they fired again.

The guns and the ammunition they fired were designed by the navy. An armor piercing round had a thicker metal shell and the fuse had a delay to allow it to smash its way deep into the vitals of a ship before exploding.

The tripods had far less armor than a battleship.

Even from that far away, Andrew could see the havoc the shell wrecked among the Martians. It tore its way right through their formation, arms, leg, heads, whole machines went flying before the shell finally burst. Andrew was reminded of the descriptions he'd read in history class at West Point about solid shot from artillery ripping through the close-packed infantry of a Napoleonic column.

"Wow!" cried Jerry Hornbaker.

"Yes, Lieutenant," said Andrew. "Wow, indeed."

* * * * *

Cycle 597, 845.2, City 3-37

Qetjnegartis was thrown violently against the safety restraints as something large smashed into its fighting machine. The machine staggered and it was barely able to regain control to prevent it from toppling over. What had happened? It was at the rear of the formation? Had one of the high-angle projectiles landed on it?

No, as it looked around it realized that something else had happened. Four of the fighting machines had been wrecked and three others seriously damaged all at a blow. The impact on its own machine had actually been part of another machine which had been torn off.

"Commander!" said one of its subordinates. "These narrow passages are death traps. The enemy can fire right along them and we are easy targets."

"Yes, yes, you are correct. Quickly, let us move into the lateral passages, out of their line of fire."

The surviving machines moved into cover behind the buildings. They were safe for the moment, but what was to be done? Over half of the fighting machines which had crossed the river were out of action. Nearly eighty percent of the drones were gone. More and more prey-creature forces were gathering with the new giant machines. Was there any way to defeat them?

"If we stay in these side laterals until the large machines approach, perhaps we can ambush them, Commander," suggested Davnitargus. "If we are very close, perhaps their large weapons will not be able to bear on us."

"Perhaps. Very well, let us try." Commands were issued and on laterals adjoining each of the five passageways on which the enemy vehicles were approaching, fighting machines were gathered. Vision pick-ups were extended on manipulators to see the enemy. They were coming on slowly; perhaps this would work.

But flying machines were overhead, circling beyond the reach of the heat rays. They were clearly directing the fire of the long range high-angle projectile throwers. Their shells were falling more and more frequently near the closely massed fighting machines. Could they warn the large machines as well?

They were nearly here. A bit closer and the trap could be sprung...

The machine stopped.

"Commander, they can see us!"

Qetjnegartis looked and saw that the tall tower on top of the enemy machine was higher than the intervening buildings. This close they had a direct line of sight to the tops of the fighting machines. They had detected the ambush. Should it still be sprung? They would have to emerge into the passageway and attack from the front. If that electric arc weapon was ready, how many machines could it take down?

The image from the vision pick-up showed the largest weapon turning to the left. What was it aiming at? The building was in the way. *Surely they aren't going to...*

The side of the building forty quel ahead of Qetjnegartis exploded outward and the fighting machine in front of it was torn to pieces. The prey had fired right through the building!

"This is no good, Commander!" said Davnitargus. "We must withdraw!"

Retreat meant failure. The only possible place to go was back across the river. The chance to establish a hold on the eastern shore would have to be abandoned. Was there anything that could be done to salvage the situation?

But then word came from the commander of the battlegroup on the eastern perimeter. The enemy force which had gathered there was now attacking. "There are over three hundred of the armored gun-vehicles, Commander," it reported. "We cannot stop such a force without immediate reinforcements."

To send the reinforcements would leave Qetjnegartis with insufficient force to deal with the current situation—if indeed there were sufficient forces now—but to ignore the request would mean the enemy would come driving in on their rear at the most critical moment. To stay could mean the annihilation of the entire force.

"Progenitor," said Davnitargus, "it was a noble attempt, a brilliant plan, but to stay here will mean our destruction; and with it, all hope for our clan on this world. We must withdraw."

Another projectile crashed through the building, but fortunately this time it did not hit any of the fighting machines. No, Davnitargus was right, to stay would mean destruction with no hope for any gain.

"Very well. All forces, this is Qetjnegartis. We must retreat. Disengage and move north. We will re-cross the river at the same point as we initially crossed. Speed is essential."

It received the acknowledgments almost immediately. Clearly all were expecting the order.

Turning its machine, Qetjnegartis fled the scene of disaster.

* * * * *

July, 1912, Memphis, Tennessee

"They're retreating, Colonel, shall we pursue?" asked Major Stavely.

"By all means, Major," said Andrew. "I doubt we'll catch them, but let's make sure they don't stop."

"You're not going to wait for an order from General Clopton, Colonel?" asked Major Bridges.

"Any fool can see what needs to be done, Major, and Clopton's no fool. Let's drive these bastards into the river."

* * * * *

July, 1912, Memphis, Tennessee

Drew Harding sat on the steps of the hotel, cradling his arm. He was filthy and utterly exhausted. A steady stream of men ran up and down the steps into the headquarters now. He looked up as the same army major he'd talked to earlier sat down next to him with a grunt. "So what's happening?" asked Drew. "Did we win?"

"Looks like it. Or it sure sounds like it if you listen to MacArthur. He's a pistol, isn't he?"

"I guess." In truth he wasn't sure what to make of General MacArthur. He'd been so absurdly confident at that meeting before the battle; pompous, even. And then during the crisis he was nowhere to be seen. His subordinates had been like a flock of chickens with all their heads cut off. With nowhere else to go, Drew had found a spot near the entrance to the hotel and dozed off. The fighting to the north didn't seem to be getting any closer, so it had seemed like a good idea.

Then, suddenly, everything was in an uproar. The sounds of battle were coming from the east instead of the north and they were getting close very fast. The headquarters staff had come boiling out of the building, carrying rolls of maps and stacks of paper and calling for vehicles to move it all. But before an evacuation could even get under way, the Martians were marching down the streets just a block away to the north. Everyone tried to find cover.

And into the midst of the chaos, MacArthur had suddenly appeared; he was immaculately decked out in his fancy uniform, decorations on his chest, and a riding crop in his hand. He'd walked through the mob like a large ship parting the waves, ignoring every shouted plea for orders. He'd strolled over to the intersection and just stood there, in plain sight, watching the Martian tripods moving past, not five hundred feet away. To Drew, it looked like he was trying to get himself killed. But no heat ray claimed him.

The sounds of fighting near the bridge grew to an uproar, and then to everyone's astonishment, the Martians had come back the way they had come, heading east, away from the bridge. A few minutes later they were followed by the most outlandish contraptions Drew had ever seen. He instantly knew what they were; he'd read about them and he'd gotten some letters from his friend, Andrew Comstock, who was helping to build them. But he'd had no idea they were ready for action or that they were coming to Memphis. They were, perhaps, the ugliest bits of machinery he'd ever seen, but at that moment they looked beautiful. Everyone stopped and stared.

MacArthur had stared, too, but then he stirred and came back to the entrance of the hotel. Everyone had gathered round. "A great victory is within my reach, gentlemen," he'd said. He didn't speak loudly, yet somehow everyone could hear him. "But now I need all your help to grasp it. Let's get to work." He'd walked back into the hotel, his staff streaming after him.

"So what are you going to do now?" asked the major.

He sighed. What he really wanted to do was to sleep for about twelve hours. "I guess I need to find Commodore Rush and get some orders."

* * * * *

July, 1912, Memphis, Tennessee

Captain Frank Dolfen, 5th US Cavalry, stumbled over the rubble, back toward where he hoped his men were waiting. The sun was sinking toward the western horizon, although it could only be seen from time to time through all the smoke. Large sections of the city were still burning and he doubted that any of the fire brigades were still functional. They'd have to let it burn itself out, he guessed.

The smell of burning; burning wood, burning coal, burning flesh, was almost overpowering. It was odd: during the fighting he'd smelt nothing. But now he could smell everything. It was like that in every fight he'd ever been in. His senses narrowed down to sight and sound.

Afterward he'd find himself covered with cuts and scratches and have no memory of how or when he'd gotten them. Like now. His uniform was torn and burned in a dozen spots, and he hurt in more places than that.

Most of them he guessed had come from at the end, during the fight in the rail yard. He'd been running from spot to spot, encouraging his men, trying to keep them fighting. Trying to keep them alive. Between dodging heat rays and dodging shrapnel from their own artillery, he'd spent most the time on his belly, crawling among the railroad cars.

He'd been quite certain they were all going to die. They were in a box with nowhere to run, and a swarm of the tripods were approaching from seemingly everywhere. A strange acceptance had filled him. It had been a good fight and they'd hurt the enemy a lot. *He'd* hurt the enemy a lot over the years. He'd been sad that the 5th Cavalry was going to die yet again. Sad that Becca was going to die, too. So young. No younger than many of his troopers, of course, but it was still a shame.

Then, those incredible, amazing... *things* had broken through the walls. Just smashed right through them, and blown the holy hell out of the Martians. Those big guns, that unbelievable magic lightning cannon, they'd simply wrecked the bastards. He'd heard rumors of the 'secret weapons' the army was building, but never really believed it. So far the only new weapons they'd seen were the airplanes and the stovepipe rocket launchers. Useful things, to be sure, but still kind of pathetic compared to what the Martians had.

But these! These things were enormous! Bigger than the tripods, big as buildings. He'd seen one of them knock a tripod over and then crush it flat under its tracks. It was glorious. Yes, *glorious*; not a word he'd had much use for in recent years, but that's what it was. He'd laughed and shouted and thrown his helmet in the air. And then the Martians were running; fleeing back the way they'd come. The troops had all cheered and come out of whatever hole they'd been cowering in to follow along behind the big green behemoths.

He'd waved to his men to come on. It was a pursuit, and that was what cavalry was for. Granted, they were all on foot now, but it still wasn't a chance to be missed. He'd shouted and led them forward.

For a couple of blocks.

The spirit was willing, but their bodies just couldn't do it. They'd been fighting or on the move between fights for a full day and a night. They had done all that could be expected of human flesh and blood. They'd tried, but eventually their pursuit had slowed to a crawl and then stopped altogether. Other troops had streamed past them, eager to finally get into the fight. Dolfen and his boys had been content to let them. Lynnbrooke had found him leaning against a wall, gasping for breath. He told him to gather the men and form them up back in the rail yard. The lieutenant, half his age, had smiled and done it. Dolfen had followed along a bit more slowly.

"Over here, sir," said someone. Looking up, he saw a cluster of men right at the edge of the yard. Somehow, they still had a guidon and the tattered red pennant with the white letters for the 1st Squadron fluttered fitfully in a weak breeze. He looked around, hoping to see others like it, but there weren't any, just a steady stream of men and vehicles moving up from the bridge and smaller groups filtering back in the opposite direction. He hadn't seen or heard anything of the rest of the regiment since they were separated at the bridge. He hoped that he and his men weren't all that was left.

And how many did he have left? He could see forty or fifty sitting or lying down. There could easily be some stragglers who had become separated during all the frantic repositioning. Maybe a few wounded who had survived and who might someday return to the ranks. But at least half were gone. Half of the officers, too. Buckman had burned up in his armored car, and he'd seen Gregory McGuiness cut down by one of the spider-machines while he was trying to clear a jam in his remaining Browning.

But it wasn't all bad news, there was Gosling, his orderly, miraculously coming up to him with a tin cup filled with coffee. Bless the man. He took it and gulped it down, realizing he was terribly thirsty. Hungry, too, as he hadn't eaten since dinner the night before. "Thank you, Goose," he said.

"M'pleasure, Captain. Helluva thing today, weren't it?"

"Yeah. A hell of a thing." He looked over his men and was pleased to see that most appeared to be in good spirits despite their ordeal. Or perhaps because of it. They all knew that they'd won a huge victory today. Maybe a war-changing victory. And his unit had played an important part. If they hadn't spotted the enemy's flank attack, hadn't delayed the Martians long enough for the new machines to arrive, if the Martians had overrun everything and been lined up along the walls waiting for them... things might have been much different. They'd done a hell of a job. And not just his boys... He looked around again, suddenly worried, but Gosling chuckled.

"She's over there with t'other ladies, sir. By the buildin' there."

He looked where he was pointing and breathed a sigh of relief when he saw the cluster of women. He handed the cup back to Gosling and walked over there as quickly as his aching legs would carry him.

Becca was standing apart from the others and he spotted her immediately. He came up to her and stopped. "Becca."

"Frank." She looked at him with eyes filled with pain and a bottomless weariness. He glanced at the other women. They had none of the jubilation that his men had. They seemed in a daze. *This was their first fight. They had no idea what to expect.*

"Are you all right?"

"Well enough. How are you?"

"Beat t'hell, but well enough." He looked toward the women. "How... how are they?"

"Beat t'hell," she said quietly. "Not sure how many we lost. I started the day with thirty. I've got twelve now. Four I know... four I know for sure were killed. Not sure about the others."

"There's bound to be some who got separated," said Frank, trying to sound reassuring. "Always happens in a fight. They'll turn up."

She nodded. "Yeah, I 'spect so. Some of the others probably just ran off to their homes. They all live nearby and they might have gone there."

"Yeah, probably." He paused. "It's a hard thing, Becca. Nothing can prepare a person for it."

"It's not my first battle, Frank."

"No, but it was theirs. And you brought them through it."

"Some of 'em."

"You can never bring all of them through. Believe me."

"No, I believe you. Don't make it any easier though."

"No."

" Frank, I need your help."

"Sure. What do you need?"

"Come with me." She led him through the smashed door of a dry goods store along the street. There was a stack of clothes on the counter. "I've still got some of the black dust on me. With all the dirt and soot and coal dust I've picked up, there's no hope of getting it all off the way we did with my mask." She looked him right in the eyes.

"Frank, help me get out of these clothes."

He blinked. "Becca. Maybe some of your girls can help..."

She stepped forward, grabbed him by the tunic, went up on her toes and pressed her lips against his. His eyes got wide, but he didn't pull away. She tasted of smoke and sweat but still very good. He probably tasted the same to her. After a minute or so she stepped back.

"Frank Dolfen, *help me get out of these clothes.*"

He took a deep breath.

"Yes, ma'am."

Chapter Seventeen

July, 1912, Washington, D.C

"We've won two tremendous victories, Leonard," said Theodore Roosevelt. "St. Louis and Memphis will go down in history with Gettysburg and Marathon. But they were both defensive victories. We can't stand on our laurels or rest to lick our wounds. That was the error so many generals have made down the centuries. We need to counterattack! And right away!"

"Yes, Mr. President," said Leonard Wood. Both men were in high spirits and the light streaming in through the windows of Roosevelt's White House office seemed brighter than it had in years. "I fully agree, but the question is where?"

"Indeed it is," rumbled Roosevelt, getting up from his chair and walking over to a map hanging on the wall. He poked a thick finger against a spot in western Missouri. "I have a lot of people urging me to liberate Kansas City."

"Yes, I know, Mr. President," said Wood, frowning. Senators and representatives from Missouri and Kansas had been bombarding him with pleas, just as they had Roosevelt.

The President turned and looked at him closely. "But you don't agree?"

"No, sir, I don't. Kansas City would be a great prize, no doubt, but another error that past generals have made is to overreach themselves after a victory. Kansas City is too far from our nearest base in St. Louis. The forces there were badly battered and are still recovering from the fight there. And the Martians might be able to call on reinforcements from their forces up north facing our 1st Army."

"Pershing says he can do it."

"Only with massive reinforcements. That will take time and we could miss our opportunity."

"So you favor what MacArthur is clamoring for? A drive on Little Rock?"

"Actually, sir, I favor a drive on the Martian fortress to the northeast of Little Rock. The fortresses are the key, sir. Not the cities. The cities are just piles of rubble now. Their strategic value is minimal."

Roosevelt snorted. "Don't say that to anyone outside this room!" He glanced over at his son, Archie, and raised an eyebrow to make sure the boy understood that meant him, too. He nodded. "While you are no doubt correct, the people want their country back. To even hint that we don't care about that would be... a very serious mistake."

A political mistake as well as a military one, eh? The election was fast approaching. The latest victories had pushed things slightly in Roosevelt's favor if the polls were to be believed. But only slightly. They needed more and this could be it. Still, to make military decisions for political reasons rankled Wood.

"I know that, Theodore. But to take the country back we must destroy the enemy strongholds. We do that and we automatically take the country back, too." Wood came over to the map and pointed to the spot where the fortress in question was located. "We've never yet captured one of their fortresses - anywhere - but at this moment, this is the most vulnerable one. It's relatively close to Memphis and that's where we have the forces to strike. The land ironclads are there, and 2nd Tank Division was barely scratched in the battle and it's there, too. To move them up to St. Louis for a drive on Kansas City, or even the Martian fortress that's closest, would take weeks, giving the enemy too much time to get ready. We can strike here! Now!" He thumped his fist on the map.

Roosevelt took a turn around the room, then halted next to Wood and slapped him on the back. "Thunderation, but you are right! We'll do it. Send the orders right away." He paused and then said: "You have no problems with putting MacArthur in command? I've heard a few... disturbing things about what went on during the battle."

"Yes, so have I, but he seems to be back in control now and there's no denying his energy. General Dickman will be in overall command, of course, but I think MacArthur will have to be the one to command the assault."

"All right, I accept your recommendation. Get them on the move, Leonard!"

* * * * *

August, 1912, north of Maberry, Arkansas

"Well, there it is, Gentlemen," said Colonel Andrew Comstock. "Our objective."

He was standing on the bridge of *USLI Albuquerque*, as it rumbled its way toward the walls of the Martian fortress in the distance. With him were Major Stavely, commander of *Albuquerque*, his aide, Jeremiah Hornbaker, the British observer, Major Bridges, and his old friend Drew Harding.

Poor Drew had lost his ship at Memphis and gotten several broken ribs and a dislocated shoulder in the process. He was currently on convalescent leave, but still faced an official hearing about the loss of his monitor. He was clearly very worried about that, although Andrew couldn't see that he had much to be worried about. From what he'd heard, Drew and his command had done a lot of damage and slowed the enemy down. But you could never tell about the navy, they were so damned touchy about their ships. The army was so much more forgiving. Lose a tank, lose a gun, they just gave you another one with no fuss. Of course, no one had lost a land ironclad yet.... When he'd heard about Drew's situation, he'd invited him to come along on Albuquerque. The man had accepted at once.

"It'll be dark soon," he said pointing toward the setting sun. "We'll attack first thing in the morning."

"With just the three ironclads?" asked Bridges. "Do you think that will be enough?"

"It will have to be. And we're hardly alone." He tried to sound confident, but in truth he was worried. All five of the land ironclads had survived the Battle of Memphis with relatively little damage, although he had cringed when he saw the spot on the front of *Albuquerque* where the combined heat rays had come within an inch of burning their way through. A heavy patch had been welded over the spot, but it was still a weak area. All five had started out on the offensive to capture the Martian stronghold, but only three had made it, *Albuquerque*, *Springfield*, and *Omaha*. *Billings* had broken down the first day out and Tulsa the day after. Both were being worked on, but neither would be here in time for the attack. Even the three which had made it were making some unpleasant sounds when they moved, and the engineers were worried about how much longer they could go without a major overhaul. The sad fact was that the ironclads were mechanically unreliable. Any hopes that they could just roll all the way to the Rockies were pipe-dreams.

Sioux Falls was on its way, too. A set of the flotation modules from one of the other ironclads, no longer needed once they had crossed to the west side of the Mississippi, had been sent to Key West. But it would be another week arriving and would not be here for the attack, either.

Still, the ironclads had a lot of support. The 2nd Tank Division was with them, although a third of their tanks had broken down on the way. There were also the equivalent of two infantry divisions - although cobbled together from about four different division - along with all the artillery, cavalry, and supply units that could be assembled in the short time they had. More troops were being brought into Memphis by rail to replenish the garrison and keep an eye on the force of Martians which had driven south along the river, breaking the connection with Texas and points west.

A signal went up from Springfield and the ironclads creaked to a halt. They were about five miles from the enemy stronghold, a long rampart encircling an area about three miles across. Some of the tanks and infantry pushed on another mile or so to protect the artillery, which would be spending much of the night getting set up and ready for the bombardment which would start the show.

"Excuse me, sir," said Stavely, "I'm going below to check on the machinery." Andrew nodded to him and the man left. Bridges decided he wanted a view from the observation platform while there was still light and climbed up there. Hornbaker went off to see about dinner, leaving Andrew alone with Harding.

"So what do you think of it?" asked Andrew, waving his hand to take in the ironclad. "I asked you that when we started out, but what do you think now that you've had a chance to look at it?"

Harding, whose left arm was in a sling, looked around and smiled sheepishly. "Well, sir," he began - there were a couple of enlisted men in earshot, so he didn't call him by name, "she - it's - a hell of a beast. When I first saw them in Memphis, they were a sight for sore eyes, but now that I've spent a few days aboard one, I'd be lying if I said I'd fallen in love with it."

Andrew chuckled. "Even so, you almost called it a *she*. What's with you navy guys and your boats?"

Drew shrugged. "Beats me. Tradition, I guess. But seriously, while there's no denying the effectiveness of the things, mechanically speaking they're a nightmare. Our ships can sail around the world with just onboard maintenance. You've lost forty-percent of yours trying to go seventy miles. Still, it's all brand new. With some improvements they might be what can win this war."

"The navy is building their own version, y'know. A little bigger than these to improve their sea-handling. Maybe you should see about getting command of one." Andrew knew it was a mistake the instant he said it. His friend's face fell and he shook his head.

"Assuming the navy still wants me to command anything after this."

"Drew, if we'd lost the battle, you might have something to worry about. They'd be looking for scapegoats. But we won the battle. Everyone's going to be a hero. So stop worrying."

He smiled and nodded. "Thanks for letting me come, sir. I would have gone crazy just sitting around back there."

"Glad to do it."

"So, are we going to win here tomorrow?"

"Damn right we are. So get some rest. It's going to be a long day."

* * * * *

Cycle 597, 845.2, Holdfast 32-4

"Commander, the enemy is taking up positions about six *telequel* to the south. There are three of the large new war machines, over two hundred of their usual armored gun vehicles, several hundred of the projectile throwers, and many thousands of their foot-warriors," reported Tanbradjus. "Their flying machines have been seen in considerable numbers."

Qetjnegartis regarded its sub-commanders gathered in a conclave room in the holdfast. Although none were grasping tendrils to form a link, there was no ignoring the great sense of tension.

"Only three of the new machines? Five were reported advancing in this direction. What has become of the other two?"

"They have halted in two different location. We do not know why."

"We have observed that the prey-creature machines are very crude and unreliable," said Davnitargus. "Perhaps they have broken down. Several tens of their smaller vehicles have halted along their route as well."

"But even with those losses, it is still an immense force," said Tanbradjus, the second in command. "Considering our own weakened state and having found no response to the new enemy machines, perhaps we should consider abandoning this holdfast and regrouping farther to the west."

"We defended the first holdfast against a heavy assault with fewer than ten war machines," said Qetjnegartis. "We still have seventy machines in operation here, plus several hundred drones, and the fixed defenses. We cannot give up this place so easily. It would be a huge blow to our strategic capabilities and the prestige of the clan."

"But you received reinforcements at a critical moment that first time. What reinforcements can we expect?"

"Nothing for at least three days," said Davnitargus. "Holdfasts 32-2 and 32-3 are sending what they can, but it totals less than a full battlegroup. Kantangnar is returning with its battlegroup as quickly as it can from the south, but it will not be here for at least two days; and we have reports that the prey-creatures are sending water vessels up the river to the ruins of city 3-118. Kantangnar may have to make a wide detour to reach here."

"Can we delay the enemy attack?" asked Qetjnegartis. "Perhaps a sortie during the night?"

"The prey are taking full precautions against such a thing, Commander. Their forces are concentrated and they are sending up the artificial illumination munitions at frequent intervals. It is doubtful that any damage we could do would balance the losses we might take in the process."

So you see, Qetjnegartis," said Tanbradjus, "We shall be over-whelmed before any help can arrive. We should withdraw this night."

"I think you are too quick to give up," replied Qetjnegartis. "If we abandon this one, we will be reduced to a mere three holdfasts. The enemy will be emboldened and we might soon find ourselves facing this same situation at Holdfast 32-3!"

"And if we try to stay here and are annihilated?" retorted Tan-bradjus. "The other holdfasts will have little defense left at all!"

"It is a risk," admitted Qetjnegartis. "But if we succeed, the ene-my will be forced to withdraw and we can rebuild our strength here."

"Also," added Branjandus, "if we are to withdraw immediately, there will be little time to destroy this facility. The prey-creatures have shown the ability to learn from our own devices they have captured. What might we learn from this place?"

A silence fell in the chamber. Clearly no one had given thought to this. Qetjnegartis had not and it was impressed that Davnitargus had done so.

"We... we can set the main reactor to overload," said Tanbrad-jus. "The melt-down would destroy much of the holdfast."

"Much, but not all."

"It is still better than...!"

"Enough," said Qetjnegartis. "I have decided. We shall defend this place. Return to your posts and make ready." It could sense dis-agreement from some, but there was, of course, no further argument. The others began moving out of the chamber.

"Davnitargus, remain a moment."

When the others had left and the chamber had sealed, Davnitar-gus looked to Qetjnegartis. "Progenitor?"

"I want to defend this place if at all possible. But we should also be prepared for a rapid evacuation, for it is entirely possible that Tan-bradjus is correct."

* * * * *

August, 1912, north of Maberry, Arkansas

"The bombardment will commence at first light," said Colonel Schumacher. "It will be a short one because we have no huge stockpile of ammunition. The primary targets will be the Martian defensive tow-ers. About one hour after the start, the artillery will pause to allow the bombing aircraft to make their attack. Following that, the land iron-clads will use their big guns to try and pick off any towers which have survived. Once that's done, the artillery will resume firing to cover the attempt to breach the enemy's walls."

The colonel paused and looked over the faces of his officers by the light of the lanterns hung around his tent. Frank Dolfen returned his gaze steadily. He was glad Schumacher had survived the fighting at Memphis. He was tired of breaking in new colonels. Almost a third of the men hadn't survived, but the regiment was still an effective fighting force. There had been no time for much in the way of replacements of men or equipment, so they only had a handful of armored cars in the whole regiment. Many of the motorcycle riders were either now on horses or had been left behind. But from the sound of things, they would be fighting as infantry in this next battle anyway.

"How are they gonna breach the walls, Colonel?" asked a lieutenant from the third squadron. Frank had been wondering that himself. "I've heard tell that it's a lot easier said than done."

"I don't have the details," replied Schumacher. "It's some device they've cooked up for the land ironclads is all I know. But while they are doing that, we, and the bulk of the infantry, are going to close up on the walls and climb to the top. Exactly where we'll do that will depend on how well they've destroyed the defensive towers. We'll try to go up where they ain't." That got a chuckle. Trying to scale the outer face of those walls with the heat ray towers shooting down on them would be suicide.

"They are going to send a few of the tanks along to support us and take out any surviving towers, and we'll just have to see how well that works. But in any case, we will get up on the walls somewhere. Once on top, we take cover and wait for the breaching. The brass seem to think that all of the enemy tripods will concentrate opposite where the breach is going to be made. We can hope they are right, but we need to be prepared to take on any that don't cooperate.

"Because our job is to get inside that fortress, gentlemen. We're to leave the tripods to the ironclads and the tanks. The infantry—and us—are to take out any of the spiders we might see, but then find a way down inside and take the place! We don't know what we'll find down there, but we have several directives from on high.

"One is to free any captives we might find. We have good reason to believe that there are a lot of our people down there. We're to rescue them. Second, we're to secure any machinery and equipment that we can. The eggheads back east want to get their hands on it. Maybe it will help them build more things like those ironclads."

Schumacher paused, took a breath and then went on. "Lastly, we've all been told in the past to try and kill any of the Martians we can find. We know that they can make machines faster than they can make more Martians. So our orders have been to finish off any downed tripods. Make sure the pilot is dead. That made sense when we were on the defensive; we didn't want any of those bastards to be rescued and come back to fight another day. But the situation has changed. We are on the offensive now. And the ground we take we are going to keep! So this time, we are going to try and take prisoners. As far as we know, no one has taken a live Martian captive. But this time we are going to try. The brass wants to have a little word with them, I guess. So tell your men. No itchy trigger fingers. Fight when you have to, but if the opportunity comes to take one of them alive—do so!" He looked around. "Any questions? No? All right. Go brief your men and then try to get some rest. We form up at three. Dismissed."

The meeting broke up and Dolfen headed back to the camp to have the men assembled. Men - and one woman. Becca was here; there had been no stopping her. Not after what had happened in Memphis. After all that had happened in Memphis. He still wasn't quite sure he understood everything that had happened, but when the new offensive had been announced, Becca had simply shown up, said that she was coming along, and that was that. Technically, she was a medic, and she did have the knowledge and the equipment to fill that role, but she carried a rifle and clearly intended to use it. He saw her standing there at the rear of the formation. She was making no attempt to conceal her gender this time and the men seemed to accept her. He wasn't sure how many of the men knew about the... change in his relationship to her, but no one had said anything to him—not that any of them would.

He passed along the information from the colonel and dismissed the men. Some bedded down immediately, but others drifted back to their campfires, probably too nervous to sleep. They were all veterans, but the battle tomorrow would be different than anything they'd faced before. Becca waited until all the others had moved off and then came up to him. "I'll be coming along tomorrow," she said.

"I know."

She stared at him and cocked her head with a strange look on her face.

"What?" he said.

"Is that all? 'I know'? You're not gonna try and talk me out of it or anything?"

"Would it do any good?"

"Nope, not one bit."

"So I won't waste my breath. I'll need it for tomorrow." He reached out and touched her arm. "But promise me one thing?"

"What?"

"That you won't get yourself killed."

"I won't if you won't."

"It's a deal."

"Good. Now let's get some sleep. We're gonna need it."

* * * * *

August, 1912, north of Maberry, Arkansas

Commander Drew Harding woke up with the bugles that echoed throughout the army. He'd spent a terrible night, just like the other ones since leaving Memphis. His shoulder ached and his ribs, too, making it very hard to get any sleep. At least he rated a cot rather than sleeping on the ground like most of the other men. The army's land ironclads had so little living space that nearly everyone had to camp out on the ground when they stopped for the night. The navy's versions were going to be large enough for bunk space, from what he'd heard.

It was still dark, without even a hint of dawn in the east. But there were plenty of campfires and lanterns around and a number of electric lamps shining from the towering *Albuquerque*, along with the blue-white glare of the welders. There was a party of engineers welding something to the bow of this ironclad and the *Omaha*. He'd asked Andrew what it was, but he'd just grinned and said that he'd see when the time was right.

He pulled on his clothes, stumbled out of the tent, and found coffee waiting for him around the fire. Several of the land ironclad's junior officers were there, along with Major Bridges. He found he liked the Englishman; he was witty and had an endless store of tales from his adventures in the far flung corners of the Empire. "Morning, Commander," he said. "I trust you slept well?"

"Not so well, sad to say. I miss my nice comfy bunk. You?"

"Oh, slept like the dead, old boy. I've got the happy knack of being able to sleep anywhere. In the mud, on rocks, even slept up in a tree a few times in South Africa. Lions, you know."

"Really. Is the colonel about?"

"Over at *Springfield* conferring with General Clopton, I believe. Bacon?" He offered a plate and Drew took it. He sat, slurping coffee and munching the bacon with some hard bread. He missed the good food from a ship's galley, too. *Definitely made the right choice when I went to Annapolis.*

Bridges was staring at him. "I understand you've known Colonel Comstock for quite some time, Commander."

"Oh hell yes. We go way back. Before the war, I was in the navy's ordnance bureau while he was with the army's ordnance department. There were a lot of inter-service meetings there in Washington and we saw each other quite a bit. Became drinking buddies. A good man."

"He certainly seemed glad to see you. I was just wondering why he treats me like a pound of week-old kippers. I pride myself in being able to charm everyone - damnation I even managed to make Kitchener laugh once - but I can't seem to break through his armor. Any idea why?"

Drew frowned and chewed on his lip, unsure if he should say anything. As he sat there, a gun went off and a few seconds later a star shell burst in the direction of the Martian fortress. They'd been doing that all night to keep an eye on the enemy. Bridges looked at him curiously in the flickering light. "Well... It's probably because you're English."

"You don't say?" said Bridges, looking surprised. "What? Did my great granddad kill his great granddad at Lexington or something? I thought we'd gotten past all that rubbish."

"No, it's more recent history than that, I'm afraid. You remember that big explosion you folks had in Liverpool back in oh-seven?"

"I do. What a bloody mess. I was in India at the time, but it was in all the papers. But what...?"

"His father was killed in the blast. He'd been invited there to observe whatever it was your scientists were trying to do."

"And he holds me to blame for *that*?"

"It hit him hard. And he wasn't even out of West Point when it happened. I guess he needed someone to blame."

Bridges nodded. "Yes, some people deal with grief that way. I've seen it in others. Well, it's a shame, but I guess there's nothing I can do about it, eh?"

"I suppose not. Just don't judge him too harshly. It's not personal."

"He certainly seems competent enough. And I guess you Yanks don't hand out the decorations like he's got for nothing."

"No, we don't. He's earned every one of them."

By this time, the whole army was stirring; companies of infantry falling in, steam tanks firing up their boilers, gunners screwing fuses into their shells. Albuquerque gave a short toot on its whistle to tell its crew to pack up and come aboard. Drew went into the tent he'd been given and packed up his valise. Fortunately, someone else would pack up the tent and the cot.

As he came out, he saw Andrew returning and they exchanged greetings. "Morning, Drew. Ready for the big day?"

"Ready as I'll ever be, I guess. So this is it?"

"Yup. The weather is looking good and we've gotten a radio message that the aircraft will be leaving on time. That was the only thing that might have delayed us. But it won't, so we go on schedule. The artillery will start shooting at first light. But come on, let's get aboard."

There was a movable gangway which could be lowered down from the ironclad allowing access, but it was very steep. With him carrying his valise in one hand and his other in the sling, it was awkward getting up.

"Here give me that," said Andrew, reaching down and taking the valise. With a hand free to clutch the rail, Drew could pull himself up.

"Thanks."

They made their way up to the bridge but then went out on the port wing to give Major Stavely room to get his vehicle in order. Bridges and Hornbaker joined them and Drew found himself acutely aware of Andrew and Bridges. He'd noticed the coolness between them before, but now every little glance and motion seemed to send signals. *Stop it, it doesn't matter right now.*

"Is General MacArthur going to be aboard *Springfield* for the battle?" asked Bridges.

"Yes," said Andrew.

"Well then, I'm glad I'm over here," said Drew. "With his staff, there won't be room to swing a cat over there!"

"He only had two people with him. I think most of his staff will stay on the ground to carry out his orders while he takes a look from up close."

"He does seem to be the fearless sort," said Drew, remembering him standing there in the middle of the street as tripods walked past.

"It's a good plan," said Andrew, "and I understand he devised it himself."

"Brilliant and brave," said Bridges. "Sounds like a dashed good combination."

"Well, he was brave at Memphis," said Drew. "Not so sure about the brilliant part."

"I guess we'll find out soon enough," said Andrew. With that, the conversation lapsed and they waited in the darkness until a faint blue line could be seen on the eastern horizon. A few minutes later, a white signal rocket soared into the sky and it was immediately followed by three quick shots from some field guns. Drew caught his breath and then the world was lit up with the fire of nearly two hundred guns.

* * * * *

August, 1912, near the Martian Fortress

Rebecca Harding looked on happily as the artillery opened fire. It was beginning! They were going to assault and capture the enemy fortress. They were going to kill the monsters, drive them away, and take back part of the land. She reminded herself that she'd heard that kind of talk before. At the Martian fortress where the town of Gallup had stood out in the New Mexico Territory. Not far from where she had once lived. They'd been supposed to capture the fortress there, too, but that had not happened. Instead, they'd been beaten and forced to flee. Step by step they'd fled all the way back to the Mississippi.

That's not gonna happen again today!

No it wasn't; today they were going to win. Today they were going to start on the long road back.

The guns hammered away, their flashes still overpowering the slowly growing dawn. Explosions sparked along the wall of the enemy fortress. There was too much smoke and dust to really see what effect it was having, but it seemed well-aimed to her with most of the shells landing right on top of the ramparts, where the enemy heat ray towers were located.

Her horse shied a bit at one especially loud bang, and she patted his neck to calm him. She had been so happy when Moses had come up, driving his wagon with her beloved Ninny in tow. She had had no idea if either of them had survived the battle, but Moses acted as though it had just been a Sunday drive in the park. Even so, he'd had no desire to come along on this new adventure.

Neither had any of the Memphis Women's Sharpshooters. One battle had been more than enough for them. Indeed, after the fighting was over, they had nearly all melted away, back to their homes - or what was left of them. A few had said goodbye to her and thanked her, but most acted as though it had all been a really bad idea and the sooner it was forgotten, the better. Oh well, they'd done more than she'd expected.

And now she was part of the real army. Sort of. She was traveling with the army, she planned to fight with the army, and no one seemed to be trying to stop her. She wasn't trying to disguise herself like the last time, and many of the men, including some of Frank's superiors, had seen her and not said anything. Of course, she hadn't signed any papers or sworn any oaths, and she doubted she would be paid like the other soldiers, but none of that mattered to her. She was here, with Frank.

Frank. She wasn't entirely sure what those moments they had spent together in the abandoned dry goods store really meant. They had both been exhausted, filthy and smelly—not exactly the sort of thing girls dreamed about. But they'd smiled at each other afterward. It had to have meant something...

A bright blue flash from inside the smoke and a long rumbling boom that competed with and won against the other noise caught everyone's attention, and a small cheer went up. One of the heat ray tower's power thingy had blown up as they sometimes did. The guns were hitting things.

It was nearly dawn now and the troops were moving into their assault positions. The 5*th* rode a mile or so around the eastern side of the fortress and then halted again. The sun peeked over the edge of the world; long black shadows stretched out in front of them and the face of the enemy ramparts glowed pinkly - they were covered with that damn red weed. The artillery wasn't hitting this part of the fortress as heavily, and further to the north there was little smoke and Becca could see some of the towers were still intact on the wall. They wouldn't be going that way.

The bombardment was slowly dying and after a few more minutes it stopped entirely. The wind carried off the smoke and dust and revealed what the artillery had done. As everyone expected, the walls themselves were intact. But it looked like all the towers on the southern half had been destroyed. There might have been one or two which had escaped, and Becca could see officers peering intently through their binoculars. There was Frank a few dozen yards away looking and pointing and talking with his officers.

Off to her left she spotted the three huge land ironclads moving forward, their tall smoke stacks spewing black clouds into the morning sky. They moved up to a position only a few hundred yards short of the wall. Then their big gun turrets swiveled and fired a few times. Explosions blossomed atop the wall. They were picking off any towers which looked like they might still be able to work. When they were finished, they reversed and backed off a bit.

"Are they retreating?" asked a trooper close by.

"No, you idiot!" replied another. "Weren't you listening to what the captain said? The bombers are on the way and they probably don't want to be too close. Those crazy fliers aren't particular where they drop their bombs!"

"Hey! Yeah, look! There they are!" shouted a third cavalryman. He was pointing skyward and everyone looked up.

At first, Becca couldn't see anything, but then she spotted a swarm of dark specks off to the east. They approached at what seemed a crawl, but within a few minutes they were nearly overhead.

"Want to look?" Becca started at the voice at her elbow. It was Frank offering his binoculars. He was smiling at her.

"Why, thank you, Captain," she said, taking the binoculars and looking up again. The specks now revealed themselves as airplanes. Large airplanes with two engines. There looked to be hundreds of them, flying in tight formations. As she watched, tiny black shapes started falling off them. "They've dropped their bombs, I think," she said. She handed the binoculars back to him.

"Okay, hang on to your hats and pray they didn't drop them short!" he said.

She'd lost track of the bombs when she looked away, tried to find them again, and then gave up and just looked toward the Martian fortress. After what seemed like far too long a time, there came a shrill whistling sound and then geysers of earth suddenly leapt up a few hundred yards in front of the walls, and then marched forward to engulf it. The roar from the explosions made the previous bombardment seem tranquil by comparison. The earth shook and Ninny snorted and shied, veteran though he was of things unnatural.

A half-mile wide section of the walls and the area to the front and rear was hammered by bombs, rocks the size of steamer trunks were tossed in the air to come crashing down again. The very air was shaking.

And then it was over. After a minute or two, the artillery started firing again, but her ringing ears could barely hear it. The ironclads started forward once more, and then Frank was shouting to get ready.

"It's our turn now!"

* * * * *

Cycle 597, 845.2, Holdfast 32-4

Qetjnegartis felt the impact of the explosives even in the deeply buried command chamber. It was annoyed when the tactical status display showed that four fighting machines had been destroyed and their operators slain. When the bombardment by the projectile throwers had ceased and the large new machines of the prey-creatures had come forward, it had assumed some attempt to breach or scale the walls was about to occur, and it had ordered the fighting machines forward to oppose it. But then the flying machines had appeared with no warning and there had not been time to pull the fighting machines back. So far, between this and the earlier bombardment, it had lost ten machines and six pilots slain or wounded. The other four had been carried back and transferred to new machines.

But what was happening now? The large machines were coming closer again and the bombardment had resumed. And this time it was not aimed at the defensive towers on the walls, it was landing in an arc behind the ramparts, apparently in an attempt to seal off the area where the large machines were gathering. Were they going to attempt to breach the walls at that point? What was the proper response?

At the same time, thousands of the prey foot-warriors were scaling the walls to either side of that area. They were taking cover on top. Meanwhile, groups of the armored gun vehicles were moving along the walls attacking the remaining defensive towers one at a time. The tactics of the prey were becoming increasingly sophisticated. Qetjnegar-

tis dispatched six fighting machines to each side of the holdfast to oppose the vehicles attempting to destroy the towers. It was tempted to
send more machines or perhaps drones up on to the walls to attack the
foot-warriors gathering there. But no, hundreds more of the armored
vehicles were poised to support them, and any fighting machine on top
of the walls would instantly be brought under heavy fire. The losses
could not be sustained and the foot-warriors were of little danger in an
open battle like this.

The critical point would be the place where the enemy intended to make the breach. Whatever they planned, they could only make
a narrow entrance. If enough power could be assembled opposite that
point, then anything attempting to enter could be destroyed. Yes, that
was the proper response.

It issued its orders.

* * * * *

August 1912, the Martian Fortress

"All right, Major, bring us forward," said Andrew Comstock.
"Stop about fifty yards short of the wall."

"Right, sir," said Stavely. He gave the order and *Albuquerque*
squealed into motion. Yeah, he didn't like the noises the thing was making these days…

"Slowly. Line it up just like I said."

"Yes, sir."

The land ironclad inched toward an apparatus that the company of engineers had just set up against the forward face of the wall
around the Martian fortress. Andrew had been very impressed at how
quickly they'd accomplished it. The captain in charge said they'd been
practicing for months. Andrew had known about this unit for many
months and even seen them demonstrate their equipment at Aberdeen
one time, but he hadn't really paid all that much attention to them. At
the time, there seemed little likelihood that they'd have any opportunity to try it out against a Martian fortress.

But then this offensive had been decided upon and a frantic message had gone out to get the 187th Engineer Company and all its gear
up to the front immediately. By some miracle, not only had they made
their way through the clogged railway system to Memphis, but then
they'd been able to catch up with the assault force and arrive in the nick
of time.

Just ahead of *Albuquerque*, there were two metal chutes erected on small scaffolds to hold them about fifteen feet off the ground.
One end was positioned against the face of the wall and the other was

pointed at the approaching ironclad. The chutes were a little over a foot in diameter. Resting in the chute was a section of metal pipe. The end facing the wall was pointed like a javelin. The other end was open and had a socket-like connection. Andrew knew that the hollow inside of the tube was packed with explosive. An identical set up had been arranged for *Omaha*, which was coming up alongside them with only a yard or two between their mammoth set of caterpillar tracks.

An engineering officer had come aboard and was standing at the very front of the ironclad, looking down and using hand signals to tell the driver what to do. A little to the left, a little right, slow down, and finally stop. Andrew decided to go and take a look for himself. He left the bridge, followed by Drew, Hornbaker, and that blasted Englishman. They came up behind the engineer, who was a first lieutenant. "How's it going?" asked Andrew.

The man glanced back, a look of annoyance on his face, but he said: "Well enough. We'll be ready for the first section in a minute."

It was longer than that, but eventually, he gave the signal for slow ahead. Andrew went up to the rail and looked down. The apparatus which had been welded to the front of Albuquerque during the night was a pair of push rods which could be lined up with the end of the explosive packed tubes. Now, using the immense mass and power of the ironclad, the tubes were slowly pushed into the wall of the Martian fortress.

The walls were simply a big mound of rock, earth, and rubble which had been piled up by the alien machines. The outer face was steep and treacherous with loose stones. Andrew had climbed the one near Gallup and knew how difficult it was. They were completely impassible to vehicles. But being loose stone rather than something truly solid, the tubes could be pushed right into them.

They crawled forward about twenty feet and then the engineer waved them to stop and then to reverse. As soon as they had pulled back, two new ten foot sections of pipe were lifted up by a crane mounted on a truck and lowered into each chute. They were then fitted into the sockets at the rear of the leading pipes. When all was ready, the process was repeated, pushing the pipes deeper into the wall.

"We'll be lucky if those pipes don't buckle," said Drew.

"The walls of the pipe are an inch thick. And they are packed full so they are nearly solid. This has been tested, and if we come straight on, it should work."

"Damned ingenious," said Bridges.

"What happens if the Martians suddenly pop up on the wall and start shooting at us, sir?" asked Drew.

Andrew glanced up at the top of the wall. The barrage was supposed to discourage the enemy from doing that, but it was still a good point. The explosives in the tubes *shouldn't* explode just from heat, but you never knew. And of course all of them were standing right here in the open. They'd be incinerated in an instant. All the gunners were on alert, of course, and *Springfield* and a hundred steam tanks were ready to provide covering fire if necessary; but none of that would do any good for those of *them* standing where they were, unprotected. I'm not necessary here, I should go back inside. But instead he stayed.

"That's why we need to hurry."

A third set of pipes were pushed in, and then a fourth. As the fifth pair were set up, a man dashed up to Andrew. "Sir, we just got a signal from Springfield that the artillery is running low on ammunition and the second wave of aircraft will be here soon. We need to finish this now."

Andrew looked to the engineer. "Will this be enough?"

"This will make two one-hundred foot lengths for us and the same for Omaha. That will be close to ten tons of explosives. It should do the trick, sir."

"All right then! Get this last set pushed in and we'll pull back. The rest of us better get up to the bridge."

As the ironclad moved forward once more, the rest of them retreated back, past the main turret, and then up a ladder to the bridge. Major Stavely met them at the pilothouse door. "That's it, sir, the charges are placed."

"Excellent. Pull back three hundred yards and we'll wait for the fireworks!"

* * * * *

August, 1912, the Martian Fortress

"Keep your fool heads down - all of you!" shouted Frank Dolfen. His troops, already lying on their bellies atop the wall, tried to flatten themselves down a little further. A couple peered at him from under the brims of their helmets, their expressions seemed to say: *okay, but what about you?* Dolfen was kneeling next to the wreckage of one of the heat ray towers rather than lying down. Well, rank had its privileges.

They'd made the climb up to the top of the wall without much problem beyond scraped hands, bruised knees, and uniforms stained red by the Martian weed that was everywhere. It would have been a terrible thing to try and do if someone was shooting at you, but today no one was. He thought back to the time - the two times - he'd done this before, back at Gallup. That time, it had just been him and that Major Comstock. This time, he'd brought a whole army with him.

He swept his binoculars in a long arc, taking in the view. A half-mile to his left, the big land ironclads were doing something very close to the face of the wall, and a large number of steam tanks were also drawn up close by. A half-mile to his right, a dozen more tanks were dueling with one of the heat ray towers, and as he watched, they took it out. A similar duel was taking place on the other side of the fortress, beyond the land ironclads. Given time, they would destroy all the remaining towers.

Behind the wall and opposite where the ironclads were at work, there was a thick wall of dust and smoke where the artillery was concentrating its fire. It was in a half ring, touching the wall not four hundred yards away and looping around to touch the wall on the other side of the ironclads. Two hundred guns were banging away as fast as they could and the explosions were nearly constant.

He could catch glimpses of Martian tripods standing or moving about beyond the wall of smoke. They seemed to have gathered, ready to oppose the attempt to break through the wall. He couldn't tell how many, but if there were a lot of them, they were going to make it very rough on whoever went through the gap first. He was glad he and his men wouldn't be involved with that. He glanced over to where Becca was laying flat. He wished she wasn't here. He'd had some hopes that maybe he could convince her to stay with the horse holders down at the base of the wall. Maybe the presence of her fool horse would make her want to stay with him. No hope there. She'd just left her horse with Private Gosling, who was holding all the officers' horses.

Lieutenant Lynnbrooke crawled over to him and said: "I went up to the edge of the wall, sir. I couldn't see anything, no tripods or spider-machines waiting for us."

"Good."

"But it's very steep. There are a few ledges here and there, but everywhere else it's almost vertical. The rocks seem all fused together, too. Not many handholds. There's a ramp about two hundred yards off to the right, but there's a whole regiment of infantry waiting to use it."

"Send back to the horses for some ropes. We'll let ourselves down that way."

"Right, sir." He crawled away.

Things were going to happen soon, he expected. And once it did, he and his men were going to have to come down off the wall and deal with whatever they found inside. He lifted his binoculars and scanned the inside of the fortress again. It was basically an empty circle three miles wide. There were some lumps and bumps here and there, but no obvious entrances to the underground parts. He'd heard that at Gallup some troops had found ways to get in. Hopefully they'd be able to it again here.

A shrill noise caught his attention and he looked over to his left. The three land ironclads were all sounding their steam whistles. He could only assume that something was about to...

He'd never seen a volcanic eruption except in drawings in the newspapers, but what happened now matched his mental image of what one must look like. The section of wall in front of the ironclads... *erupted*. The top part of the wall lifted up into the air, almost in a single piece, while two huge clouds of rock, dust, and smoke blasted out from the front and rear sides of the wall, spewing debris for hundreds of yards. Then the upper part disintegrated into another boiling mass of flying junk. Boulders tumbled end over end and came crashing down again. Smaller rocks were flung great distances, a few thudding down only a hundred yards away.

The wall beneath him was shaking and the clouds of dust all merged into one and drifted slowly eastward. The noise blotted out all other sound, even the artillery bombardment. He knelt there staring as the dust slowly settled. The artillery fire died away and the cloud from that dispersed as well.

What was revealed was a huge ditch blasted through the wall. All the rocks and dirt from a big section had been blown in all directions. He couldn't see down into it from where he was, but the land ironclads were starting forward, so apparently they thought they could make it through. The Martian tripods had stood as still as everyone else during the explosion, but now they started forward, too, directly toward the ironclads. Could they get through and deploy before they were overwhelmed?

But then a buzzing reached his stunned ears and it quickly grew to a roar of another sort. Looking back he saw a swarm of aircraft coming right at him. They were flying scarcely higher than the walls, and a moment later they swept over him so close he felt he could reach up and grab one. Hundreds of them! *Selfridge and his boys must be with them.*

Lynnbrooke was back tugging at his sleeve. He pointed toward the edge of the wall. The men were getting up from where they lay. Dolfen wrenched his attention back where it belonged. He shouted at his bugler: "Sound the advance!"

* * * * *

August, 1912, the Martian Fortress

As the dust and smoke gradually thinned, Andrew Comstock tried to see what the explosion had done. Had it cleared a path which the ironclads and the tanks could traverse? It was essential that the tanks could make it, too. General Clopton had convinced MacArthur that as impressive as the ironclads might be, they couldn't win this battle by themselves. They needed the tank support, so they had to get inside the fortress.

Slowly, slowly the air cleared and revealed what the engineers had wrought. An enormous divot had been made through the wall. The upper half had been gouged out for a width of perhaps fifty feet - barely wide enough for an ironclad. Just as importantly, the displaced dirt and rock had been scattered on either side and formed what looked like a passable ramp up into the breach. There was no way to tell if there was a similar ramp down on the other side, but there ought to be.

Only one way to find out!

A toot from Springfield indicated that Clopton agreed. Forward!

Albuquerque would lead the way and Major Stavely got it up to full speed as quickly as possible. The British-designed steam turbine spun, the electricity it produced powered the big Westinghouse motors, and they turned the Baldwin-built caterpillar tracks. Human ingenuity on the move! They reached the edge of the debris field and started up the ramp, crushing down the rocks and boulders and hopefully creating an easy path for the tanks to follow. He was able to see through the gap now, and what he saw put a lump of fear in his throat. A seemingly solid phalanx of tripods was coming the other way, maybe a half-mile in the distance. Swarms of the spider-machines were all around them. Could they get through the hole before the Martians put a stopper in it?

"Sir! Here come the aircraft!" Hornbaker shouted at his side. Andrew looked through the rear door of the pilothouse, and to his relief, the promised air support had arrived. Squadron after squadron of the small attack planes swept in at low altitude, spread out over a wide arc. Past the ironclads, over the walls, and straight against the enemy, closing in on them from three sides.

"Right on time!" cried Drew Harding. "First the bombers and now these. They taught us at Annapolis that no battle plan ever works right."

"Taught us the same thing at the Point. Guess there's a first time for everything, eh?"

The aircraft bore in on the Martians, machine guns chattering. The tripods halted and formed a tight mass, facing outward. Their heat rays lashed out and the formations of planes were turned into balls of fire. Dozens fell in the first seconds. More followed. Flaming wrecks fell to the earth everywhere. Only a few made it close enough to drop their bombs. Fewer still hit anything, and only a couple of hits were on tripods. Andrew felt sick to his stomach.

But the sacrifice of the fliers had bought precious seconds. *Albuquerque* crested the top of the gap and headed down the other side and onto the flat ground inside the fortress. *Omaha* was right behind and swung right, *Springfield* swung left. Twelve and seven and five-inch guns roared out and shells tore through packed enemy machines. A dozen tripods went down in seconds. The ironclads reloaded and fired again, smashing more of the hated foe.

With most of the aircraft destroyed, the Martians now turned against the new threat. Dozens of heat rays stabbed at the metal giants and Andrew ducked away from the red blaze that came in through the quartz blocks in the pilothouse view slits. The guns on the ironclads roared out again, and some of the deadly rays were silenced. But they were under the concentrated fire of the whole Martian force now and damage reports were coming in as some of the rays cut through the armor in spots. Major Stavely ordered steam to be released to lessen the effects. A hissing cloud engulfed them.

They were blinded now and the steam would only help them for a few moments. "Maybe we should turn!" cried Drew Harding. "Show them some undamaged armor!"

"Worth a try," said Andrew. "Stavely bring us left!"

The major gave the orders, but a moment later he shouted: "Track number two is out! We can only turn right. Turning now!" The ironclad shuddered and groaned as it dragged itself around sideways. After a few seconds, it lurched to a halt. "Number four is out, too! We're stuck!"

"Damn!" Blind and immobilized, they were sitting ducks.

But then the red glare faded completed and a host of new sounds filled the air. Cannon fire. Smaller cannons to be sure, but a lot of them. Andrew poked his head out of the pilot house, and when the wind pulled the steam curtain away for a moment he saw dozens and dozens of tanks pouring through the gap in the wall, their guns blazing. The 2nd Tank Division was charging into action.

"Secure steam!" gasped Stavely. The hissing died away, and after a moment they could see again. There was *Omaha*, off to the right, its guns still firing, still killing Martians. To the left was *Springfield;* Andrew was dismayed to see black smoke boiling out of a hole in its side, and its observation platform gone. But some of the guns were still firing. And all around were steam tanks. Mark IIs with their single guns and Mark IIIs with three of them. Even a few of the large, but notoriously unreliable Mark IVs had made it through. All were firing steadily at the enemy. There didn't seem to be all that many of the enemy left now; maybe thirty or so.

"Sir! Look there!" Hornbaker pointed.

"What?"

"Spider-machines! A whole bunch of them! I think they're going after *Springfield*!"

Andrew looked through smoke and saw: a moving carpet of the smaller machines, and yes, they looked to be heading directly toward the flagship.

"That's how they sank my monitor, Andrew," said Drew Harding urgently, his face twisted with remembered anguish. "They got aboard and down inside and blew up the magazine."

Andrew turned to Major Stavely. "Major, can you put some fire on those things? The machine guns, maybe?"

"I can do better than that! Doctor Tesla's cannon is still undamaged. It's ready to fire!"

Andrew's face lit up. They'd been too far away to use it at first, and with all the damage he'd assumed it was out of action. But it wasn't! "Yes! Tell them to fire at the spiders!"

Stavely passed along the order and just a few moments later the turret with the Tesla Gun swung around and the blue-white lightning burst forth. It leapt to one of the spider-machines and then another. And then another, more and more, a dozen, two dozen. They writhed and shuddered, and many of them exploded in a display that to Andrew looked like kernels of corn on a frying pan. When the lightning winked out, the field was littered with wrecked spider-machines. Many of the survivors stood frozen while fire from the tanks picked them off.

"Sir? Sir?" said Stavely. "I think the rest are pulling back."

Andrew looked out and indeed some of the remaining tripods seemed to be retreating.

"Looks as though you've broken their back, old boy," said Major Bridges.

"Yes, yes, I think you're right!"

* * * * *

Cycle 597, 845.2, Holdfast 32-4

"Qetjnegartis, we must retreat! This fight is lost!"

Qetjnegartis listened to the message from Tanbradjus and then looked with growing dismay at the tactical display in the command center. Everything was happening so fast. The attack of the prey-creatures had been more relentless and devastating than anything it had encountered before. It had been expecting a slow and methodical attack such as it had faced at the first holdfast. A step by step assault with time to react. But this! The large projectile throwers, the heavy flying machines, the explosion which breached the wall, and then the onslaught of the lighter flying machines, the huge vehicles and the smaller ones. All one right after the other with no pause.

They had less than thirty fighting machines left, and while they had disabled two of the large prey-creature machines, they were still firing their weapons and were supported by nearly two hundred of the smaller vehicles. At the same time, thousands of the foot-warriors, many carrying explosives, were roaming inside the holdfast's walls. Some were attempting to blow open some of the small access doors, clearly trying to get inside. How long before they succeeded?

"Qetjnegartis, I am ordering the fighting machines here with me to retreat," said Tanbradjus. "If I do not, we will all be destroyed."

Qetjnegartis's tendril stiffened on the interface rods. Was this a deliberate challenge to its authority? It doubted that Tanbradjus would be able disobey a direct order if given one, but this was still a breach of protocol.

Perhaps the circumstances warrant it.

Yes, there was no doubt the battle was lost. Further resistance would only mean needless losses, which they could not afford. Losing the holdfast was a severe setback, but losing it and all the defenders would be immeasurably worse.

"Very well, all units will retreat to sector 3-28-243. We will reassemble and then head west."

"At once, Commander," said Tanbradjus. "A wise decision."

The communications link was broken. Qetjnegartis looked to the other two clan members in the control chamber. "Go to the hanger at once. Rendezvous with the others. I must set the reactor to melt down."

"But Commander, that can only be done manually. You may be trapped here. Let one of us do it."

"You have your orders. Carry them out."

"Yes, Commander." The two transferred into travel chairs and moved out. As Qetjnegartis was about to do the same, a message arrived from Davnitargus.

"Commander, I will bring the remains of my battlegroup to the hanger exit to cover your retreat."

"No, I may be delayed. You shall retreat with the others. I will join you later."

"But, Commander..."

"Obey me, Davnitagus!"

There was short delay, and then the bud responded. "I obey, Commander."

Qetjnegartis transferred into a travel chair and headed for the reactor chamber.

* * * * *

Captain Frank Dolfen led his men across the flat central area of the Martian fortress, looking for some way to get in. Off to the south there was still a hell of a fight going on and he could not help but think that if that fight was lost, all the people on foot were going to have a hell of a time getting out of here again. Coming down those ropes had been quick and pretty easy. Going back up them would not be.

That wasn't his concern at the moment, however. His job was to find some way inside the enemy fortress. He spotted other groups of men clustered around some of the lumps and bumps he'd seen earlier. Sometimes an explosion would erupt from one of them. Were they blasting their way inside? He couldn't tell. Colonel Schumacher had split up the squadrons to cover more ground, and to Dolfen it almost seemed like he considered this some sort of contest. Who could get in first and start capturing great stuff?

They came across a few wrecked tripods but the Martians who had piloted them were either dead or gone. They also found some of the spider-machines, still very much alive. One killed two of his men before they took it down with massed rifle fire. Several others were frozen in place and they just slung bombs on them and blew them up. He guessed they were supposed to capture those, too, but he'd seen the frozen ones come back to life before and he wasn't about to take chances with them.

Becca was still with them and still unharmed.

They reached the center of the big flat plain and Frank tried to decide where to go next. Further north there were still a few of the heat ray towers functioning on the walls and he didn't want to tangle with them. Best leave those things to the tanks.

"Sir! Over there!" Lynnbrooke grabbed his arm and pointed. About a hundred yards away, a tripod seemed to be climbing out of the ground.

"Down! Everyone take cover!"

The men hit the dirt and brought up their weapons. But the tripod was facing away from them and rapidly moved off to the north. A few shots from distant guns burst around it, but it kept moving. Dolfen quickly looked around to make sure there weren't any others coming out of different holes. There weren't, but he saw that twenty or thirty tripods a half-mile to the south were also moving quickly away from where the battle had been going on. Steam tanks appeared to be in pursuit. Had they won?

"Another one!" hissed Lynnbrooke. A second tripod appeared in the same spot as the first. It too moved rapidly away.

"Looks like we've found a way in," said Dolfen. "On your feet! Let's check it out!" They advanced warily, and as they got closer, they discovered a ramp leading down into the earth. It was a big ramp, obviously designed for the Martian tripods. At the bottom there was a huge metal door, but it was wide open.

"Somebody forgot to lock up when they left," said Lynnbrooke.

"Well let's get down there before they remember! Send out a few runners. Find the colonel and tell anyone they meet to come over here." There were bands of troops all over the place and it shouldn't take long to find reinforcements. The rest of them moved to where the top of the ramp merged with the plain and then started down, weapons ready. They had a few of the stovepipe launchers in addition to a machine gun and their bombs, but they really didn't want to take on anything tougher than a drone if they could avoid it.

They reached the bottom and found themselves on the edge of a huge underground space. It was dimly lit, but they could see rows of tripods standing near the far wall. All the men tensed and crouched down, but Dolfen looked at them closely through his binoculars.

"I think they're empty. Like those once we saw near Little Rock. Spares, I guess."

"If they're not, sir," said a trooper, "an' we go out there, we're cooked for sure."

"If they have Martians in them, they'd be outside fighting. Now come on."

"What about the doors, sir?" asked Lynnbrooke. "Wouldn't want to get trapped down here."

Dolfen looked over his men. "Sergeant... uh, Wilkerson, stay here with your squad and see if you can find something to jam the doors with. Blow 'em up if you have to, but keep them open."

"Yes, sir."

Leaving the squad behind, the rest of them, about a hundred men, started across the open space. As their eyes adjusted from the bright sunshine outside, they could see well enough. Near the parked tripods, there were a number of smaller three-legged machines. Bigger and differently shaped than the spider-machines, they were as silent and inert as the bigger ones. Nonetheless, none wanted to linger in the vicinity and they were nearly jogging by the time they reached a set of smaller doors on the far side.

The doors led to a corridor which went off in both directions. Dolfen looked one way and then the other; they were empty. The corridors curved slightly so he couldn't see very far. But the one to the right was sloping slightly down, while the left-hand one sloped upward. Part of him really wanted to go back up, but something told him the things they were probably looking for were farther down. Some faint noises made him look back the way they had come and he saw more troops coming down the ramp. Good, they weren't on their own anymore. Making up his mind, he went down the corridor to the right.

The corridor was about twenty feet wide and twenty feet high. But the walls curved inward toward the top making it a sort of flat-bottomed tube. There were doors at intervals set into the walls, but they were all sealed and he didn't want to waste time trying to blow his way into them. Clearly this place was going to take a lot of time to explore, but he wanted to try and find the main parts of it as quickly as possible.

Down they went and then they found an intersection with one ramp going to the right but more steeply downward, and another to the left leading upward. After a little thought, he took the one leading down. It went down about thirty feet, he guessed, and then got broader. A set of heavy doors were standing open and he sent some men ahead, while he followed more slowly with the rest.

Now they came upon some sections where there were windows in the sides of the corridor. Looking through, there were rooms filled with what looked like machinery and perhaps laboratory equipment. He remembered a photo in a newspaper of Thomas Edison's lab and it was kind of like that—only different.

"Looks like we're finding the stuff the generals want, Captain," said Lynnbrooke.

"Yeah, looks like. But I have no idea…"

"Captain!" One of the men he'd sent ahead was running back, he looked… upset.

"Trouble?"

"Uh, no, sir, no Martians, anyway. But… but we found something…"

"What?"

"Uh… people, sir, but they're… they're…" The man swallowed and turned away.

Suddenly Frank knew exactly what they'd found. He'd heard rumors… He gritted his teeth. He didn't want to see this, but he had to. But Becca was back there and she didn't have to see this. She was tough as nails, he knew, but she still didn't have to see it. He turned to Lynnbrooke and said loudly: "Lieutenant, I'm concerned about our rear. Take a squad back to that intersection and stay there." And then more softly: "And take Miss Harding with you. Don't take no for an answer, you understand?"

"Uh, yes, sir." He moved toward the rear. He thought he heard Becca say something, but he couldn't catch it and she didn't speak again. When he glanced back, he saw her going with Lynnbrooke and the others. Good.

He led the way forward, further down the corridor. There were more chambers with the windows, Big ones. And inside…

"Oh, God…"

* * * * *

August, 1912, inside the Martian Fortress

Becca Harding looked back several times, but all she saw was the tail end of the group of troopers heading the other way, and they were soon lost to sight around the curve of the corridor. She had a good idea of what was back that way. Holding cages. Holding cages for the people the Martians used as food. Sam Jones, the soldier who had been rescued from the Gallup fortress, had spoken of them - shrieked about them, actually. They eat us! She didn't want Frank coddling her, but somehow this time she had no real desire to fight him over it. She followed Lieutenant Lynnbrooke.

They went back to the intersection and waited. She'd seen more soldiers following them down the ramp into the fortress. They ought to see some of them soon. Had they won? It had looked like it. They were inside the enemy's stronghold and the few remaining ones they'd seen outside were all running away. They'd done it! Captured one of the fortresses, liberated some of the land. For the first time all day she started to relax...

"I hear something, sir," said one of the men. They all paused and listened. At first she couldn't hear anything but her own breathing, but then she heard something else. A clicking sound. Metal on stone maybe. Not leather boots, surely. But where was it coming from? Four corridors went off in different directions and the sound was echoing off every wall. She raised her rifle. One of the men had a stovepipe launcher and he made sure it was ready. The lieutenant had his pistol out.

The sound was definitely coming closer. Becca turned this way and that, but she saw nothing. The lieutenant sent a man down the way they had just come—the only direction the noise couldn't be coming from—to tell Frank what was happening and to get some more men.

Suddenly the sound was clearer and coming from the ramp leading up. They spun to face that way, just as a machine came into view. It was a medium-sized tripod machine, not a spider and not one of the big ones; it was like one of the parked ones they'd seen earlier. The top was open and she glimpsed part of a Martian inside.

She fired her rifle, but the bullet bounced off the metal skin. Two others fired as well, but with no more effect than her shot. The stovepipe man was raising his weapon when flame burst from the machine. A small heat ray blasted out and swept across the group.

"Look out!" cried Lynnbrooke. He flung her down to the floor and shielded her with his body. A half-dozen screams filled her ears. She landed heavily and Lynnbrooke was on top of her for a moment before he rolled away, his clothes burning.

She twisted around, expecting the next blast to kill her. But the machine had already turned away and was heading down another corridor. She'd dropped her rifle, but then she saw the stovepipe launcher lying on the floor. The man who had carried was lying dead beside it, his head a smoldering mess.

She leapt to her feet, scooped up the stovepipe and pointed it at the retreating Martian. She'd insisted that the troopers show her how it worked and with an odd calmness and clarity, as though she had all the time in the world, she placed the tube on her shoulder, aimed, and pressed the firing button.

There was a loud *whoosh* and the rocket sprang from the tube and hit the machine, blowing off one of its legs. The thing crashed to the floor and skidded along for a few yards. The grey shape of the Martian tumbled out and rolled up against the wall and laid there.

There were shouts and the sound of feet pounding up the ramp, but she didn't turn to look. Instead, she picked up her rifle and walked toward the Martian.

* * * * *

Cycle 597, 845.2, Holdfast 32-4

Qetjnegartis had been surprised and horrified to encounter the prey-creatures inside the holdfast. So soon? They were inside already? It was on its way to the reactor room when it ran right into a group of them. The travel chairs had all been fitted with the same sort of heat rays as the drones carried, but it had never expected to need it. But it had and it fired at the prey and thought it had brought down them all. But then something had struck the travel chair and now it was lying on the floor, stunned.

It heard a noise approaching from behind and pulled itself around to see one of the prey-creatures approaching with a weapon. Qetjnegartis was unarmed. There wasn't a thing it could do to defend itself.

The creatures halted a few *quel* away and aimed its weapon.

Well, the disaster is now complete. The clan had been dealt a devastating blow. There were scarcely a hundred adults left on the planet and only the three holdfasts. It would take several years to rebuild their strength to even what it was a few days ago. Would they be given those years? It seemed doubtful. The prey-creatures grew ever stronger, ever more resourceful. *And they will have this entire holdfast to study.* It would not be able to melt down the reactor and the place would remain intact.

There were still many other clans on the target world and most were in far better shape. Eventual victory might still be possible, but the Bajantus Clan would play little if any part in it. Command would fall to Tanbradjus, and it had serious doubts about its wisdom. *It was wiser than me on the question of defending this place. Perhaps things would work out.*

The wait for death seemed interminably. What was this creature delaying for?

* * * * *

August, 1912, inside the Martian Fortress

"Becca!"

She heard Frank's voice from behind her, but she didn't take her eyes off the hideous creature lying before her. Her rifle was pointed straight at it and all she had to do was squeeze the trigger.

"Becca, they want us to take prisoners. This one's helpless."

Still she didn't turn. The hate in her was a boiling acid, searing her soul. These awful things had come here, killed her parents, her grandmother, her friend Pepe, destroyed the farm, her whole world, killed countless others, and would kill her and Frank if they weren't stopped. Why should she spare any of them?

"Becca, you've already killed one of them face to face like this. That's more than most people. And if you kill it, this one will just be another dead Martian. We've gotten plenty of those in the last few weeks. A live one might help the scientists learn better ways to kill the others. Don't do it, Becca."

Her hand tightened on the stock of the rifle.

"I want to kill it, too, Becca, believe me. After all I've seen, I want to kill them all. But if we can learn anything from this one, we should. And frankly, girl, after the scientists get their hands on it, this one might wish you'd killed it."

That got through the wall of hate in her brain. Yes, shooting it now was just a quick death. But life for this thing as a laboratory animal. Poked and prodded and given electric shocks just to see how it reacted. That would be punishment for its crimes that went on and on and on. So no, not mercy, not mercy at all.

She lowered the rifle and she heard Frank sigh.

She spun around, brought the rifle up to her shoulder and said: "It's all yours, sir."

* * * * *

Colonel Andrew Comstock leaned against the rail of *Albuquerque*'s bridge. It was slightly deformed thanks to a heat ray, but it had cooled off now and he rested his weight on it. The whole front half of the ironclad was looking a bit deformed and decidedly shabby. All the paint had been burned off and the metal underneath was discolored in those strange patterns that extreme heat could cause. Half the guns were out of action and with the two right side track units damaged, it wasn't going anywhere any time soon. Repair crews were looking things over, but he suspected it would be weeks—or maybe months considering the lack of facilities - before it was ready for action again.

Andrew felt pretty much the same as the ironclad. He was exhausted and he could feel his muscles quivering. The non-stop action of the last few weeks, getting to Memphis, fighting the battle there, getting here, and the fighting today, had worn him out.

But at the same time, an exhilaration filled him. They had done it! They had beaten the Martians in an open battle, driven them off, and captured their fortress. Reports that were coming in said that the whole thing was intact and that they had even captured some live Martians. This was the victory everyone had been hoping for.

They'd paid a price for it, his eyes went out to look at the still smoldering wrecks of the aircraft which had provide the vital, but so costly, diversion which had allowed the ironclads to get inside. A lot of other men had been killed, too, but nowhere near as many as in past battles. Yes, it was a great victory.

"Quite a thing, wasn't it?" asked Drew Harding, coming up beside him.

"Yes, quite a thing. What do you think of the ironclads now?"

Drew nodded his head. "They won this fight for sure. They may be what we need to win the war."

"We're building more of them. A lot more. This was just the beginning. The first step on the long road back."

A shout from above made them look up. A man - a braver man than Andrew - had shinnied out on the pole which stuck out from the side of the observation platform forty feet overhead, and attached a new line to a pulley mounted there. The heat rays had burned away all the old lines. He threw the line down to two men waiting below and they attached it to the pulley there. Then they hooked something to the line. There were more shouts and then one of the five-inch guns on *USLI Albuquerque* boomed out with a blank charge.

All around them on the vast round plain of the captured enemy fortress, men stopped whatever they were doing and looked that way. A bugler started playing *To The Colors*, and a dozen more joined in, the sweet sound echoing off the walls. The men at the line pulled and the flag ran upward.

Andrew and Harding came to attention and saluted. Thousands of other men did as well.

The flag reached the top and the breeze caught it and displayed it. The Stars and Stripes gleamed in the afternoon sunshine, waving over land that was America once more.

Epilogue

November, 1912, Washington, D.C

"The results have come in from Ohio," said George Cortelyou. "You are reelected, Mr. President. Congratulations, sir."

A cheer went up from the crowd in the East Room of the White House. Theodore Roosevelt's campaign manager shook his hand and then gave way to let all the others do so as well. General Leonard Wood fell in near the rear of the line.

There was quite a crowd here tonight, far larger than past elections. Roosevelt usually disdained this sort of thing, but it was clear that tonight he was in a far more ebullient mood than in past years.

That was probably because this had been the toughest election he had ever faced - and the President loved a political fight. And also because the war was going far better than anyone could have hoped just a few months ago.

The huge defensive victories at St. Louis and Memphis had been followed up with the capture of the Martian fortress near Little Rock and the liberation of that city. Then the enemy had evacuated and destroyed their fortress near Kansas City, and another near Des Moines, and abandoned all that ground without a fight. To all appearances, they were falling back toward the Rockies.

The news had electrified the country. The peoples' confidence in Roosevelt had been restored and Nelson Miles' single-issue campaign based solely on the lack of military progress lost ground steadily.

Still, it had been a near run thing. The Supreme Court's ruling that the refugees from the overrun states could cast absentee ballots from those states had seemed sure to give the election to Miles. But the victories had caused a dramatic shift to Roosevelt as those people felt there was hope they might see their homes again soon after all.

Wood hoped that they wouldn't be disappointed.

The road back was going to be long and not nearly fast enough to suit most people. Wood was determined that they not make the same mistake as they had in 1910 and leave their lines of communications vulnerable to enemy raids. The armies were not going to just rush forward to the Rockies. The railroads would have to be rebuilt and powerful fortresses were going to be constructed every twenty or thirty miles along them to keep them safe. That was going to take a lot of time and a lot of effort. Wood secretly doubted they would be ready for a final assault on the remaining enemy fortresses before the 1916 election.

And it might not happen at all depending on what happened to the north. In September, there had been a serious attack along the Superior Switch defense line. 1st Army had very nearly been forced back. Only by sending every man he could lay hands on to help had the line been held. The British in Canada were reporting alarming concentration of enemy forces along their front.

The north was Wood's biggest worry now. They knew that the strength of the Martians was determined by how many Martians they could produce, not how many machines. They'd killed a hell of a lot of Martians from the two landing groups in the United States and both groups were weak now. But they knew that there were at least two more groups in Alberta and Alaska, and one more in Greenland. None of those had been involved in much fighting. How strong had they grown? Would he awake one morning to find news that ten thousand tripods were coming down from the north? If even a tenth of that number appeared, it could derail any plans for a drive on the Rockies. Still, the recent victories gave them a chance even if the worst happened.

"Good evening, Leonard."

The voice at his elbow made him turn and there was Elihu Root, the Secretary of State. "Good evening, Mr. Secretary, how are you?"

"Well enough, well enough. A great night for sure. And you? How goes the war?"

"As well as can be expected, sir. We'll be consolidating for the winter, but building up for offensives in the spring. How's the rest of the world?"

Root shook his head. "Confused is the only word that comes to mind. The British are holding on all their various fronts. The Japanese have occupied a lot of China's coastal cities and are holding them. China is a mess, as always. We're getting some very strange rumors from Russia. They've lost Moscow but seem to be holding on to Ukraine and the areas around St. Petersburg. And Poland is in revolt. We aren't sure what the Kaiser is up to in South America, he's playing things very close to the vest there. And the French... well, that's why I wanted to talk to you. What are you hearing from Funston down in Texas?"

Wood stiffened. Fred Funston was a very touchy subject these days. Roosevelt and he had secretly decided to relive him once the election was over. "He's destroyed a small Martian stronghold down near Corpus Christi and stabilized his lines. We still don't have reliable rail connections with him. We're hoping to rectify that in the spring."

Root frowned. "The reason I ask is that we've been getting some rather... disturbing rumors about diplomatic agreements being made directly between the French and Governor of Texas."

"Supposedly there were some French troops involved with the attack on the stronghold..."

Root's voice fell to a near whisper. "And have you heard that there was a referendum on the ballot down there? A referendum, which if approved, would give the state legislature the power to secede from the Union?"

Wood snorted. "Didn't they try that once already? Didn't work out so well as I recall."

"It's no laughing matter, Leonard! If they throw in their lot with the French, it could be a real mess. Other western states could get the same idea."

"Well, the surest way to avoid that is for us to reopen the railroads and give them the support they need." Wood didn't mention the fact that he had argued strongly against giving them the support they needed, nor that it had been the right decision at the time. "We'll be making that a top priority next year."

"Next year might not be soon enough. Isn't there anything you can do...?"

"Elihu! Leonard! Good to see you!" Without his noticing, the line had advanced and they were now at the head of it. There was Roosevelt beaming and booming. He grabbed their hands and shook vigorously.

"Congratulations, Theodore," said Root.

"Congratulations, Mr. President," said Wood.

"And congratulations to both of you! We wouldn't be here but for all of your hard work! You both have my thanks."

"There's a lot more hard work ahead," said Wood.

"True! True! But tonight at least we can relax and pat ourselves on the back. The work can wait until tomorrow!"

* * * * *

December, 1912, Washington Navy Yard

"And it is the unanimous finding of this inquest, that the loss of *USS Santa Fe* was due to enemy action in the course of carrying out its assigned duties. No blame for her loss can be assigned to any person. This proceeding is concluded."

Commander Drew Harding let out the breath he'd been holding. He sprang to his feet as the panel of officers left the room and then accepted a handshake and congratulations from the lieutenant who had acted as his counsel for the hearing.

That hadn't been nearly as bad as he'd feared. His friend Andrew had been right: with the war going well, no one needed to look for scapegoats and they'd been willing to give him the benefit of the doubt. Still, it was a hard thing. He'd lost his ship and no one would ever forget that. Nor that somehow he'd been the sole survivor. And even if everyone else did forget, he wouldn't. He'd been writing letters to the families of his men for weeks.

He left the hearing room in the big headquarters building and headed toward the personnel offices which were in a wing on the opposite side and two floors up. He trotted up the stairs, not at all troubled by his shoulder or his ribs; they were all pretty well mended. He walked down a hallway to a specific room and rapped on the frame and then went in.

Inside he found a navy captain at his desk. The brass plate on it said: *Winthorpe*. He looked up and smiled. "Well, Harding! Good to see you. I assume all went well?"

"Yes, sir. As well as could be expected."

"I assumed that by the fact that you are here and not in the brig," Captain Winthorpe laughed. The smile faded. "So now you come to me looking for work."

"Yes, sir, I need a new assignment."

"Well, you had your own ship, so I can't very well assign you to another one in a subordinate role. But we don't have any ships in need of a captain just at the moment. In a few months something might turn up. In the meantime, I can give you a desk assignment somewhere. You were in the ordnance bureau a few years back, weren't you? Maybe I can find a posting there."

"If that's all that's available, sir." He didn't much like the idea and it must have shown on his face.

"Or..." said Winthorpe slowly, "there is another possibility."

"Sir?"

"I understand you got a close up look at the army's land ironclads out at Memphis this summer. What did you think of them?"

"They're small, cramped, and mechanical nightmares. But there's no denying their effectiveness, sir." Where was Winthorpe going with this?

"Well, as it happens, the navy is building its own version of the contraptions."

"So I'd heard, sir."

"And we need commanding officers for several of them. It's proving hard to find men willing to take the posts."

"Really? After Memphis and Little Rock, I'd have thought they'd be lining up for the positions."

"Ha! Well you'd be wrong. Too new, too different, the experienced officers are afraid of what a posting like that might do to their careers. And I'll be honest with you, Harding, taking command of one of these things might be a bad career move. If the war ends soon, you'll be in command of a white elephant which nobody wants."

But I'll be in command of something. Something that can hurt the enemy.

"I understand, sir, but I think I'll take my chances with that. If the position is available, I'd like it very much."

* * * * *

Cycle 597,845.5, location unknown

Qetjnegartis watched the prey-creature writing mathematical equations on a black panel with some sort of white stick which left marks on it. It had taken only the briefest amount of study to realize what the marks meant: basic numbers using symbols for one, two, three, and so forth. Surprisingly, the creatures used a base ten system just as the Race did. The operational symbols had taken a bit more study to unravel: addition, subtraction, multiplication, division. They had used actual objects to make the connection between the symbols and what they represented.

More difficult to puzzle out was just why they were doing this. Eventually, the only answer Qetjnegartis could arrive at was that they were trying to communicate with it.

When it had first been captured, it had expected a quick death, either deliberately or accidentally, as these creatures experimented on it. But they had been very careful, and while some of the examinations had been unpleasant, none had proved lethal. Five other clan members had been captured along with it on that disastrous day at the holdfast. Three had been badly wounded and died within days. One of the others had clearly become mentally unhinged by the ordeal. It had stopped eating and died soon after. The last one had been taken elsewhere after twenty days and it had not seen it since.

Qetjnegartis had been alone after that with little to do but contemplate its fate and watch the prey-creatures make their symbols. They were feeding it; blood from some non-intelligent animal it assumed. But it wasn't being filtered, and between that and the close contact it was having with the prey-creatures, it expected to become ill with the local pathogens sooner or later. A bud was growing in the sack on its flank, and if it lived long enough to do so, it planned to transfer its consciousness to the bud at the proper time. It had no intention of creating a new member of the Race under these circumstances.

Another option was to cease eating and simply die as the other one had done. There were certain attractions to that path, and it would remain open, but it would not take it yet. It supposed that this could be considered a chance to learn about its captors. *A shame Ixmaderna isn't here instead of me. It would have welcomed the opportunity.*

It wished it knew what had happened to the others. Had they escaped? Were the other holdfasts still surviving? How was the overall course of the war going? The reverses suffered by the Bajantus Clan did not mean the war was being lost on all fronts. But there was no way to find out. It was completely cut off and isolated. It was very unsettling to be kept in such ignorance.

It was also becoming boring. Boredom didn't come easily to the Race. With memories stretching back thousands of cycles, there was always something of interest to contemplate. Even so, the enforced inaction was difficult. The desire to work was an integral part of every individual.

The prey-creature was standing very close to it now, holding out the white stick and shaking it. Was it annoyed at the lack of response? Qetjnegartis looked at the black panel. The creature had wiped away all the other writing and only one equation remained. It recognized the symbols from earlier sessions:

$$1+1=$$

The Race did not make a lot of use of written records. The perfect memory of each member and the ability to pass on information and even memories to new buds meant that nearly everything of import was remembered by multiple individuals. There was a written language, too, and all items of basic knowledge had been recorded in the event of some great catastrophe, but it was rarely necessary to refer to those records.

But for these prey-creatures, such record must be utterly necessary. It remembered Ixmaderna's lecture about the short lives and inability to pass on information to offspring and their long maturation period. To them, these written symbols were vital.

The prey-creature came closer. At first they had kept Qetjnegartis at bay and sometimes even restrained, until they realized how physically helpless it was. Now they simply placed it on something flat. There were always armed warriors present, of course.

The prey-creature was making noises. They were always making noises and this was clearly how they communicated with each other. Qetjnegartis doubted that it would ever be able to decipher whatever passed for a language, and was certain it could not reproduce the noises. But communication through symbols, that might be possible.

Possible, but was it desirable?

What can I learn from them? More important, is there anything they can learn from me?

That was clearly why they were doing this: in hopes of learning something useful. But they could only learn things of use if it decided to give them to them. I control that.

So there seemed to be no harm. And the boredom was becoming

intolerable.

Qetjnegartis reached out a tendril and wrapped it around the white stick. The action seemed to surprise the prey-creature because it jumped back and made a loud noise. Qetjnegartis ignored it and dragged itself closer to the black panel. Remembering the proper symbol, it took the stick and awkwardly scratched:

2

* * * * *

Cycle 597,845.5, Holdfast 32-3

"The prey-creatures are not pursuing us, Commander," said Davnitargus. "I have led scouting expeditions as far east as City 3-118. The prey-creatures are there in considerable strength and they have their own scouts sent out nearly to the mountains, but there is no evidence they are preparing for a major expedition westward."

"That is very odd," said Tanbradjus. "They must surely know they hold the advantage. Why do they not exploit it?"

"The local winter is coming on," said Davnitargus. "The prey-creatures have difficulty functioning or feeding themselves in low temperatures. Experience shows that they probably will not attempt any major operations until warmer weather returns."

"That is good to know. It gives us a chance to rebuild our strength." Tanbradjus paused and then went on. "I am relying on those of you with experience on this world to guide me when necessary. With the regrettable loss of Qetjnegartis, I will be relying on you in particular, Davnitargus."

It regarded the new commander closely. Was this some veiled statement that it doubted its trustworthiness? "I serve the clan and Race, Commander," it replied.

"As do we all. But I shall speak plainly, Davnitargus."

"That is usually best."

"It is known that those budded on this world lack the inherent submission to superiors that exists on the Homeworld."

"Indeed?"

"Yes. Some find this extremely disturbing. But the situation is what it is. You are the senior most of all those budded on this world. I will expect you to keep the others in line. Can I trust you to do that Davnitargus?"

"Of course, Commander."

For now.

December, 1912, Little Rock, Arkansas

"Merry Christmas, Becca."

"Merry Christmas, Frank."

They didn't have champagne, they didn't even have wine. They were forced to clink tin cups half-filled with bourbon, but neither one minded. They were alive and together and nothing else really mattered. The 5th Cavalry was stationed in the remains of Little Rock now. The town was slowly being rebuilt and refortified. The rail connection east had been repaired and concrete fortresses were being built all along its length. Two divisions of infantry were defending the place along with four battalions of steam tanks and a lot of artillery.

The cavalry had been conducting scouting missions west all through the fall to keep an eye on the Martians, but aside from small scouting parties, they hadn't seen much. Half of their job had been to turn back parties of civilians who somehow thought the recent victories meant they could go home again. It wasn't easy convincing them that it would be a very bad idea. Becca had gone along on those scouts and no one had complained.

"Remember our first Christmas together?" asked Becca.

"The one in the Pueblo cliff-dwelling?"

"Yes, we didn't even remember it was Christmas until the day was nearly over. No tree, no presents—no bourbon."

"I've spent nicer ones, that's for sure. I wonder whatever happened to those people," said Frank. "The civilians we picked up who wouldn't go on to Ramah with us."

"Dead probably." She got up and went over to the fire and poked at the logs and threw another one on. The army had taken over a lot of the abandoned property in the town—the buildings which hadn't been too badly damaged. Frank's captain's rank had rated him a modest town house with a nice parlor. There was no electricity or running water, of course, but they made do.

They made do. They were sharing the house and no one said a thing. Becca's mother—or her aunt—would have been absolutely scandalized, but neither one of them gave a damn about such things. Frank had asked to marry her, and she'd said yes, but then when they checked the regulation, they found that as a married dependent she'd technically be barred from serving with the 5th out in the field. But as a camp follower, well, the regulations were reassuringly vague about it. So they'd let things be.

"Oh, speaking of presents," said Frank. "I have something for you. Came last week, but I've been saving it for today." He pulled a sheet of paper out of his tunic pocket and handed it to her.

"What is it?"

"Read it."

She unfolded it and held it so the firelight fell on it. She squinted, frowned, and shook her head. "It's written in *army*, Frank, what does it mean?"

He laughed and took it back. "Congress recently approved a bill to give veteran army nurses officer's rank. So they could boss enlisted men around, I guess. When I heard about it, I had a little talk with Colonel Schumacher. He pulled some strings and this, young lady, is your commission as a second lieutenant in the Army Nurse Corps."

"Really?" She snatched it back, a look of delight on her face. "A lieutenant? Me?"

"Sure enough; you'll get the pay, too. 'Course you already were a lieutenant with your sharpshooters."

She snorted. "A make-believe rank for make-believe soldiers."

"You sell yourself—and all your girls—short, Becca. They fought and some of them died. Nothing make-believe about it."

"No. you're right. Some of them were good soldiers, too." She held up the paper. "But this is for real? I'm a lieutenant?"

"Well, in the nurse corps you are. You can't really command troops in a combat situation."

"That's all right, don't really want to. As long as it means I can keep comin' along and fightin', I'm content."

"As long as Schumacher is colonel that's what it means."

"Then we'll have to make sure he stays alive!" She held up her cup. "To Colonel Schumacher!" They clinked them together and drank.

"So what happens now?" she asked.

"Well, I was thinking we'd get drunk and then go to bed." He reached out a hand and pinched her.

"I meant with the war, you goof!"

"I doubt much will happen during the winter. They'll want to get everything fortified and set up for a spring offensive."

"So we'll be movin' west in the spring?"

"Seems likely."

"Good," she said. "We took some of ours back this year. But we ain't gonna stop until we have it all."

"Amen to that."

* * * * *

January, 1913, Washington, D.C.

"Happy New Year, dear," said Andrew Comstock. He took his wife in his arms and kissed her.

"Happy New Year, love," replied Victoria. She smiled, but he could see that she was troubled. The birth of their daughter three months earlier had gone well. Little Arthur and Elizabeth were sleeping soundly despite the noise of the revelers roaming the streets of Fort Myer. So that wasn't the problem.

"I'm sorry about the new assignment, but it will be months before they're ready to take the field. We'll see a lot of each other."

"But then you'll be going back to the war."

"I'm a soldier. It's my job."

"You had a job in the Ordnance Department. Not a combat command."

"My Ordnance job didn't exactly keep me out of harm's way."

"No, it didn't! But why do you have to be in the front lines? Just the other day you told me that that pilot friend of yours..."

"Tom Selfridge?"

"Yes, him. You said he'd been taken off flying duty and sent back to train new pilots. Why can't you do something like that?"

He shook his head. "Piloting is the most dangerous job there is, love. They have about a seventy-percent casualty rate. Tom barely survived the battle at the Martian fortress. The high command thought he had taken enough risks. But my job is different; the land ironclads are the most powerful and safest combat command I could have. We took on seventy tripods with only three and won. I'll be commanding a whole squadron. Six of them. I'll be as safe as any soldier can be."

She sniffed and turned away. "How much longer will this go on?"

"It is going to take a while to clear the Martians all out. But we will."

"We're really winning? There are all these statements from the President, from the government, but I don't know what to believe."

"Yes, we are winning. We hurt them very badly this year. We'll hurt them even worse in the spring. Someday the war will be over and we are going to win."

She moved into his embrace again. "You promise?"

"Yes, I promise."

The End

Look for more books from Winged Hussar Publishing, LLC – E-books, paperbacks and Limited Edition hardcovers. The best in history, science fiction and fantasy at:

https://www. wingedhussarpublishing.com

or follow us on Facebook at:

Winged Hussar Publishing LLC

Or on twitter at:

WingHusPubLLC

For information and upcoming publications

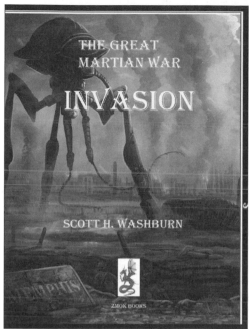

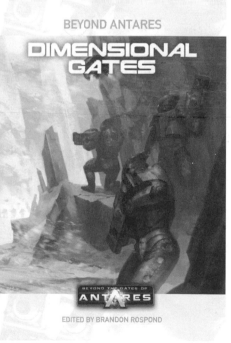

Find out more about the game,
All Quiet on the Martian Front at
quietmartian front.com